TOWARDS POLARIS

TOWARDS
POLARIS

A Novel of the Adirondack Foothills

MASON SMITH

Syracuse University Press | May-Reverse

Copyright © 2005, 2006 by Mason Smith
First Copublication Edition 2008
08 09 10 11 12 13   6 5 4 3 2 1

Syracuse University Press, Syracuse, New York 13244-5160
May-Reverse, 68 North Point Road, Long Lake, New York 12847

Previously published as *Florida* (Xlibris, 2006).

The paper used in this publication meets the minimum requirements of
American National Standard for Information Sciences—Permanence of Paper for
Printed Library Materials, ANSI Z39.48-1984∞™

For a listing of books published and distributed by Syracuse University Press, visit
our Web site at SyracuseUniversityPress.syr.edu

ISBN-13: 978-0-8156-0906-3   ISBN-10: 0-8156-0906-X

Library of Congress Cataloging-in-Publication Data
Smith, Mason, 1936–
[Florida]
Towards Polaris : a novel of the Adirondack foothills / Mason Smith.
— 1st copublication ed.
p. cm.
ISBN 978-0-8156-0906-3 (pbk. : alk. paper) 1. Adirondack Mountains
(N.Y.)—Fiction. I. Title.
PS3569.M5378F55 2008
813'.54—dc22
2007051024

Manufactured in the United States of America

In memory of Louis Curtis and Sooky Smith,
members of the combo *The Parking Lights,*
Gouverneur, NY, 1949

★

His hope has taken on her shape,
and he can no longer wish it to have another.
—Thomas Mann

Area of the Action, Northern New York. Sketch by Leo Weller

Genealogical Information, supplied by Leo Weller

CHARACTERS in "FLORIDA" by family

The Wellers —
Farmers and merchants in the heydays. Most got educated and left. Leo and Leo's father are still here. Then there's Aunt Sarah, dear old battleaxe who lives near NYC.

The Sochias —
Anybody in the Falls might be related to them. Our hero Robert and JoAnn (Sochia) Hubbard are first cousins. The family's proud of hot blood, relish doing dirt to each other.

The Stampines — Dying out — or are they?

The Old Man — with wife #2

wife #1
Neil, Bess, Clarence (among others) raised in a log cabin on the Lake Rd. No progeny. Too good for this world

Milly — stolen away by New York artist. "Not right" after childbirth, died in Brooklyn

daughter went bad (got married too many times.)

grand-daughter unknown to Milly's surviving siblings (but not to Aunt Sarah!)

The Community Chorus
HQ: Rideau's Roadside Rest.
Eugene and Mavis, owners
Amos Cheney, retired plumber
Millard Frary, still milks 5 guernseys
Lenny LaBounty, broke mechanic
Billy Atkin, loudmouth
Murdock, telephone lineman, lots of seniority and spare time and company van for visiting.

The Deputy Sheriff T. O'Neil.
Awkward fellow. Too literate. Thought by becoming a lawman he'd got to know what's going on. Wrong.

Harry LaFleur, strong silent type who stands by JoAnn w/o reward.

"Duke" Arquit, grocer and Supervisor. Also sells hunting equipment, incl. a nice Colt's Revolver.

1

Say One Thing and Do Another

Leo Weller, manic and irresponsible, big-eared, relishing the bright day and impending babble, jogged up the main street of Sabattis Falls in his bomber-pilot helmet, the metal goggles over his forehead, scarf twirled around his neck, mittens pumping the air ahead of him athletically. He was headed for Eugene's, or, as the sign over the low roof said, Rideau's Roadside Restaurant, to hear the verdict in the Sochia trial.

It was the middle of the day, a skiff of fresh snow on the sidewalks, tracks of schoolkids all going north, deep blue heavens up above. Hot sunlight crashed over him between the drugstore and the bank, then between the bank and the grocery store, then between grocery store and restaurant. He could have stayed with Père (that is, his father), back in the office of the Feed & Coal, where they'd heard on the radio that the court would reconvene at one; could have walked back home with him and made sandwiches and waited for the verdict there, but his Père was less interested than Leo in Robert Sochia's fate; far less in ignorant jabber about it at Eugene's. Unfair word. Not ignorant at all.

Eugene's regulars would be there in force, every man whose time was his own and some whose wasn't. Along with the usual raft of pickup trucks in front of the restaurant he noted the telephone company van and other vehicles facing his way across the street; also a recent splash of Lenny LaBounty's tobacco-juice in the snow by the cement step. He shoved the door inward, to be blinded by fogged glasses and darkness within.

Warm. Crowded. Somebody in green, sub-average height like
his own—Billy Atkin?—had to step back from the shuffleboard
table to let him by. Wool jacketed mossbacks shoulder to shoulder
along the bar. He stood a moment warming his lenses between
thumb and forefinger. Would he even find a place? Ah yes. Lenny
was having his lunch at the near end of the bar, as usual, where he
could spin around and see if anybody had pulled up to his dead
gas-pumps across the intersection, and Amos Cheney had left him
space to spread his elbows. Leo claimed the empty stool at once,
nodding left and right with a big grin of excitement. But Amos's
slow blinking at him, his wrinkled brow under cap tipped back,
the lack of a vocal greeting from anybody, in fact the overall quiet
in the place, reminded him the proper mood was basically black
and unforgiving. Robert Sochia had shot a person dead, after all,
even if it was only his own worthless cousin, who couldn't have
asked for it any harder. And even if it was over a year in the past:
this trial, now ending, was the second. Still Leo beamed at Eugene
who set him up his Coke without a word.

The radio was on, little brown plastic thing on a shelf behind
Eugene, as Leo supposed other radios were on all over town—in
the bank and Arquit's store, the Senior Citizens across the street,
in the office of the school; in many kitchens linked to one another
by telephone. The jury, in Malone, seat of the next county over,
had only been out since ten o'clock, but the announcement which
Leo and his father had heard, that the court would reconvene at
one, seemed to mean that they were already done deliberating.

Père had raised his eyes at this, met Leo's; they had read each
other's mind: that was quick!

But then, why should the jury take any longer? Why should
they take ten minutes? Ain't that what the whole town's been saying?
(Leo and his father liked to speak the vernacular, to think it too:
the ain'ts and he-don'ts and ennaways. Leo's father was raised bi-
dialectal on the family farm.) Because look: fellow shot his cousin
from the porch steps of his house, with a deer rifle with a flashlight
held along it to improve vision. Not only that, the killer was a
well-known poacher, drug dealer, and ladies' man. Don't that tell

you ennathin'? Besides, it was a lie (one of many) that that was Robert Sochia's house, an important untruth because to defend one kind of house, your own, you can shoot people, and to defend the other kind, somebody else's, you can't. It was his father's house (father absent in Florida). Robert's sister, not Robert, was living in it, with her baby. Robert was living where his hostess, another liar, testified he wasn't living and had never even stayed overnight. Granted, the dead cousin was violent, granted he'd threatened to kill Robert for years (and in a crescendo of threats that particular night), but all he'd have done, if he hadn't been shot—everybody knew this, if they knew anything—was to break his excellent nose at last, a thing so long promised it'd have been about time.

And so on. So obviously Robert Sochia was guilty. It had been obvious last year in the first trial held right in Moira where it belonged, Olmstead County's own county seat. But that one ended in a hung jury, after three days of all the sensible jurors ganging up on the one who still couldn't see it, the one the foreman of the jury (sore loser) let out had fallen in love with the defendant. She wasn't a real North Country person, he said. An outsider, come up here from Kentucky, of all places. A college person. A bleeding heart. He didn't say it, barely, but she was a Jew besides all that. There was no reasoning with her, anyway, so there had to be this second trial.

The radio was marking time with music. Eugene had it turned down, the men along the bar keeping their voices low so he could catch when the reporter's wry voice came on again and turn it up. The shuffleboard game proceeded quietly at the long maple table under the street-side windows, their blinds shut tight against the glare of day. The Red Cap clock over the mirrors and bottles approached one-thirty. Leo noted that his sense of time was off. He had skipped his medication this morning, liking to live fast on occasion. The doctors over at Ogdensburg had made clear (so had his reading in the medical literature) that he was on drugs for life, but he knew himself, he wasn't worried about a low today. He was keen. He picked up the sense of a drama in the game behind him, kicked the stool and rotated, brushing elbows both sides without apology.

Mavis and Billy were at the near end of the board, by the door. The score, on the illuminated scoreboard arching over the middle of the table, was even, 20-20, but Billy wore a gloating smile. There was a clutter of weights at the other end, the deepest of them evidently Billy's. Mavis was passing her last weight from hand to hand, considering.

The radio music had given way to chatter. Still not the female reporter in Malone, but preliminary perhaps. Eugene uttered a short burst of syllables hard to separate. Amos said, "Ay?" and looked closely at him. Eugene said, "I say," and repeated the utterance, still garbled. Millard said, "He says, 'Innocent, you think?'"

"Oh, I suppose," Amos said. That was what the town expected, in spite of the facts.

Billy, swaggering back to his stool, cried, "Shit-yes, he's innocent! There's women on this jury too!" and laughed at his wit. Mavis frowned, shook her head, and zinged the last weight (known as the hammer) down the board free-hand, lickety-hell. There was a burst of loud clicks, like a string of firecrackers going off, and heavy thumps as weights banged off the end and sides and fell in the gutters. Everybody turned around to see what was left on: only two weights, Mavis's hammer still hopping and spinning, narrowly bettered by one of Billy's that didn't get touched at all. "Best I could do," Mavis said.

But the thumping and banging went on for a moment, like an echo of shuffleboard violence coming out of the radio. Chairs and tables being rearranged? And then they were hearing the echo of that dignified high-ceilinged dark-wood courtroom in Malone, a door closing, some shuffling and coughing. Almost immediately, the gavel banged, the sounds subsided halfway, a nasal voice rose and fell, blurred. There was a long pause, followed by a rising stir that could have been Leo's own eager heart, and everybody else's down the bar. He loved this, living right in the very forge of a story. What next? Turn page.

The reporter let that stir-sound go unexplained for a moment. They just heard the reporter breathe a sort of surprised or laughing

"Well . . . !" and then some whispering, or murmuring. Then male voices, questions, answers, more silence except for the stirring, some unexplained delay. Then the reporter came on again explaining, "Well, that was Mr Sochia coming in. The defendant, coming in to hear the verdict. Led by the deputy sheriff, Mr O'Neil, who is also from the defendant's home town, Sabattis Falls. And you heard the reaction of the people in the courtroom. It was to his—" She stopped in mid-sentence, apparently covered the microphone and spoke to somebody with her. Then she was back. "To his attire, actually. Kind of a surprise, what he's wearing."

It wasn't perfectly clear that the reporter took this whole thing as seriously as she might. Leo saw Amos's mouth tighten with disapproval. Robert Sochia had fled from his cousin, his long-time nemesis, from bar to bar that night, and finally to that house of his father's that a sister was living in with her baby, and then in rank cowardice, albeit after warning Raymond clearly enough (neighbor Neva Day testified to that) by shining a six-celled (deer-jacker's) flashlight on the rifle so Ray would know he had it, when Raymond ignored the warning and charged up the path anyway, put a bullet through the madman's lungs. There was real enough blood on Robert Sochia's hands. But they all strained to hear, they all looked right at the radio as if to see, what was so surprising about Robert Sochia's "attire."

As she now said, the reporter had covered both of these trials in their entirety for the Moira radio station, and they had touched her funny bone more than once. When Neva Day scolded the judge for not letting her say all that she had in mind to say. When Johnny Pelo told how Robert had often stayed overnight at the Pelos' house, especially when the two of them were going hunting in the morning (*he was a friend*, Johnny said, *the children loved him*), and then the very next witness, Helen Pelo, Johnny's wife, swore up and down that Robert Sochia had never spent a single night in their house. And yes (since the D.A. pointedly asked), her husband was a liar if he ever said he did!

"Well now in both trials," the reporter said, "last year's and this one, up to today, Robert Sochia has always appeared in a dark

suit, white shirt, tie; clean-shaven, his hair cut short, looking pale
and serious. Looking slight, shy, possibly—or plausibly—timid."
(An unmusical snort here from some of the chorus in Eugene's.)
The reporter had gotten the impression, she said, of a person of
ordinary or less than ordinary height, slighter than ordinary build,
without much color. "I'd say, really, *sallow*. To tell the truth," she
said, "Robert Sochia always looked tame as a lamb, to me. But just
now, for a second, I wondered if they'd brought in the wrong
person, or this wasn't the right room. I really didn't recognize him
at first!" She was clearly enjoying if not exaggerating her surprise.
"Let's start with the hat. Normally, you know, men don't wear
hats in court. Well: he's wearing a high-crowned, flat-brimmed,
black felt hat, with a beadwork band. Sort of, if I can say this, an
Indian-looking hat. Or a Hoss-type hat. Really, under the
circumstances, a sensational hat."

In Eugene's, resigned smiles and head-shakings were breaking
out along the bar. Leo's smile opened wide at this evidence that
Robert was not going to disappoint. He was going to do something
you couldn't predict, give them something to talk about. But she
was going on: "Then the jacket. A double-thickness, real thick,
with like a cape over the shoulders, wool jacket of red and black
plaid. Not the trite buffalo check that hunters all wear but more
interesting, a plaid, but only red and black. A quieter red. But I
mean thick wool. Thick. Dark gray wool pants, with threads of
green and red woven through the gray. Malone pants? This is
Malone, why not? And leather boots, old, oiled beautiful reddish-
brown leather. Red Wings, somebody says. And you know? In
these duds he doesn't look so small or slight anymore, he really
looks taller. Stronger. Healthier. *Braver.*

"And—" She paused for a second, but the guffaws were
forestalled, the chorus waited. "—Perhaps I should have said this
first, but it was on the far side of his head and I wasn't sure I'd seen
it, but I see it now, sure enough"—she stifled a laugh—"he has a
gold ring in his ear! No uptight little Cheerio, either, no-no. Maybe
not *gold*, I guess brass, but *Jeez*, maybe an inch and a half, two
inches in diameter. What can I say? This is a new and different

Robert Sochia, folks. I'd—" She did laugh now, a short laugh like a cough. "I'd swear his hair has grown shaggy. Shagg*ier*, anyway. Frankly it'll go better with the get-up when it grows a bit more. And I don't think he shaved this morning."

Billy Atkin couldn't stand it any more. He leaned forward and turned his round head to ask everybody up the bar, "Did Sochia ever have a ring in his ear before? When he brought Carol back from California?" Carol was the dead cousin Raymond's wife, who had run off with Robert Sochia at one point in the past. Lenny hollered down to him, "No, no, no. Carol never went to California wiv him. He parked her ass in Rochester, put her to work to support his travels."

"That ain't what I asked," Billy said.

"That's what really pissed Ray off," Lenny said, ignoring him. "Not taking her all the way wiv him. Parkin' her ass in Rochester, puttin' her to work."

The reporter was going on. "He's just standing there looking out over our heads, at these tall windows behind us, where the sun is really pouring in. It's actually hot, this sun, no matter how cold the air outside. Ha! His lawyer and the sheriff want him to sit down, they want him sitting down so he can make a show of standing up when the judge comes in. Or to make him less conspicuous? But he's ignoring them. They want him to take off the hat. He doesn't seem to hear them. Will one of them just *lift* it off him? No. They won't."

All this time there was continuous loud muttering among the public in the courtroom. And now the clerk called out order, the judge in his black robes swept in, paying no notice to Robert Sochia. The jury were called and came in and filed to their places and sat down and then they saw him. Some of them looked at him with a certain petulance and most of them avoided looking at him at all, and the reporter surmised that they and the judge had been forewarned. The foreman passed his note to the judge, the judge read it and laid it aside.

This via the reporter. Then all they could hear in Eugene's for a moment was the microphones being moved to where they could pick up the foreman. Down along the counter, glasses and bottles were held halfway to open mouths. The reporter said nothing, waiting. Leo wondered, Did Robert and his lawyer already know how they found him, know the verdict in advance? There was suspicion in the town that, this time, some deal had been made. The prosecution hadn't seemed to have its heart in the process, toward the end. This squalid case had last year cost the taxpayers of Olmstead county three hundred thousand dollars or more, a total waste, and it looked like you couldn't get a murder conviction anymore no matter what. Maybe there was a deal.

The judge asked the foreman to tell how they found the defendant.

The foreman said that they found the defendant not guilty. A couple of shouts and sobs came over the air from the courtroom, renewed stir and movement. In Eugene's the bottles and glasses were held in suspension for another beat, with various nods and slantings of eyes, bitter or devilish smiles, mild snorts and ejaculations; then tipped up and drained, each drinker with his own kind of relish and finality. But then the glasses and bottles were put down noiselessly, because the reporter was speaking somewhat urgently. Robert Sochia, she said, was already out the gate in the railing, before the courtroom public could get to its feet. He was out the side door of the second-floor courtroom, his lawyers following trying to slow him down, reporters ("including me," she said) in hot pursuit, except that the public, getting up and putting on its coats, was blocking the way. "Fortunately, maybe," she said, "we're already set up out there, for interviews after the trial. But I don't know if we can stop this guy. Jeanine, you there? Watch out, here he comes!"

Most of Eugene's habitués knew that courthouse better from the outside anyway, Malone their shopping and hospital town. They could see the gray stone building clearly, the wide granite steps. Leo exerted himself to imagine: was anybody there to greet the innocent RS? One big show of family support, last year, had been enough for Robert's father, Royal Sochia. Phyllis, Robert's mother, had gone to Florida at Christmas, supposedly to persuade him to come up for the second trial; but instead she too had stayed down there, evidently held by what Billy Atkin called "Royal's superior attraction." Robert's friend Johnny Pelo was in jail, for trying to keep up Robert's business for him while he was away. Leo pictured Robert and his scrappy, pugnacious attorney coming out into the bright sun and cold on the steps, into a barricade of wires and microphone stands, the reporter for the *Tribune*, this radio crew-member "Jeanine," perhaps, and nobody else.

But it wasn't exactly like that. The reporter had scooted down stairs to the Bureau of Motor Vehicles and out into the alley and around front, and now she described the crowd flooding out the doors and turning back, filling the steps and waiting for the principals to emerge, "if they are coming at all. Where are they?", and Leo figured, Sure, because Grogan, the lawyer, slowed Robert down in the lobby, tackled him and held him back, told him he would have to hold his water at least 'til they brought him his car, out of wherever they stored it, anyway; so let the people go out ahead; because surely Grogan had a word for the press and the public, if Robert did not, publicity being about all he was likely to get for this successful defense.

So then there they were, fireplug Grogan blinking and glad-handing as the D.A. came out beside him, Robert taller behind them both, shaded under that new hat. He was not smiling, not accepting congratulations, not looking at anybody. "Not even there," the reporter said. "Gone already. The jail is attached to the back of this courthouse, you know, he's been here long enough, and he seems to be looking and yearning right over the street and the town to the south, maybe the Big South Woods out there, invisible, his old stomping grounds."

In Eugene's they could hear Grogan's voice, fuzzy, and, closer, what might even have been Robert's breathing, or somebody's, as if the microphone were held right up under that slender, sensitive, well-protected nose, and now they could hear the female voices asking one over the other, "Where are you going now?" "What are you going to do?" "How does it feel, to be free to go—go anywhere you want to?" "Are you going back to Sabattis Falls?"

Which made Billy Atkin exclaim, "'How does it feel?' Jesus Christ! Here! Do you want to feel it?" Robert's voice didn't come on in answer. Billy had caused them to miss something Grogan said, perhaps to Robert, and then there was a pause and a shuffle; it sounded as though Grogan was preparing to make a speech. The mike was pushed close to the lawyer's mouth and he intoned, loudly and sonorously, as if right in their ears, "First . . . first . . . first, I would like to say that this is a great day for justice in the North Country. For the sanctity of private property and the absolute right to self-defense." He left a pause for further attention to accrue to his person. "As some of you may know, I took on this case without expectation of payment, in the interests of seeing Robert Sochia get a proper defense. And to teach my good friend the District Attorney here when, and when not, to bring a charge of murder. And how, I may say, to try a case when he does so. And I think that we have been successful in these matters. He can correct me if I'm wrong. But there is another issue here and you may think I have been unaware of it, the peace and well-being of the little community of Sabattis Falls. Well, I have not been unaware of that, nor unconcerned. And I know that the people of Sabattis Falls have been concerned over what might be the consequences of this acquittal today—which is and I think everybody knows it, the right and proper conclusion—what might be its consequences for the peace and well-being of that town. The reporters here have been asking whether Robert Sochia is going to go back to Sabattis Falls. At my request, he hasn't answered that question. Well, now, I am happy to answer it, and to tell you, and to tell those good people over in Olmstead County, in Sabattis Falls, that *as a firm commitment to me*—and I believe I can say without prejudice that he owes it to me—Robert Sochia is not going back there. He is not going to attempt to live in Sabattis Falls, among the relatives and friends of his unfortunate cousin. He is going straight—*straight*—to Florida."

A reporter in the background said, *"Florida?"* It sounded like the radio newscaster herself, her tone of amused amazement. But the lawyer went on quickly, "That's right, Florida. Nothing surprising about that, he has family there, his father and mother. He's lived there in the past himself."

This produced a concerted chuckle along the bar, that changed into outright laughter when Grogan went on, "He can find work there quite well, as he has done before, in his trade of paper-hanger and interior painter." Billy stood up on the rungs of his stool and cheered, "Florida!" while one of the reporters asked something unintelligible and then Grogan said abruptly, "No. No deals were made. He's a free man, he has every right to go where he pleases and live wherever he wants to. He's a free man, but in the interests of peace, and, as I say, as a *firm commitment to me*, made in good faith and I might say in gratitude—"

"Floridaaaa!" Billy cheered.

"—he's going directly to Florida." Then the lawyer overrode more questions, saying, "no, he is not going to Sabattis Falls at all. The people over there—" He let out a breath, in place, apparently, of what he might have said about the people over there. "—can relax. He is not even going to pass through that town."

Billy sat down at that. The men along the bar shook their heads, grinning at each other.

Mr Sochia's car, the reporter said, was being brought through the alley beside the courthouse. It turned tightly, crossing over a corner of the sidewalk, and parked at the curb at the foot of the steps. Their own deputy sheriff Terence O'Neil got out and stood by the driver's door, holding it open. They could see that car, too, knew it well, the once-upon-a-time two-tone green Fifties DeSoto Robert had brought back from California (bringing Ray's wife back too, somewhat fatter than when last seen), its self-closing headlamps still working then and not a speck of rust. Not that you would have noticed the rust, when the thing was all painted up with swirls and curls, flowers and flames of color, as decorative as the long triangular patches of Indian prints in the hip-hugging bell-bottom jeans he wore. The Hippymobile, Billy called it. That hand-painting hadn't stood up to the North Country elements, just like quite a lot else about that hippy style of life.

Now Robert's DeSoto was more or less two-tone-green again, deeply faded, between the holes and blossoms of rust.

Apparently as soon as the car was there at the curb he struck right down the steps for it, the crowd parting well beyond touching distance. The reporter described the deputy sheriff pointing to something on the windshield as Robert walked around him and the wide door to get in. "Mr Sochia's ignoring this, whatever it is that the sheriff's pointing out. Inspection sticker, maybe? He hasn't said a word. Hasn't cracked a smile. If he thanked Mr Grogan for saving him from prison I didn't hear it. Ducks his head to look around inside the car and oh wait, he's speaking to the sheriff. Deputy sheriff. Reading his lips, or kinda half-hearing, half lip-reading, I'd say he might have asked the sheriff, 'Where's my rifle?' Well sure, now I think of it, they've gotta give him his gun back, don't they? That thing's no more guilty than he is! Deputy Sheriff O'Neil's pointing to the trunk. Robert Sochia isn't satisfied with that. Deputy Sheriff O'Neil now shuts off the car and takes out the keys. They're opening the trunk. I can't see anything now, but they just take a peek in there and the sheriff shuts it again. Robert Sochia's apparently satisfied. Huh. Gun in the trunk? I'm just guessing, folks."

Billy Atkin bawled "Oh Jesus yes, you can't expect the boy to go around unarmed!" Amos rubbed his furrowed brow and looked at Millard Frary, shaking his head.

Robert Sochia took off his hat and just briefly turned his face up to the sun while the sheriff spoke closely to him for a moment, and then he slipped into the car. In Eugene's while the reporter stumbled to express her sense of unfulfillment they heard the soft sputtering of the old Turbo-Glide accelerating slowly up that hill and could see, could virtually smell, the cloud of blue oil-smoke that would be rolling up behind it.

"Well? That's the end of it, I guess," she said tentatively. "Everybody's left standing here on the steps, in the sun, wondering what just happened. What it means, you know? Is anybody celebrating? Is anybody mad?"

Eugene snapped the radio off. It took a moment for the people at the bar, other than Billy, to resume supplying their own commentary. Amos said, with a meditative rub of his chin, "Going to Florida, ennaway."

"Yuh. Yuh. Going to Florida, by golly."

"Yuh. Going to Florida."

"Hee hee hee."

Somebody looked at the clock and said, "How long, fellows? Half an hour? We best be watching the street."

"That's right," Billy Atkin said. "Say one thing and do another. That's any of them Sochias right through." His neighbor swatted him on the back of the head with his cap. Billy leaned away from him and said, "You a Sochia too, God damn it?" Several others were sitting up, zipping up their jackets, backing off their stools. On their ways out, they too beat him about the head and shoulders with their caps, in turn. He put his head down on the counter and covered it with his arms and hands, laughing.

2

Don't You Worry, Neva

Neva Day remained in her place on the third bench of the courtroom, with her small mouth pressed to its smallest. She shrugged back around her shoulders her gray, fur-collared coat, which she'd never taken entirely off, knowing this session would be precisely as brief and unsatisfactory as it was. With her lips pressed so tightly she prevented herself from saying to the young person beside her that she didn't know what the world was coming to. She did know. It had come to it, a point at which not only wasn't there any justice, but worse, there wasn't any virtue high or low and people who still cared for either might as well keep their mouths shut. Gloves, handbag. The blue straw hat with short veil had never been off. She didn't have to straighten her back, it was always straight. She was ready to go now, if Julia was.

Her companion rose beside her in her purple bell-bottoms and scoop-necked black jersey (she *would* not dress properly— Neva had given up on that), turned around for her pea-coat and twirled herself into it, swinging her long cape of hair free of the turned-up collar. She hugged Neva's arm and pushed her with the aggressiveness of a city girl out of the pew and into the stream of people moving toward the hall. Neva would have waited for somebody to stop and offer her room.

At least Julia agreed about not wanting to get caught anywhere near *him*, in the crowd around him and his lawyer, who was probably crowing. "Let's get *out* of this place, Neva," the girl said, and dragged her out of the traffic, down the granite steps toward the motor vehicle bureau in the basement. They followed the hall straight to the glass door at the end and emerged in the alley, alone!—except that that revolting ugly car of *his* went by, only inches in front of them. When she'd recovered from the fright, Neva demanded, "Who was that driving that thing!"

It was that useless Terence O'Neil, never mind indeed. Neva was glad to be hurried away across the courthouse parking area, always full, to the side street and down a block to the village's other lot where they had left her car. Amazing to Neva, to find herself the dependent follower of this child. More than that, to find herself in any sort of intimacy with such a creature. Neva hadn't ever had a confidante, not in her fifty years, nor been one. Not even with Mrs Bryant, though she called her Nanna, the Weller family's intimate name for her. She might have worked for her for twenty years, might share with her every value and opinion—about the dirty Democrats, the state of morals, the only way to do dishes—but she would never have presumed to call herself Nanna's confidante. The intimacies *this* person somehow brought Neva to share would have shocked them both. Neva still disapproved of her in a hundred ways, mind you.

Julia was in a great hurry now, and Neva had to trip along faster than she liked on the frozen slush. (Proper sidewalk-shoveling was a thing of the past. Some kind of a *tractor* had been over these sidewalks, instead of anybody who cared.) Neva knew how some of her acquaintances reacted on hearing that the new practice teacher was living in her home, indignant at the very suggestion. "Neva Day does not let rooms!" Not that there was anything wrong with letting a room, but in a town like Sabattis Falls you know your neighbors. "Who is she, this tenant, if you please! I don't believe it!"

This was exactly what she couldn't get across to the judge, this year any more than last. In a town like the Falls, you *know*. You don't have to *see* everything that happens, you don't have to be present, *in person*, to know it perfectly well! She knew all the jury needed to know and a good deal besides, and unlike other so-called witnesses she was prepared to tell it. And he wouldn't let her! The white-haired old tyrant! "Confine yourself to yes or no, if you please, Mrs Day"! Patiently, condescendingly explaining to her that she must only answer the questions asked! For goodness sakes, why? When the questioner doesn't know enough to ask the right questions! When if you answered the questions he does ask, you would give the wrong impression, you'd just be helping him pull the wool over everybody's eyes! Go up there and take the oath to tell the truth, and then be allowed to say no more than Yes or No! That's not the truth! They got through this second trial from beginning to end and the word *drugs*, if you please, never fell upon the jury's ears!

None of this did she say. Julia had heard it all many times, and it took all Neva's breath to walk so quickly.

The Ford was easy to locate, its high black roof visible over the tops of all the newer cars. Neva got in on the passenger's side; her roomer was welcome to the driving. Of course she didn't let rooms! She had a husband and teen-age girls of her own, and she wasn't so improvident that she needed the money, welcome as it might be. But there it was, she was renting her garret room to the new practice teacher, already a scandal before she had moved in. A scandal, yes, for going to The Rapids on a Saturday night with her professor friends and their wives from the state college in Moira, in the middle of hunting season *and* a murder trial, and not a brassiere on a one of those women! Neva hadn't seen this, of course—she wouldn't go in that place!—but she had certainly heard about it. There was a fight, as usual; young men showing off for those half-dressed college women. And Julia got herself right in the middle of it. She stopped it, they said! Neva could not imagine and did not want to imagine. Well, she could, now that she knew the girl. That's exactly what she would do. Get in the middle of everything.

But there it was. She did let her have a room, at Mrs Bryant's more-than-request. Neva's telephone-friends were dying for an explanation but she was sworn to secrecy and couldn't say a word. Now the child had wormed her way into her family, her life, even, though this was hard to admit to herself, her affections. And she *still* couldn't get her to wear a proper foundation. She was wearing her net halter now, as usual, no control or support at all! Julia was like Neva herself, large-breasted for her small size. But Julia was not naturally firm and well-supported, as Neva was, thanks to hard work, good posture, and proper garments. The poor thing had stretch-marks already! And said she didn't care!

Neva had been Mrs Bryant's companion for much of her life, starting in her girlhood, when she helped Mrs Bryant at her summer camp at the lake, and later when she went to live with her in Westchester County through the winters. Nanna was a North Country woman herself, the best of them, a Weller, and she always said that she wouldn't have any but a North Country girl for her companion even if she did have to live in Sodom. Neva would never have left her; she was proud to have disappointed many a suitor. But finally Nanna told her that it was time for her to marry and raise her own family and made her go home. Even now, Neva opened up Mrs Bryant's cottage every June and closed it for her every September. If Julia was in some way Mrs Bryant's ward or protégée, Neva did not need to know a thing more. If Neva had any idea, any guess, what the connection between this girl and Mrs Bryant was, she would think it wrong of herself to pursue it. She just let it lie. Period.

The girl drove humming, lightly drumming on the wheel, or waving her head back and forth, or mouthing with her beautiful mouth (such lips and teeth!) to Neva what a beautiful day it was. It was beautiful. Neva stirred out of her huff to acknowledge it. Especially here, west of Malone, where the road rose above wide, smooth snow-fields that disappeared over the horizon south and north, one of those places where you can look down to the north twenty-five or thirty miles on a day as clear as this and see the St. Lawrence River and Canada.

But to Neva nothing was now as beautiful as in better times long gone. In the summer, nowadays, this was a huge vegetable farm, nothing but tilled dirt and infinite rows of some single kind of plant as far as the eyes could see. Broccoli. At harvest time you'd see, of all things, here in the North Country, migrant stoop laborers from God knows where, all kinds and colors and caravans of them, gypsies! and rubbish of leaves of cabbages or something all over the bare dead ground; and the smell of it!

To Neva there was only one right kind of agriculture, a dairy farm, family-sized, like the one Nanna and the rest of the Wellers grew up on.

The larger view suddenly gone, and the run-down, poorer farms of the present, intermixed with modern homes, passing on either side, she came back to the present disgrace and danger. Yes, danger, though Julia made light of it. Neva had tried her level best, right in front of him (and looking him in the eye, too!), to put that villain away for good, and they, the people who had had him behind bars, who had not let her finish, had turned him loose to get even with her. They had as good as told him to do his worst, his worst wasn't bad enough. What was to stop him from coming back and—doing something to her daughters?

If she said this aloud, she'd just get an argument from her driver. Julia pitied the murderer! She claimed to "understand" him! She was a very insightful girl, Neva would admit, but too sure of herself by half. She "understood his fear." Well, of course he was afraid! The whole town had always known he was a coward, from when he was a little boy. His own father called him a coward, because he wouldn't ever defend himself from that Raymond. Julia pitied him for that, too! Now she was all concerned about what would happen to Robert Sochia if he ever came back. If he dared! Julia insisted that he had a perfect right to come back, and she was furious about the threats she heard. Well, don't go to bars!

What did she know about him or this town! He had done it before, what Neva was afraid of. Gone off with, taken away with him, the last young girl you'd think would have anything to do with him. It was *not* ridiculous to be afraid of this! She sniffled, found her hanky in her purse and used it.

The young woman said, "Oh, Neva!"

"Don't you 'Oh, Neva' me! A snake like that doesn't forget! They won't be safe outdoors!"

"Don't you worry about your daughters, Neva. I won't let him lay a finger on them."

There! That kind of assertion, really! Julia smiled her beautiful smile. She was really a blessed child, such eyes and eyebrows, such a perfect nose, not pretty, *beautiful*; moreover she *was* wise, in some ways; Neva had been impressed many times by her perception of her, Neva's, feelings, feelings she had never expressed to anyone, not even Nanna! She *was* wise, beyond her years. But what assurance! She had no right to be so sure of herself! What could she, a newcomer, a visitor, a stranger, a mere college student—!

Julia kept glancing at her (between glances at the road—she had such quick-moving eyes). And then they both laughed, Neva guessing they both were laughing at Julia's "I won't let him." Julia patted Neva's tightly skirted knee, rubbed it, squeezed, and Neva was comforted in spite of herself. Neva opened her purse again and put back her hanky. It was just an encouraging joke, meant to make her feel better.

They came into the Falls from the north, past scattered, mostly unfarmed farms. The big elms and maples of a cemetery lined the road just as it crowned over from the gentle climb toward the mountains and started to descend through the town, toward the river. They passed a few houses on both sides, then the Catholic church where Robert Sochia used to be an altar boy. One of the scandals about him was how he had corrupted the priest, taken him jacking deer and poaching trout, for heaven's sake! Opposite the school they turned left onto Neva's street. In the second block they pulled into her driveway.

Neva took in a breath, through her nose; she let it out the same way. On the opposite side of her house that night, she'd heard the car, the shouts, she'd run to her bedroom window. She'd actually seen the murder! She'd told the truth about what she'd seen. She'd tried her best. She gathered up her purse and unlocked her door. She thought that she and Julia would go in and make a pot of tea. Then, after they had sat together a while in her warm kitchen, Julia would take her second cup of tea up to her room, and Neva would call one of her friends.

But Julia sat behind the wheel doing up her hair, pulling it back and clasping it behind her head. She remained bent close to the steering wheel, her face hidden, her fingers fluttering on the horn-rim.

"Why, what is it?" Neva asked.

"I have to go with them," Julia said in a very low voice she had when she was tired.

"Who!"

"Behind us. Didn't you notice? Across the road."

It was that black thing, older, an antique, Raymond Sochia's car, the one that he had come in that night. Now it was his nephew's, Peter Hubbard's, and the same trash was in it that was with Raymond Sochia then. Hmph! As soon as the shot was fired, they were gone. Backed out of that driveway as fast as they could go! Now the same two were always hanging around for Julia. They didn't have the manners to come to the door and ask for her.

"I have to go down there with them, you know, Neva."

"No you don't!" She knew where Julia meant. The Rapids, that JoAnn Sochia's place. Or whatever her married name was now. Hubbard. Once a perfectly nice hotel but now nothing but a place to drink alcohol, a den of iniquity—

"Today of all days, I have to go."

Julia rolled her lips together briefly, as she always did when getting ready to explain something to Neva as if Neva were a child. "I know you don't like these people Neva but they are human beings and I care about them. I have to help them today of all days and tonight of all nights. I won't be home until late. Do not wait up for me. Do you understand?"

The child might be speaking Greek sometimes. Neva was made to feel beyond the pale, outside the human race somewhere, if she failed to understand. Help these boys what? Resist JoAnn Sochia— Hubbard—who wants them to make sure Robert Sochia doesn't have any illusions about coming back to this town. What was wrong with that? Neva had tried her utmost to the same end! They could all clear out, if she had her way, leave this town to be what it really was: a peaceful little town of maple-shaded streets and modest houses and decent hardworking people with something more on their minds than making trouble!

But there the little hussy went, with an unwanted peck on Neva's cheek, and not shutting the car door properly. Neva reached across to shut it, then looked around to see her get into the back seat of that car, with those two in front. And somebody else in back? Neva thought she saw another head, briefly, through the small high back window. Who would that be? *Three* men. Hussy, yes! I'll say it again!

She had tried, as she knew Nanna would want her to do, to control Julia's comings and goings, the company she kept. As God was her witness, she had tried. Loyal Weller, Mrs. Bryant's brother, had assured her that it wasn't her responsibility. His sister could not ask it, that was all, Mr Weller said. Well, she couldn't do it anyway!

3

Gokey Road

Pictures of the deceased Raymond Sochia, framed and unframed, made a little shrine to JoAnn's lost brother behind her bar. Propped on the glass shelves in front of mirrors and bottles, Raymond beside his car with a beer, half in bright sunlight, half in tree-shade. A younger Raymond in an unnatural-looking suit, the collar almost up to his ears. Raymond in the Navy, his sailor hat tilted back behind a cowlick of short black hair over a low worrying forehead and black handsome eyebrows that almost met over his nose, with a big smile and a broken tooth and a pack of cigarettes rolled up in the short sleeve of his white tee-shirt.

Wandering loose about the place Leo Weller banged a weight over the dead switches of the bowling machine and noted that Julia, seated on a bar-stool between her protégés, had a finger in a belt-loop of each. Smart girl, keeping her attentions equal.

It had been against Leo's hip that Julia bumped when she slid into Peter's car, against his shoulder she had gratefully slumped. He'd found the boys up there by Neva's waiting for her and had invited himself into the car despite their scowls. He and Julia were chums. She had a special place in her heart for him, and rightly so: fellow artists!

The silence in The Rapids was as who should say deafening. Leo liked it when everybody was wired up like this. Julia periodically whispering something to one of the boys, then, after a pause, something to the other. Probably the same thing. JoAnn in her usual slack-time place, a stool on the outside of the bar opposite them, with a view out the window toward the bridge, not even looking out. Everybody pretending nothing was up, while on the say-one-thing-and-do-another principle, Robert Sochia was long overdue. Leo didn't snoop very closely but suspected the boys were hoping he might actually be too frightened to show up, and Julia was reminding them that that was not the point. They shouldn't wish.

Robert's mother had been north at the beginning of this second trial. She'd visited Robert in jail, and told him everything she heard in the bars (where she hung out until closing every night; she heard it all). And so, being the coward he was—"I've always admitted it, he has a yellow streak about yea-wide, right up and down his back, that kid of mine"—her son was coming straight down to Florida if he got off. That's what she came up to do—get him to come south, for safety's sake. His father could put him to work. Would be glad to, his mother said.

When the telephone rang, JoAnn left her stool, skirted the end of the bar, picked up the receiver without a word, shook her hair out of the way and put it to her ear. She listened with her lips sweetly closed as if to kiss a child. "Oh really," she said without animation. She listened a moment more, then gave a two-note pizzicato "Thank *you*," and hung up. Seated again on the outside of the bar she lowered her eyes to her newspaper.

Peter called, "Who was it, Ma?"

JoAnn said without looking up, "A small, neat, dark-complected woman just stepped into Arquit's, asking directions to the Gokey Road."

Peter said, "Huh."

His mother went on, with no apparent interest. "In high boots and leather gloves and a hooded coat, driving a late-model car. A Buick, Marlene thought."

"Was that Marlene?" Leo asked. Marlene Lucas worked at Arquit's, but she was no friend of JoAnn's.

"No. Germaine."

He whistled. Excellent transmission. Marlene calls Germaine, Germaine calls JoAnn, and the Buick, supposedly heading for the Gokey Road, hasn't even passed the window yet.

The Gokey Road, now. The Gokey Road was the address of nobody nowadays, a narrow gravel road leading off the highway south of town, between rocky old pastures grown to brush, past one sole house-and-barn, then turning into a virtual gully, unused even in the summer, down through the woods to the river road. It was a dead-end at this time of year: the snowplow turns around a mile past the empty Pelo place. What middle-class out-of-towner would know the Gokey Road existed?

It did have one point of architectural interest, what Leo called the Pelosphere, or, interchangeably, the Pelodome, a crazy spherical building of sticks and shingles that Johnny Pelo and friends (eminently including Robert Sochia) had put up, over the scorched foundations of the small, Civil War period farmhouse Johnny had inherited. Which, going backwards historically, had burned down soon after the owner's friend had come back from California with, in addition to the plans or vision for any such building, somebody else's borrowed wife. Johnny and Robert, a couple of would-be hippies, with a dozen dope-smoking high school kids to help, put that thing up, probably with Helen Pelo calling out the directions about what goes where, because neither of the head carpenters would know how to make a cross of two sticks.

Pelodome, Pelosphere, the Pelos had lived in it until Johnny dumbed himself into jail right behind Robert, for continuing to sell their manure-pile crop of marijuana. Helen had been deemed an unfit mother, by association. Then Johnny jumped a work detail to go see the kids, wherever they were, and got sent to a real prison, Dannemora no less. At least he was still in God's Country, relatively close-by. They heard the bridge grille-work buzz, and Leo went on past JoAnn to watch a maroon sedan, trailing its flag of steam, tilt up and climb the glistening street to the south.

Peter Hubbard had slipped off his stool, too, to watch. Now he re-straddled it and Julia hooked him up again. On the other side of her, Francis offered, "Maybe she was from Social Services, something to do with the Pelos and their problems. Social Services drive them kind of cars."

JoAnn's look suggested it wasn't worth saying this aloud.

Leo wondered, did JoAnn have an idea who that was? He did, now he'd had a glimpse of her behind the wheel. One of the lady jurors wore her hair in a bun like that. First trial. Leo had been to court, he'd studied that jury, as one does. After the mistrial of course he'd tried to guess which one it was that hung the jury.

He met JoAnn's eyes and raised his brows. Small, dark-complected, with a bun. Could it be? Was the foreman right, after all? Did that jurywoman fall in love with Robert on the witness stand? Or words to that effect?

Without raising her eyes from her paper, JoAnn said, "You know, Peter, if you were curious . . ." Now she did turn her head, and calmly looked at him. "You could follow that car."

"You could not!" Julia said, sitting up straight and yanking both their belts.

"Later, Ma," said Peter.

"Okay!" JoAnn said brightly, as if she didn't really care. "There's no hurry, is there, Leo?"

As it got dark, Leo had to cup his hands around his eyes and hold the edges of them against the plate-glass window, to identify (or not) the passing cars. Crossing the bridge, both ways, south and north, they were briefly but deceivingly lit by the mercury-vapor lamps at either end. Never the DeSoto, by golly. But never the Buick coming back through town either. It made you wonder. Rendezvous? Leo went home for supper and to report on things thus far; came back. JoAnn with a bored look and a hunch of her shoulders signaled no change. The bar gradually filled up, and the noise increased to normal and beyond, and it was pretty clear by the time he went back to the Feed & Coal, to walk his father home, that nobody would go out to the Pelo place to "investigate" until well past their bed-time. It was Peter's and Francis's job, as Ray's designated rememberers. Nobody was going to do it for them. They just had to get rid of their watcher first, and Julia was probably good until closing time. At that point, she'd make them take her back to Neva's and command them to go home themselves. But their balls would be so blue from her kisses goodnight that they'd have to disobey.

This was the Wellers' custom. After their bachelor supper, in the house by the bend in the river, Mr Weller would do up the dishes and go to his study while Leo climbed the former servants' stairway to his room and played his trombone for an hour. Around eight o'clock, when Eugene's and The Rapids would be filling up, Mr Weller would hear him trundle down the front stairs. In a moment, togged up for icy blasts, Leo would lean into the study to say "Ta-ta, Père," and then set off for either "the restr'n't" or "the hotel," or both. It was a harmless habit. He didn't stay much more than an hour, nursing an ice-filled glass of Coke. Talk was his life, not just in the bars but in kitchens, stores, the bank, the gas station. Leo was all over the town, shoveling, gardening, gabbing, friend of all, tolerant enthusiast of character, the more pathetic or outrageous the better. Reminding his father gaily of his own teaching, "Takes all kinds to make a world!"

The doctors in Ogdensburg had put it in the plainest terms: the life of an artist, the great world, mansion, luxury car—these dreams of Leo's youth were not possible. He would have to compensate, to experience certain things vicariously. It could be done. He was a smart, well-informed patient, a scholar of his own disorder. They challenged him to do it. He picked up the gauntlet with a willingness which was somewhat worrisome itself. Was he perhaps too eager, too ready to give up? But his quiet father was, at bottom, proud of how he handled his limitations.

Was it the mother, rest her soul, born wealthy, to a father who killed himself after the Crash? She affected the best of sportsmanship about that, and became, Mr Weller felt, unnecessarily earthy in her straitened circumstances as his wife. He was never quite sure her self-deprecating good-humored vulgarity, apparently intended to show her pluckiness in adversity, wasn't really a reproach to him for failure to lift her back into her girlhood station. Was it something about himself? Or was it the knock on the head? Not quite out of high school, Leo had veered off the road and crashed the family sedan into a milkhouse, upending the new bulk tank within. He had remained mostly unconscious for two weeks, occasionally uttering a burst of hilarious vulgarity much like his mother's, then relapsing into coma again.

He came through it, and seemed himself, but his attempt at music school failed. And soon after that, while he was helping Lenny LaBounty change tires, he got detached from reality at times. There had been a series of extremely manic spells, when Leo, for instance, broke into the studio at the radio station in Moira where his school-friend and band-member Lem Schofield was a disc-jockey, and took over Lem's show, putting records on the turntables and grabbing the microphone. Lem played along with him, and that was said to have been a very funny program, but the boy had been far out of control. Another time he had walked into the Ford dealership in Moira and ordered a Lincoln Continental, leaping straight into the life of the successful bandleader, the stately Lincoln sweeping up under the *porte-cochère* of a collonaded Southern mansion, a glamorous woman waving from the door open upon a glowing, chandelier-lit interior. After a few of these outbursts Leo spent some time in Ogdensburg, willingly and happily enough, tremendously excited by the other people he met there, thrilling, wonderful people, he claimed.

At one point the doctors assigned him to a locked ward, in the basement level of the hospital, with people who wouldn't use the facilities, wouldn't wear their clothes. Leo got a shower once a week down there. But he made a point of wearing a sportcoat and tie every day on that ward, held his head up, somehow maintained his cheer. He told his parents it was only a test. The doctors were only demonstrating something to him. And perhaps he was right. Soon after that they sent him home, in a sort of parental custody. He'd gone back for short periods once or twice since. Time passed. His mother dwindled away. Here they were. It was a life of habit, mostly.

While Leo was making his rounds, his father would let his small slabwood fire die down, close his book and leave the house himself. He crossed the bridge and, turning the other way under the streetlamp there, passed the entrance to the town's so-called Recreation Project, in summer a tourist campground right in the village, built along a rough stretch of bouncing water with federal money and youth labor. Always a lighted window down there in the log cabin where Clarence Shampine wintered, free of charge, informally in return for clearing the snow off the little skating rink. Mr Weller followed a curving back-street uphill to the office behind which the sheds and outbuildings of the nearly defunct business scattered along the dark hillside on two levels. Inside, behind storefront windows on the street, beyond some counters of hardware, paint, stove-pipe and plumbing supplies, he turned up the kerosene pot-burner and sat down in his overcoat at his desk. He refilled his little thin-stemmed pipe. Respectful of Leo's mother's ghost, who would have no alcohol in the house, he kept his bottle with a glass in the deep bottom desk drawer by his knee.

Here he scratched out in a jagged hand his correspondence with the family, the sisters married to professional men, the brother a doctor in Springfield, Mass, the nephews far-flung from the CIA to Brown University and the University of Texas and Cornell; here every spring he crated up in handmade wooden crates the metal gallon cans of maple syrup the tenant farmer Opel made in the sugarbush on the family farm, addressing them in ink on wood to all the same recipients. Here with his pipe in his teeth, his cardigan and corduroys dusted with shavings, bent over on his Cascade chair, he carved his famous canoe paddles, with a hatchet and jack-knife, block plane and broken glass, keeping the succeeding generations of youngsters in the family supplied with paddles that reached to their eyebrows, new ones every couple of years as they grew. (The paddles hung from rows of paired nails in the shingled porch walls of the family's three cottages at the lake.) From time to time he braced the emerging paddle against the leg of the desk and sighted down its length. He swept up the chips and shavings and carried them home in a paper bag to start his fire next evening.

During the War he had become a naval officer, ultimately a sea-captain, in very perilous seas indeed. Since then he had done what seemed to be given him to do: presided over the long decline of this business (preferable, he thought, to a short one); maintained, with some financial assistance from his siblings and the irregular rent payments of an illiterate and foolish tenant farmer, the family farm a few miles out of town to the northwest; and, now, made a family for Leo. With the upkeep of the good house they lived in, across the lower bridge, and service on the school board, this was enough to fill out his modest requirements for responsibility. Leo, more than he, kept the house painted and the paths and driveway shoveled and the shrubbery trimmed impeccably. Leo gardened for others in the town too, carrying his tools in the satchel his mother had bought him for his music, when he was a music student years ago.

You took the situation given. He could not see how else to behave.

4

Like an Actual Citizen

Librarian at the state college in Moira, two children, engineering professor husband, who drank, small new house on a circle road opposite one of the dorms. She'd found the North Country basically closed and unfriendly, scary and inexcusable in its received opinions except on grounds of isolation and powerlessness. Nevertheless it had become home. She had grown to love the terrain and the seasons and her co-workers and friends, and she lived her reasonably good life in silence, or in secret, as it were, except for mild and risk-free activism. She didn't go to Selma, she went to coffee houses. She marched in *local* marches, and gave money, too little, to various causes. When, after eight years of living and voting in the north, she was called for the jury in the Sochia trial just like an actual citizen, she could hardly believe it. She told her husband, with her typical single chirp of laughter, "I thought they knew about me!" And even though he told her she was stupid not to plead the debilitating migraines that even a single violent scene in a movie, for instance, would trigger in her, she refused to seek to be excused.

The trial was eye-opening. It had never occurred to her, before, that the adversarial system wasn't much good as a way of discovering truth. Far from it, the adversarial system encouraged and tolerated transparent falsity! What she saw was two incompetent hack lawyers each trying to set up a preposterously one-sided account of things, the witnesses playing dumb or invoking the Fifth Amendment, the judge terrified of a mistrial, and nobody in humble pursuit, as she was, of the real, complex story! Usually she could not even guess the *purpose* of a series of clumsy questions, which the judge had to rephrase so that he could allow them to be answered. If an interesting line of inquiry did begin to take shape, it was sure to be aborted, after objections and conferences at the bench, to her complete mystification. The defendant could hardly be induced to speak in his own behalf, honestly or dishonestly—to explain himself at all. The only things she felt quite sure of at the end— and not because they were proved—nothing was proved—were, first, that the accused had had every reason to be afraid (*she* certainly would have been), and second, that he had fled as far as he could, to a place in which, whether or not it was his actual home, he had a right to refuge. Here it became personal. She believed very firmly that everybody had to have someplace he or she could *go*.

The jury deliberations had cost her so much menstrual cramp and migraine that she felt, at the end, almost as though she had given birth. The foreman in particular was a self-righteous bully and considered it his duty to bring everybody into agreement by loudness and interruption if adequate, by insult and ridicule if necessary. But given the two things she felt certain of at the end of the trial, plus her particular horror at what goes on in jails, she simply could not agree. No one could know how sorry she was to be alone in her view. When afterwards the foreman let out his libel about one of the women jurors falling in love, she was insulted and demeaned, but not identified, thankfully. Only Phil and her friends knew it was she, and they threw her a little party to celebrate.

A year had passed. The reports of the second trial which she heard over the radio brought back all her distress over the first. She'd have liked to feel a little satisfaction that she had given this young man a second chance, but he didn't seem to be doing any better with it. He had the same stupid pug-nosed lawyer, against the same inarticulate district attorney. There were the same phlegmatic witnesses, except for the same Mrs Day who wanted the law to clear the town of the whole younger generation, not just Robert Sochia. Even the same lies! Except that John Pelo, whom she remembered as handsome and nice, with shoulder-length brown hair and a superb, drooping mustachio, in a silly leisure suit, not bright but at least convincing as Robert Sochia's real friend, was now described as close-cropped and shaven, respectful and obedient, accompanied by two uniformed keepers because he too, dear lord, was in jail. But there was a different judge and a different tone and a higher speed to the second proceeding and it all seemed comparatively perfunctory.

She was at home, alone, eating lunch at her kitchen counter, when the court reconvened for the verdict. She knew the reporter well, from various groups they were involved with. She chirped at Georgia's account of the hat, the new outdoor clothes. She'd never believed him in the suit—how dumb did the lawyer think the jurors were? Now, with this new image of Robert Sochia bursting out of the lawyer's control, there was hope. He might have a sense of humor, for instance! In came the jury and the judge, and at the foreman's word she cried out, "All right!" like one of her daughters' friends, but in her own ironic drawl. She was surprised. She had done something after all.

Now he could go home. Back to whatever that world was, that he was at home in. Not a world she would be at home in, but he could stay in it and live in it and redeem himself, if he felt so inclined—an idea which would extract a cynical snort from her husband. And here he was! Outside in the sun. She listened intently, everybody asking questions at once. But as in the trial he spoke with his mouth shut. Good. She didn't want to hear him happy, full of his victory. When the lawyer came on instead and said *Florida*, she put down her fork with a snap. He said it again and she objected, "Florida?" thinking of her parents, Phil's too, carefully aging couples both. "That's where people go to *die!*"

The lawyer went on, big frog in little pond. "Florida, forfend!" she cried. "He can't go to Florida!" She pressed her temples with the tips of her fingers. What did she care? But it was just so wrong. That trial was about the *place,* the whole culture, the blood, the voices. They were *natives*. All those people had been so *out of place* testifying about themselves just in the next town north. *None* of them should *ever* leave home! *Robert Sochia doesn't get off this easily!*

She pushed off from her counter, ran to her bedroom, pulled on her duofolds under her skirt. Knee socks over them. At the hall closet her mukluks, parka and driving gloves. Oh this was silly, this was going to bring down mockery on her. He wasn't even going to pass through Sabattis Falls so nothing mattered and she was just going for a drive. The girls would be coming home from school in two hours. In the bright kitchen again she thought, "Leave a note? Saying what?" The girls would be unperturbed. She grabbed an orange; two oranges; stopped and looked at the phone. No. She passed out through the breezeway, into the garage, and hauled up the door.

Ten miles to Chittenden, six more to the Falls, plenty in which to change her mind. On the car radio she heard him take off in a cloud of blue smoke. *I'll never catch up with him. I can't stop him. I just want to make him look me in the eye and say Florida.* She'd simply tell him: "If you were going to go to Florida you should have gone before you shot somebody. Now you have to stay. Get it?" Anyway Robert Sochia didn't say he was going to Florida, the lawyer said it. But she wouldn't find him, she would just see the town, perhaps settle her stomach. It was a nice day for a drive.

She didn't want to come right out and ask where she might find Robert Sochia. And she'd forgotten what little she knew of the town from the crude charts and maps that were shown in the trial. She did remember the odd name of the road the Pelos lived on, and asked for that. So okay now, back in her car: "Cross the bridge, keep going south, watch for the sign."

She drove slowly up the hill, past small houses, some poorly kept, some well kept. You didn't have to do the same as your neighbors here. You left whatever junk you might ever need in your yard just like Alaska. Over the crest of the hill she passed roads with other names. Nobody mentioned other roads. Nobody tells you distances. A mile or more beyond the town she guessed she must have missed the Gokey Road. Then she came to it in the middle of nowhere, just a lane between snowbanks stuffed with scrawny small leafless trees. Biting her lip, she turned and went creeping along, wondering what you did when you met somebody. Over the banks on both sides it looked like old pastureland grown

up to brush. The only promise of anything ahead was a power line
or telephone line looping barely above the brush.

She didn't quite register the dome at first, perhaps because she
saw it first as the oddly-shaped end of the weathered gambrel-
roofed barn which stood back from the road beyond it. Then it
was right beside her, separate, just over the snowbank which ran
straight on toward distant woods. Her tires were loud on the very
cold snow, creaking as she stopped.

She'd passed it and now backed up abreast of it. It was not
high, not large, but it was *round*, an actual geodesic *dome*. So
they *were* hippies! That's just what they had looked like, hippies
washed up for court; but she had never quite credited real hippies
in the North Country. There were indeed no windows in it low
enough to see into from the ground. The door she could just see
over the snowbank was padlocked, and the red curtains behind
its panes were closed. But an uncertain-looking home-made
ladder, of two-by-fours with short pieces of board nailed to them,
leaned against the roof, or whatever she should call it, the upper
side of the dome, where a tarpaulin tied with clothes-line covered
some sort of raised triangular opening, like a sky-light. She edged
her car to the other bank as if to leave space for someone to get
by, but that would be impossible. She bet no one would pass by
here in a week, anyway. She got out and at once felt the slide of
cool air from the rising land across the road, and she pulled up
her hood.

An actual Buckminster Fuller geodesic dome! Nay, more than a
dome, almost a sphere—when she stepped tentatively up on the
lower slope of the snowbank she saw that the sides rounded in
under it. On the concrete pad underneath, scoured bare of snow
by the wind, she saw a wringer washer, propane tanks, a small pile
of fire-wood, uncovered, almost black from weathering.

The brilliant silence seemed intentional, directed at her or
caused by her. She tested the snowbank higher. It held her weight
a moment, then broke through and she went in over one mukluk
to the knee. Wobbling, she was confused by a sound, frighteningly
near. Then she couldn't hear it, and looked around, and immediately

she saw, spray painted in yellow on the chained and padlocked doors of the sagging barn, in a looping script:

NOTICE!! I have ben looted, spied on,
shot at, burned out and thats enuf!
Do not trepass upon this propaty on pain
of getting shot! This mean YOU!

She trembled *in situ*, lacking the balance to run away right then. She steadied herself and asked, *Do I want to know these people?* She heard the sound again, the voices of kids, or women, some fresh-sounding murmur of conspiracy. *Chickens?* There was a low building between the dome and the barn, perhaps a chicken coop in very fact and the sound was that distant. Then, no, it was right here near her. Not children, nonsense! She waded over the bank toward the house, dome, whatever, and kicked around toward the sound coming from under the snow. A black thing sprang up, quivering: the torn-off end of a black plastic pipe, running a polished knob of water like the glass head on a cane.

"All right, you guys," she said. Her heart was pounding, but it was only water. Springwater. It must come from across the gravel road, higher on the hill. If she wanted to she could have a drink, and it would be pure and good. She squatted on her heels and held the pipe away from her, then near, and sucked from the top of the liquid knob. It made her realize how dreadfully chlorinated the water in Moira was.

She was pleased with herself. So far, she had stood up to bullets, chickens and a snake. It was gorgeous in the sun, and under the dark-blue sky the clear air just above the dome vibrated with warmth, and swirls of vapor rose from the cedar shingles. She couldn't see between the curtains in the door. The padlock didn't drop open at a tug. But there was the ladder. She stamped herself a way to it.

It sprang as she climbed on hands and knees but grew stiffer higher up. At the top she was looking over the globe like a sailor. Astonished, she saw Canada. Why, you might see the lights of

Montreal from here! And in the foreground, the ruddy, bud-tinted, snowcovered land spread out below her, the valley of the invisible Sabattis, the outskirts of the little town, woods and farmland beyond. She was warmly dressed. Comp time. When did she ever get to sit on a roof? She reversed herself on the ladder, made herself comfortable, facing the sun, arms around knees. Her eyelids fluttered to manage the brilliance. Only two bony points on her bottom were cold. Where were Helen Pelo and the children? Why would he come here? He's going to Florida. Wait for a while, just in case.

5

Throwback

Leo said to his father in the office of the Feed & Coal one night the following week, "You seen those old pictures in the town building, Père? The ones that Randall Garner found at the dump and hauled home in his station wagon?"

His father had not. Didn't know what Leo was talking about.

"Old pictures from the bank."

"I thought you said dump."

"The bank dumped them. Garner retrieved them. History is a hobby of his. He took them to show Ida Tharrett, and Ida figured out what some of them were of, and typed up little captions, and got somebody to frame them. She's hung them up in the hall around the Town Clerk's office. Our town in its heyday."

"Oh? The bank had them, you say?"

Mr Weller had his opinions about the bank. The little one-town bank in which the Jenkinses and Purryers and probably Wellers too used to write themselves notes any time they needed to, and paid them off when they wanted to. The little red-brick cube, separate from neighbor buildings, had not burned when much of the rest of the Main Street buildings had, in the thirties. Some years ago a bigger regional bank bought it up, along with a lot of other little banks, in preparation to be bought out later, itself, by a still bigger one, and now an out-of-state seacoast conglomerate bank had riveted its plastic banner over the door. The conglomerate bank wasn't there to do business either. What the conglomerate did was take money out of all these little banks in little towns where the people thought they were keeping it but couldn't seem to borrow any of it back when they needed it, and lend it to South American governments, which wouldn't pay it back, ever, but that didn't matter because the US government would. But apparently this took more space than doing business did and so they had to move all the original little bank's archives and quaint furnishings in two dump-truck loads to the landfill out on the Lake road, where the town supervisor, Duke Arquit, set Clarence Shampine to work sometimes. And now Leo was telling his Père what Clarence, seventy-two but still living in his boyhood anyway, happened to see in amongst that stuff at the dump: some old photographs of horses and logs and ice and snow—

"I thought you said Garner," Mr Weller said.

"I did say Garner. Clarence is too nice to just up and steal something from the dump, you know. But he did pick up a picture of one of those overtowering loads of pulp and logs on the double-bunked sleds, the horses looking like Shetland ponies next to it. Took it back to the warm-up shack and tacked it right over some of the other-type, more conventional-type pinups that Armand Lucas has plastered the shack with, that Clarence don't like to look at. Pretends to be quite upset by. But Armand says they keep the wind out."

"And Garner—"

"Oh, yes, the connection, which don't matter, but Randall Garner, yes. Where *Garner*, since you insist, saw it and asked Clarence where it come from. And Randall Garner ain't so nice as Clarence, he don't see any reason not to load up his station wagon with the photos and bank records and old loan-notes. Took them home and spread them over every horizontal surface in his little house, driving his wife crazy with them. She's not speaking to him, but he don't care. He ha'n't done a lick of paying work since. Wild for the past! But to give him credit he took the best of the old pictures over to Ida, kinda suggesting she do what she did do, turn the town office and the halls into a regular museum of the olden times."

"Well. I haven't been over there," Mr Weller said.

"No. But you know who I think has? Must have? Which is why I brought it up. Know who has?"

"Clarence, I would imagine."

"Oh well, Clarence. Clarence might be mooning around there hoping somebody'll ask him to explain how men could build such loads, or horses move them, yes. Or if wa'n't anybody there, explaining it to nobody. But I think those old photos may have inspired somebody else."

"Who?"

"Who'd you think? Hero of the present composition, which we're all working on."

"I didn't know we were all working on your composition."

"Manner of speaking," Leo said. "Robert! Duh! Because he's picking out a new style for himself, or more accurately, an old one. He was starting toward it when he came out of jail in hunting clothes instead of flared bell-bottoms or the undertaker's outfit he let himself be tried in."

Mr Weller understood that Robert Sochia had been seen around town. He had protection, it seemed, in the form of a late model Buick sedan that was always parked at the Pelodome at night when the boys went out there to set fire to it. So all they had done, to Mr Weller's knowledge, passed on to him by Leo, was let a speck of lead or two fly through the roof, up high where it wouldn't disturb anybody but a few carpenter ants.

"I don't picture Robert Sochia hanging out in the town offices," Mr Weller said.

"Well, no. But you'd think he was, to see him nowadays. He's harking back, is what I mean, to all those fellows in the woods, the camps, tents, around the chuck wagons in those pictures. Loggers. River drivers! You look at those pictures, Father, and you realize what a bunch of individuals our old boys used to be. Used to let their hair grow any length it suited them. Every man his own notion of a beard, a mustache, hat and neckerchief and boot. Suspenders, long-johns, vest. Makes you realize what we've come to. We ain't like that any more. We're pussy-whipped to a man, compared to them old boys."

"H'm." Mr Weller didn't see the need of bringing women into it, or of blaming them for the modest requirements of conformity

which civilization brings. But to take up that issue would be to
acknowledge what he preferred not to have heard, Leo's bad
language.

"I see him here and there. He appears in the odd place,
unexpectedly. He hasn't really grown a beard but he don't shave
either. There's always just this growth that looks like the first one
of his life, dark, thin, curly, on his chin and upper lip. He looks
almost comfortable now, natural. Couple of grouse feathers stuck
in the beaded band of that high-domed hat. He's been visitin',
you know. Heard about that?"

The DeSoto had been parked out by the Pelosphere all week,
a nice big space shoveled out for it, big enough for it and the
jurywoman's Buick both, side by side, at night, so the would-be
arsonists could drive on by and turn around, a half-mile beyond,
where the snowplow does.

"Visiting?"

"Yes, all over the countryside. Visiting old girl friends, is the
general assessment, when their husbands aren't to-home. Doesn't
talk much, they say, takes a hot doughnut out of the fat and a glass
of cold milk and sets at their kitchen table and listens, while they
give him hell. They all tell their husbands they give him hell. Say
he sets there and takes it, humbly. Has nothing to say in his own
defense, which we already knew. Say he seems to be listening for
something, or looking for something. Waiting for something. Maybe
for the right one to take to Florida with him when he goes. That's
what the fellows in Eugene's think. He always took somebody
with him, you remember, when he went somewhere."

"Yes, I remember that," Mr Weller said.

"The nicest, the sweetest, the most innocent et cetera et cetera.
The last one you'd think would et cetera et cetera. Billy Atkin says
it'll be Helen Pelo, just because if she ain't the last one you'd think
would go with him, who is? On account of, as Lenny LaBounty
puts it, 'He got her friggin' husband into Dannemora! She lost
cust'dy of her kids because of him. Him and his friggin'
mary-juwanna!' Billy says 'Hee hee, that's just what I mean.' But
we don't even know if he's been to see Helen, yet, don't know if

he's dared to go there. I mean, to her mother's where she's staying. You know old Lila! But oh! I gotta tell you what Old Herman said. I'll get back to Robert harking back in a minute. All this talk about which woman Robert's going to take to Florida: way down the bar, somebody croaks, 'Horse manure!'

"We all looked down there. Somebody in the dark, beyond the glare of the windows. 'Horse manure!' again. Eugene says something, you can't tell what. Billy leans back and peers into the gloom down there. 'Who's that?' 'I say,' Eugene says, better this time, 'Old Herman.'

"Billy says, 'Who keeps sayin' horse manure? That you, Herman?'

"It was Old Herman Plumadore. He'd swung himself across the street from the Senior Citizens half an hour before, said nothing, taken a stool by himself, around the bend near the Does' room, where he could lean his crutches up against the wall. Looked tiny down there, folded up under that old floppy-brimmed felt hat. Got the last metal guide's license still pinned to it. Opens his mouth and lays his head back and hollers, 'You ain't even close!'

"Billy says, 'What you talking 'bout, Herman?'

"'Girl. You say he come back here for a girl. Horse manure.'

"Now we all waited politely for him to elaborate. He just sits there, tiny old spider with one leg plucked off, motionless beside his crutches. Chewing something distasteful between nose and chin, which come near touching. Suddenly yells, 'Somebody up the bar there said the boy never really lived here. Been away in jail or somewheres else too much to ever really lived here.' He chews, frowning. 'That's a lot of horse manure too.'

"We waited. Herman waited. Looking sharply at us all, blinking slowly. Then he shouts, shaking his small body with it. 'Listen to what I'm telling you!'

"His jaw's just moving, as if he has a tiny nut or a seed he's softening between his store teeth. Takes his time, then bursts out again, sudden: 'That God-damned young outlaw, for all he ain't but only twenty-three or twenty-four, such a matter!' He rested, chewing, blinking. Just a little zigzag of gray worsted under the old guide's hat. 'I don't make no excuses for him.' He waved an arm, like he had no more use for Robert Sochia than anybody else. He sipped his beer, quite dainty. Said, 'That boy knows this country.'

"About then Harry LaFleur zips up his fireman's jacket, ready to go down to JoAnn's. But before he can get up, Herman barks, 'Better than anybody sitting at this bar!'

"Now that might be taken as a challenge, father, by some of these boys. There's a few old huntsmen there, Amos and Millard for two. LaFleur's been outdoors himself. Old Herman paused so long this time that some of the boys stirred, looked away, figuring he was all done.

"There was a kid in there that's been away to Louisiana or Texas or somewhere, tried the oil rigs I guess, and just come back to town, didn't know about Herman's amputation, and he asks, 'Old Herman getting mixed up, is he?' And Billy looks at him like the veriest stranger. 'Jesus Christ, Bently, how long you ben away?'

"And Old Herman bursts out finally, 'No woman amounts to nothing alongside the country that a man knows.'

"Eh? Eh?" Leo said, hoping his father appreciated the line. "'No woman amounts to nothing alongside the country that a man knows.' Old Herman's a pisser."

Mr Weller observed that there was talk they were going to have to take off the other leg. Old Herman, the great repository of the stories of the old times in Sabattis Falls. Too late already, perhaps, for the oral historians from the college and their tape machines.

Leo said, "But back to RS, what I was trying to say is, he looks like something not of the present day, to me, something out of the dim and distant past. Kinda like them fellers in the old pictures the bank threw away. Of course without the bedbugs. Without the lice. No woman'll ever have to strip Robert Sochia naked and stand him in a wooden tub on the back porch and scrub him head to foot before she could let him in the shack. Robert was always clean. Makes me think of our own almost-mythical Jean Ste. Jean Baptiste."

That was quite a far-fetched comparison, Mr Weller thought. Sa' Bateese. A profane and historical man like any other, no doubt, but unremembered now as anything but demigod, who rode the rapids singing, and died the day before his marriage, and floated up among the logs above the dam and gave the town its name. Whereas it was commonplace reality then: men died on the river drives every spring. You could get kicked in the head by a cow, too. He'd lost a cousin that way.

Mr weller discovered he was drooling around his pipestem. Bed called to him. He took the pipe out of his mouth and wiped his lips on his folded handkerchief. He'd had something else on his mind for several minutes. "You say he's visiting old girl-friends when their husbands are away. That seems foolhardy, considering."

Leo, kindly holding the door for him, said, "Robert's allowed to be foolhardy, ain't he? What d'you care?"

Outside, the town was dark, they would not have known there was a town around them, the sky fully spangled with stars. They walked looking up, using the Milky Way as a path between treetops and so between trees. And so between snowbanks, down the middle of the invisible street. They were on the lighted bridge over the running river when he put his question, though still indirectly.

"Oh, I just wonder what they're telling him. Those other women."

"Meaning, Do you suppose they've mentioned Little Miss Liberation? The Braless One?"

"All right."

"The one that has Peter and Francis wrapped around her little finger? That won't let them harm a hair on his head? That one?"

"All right."

"Naw. Guess!"

Mr Weller said, "I wouldn't want her to get involved in any of this business of his."

"No."

"Seriously, Leo."

"You don't think she can take care of herself? You're just like Neva, Father, worried about her daughters."

Harking back, was he? Mr Weller had never thought it very healthy, the way the town lived on its past, celebrated its rough, pioneer character. This wasn't frontier any more, it was backwater. True, it once was half wild. The town sits right on the edge of the Big Woods, just past the band of sandy soil that was once the verge of a great northern sea, where the river that once fell into that sea had deposited the sand and gravel that it had worn and carried from the mountains. And where, he supposed, the old sea had thrown it back up in dunes and beaches. Then the whole range of mountains, made of the oldest rock in the world, had been lifted up again, beaches and valleys and all; and the river, or another, cut through it yet again.

It was that river that had carried the logs down out of the mountains, that had provided the power with which they were sawn into lumber, at the first place on it where there was breathing room enough for a town, and soil enough to feed it and its horses. Or just almost enough, for almost but not quite a town. It was never incorporated. The town barns and offices still bear the name of the surrounding township, Kildare, not Sabattis Falls.

It was never really settled in the ordinary sense. As for such farmers as cleared and built and farmed here, the better land below to the north, like the Weller family farm, was already taken fifty years before they came. Mr Weller suspected they weren't really farmers at heart anyway, but wanted to be higher up and closer to the hills and streams and deer and trout. Most of the men who came to log the woods to the south, along the river and the tributaries big enough to float logs in the spring, were young and single. A lot of them were French-Canadians with homes and families elsewhere, and a lot of the rest were Indians. They outnumbered the first women twenty to one, so if they thought of marrying they probably couldn't, and if they did marry they couldn't settle, because as soon as the logs in any given purchase were gone, the company went broke or moved away.

Even by the eighteen-eighties and -nineties, the marketable timber within reach of the mills at Sabattis Falls was all gone. The Jenkins family that had built The Rapids as a hotel for the well-off summerpeople going south to the resorts, to Paul Smiths and Saranac Lake and Lake Placid, had to start up a chair factory, gone now too, just to keep the town alive at all, keep its school and bank and churches going.

And then the markets opened up for hemlock bark, and pulpwood, and the logging railroads came. The roads went further in the woods, and the town kept on, wintertime by wintertime, telling its stories of strength and skill and courage, of competition between Frenchman and Frenchman, Frenchman and Indian, of great ax-handlers and fearless river-drivers, of powerful teams of horses, powerful cooks, of foremen good and bad and women likewise, he supposed. The crazy Bateese and all his imitators since.

It didn't matter that people now gave their souls to the unions at the plants at Massena, or to Niagara Mohawk or the government or the college, or the damn teachers union, all to get more than their more independent and harder-working neighbors. Or if what was left for anybody else was to pound nails or service vending machines or sell cars. Or nurse or cut hair. The town (a large part of it) still pretended to be a lumbering town. It was the kind of thing that had made a permanent child out of Clarence Shampine, who was a boy when they quit using horses in the woods and never looked forward since. Mr Weller sympathized but he couldn't admire it. The milk was spilt a long time ago.

As for why Robert Sochia seemed to be having trouble starting his trip to Florida, Mr Weller tended to agree with Old Herman Plumadore. Mr Weller knew well what it was to come back to the North Country from an enforced absence—in his case from tending a slow and virtually unarmed ship across the cold northern sea in time of torpedoes, without benefit (as he there discovered) of genuine prayer. He remembered how the North Country looked to him after that and ever since: the only right and proper country

that ever was, in every form and line and color. The works of
humankind upon it, to be sure, were mostly a shame and a disgrace,
certainly all those wrought since about 1899. But the country
itself! The family had come from the Lake to the station to get
him, the summer of the Armistice, but he wouldn't let them drive
him right back to camp straightway. He made them take him past
the old farmhouse, down every road past every cemetery and bridge
and fishing brook he'd ever known, before going up the winding
one-lane road southward to the lake, where the whole extended
family waited to welcome him back from the war. He saw the
landscape that day with the most uncanny clarity—every leaf and
twig—and everything he saw felt like an intended blessing. He
would never forget, it was that way to him still, every day.

That was summer, but if it had been winter, as it was for Robert
Sochia, the country would have had the same effect, or greater; the
works of humankind half hidden under snow, the sun picking out
the ruddy color of the maple buds in the woodlots, the dark green
of the scattered spruces, and the silver tops of silos; the transpiring
snowbanks pulling away from the salt gravel on the shoulders of
the roads and the road-sand making a warm brown mole down the
middle of each lane, curving and undulating among the roadside
trees—*few as are left from the widenings; the butcherings of the con-demn
roadbuilders.*

He'd never resigned himself to the slaughter of the lovely
low-spreading maples that had shaded the front of the family
farmhouse, convenient to the road in horse and buggy days. That
road had been paved as long as he could remember, but it needn't
ever have been widened, less and less traffic on it as the years went
by and the farms gone or going to ruin. But the town got some
money from the state to rebuild roads, money enough that it could
make a profit on every mile, so rebuilt every road it had, no matter
if it stripped bowerless and made forlorn and naked every lovely
white clapboard, green shuttered farmhouse in the countryside.
They took the front piazzas right off some of them, *the sons of
bitches . . .*

6

Chrysler-product

On the second day after Robert Sochia was acquitted, he had pulled alongside Lenny's pumps with the DeSoto, wanting gas and an inspection. That was a kind of a comical scene, witnessed from Eugene's because Clarence Shampine had been inside the garage, his truck just rising up on the hoist when RS arrived. Sochia paused at the office door, looking across to the restaurant as if he wondered how many of the old boys were in there looking at him. Lenny's old arthritic German Shepherd, Queenie, brought a chunk of ice or stone or cinder, whatever it was, and set it all slobbery on the toe of his nice clean boot. He stooped down and tugged it out of her teeth, letting her wag his arm back and forth a bit before she let it go. And then he gave it a wicked fling, right at them, across the intersection all the way to where it skipped in between the vehicles and banged against the aluminum clapboards of the place.

They could already hear the bulk-milk truck coming, or feel it shaking the ground. Queenie forgot her arthritis and came after the cinder, pell-mell. As the truck roared through, they saw her legs running toward them, hind legs around fore, right under the belly of it. At least one man moved toward the door, furious. But she appeared still running after it had passed. She scrambled in between trucks, grabbed the chunk, turned and shot snow against the building from her feet as she tore back to Lenny's. Robert was inside by then and she just circled around herself on the step again and lay down.

What was comical was Clarence Shampine's rapid escape from the vicinity of the murderer. Lenny's big door had barely come

down behind the truck when it was flung up again, Lenny exposed
hauling on the rope to it, and they saw the tail end of the pickup
bounce off the ramps before they hit bottom. Clarence has no
affinity for machinery, can't keep a clutch in a pickup truck. He
jerked and jerked that truck straight back, across the side street,
until he drove his rear bumper into the snowbank there. Then he
put the truck through all three forward gears trying to get away
from it. But he only spun. It had him.

Until Lenny and Robert Sochia both came out of the garage,
walked across the intersection, and, one on each side, got his doors
open and pushed on them while he clutched the wheel, looking
neither to left nor right, and gave her the gas. Lenny yelled at him,
"Take her easy, for Christ's sake, Clarence! Easy!" When he let up
enough to get some traction, both pushers had to skip for safety,
not to get whacked by the hind end of the truck slewing around.
Off he went down that side road, which is the way to the old
sheep-farm where his sisters live. Probably went there and told the
story on himself and got ridiculed for it.

Lenny had come into the restaurant eager to share his brief
conversation with RS. "You know what he wanted? He come and ast
for a 'spection. He could use a tune-up too, but he wants a 'spection.
I told him, 'It would be a good idea, certainly, it would be advisable,
to get that old fucker 'spected. Suppose you was to get pulled over
on the way to Florida. As,' I says, 'I see by the radio that you was
goring to do.' I says, 'Is that true, Robert? Are you goring to push
this old Chrysler-product all the way to Florida?' And you know
what he tolt me? I'll kiss your ass if I'm lying to you. He said, 'Not
alone.'" Lenny tipped his face up and rubbed his grimy cap all over
it, grinning up into the cap. "I love it. Not. A. Lone!"

Then later in the week, word was that somebody had slashed
the DeSoto's tires, where it sat, uninspected and unused, out there
by the Pelodome, while Robert went snowshoeing, according to
reports.

It didn't seem to bother the person supposedly going south.
When he needed a car he drove the J.E.W.'s Buick, herself beside

him. But it bothered Lenny LaBounty. He declared, "He ain't goring nowheres wiv that old D'Soto's tires flat."

Lenny hadn't been anywhere himself, except on foot, a triangle between Eugene's, the garage across the street, and his grandfather's house just beyond Eugene's and Mavis's house, which was next to the restaurant. He wasn't allowed to visit his own home, down on the river road. On one occasion he had thrown the telephone through the picture window, and his wife Terry had sworn out orders of protection against him. He was just working and sleeping, trying to get out of the hole. Eugene bought Lenny his Red Man chewing tobacco in bulk and gave him credit for food, and he paid cash for a beer to soothe his ulcer. He would have his inspection license back in a week or so. No telling when he would get credit with Shell again but he made little money on gas anyway. He worked long hours and was a good mechanic and welder but he didn't charge enough for his service, especially to people he knew were as poor as he was. He wasn't in good health for so young a man. He needed dental care. He needed Terry to run to Moira for parts, but there was a fellow hitch-hiking all the way from Winthrop in a suit to visit her, or calling her all the time. Terry would probably straighten herself out eventually but it was hard for Eugene and the others to see Lenny ever doing any different.

Lenny announced, "You know what, men? I'm goring out there and fix them tires. Who's goring to fix them if I don't? He can't even put on the spare and bring her in, wiv *two* flats." He added, finishing up his hamburger, "I never had no trouble wiv Sochia. He always treated me like a white man."

Here it was a sunny afternoon, melting a little, a sparkle off everything, the sky a mile up and dark blue. He had enough gas in the wrecker. Eugene fished a cold six-pack of Bud out of the cooler for him to take along and share with the outlaw. Lenny said, "He ain't goring to be there. I know that. I'll just jack her up and get the wheels off, bring 'em back here. But sure, all right, I'll take it along, in case I do see him." He went across to where his wrecker, made out of an old blue Dodge truck, with a big block of concrete on the back to give it heft, stood by the pump to block anyone from pulling up for gas.

Out on the Gokey Road, he halted the noisy, unmuffled wrecker next to the Pelosphere, left it running for the warmth, and opened a beer. He put his elbow out the window and drank. He noticed a wobble in the sky over the stovepipe. The DeSoto was over to the right-hand side of a shoveled parking-space (room for the J.W.'s Buick beside it). By the tilt, it was the right-side tires, against the snow, that were flat. He could see how the snow was messed up on that side where somebody waded in there to deflate them.

He got out and slammed the door. Leaning back and holding one hand over his side, where the ulcer pained him, he went around the front the end of the car, looked back along the low side. The wheels were right down on their rims. "Now that's an awful thing," Lenny said aloud. "That's childish."

He brought his shovel and jack from the wrecker and dug a couple of shovelfuls out from under the front bumper. "They ought to stand up and say something directly, if they've got something to say, 'stead of this shit. Far as I'm concerned, you had the courage to come back and stand up to 'em. Now if they wasn't goring do nothing about it, time to let bygones be bygones. You done some time just waiting for them trials. You done a year, rilly, and you were innocent!"

He set his cap back where it belonged and was scuffing a wider work-space beside the front wheel when he saw Robert's shadow, crossing the snow in front of the car and folding up onto sloping wall of the house. There he was, hatless, a bandanna around his neck, the rifle under his arm. His hands were red and there was deer hair sticking to the turned-up cuffs of his wool jacket. He stood the rifle by the door.

Lenny paused, grinning, then went on around the front of the car and back to the wrecker, continuing without a hitch. "I says to them, I says, 'He's settin' out there waiting for yous. He's givin' you the chance. He's putting off his trip, 'parently, just so's you can get your two cents in. Look out he'll be gone, soon's we get his car inspected. Pretty soon I'll have my license back and we'll slap a sticker on 'er, and away he goes to Floridy and you're settin' there with your finger up your ass."

On the way back he brought along the six-pack and set it down for Robert. Robert was rinsing off his hands and forearms, in water running from a black pipe sticking out of the snow. Lenny put down his tools. He went on, enjoying the quick action of the beer he had drunk so fast, enjoying the outdoors and the light, kneeling by the front wheel, getting ready to work.

"Now I heard your tires was flat. I says, 'How's he supposed to go to Florida wiv his tires slashed?' Now— Well shit too, look at this, Robert. They didn't slash your tires at all. All they done was cut off the valves." He leaned back to check the rear wheel. "Bofe of them. Somebody's got a good pair of nippers. Shit, this'll be nothin' to fix." With the pry-blade end of the lug-wrench he popped off the wheel cover. The lug nuts were seized with rust. He stood with both feet on the wrench, stepped off comfortably when the nut screeched. He loosened all the nuts that way and then, serious, workmanlike, he slid the jack under the frame and raised the front end.

He took the front wheel off and rolled it around and threw it on the truck. He got in and cut ahead into the road and then backed the wrecker in line behind the car, blocking the road. He pulled the tow cable free and hooked it under the bumper of the DeSoto. Robert had brought out a stool and was sitting on it, leaning back against the shingles, his boots up on the rungs.

From here Lenny had to speak a little louder. He said, "I told them, I says, 'Shit, he isn't even fuckin' wiv anybody's snatch, what you got to complain about?'" In the truck again he raised the cable to vertical and lifted the rear end of the car. He pulled off the rear wheel and rolled it alongside the truck and after a pause to get his breath, heaved it on. He lowered the cable carefully, stopping once to look under the car. Robert brought over a couple blocks of firewood from the cement pad beside the house, and Lenny kicked them under the rear axle. He lowered the car, secured the hoist on the wrecker.

"This other one they's so interested in. I don't get it. Do you? I don't get it, myself. I would do anything just to have peace in my house. I never runned around, never in my married life, not 'til I was done awful wrong to. Before I was married, yes, sure, wanted a certain amount of esperience. But chase after anybody else when you got it perfeckly good right to home? You know it? That's greedy, that is."

Robert inclined his head in what Lenny took to be agreement.

"I mean, it isn't as if Peter Hubbard don't have no business of his own to 'tend to. You know what I mean, Robert. You know Patty. Now that's an awful thing, to leave that woman unsatisfied. You know that, well as I do."

Robert tilted his head again. Lenny jumped up on the running board of the wrecker and gave him a wave. Robert, siting on his stool, held up the six-pack. Lenny told him, "Eugene sent that up for bofe of us. I better not have no more of it." Robert nodded and put it back down.

When Lenny got back, with new valves in the wheels and thirty-five pounds of air, Robert was nowhere to be seen. Lenny looked around, detective-fashion, and saw where he'd waded and tramped a path back toward the barn. The barn was where he'd hung the deer, most certainly. Maybe he was out there now, finishing what he'd been doing. Lenny decided he'd keep that to himself, the blood and hair. Let Robert have his venison in peace.

He thought of leaving the wheels for Robert to put on. Robert could use the car jack and wrench out of the DeSoto, if there was any such. But even supposing he had the tools, would he do it? He couldn't really imagine Robert changing a tire. He'd rather steal or smuggle or sell something illegal. He always paid Lenny to do his car work, right down to wiper blades and antifreeze. Lenny could remember that DeSoto with all the hand-painted designs in many colors, the whole thing covered with stars and waves and patterns. Psychedelic, they called that sort of decoration. He had to get his floor-jack out from under it anyway, might as well put on the wheels. One of the old stories about Robert came to mind. How one night when Ray was harassing him, Robert ran over to

Risdonville, to the Hilltop Inn, just to keep out of Raymond's way. This other famous poacher, Joe Votra, a husky fellow, scared of nothing or nobody, supposedly asked him, "Why don't you fight him just once? You're half again his size, why don't you fight him, for Christ's sakes? That'd be the end of it." But Robert said, "I don't fight with my hands."

Or he *supposedly* said it. Like "I don't work with my hands." He might have supposedly said that too. But you never knew what he really said. Lenny took those stories with a grain of salt.

He didn't talk to thin air this time. It was later in the day and he was colder. He put the wheels on, let the car back down, threw the floor-jack back on the wrecker. But then he had to have a good look inside the old car from the Fifties. It had a dashboard such as you didn't see any more, all hard metal, straight across, symmetrical, chromy. A big flat steering wheel, with a full circle horn ring you couldn't miss with your thumbs. He yanked open the door and slid in on the wide slippery seat. Aw, he thought. He could eat the whole thing. The keys were in the ignition. He turned them, thumped the pedal, pushed in the clutch, and tried the starter button. That was kind of a nostalgic thing right there, a starter button. The engine turned over, none too fast. It fired one time out of eight. He had to bring the truck in alongside it and jump it. Then he raised the hood and took off the air cleaner and, with a screwdriver from the bib of his overhauls, adjusted the idle. He listened. He shut off the ignition, snapped off the distributor cap retainers and turned the engine over by means of the fan belt until the points were fully open. He cleaned them with a tiny file from his overhauls, then set them by eye at about thirty thousandths. He started it up and adjusted the idle again and dropped the hood. "There," he said. "But I ain't goring to put no sticker on 'er less you bring her in. You got to do *sumfin'* for yourself, Robert."

7

Himself Surprised

Robert Sochia had shown no surprise at finding her perched on the roof of the dome (like the spot on the egg that tells the sperm where to come in, as Leo saw it when she described the scene to him). Her first impression of him, when he'd come out from behind his car and climbed the ladder to her, had been favorable. He looked more like a real person, more like a person of the country he supposedly belonged to. He looked, she said, "*authentic.* That's a big deal with me." In her embarrassment she'd taken the second layer of his Filson coat between her fingers and told him, "This is much better." The ring? It *was* gold, she guessed. Not as huge as she'd imagined. It . . . worked. It made a statement: I'm not going straight.

He showed no recognition. Nothing. He just pulled off the tarp on that upward-looking window-thing, took out a big ring of keys, went back down the ladder and presently came back up under her, inside. He stood on the bed and lifted her down, "like a cake," she said, into a sort of loft. And then climbed down and went about heating the place up without a word.

When they were sitting by his old friend's two-barrel stove, and she had identified herself, and made some small effort to explain herself, to no particular reaction, she had asked him if it struck him as at all strange that they were thus. Herself, the older woman, the juror, alien in ten different ways, and himself, the emigrant to Florida, here in Helen's and Johnny's two rocking chairs, with their warm toes touching together on the padded footstool, sipping hot chocolate made with springwater and powdered milk. Didn't it seem at all strange? She was *very* conscious of the strangeness of *her* being there.

Maybe he hadn't learned how to feel free, yet. To respond to anything. To use his face. What first occurred to him to say was, "You can always come back to this town and find some shack to hole up in."

He was only thinking about the place? He took no notice of her? That set her straight. But he went on, just following the train of thought. "And some woman to cook for you."

"Oh!" she said. She *was* a part of the picture. "I'm supposed to cook?"

She could see that he didn't know how to take her sudden, chirped remarks. She was needling him to keep things clear. But no, he hadn't been thinking of her then, either. Or food. It wasn't impolite, it was just that his thoughts were elsewhere. He did say there would probably be some canned stuff in the cellar-hole, unfrozen, and he scuffed up, with his heel, the worn and dirty rug, exposing a trap-door.

She exclaimed, "Hey, that's an actual Navajo rug, I believe. That ought to be cleaned and mended and hanging on the wall, not trodden underfoot!"

He kicked the rug over the trap door again. "Look. The edges are frayed, but they could be repaired, there are experts who— Oh well." Very irrelevant to this situation but she couldn't help it.

What he said was, "If anybody comes out here tonight, you'd be safe down there."

"Oh!" She wouldn't be safe elsewhere? Let me out of here. But she controlled herself. *That's* what he'd been thinking of. She recovered enough to say, "I'm supposed to stay the night?"

He said, "Aren't you?" At which she laughed. Pure nervousness. She hadn't even thought of this, that he might not be *safe*, if he came back. *That's* why he might go elsewhere. And it dawned on her, too, maybe he hadn't even known he was going to get out his keys until he found her on the roof. Until he climbed up there and checked her out. He hadn't done that right away, as she now recalled, he'd kind of peeked from behind his car. Had he been afraid of *her*?

They ate canned ravioli and lima beans from down below, and she told him, as regarded the night, "I'm not going down there. I don't go into dark holes. So you had better tell me what's going to happen."

"Cars will come by."

"And?"

"With your car here—"

"Supposing it's here."

"Shots will be fired."

"Jesus." She might be Jewish but this was her emergency invocation. She felt the blood leaving her face.

"Into the roof. Maybe just over the roof. They'll try to scare us."

"This whole place is a roof, what do you mean? Come on," she whined, "guns, really?" But he meant it, and steeling herself she said, "That's with my car. Without my car, what?"

"They burnt the house that was here before."

"Jesus. I'll just go home. Be straight with me, Robert."

That was the first time she'd said his name or acknowledged she knew it. To equalize she said, "You can call me Marjorie." Her last name didn't seem important.

He got up and awkwardly shook her hand. Manners learned in grammar school and never used since. Was she so teacherish?

"I came because I didn't think you ought to go to Florida, but what do I know? Maybe you should."

He didn't say anything to that.

"If I stay here they'll only shoot the house. If I go they'll burn it. I can't believe this. What'll *you* do, defend your home again?" She pressed her mouth so that her chin wrinkled. She remembered the rifle presumably in the trunk.

But he didn't take offense. Perhaps he didn't get it. After a minute he said, "One night."

That was touching. He was talking to himself. He really didn't know what he was going to do, how he was going to react. She was glad he didn't say, "It's up to you."

She wandered around the dome thinking about it. She was just barely glimpsing what she had missed in the trial. She'd missed the whole matrix of reality and identity and *place* that she knew must underlie the event she was supposed to judge. Authenticity, as it was called by those who thought they couldn't have it, because they had irony instead. If she went home and he went to Florida there was no such thing.

Then too, if she stayed with him in the dome that night, the whole town would think what the foreman of the jury thought.

So? She could give him that much, couldn't she? For a little bit of *meaning*?

She ought to go. She should. Her husband would mock her relentlessly if she stayed—not that he'd *care*. But it was a matter of principle. Anyway, "obviously," she didn't go. She presented it to Leo as something inexplicable, without excuses, almost funny. "And there did come a time, as they say in trials," when they climbed up there lay down together under Johnny and Helen's blankets. He in his clothes. She, actually, in her long-johns; her skirt and sweater carefully draped on a hanger, hung from one of the hubs of the structure. They lay on their backs, side by side on a mattress on the floor of the loft, looking up at all the triangles of two-by-four and plywood, lit by the gas light downstairs which he left burning. She'd have made the bed, formally, for them, but she found no sheets. He didn't talk. She guessed he wanted to listen to the wind. So she tried sleep but found herself tense like him and listening too.

They heard the crunching sound of a car coming slowly along the road, then gravel tinkling in its hubcaps as it slowed to a stop. Whoever it was didn't even get out of their car. They sat there a long time, their motor idling. Finally the engine revved up high, then quieted down. She imagined a big-engined pickup truck. At that moment somebody fired two shots, too quickly for both to be aimed, or maybe from two guns. She grabbed him and ducked her head into his chest. Dust, or something, drifted down over them. They listened to the whine of the truck in reverse, all the way back to the highway.

She relaxed, a little. "Will that be all?"

"All for that bunch," he said.

"There might be a parade?"

He could imagine various parties who would come out to see for themselves. The strange car, beside his, in the space he'd shoveled; dim light behind the red curtains on the door-window; smoke curling out of the stove-pipe against the starry sky.

Was that a smile on his face? It would be about the first noticeable expression. She couldn't tell. "Ah'm no hero," she said, and she climbed over him, away from the road, even though that was the colder side, away also from the warm air rising past the edge of the loft.

On those first days she left the dome well before daylight to get back to Moira and make breakfast and see her daughters off to school. She told Robert her plan, and she told her husband too. She'd drive to work at the library, return to her house for lunch, and while eating her yogurt and grapefruit, she'd marinate chicken breasts or whatever for dinner. After work she'd come back to the house and leave two servings in the dish beside instructions for her husband to cook them and make a salad. Then she'd come to the Falls with the other servings and salad-makings and couscous or rice. Robert had to be there between five-forty-five and six-fifteen or she would eat without him. And the house had to be warm, please.

She sautéd the chicken and steamed the couscous in Helen's pans, and served them on Helen's thick old white china plates, and they sat with their plates on their laps in the rocking chairs. After the first night there was always cold fresh unpasteurized milk in a stainless pail in the gas refrigerator. (Leo knew where that came from, the raw milk and the pail, and probably doughnuts or gingerbread too: from Grace Frary, and unbeknownst to Millard.) Both put their feet up on the stool in front of the stove, so they were partly facing one another. They ate not saying much and when they were finished she'd put her plate down on the floor and take up her sewing and say, "All right. Talk."

She'd found, in some angle of the dome, a paper bag full of scraps of cloth, and she began to piece together, while she listened, a quilt, or comforter, which she thought she would either give to Robert at the end, or leave in the dome for the Pelos.

He didn't start talking right away. Fresh out of jail, he hardly wanted to dwell on the past. But that was their deal. "For instance, California. Start with that, why don't you? I think I can guess what you went out there for." He still seemed blank, so she specified. "Marijuana, wasn't it? Start with that."

He'd already been wearing his hair shaggy, around his ears and the back of his neck. He was already wearing worn-out, bleached jeans, patched in the knees with bits of other materials. He thought he'd invented these things. They were just what seemed natural and comfortable and independent to him in this place where everybody else was wearing butch cuts and khakis. But then in the glimpses he would get on TV and in magazines he began to see *really* long hair and beards on young men out west, people trying to look like Jesus, pony-tails, and the really widely flared and colorfully patched jeans, and at first he had hated these images, they were ugly, ridiculous, maddening, but then he listened to the music they had, saw the dust jackets on the albums, and the posters, he saw the girls or women, how they went without bras in those long thin dresses, their beads, their braids, their bare feet in sandals. He heard about how they lived and what they thought, and, sure, about the risks they took with the things they ate and drank and smoked that changed the way they saw and heard and felt and might mess up their brains forever, but they weren't worried about forever. He saw their insolence at police and politicians and how it infuriated the businessmen, the government which was running the war that at first he had been too young for and then he wasn't and he could have been drafted to fight in the dark in some jungle where he wouldn't know when his throat was going to be cut. The hippies out in California hated the war, they shouted out against it, they marched and sat in official buildings and got jailed and talked about making love instead of fighting and he realized that he hadn't been hating these "freaks," he was jealous of them, they were way ahead of him; *far out*, as they put it.

And so he didn't have any choice. Once he saw how far behind them he was, in everything, tied up in this narrow-minded town with its feuds and jealousies and dead opinions, his own horizonless outlawry, he felt ashamed. He could hardly wait to go out there and learn about it and get back here with it. All of it. He thought it would only take him long enough to let his hair grow down his back, to learn how to get the stuff, to grow it, use it, trade it, learn what went with it, and he would have absorbed the rest. The togetherness, the cool. That different perspective on life they had that he thought he had too, that explained to him why he was an outlyer, an outlaw. He'd be much more of one when he returned.

Carol was a nice person, married to Ray but in love with Robert too. He didn't ask her. It was her idea to go with him, part way. They both worked for a while in Rochester.

"Oh?" The jurywoman asked. Work hadn't been mentioned in the trial. "Doing what?"

He didn't like to tell her. He had a trade, he said. It wasn't really a trade. He could do it. You could find work at it. Little jobs. It wasn't like a regular job. You worked in houses, alone. You did some painting along with it. It was clean. "You don't have to apologize for being able to make a living," Marjorie said. But he obviously was embarrassed. Then he left Carol there in Rochester—she didn't have the urge that he had—and got out where it was.

"Where specifically? Haight-Ashbury I suppose."

"Big Sur. And some other places. Stimson Beach, Bolinas."

She was impressed. She knew of these places by name.

He just wandered in among the "freaks" and "heads." He never called himself that. Nor hippy. But they took one look at him and called him brother. He didn't have to do anything. He didn't even have to say anything. He looked all right to them. He just did what they did. When he didn't understand something, he asked. Usually he found out that they didn't understand it either, they were just doing what they saw done. If he didn't know something, usually they didn't know it. There were some with ideas, who talked a lot, who were leaders. In fact, after a little while, it seemed to him that he was singled out. He was treated almost like a leader

too. Not because he had ideas or talked a lot but maybe because
he knew how to do things. But there wasn't much to do. It was
such easy living. He didn't know why but he seemed to be
respected, for once in his life.

"You were a good head." She knew the terms.

But no, this was serious, he was remembering. It had been
very different out there, the way people gave you a break to start
with. He thought what they caught on to was that he had a place
that he belonged to, far away, that he knew and that he carried
around with him. This place, around here, he told her. This place
was what made him different, to them. He sounded different. He
knew different things. That was all it was.

"You're very modest," she said.

It made him different from them because they were all sort of
alike, he said. It didn't matter who you were talking to or smoking
with or even a part of you passing the time of day inside a part of
them, they all acted the same and sounded the same and did the
same things and said the same two letters when you asked them
where they came from. They were kind of like a swarm, he said,
made up of little moving clouds of pleasure and predictable opinion
without a real name or even hardly a separate identifiable body
attached to them. They thought they were already in some future
where you wouldn't have people or places or the old-timers and
their stories but just The Brothers and The Sisters and The Earth,
and the only Time there ever was or would be was Now. So that if
the sun came up over those dried-up and burned-off mountains, it
was the only time it ever had, and if it sank behind the ocean some
time later, it was the only time it ever would.

"And they said, 'Like, *wow!*' every time it did, didn't they? But
those *are* beautiful sunsets, over the Pacific, I'm sure." When he
didn't reply, she said, "But when you've seen one, you've seen them
all." And then, "I'm sorry. Talk."

He drifted and listened and lived on the beaches, up creeks, in
shelters made out of anything that drifted up or could be hauled
down the canyons through the live-oak and poison oak. He hardly
wore clothes. Some of them sometimes got dressed up and went

out to San Francisco, to the Filmore, or to Kezar Stadium or Berkeley or Stanford or to the military base down the coast, Fort Ord, to take part in marches, demonstrations. There were people back up in the hills who had cars, or VW buses, they could use. Yah, he did that stuff. "The electric acid kool-aid thing?" Yah, he was there. "Ken Kesey?" Yah, he saw him, saw how people sucked around him kissing his feet, everything he said saying 'Right Ken, right.' That was all he needed to see of Kesey. He got used to California. To the appreciation people gave you, strangers, the smiles of people in those crowds. The whole atmosphere, which was different. The way they were, the people. To the easiness. To the touching. He adapted to it, he told her.

"I imagine you did," she said, rocking slowly. "If they must be interchangeable, those California kids, it's nice they have those great tans, that flaxen hair, those long legs. Nobody's fat and pimply, isn't that right? You could adapt to that. Sorry, go on."

He even thought that it was better there sometimes. Their idea of life. No hatred, no jealousy, no fighting over women. No family pride and hostility. No Raymond to nip and tear at him. He sometimes thought that he would never come back to this. Even if you were black, you were all right out there. They would smile at you. They would touch you. And there was no shame in two men looking in each other's eyes or putting their arms around each other. It got to be normal to him. It all did.

"You let yourself like people! You let them like you!" Keeping her head down on her stitching, she said, "But that isn't the word they used, is it?"

"They said the other word a lot."

"Harder to say here in the East, isn't it. Love, love. Why *didn't* you stay?" She sighed, flicked a wry smile at him, got down on her heels and opened the door of the stove. She put in two more pieces of wood, wet from the snow that had been crusted on them, now melting.

"You wanted to bring that home too, hmm? The no hatred, no jealousy, no fighting over women? The touching and the looking in men's eyes and everything? Because that would be even more outrageous than the other stuff, the little bitty pipes and hookahs and all. Because *here*, you'd have all that and your special place too, your woods and your deer and your trout. Some shack to hole up in and some woman to feed you, as you said. And your own townsfolk who could be relied on to shake their heads about it, take due note. Instead of those people in the Garden of Eden who didn't even pay any attention. Except don't I remember that they tried to close those free beaches? Didn't they get the sheriffs to chase you all off into the poison oak or make you put some clothes on?"

He didn't take offense, but she felt she should explain her superficial information. "It was all on television." He hadn't been on those free beaches near the city but on beaches further south and further north, remoter, harder to get to, secret almost. Far away now, not even real to him anymore, she supposed.

She had been looking at the fire, letting the new pieces get going. Now she closed the door and stood up, spanking her hands. "Well," she said. "You did come back. And what did you do then? What was *this* all about—?" She indicated the structure they were in, reddish like the inside of the whale in Pinocchio. "Now, it's my bed-time. Tomorrow night you have to tell me all about that."

Since that first night, there had been no more harassment. They slept close together, comfortably nested, until, grown too warm or too confined, he flung himself on his back. She knew he felt entitled to a woman, felt that his birthright was coming to him in such form. He was waiting for that. They both knew the woman wasn't she. She'd made that clear, but she regretted it a little, and regretted his acceptance of it, as she grew comfortable with him.

She told this to her husband, who scoffed at the whole project of course. Their relationship was very frank, meaning he didn't bother to conceal his infidelities. They both agreed that if he was bound to have them, this was more respectful of her than secrecy. She didn't know that she would necessarily show him the same respect, but she had nothing to hide. She said, "I might as well be hung for a sheep as a lamb. But you know me."

8

Maestra!

The gym was divided in half by a curtain, and one half of the bleachers had been rolled out and turned to face the stage behind several rows of chairs on the floor. The basketball goal had been swung up out of the way. They sat in the third row of chairs, Leo passing whispered comments in Mr Weller's ear sometimes a little too loud for privacy. The band members came in at the side entrance and tromped up the chorus risers onto the stage, looking quite happy and confident, nicely dressed, their instruments gleaming. Some boys slid closed the big panels at the back that opened onto the hall of classrooms, and Mrs Higgins placed an open bejewelled hand on her bosom and said, "I hope you can hear me."

Leo wouldn't have missed this concert, Julia's first. "Be there or be square," she'd told him. Mr Weller attended out of a school board member's sense of duty. He could hear Mrs Higgins quite well but didn't want to. What she was about to say would be self-congratulating, fulsome praise for these students and their musical achievements, which the students would then proceed to contradict.

It isn't a notably musical town, perhaps, and he no great judge, but what these long-tenured music teachers got out of the children struck him as poor moaning embarrassment, mostly. These teachers themselves had tin ears, he could tell that much. They couldn't play the piano, either one of them. They didn't get the stage band to tune their instruments. Secretly he laid some of the responsibility for Leo's troubles at their feet.

They had mostly let Leo teach himself the trombone, and though he did very well, he played off the side of his mouth, the

way a stereotype gangster talks. When he went on to the music
school at State, full of his dance-band dreams, the first thing his
horn teacher there did was make him change his embouchure. He
had to break down the complicated musculature of his lips, which
had produce the rich, warm tones he was famous for at the high
school dances, and try to build it back up correctly, with the
mouthpiece in the center. He lost everything he had achieved on
his own, a great deal. It was a disaster to Leo's eager hopes—not
wholly realistic hopes, perhaps, but still—

Mr Weller was subject to musical sentimentalities despite
himself and, to be fair, there were always enjoyable moments in
the singing parts of the recitals. And it was interesting to see the
students dressed up. Among the boys, there were unexpected
neckties and shined shoes and even a certain pleasure in wearing
them, in some cases. In others, apparent trade-offs with their
parents, as if they had agreed to wear a collared shirt if they didn't
have to tuck it in, or to wear pleated pants if they didn't have to
wear a belt. The girls positively leaped at the chance to adopt more
adult clothing, announcing a maturity verging on the inappropriate,
or so it seemed to him.

While the noise of conversation abated Mrs Higgins went on
about the exits and the rest rooms. Tonight's stage band concert
was going to be something special. We were going to have our
practice-teacher, still a student at the School of Music at Moira
State, conduct the band. We had never done this before, but Miss
delBorgo had been working with the band during Mrs Jones's recent
absence. (Mrs Jones had been diagnosed with cancer, it was said.)
Needless to say, she had been a godsend. We were very proud of
her. Mrs Jones was not missing. She was home again and you would
find her back there in the brass section, filling in where she was
most needed.

With that, Mrs Higgins gave the program over to Julia, whom
Mr Weller's eyes had already been following in surprised approval,
as she moved up and down the risers with microphone stands and
cables, in and out of the wings with the arms of kids. He'd been
glimpsing one little deft transaction after another, the children

beaming, laughing, pleased. Obviously they loved her, and he could
see that she, whom he'd always thought a somewhat messy young
person, was transformed in this context into a confident, brisk,
persuasive leader. And quite irresistible, in a plain black dress with
a full skirt, a modest neckline and short, loose sleeves, and tiny
black low-heeled shoes. "My goodness," he said to Leo beside him.

Who cocked his head at him as if to say, "You hadn't noticed?"
She was aglow, pale but rosy-cheeked. He was a poor observer of
details but he took the effect and tried to isolate its causes. Her
hair was bound up complexly, and her neck (had he ever seen it
before?) long and slender, like her calves and ankles (also never
before noticed). Moving so swiftly here and there, unconscious of
onlookers, helping her orchestra get settled, music correctly placed,
mikes in position for the solos, she was bewitching to watch.

Now facing the band, beside her own music stand on her little
platform, she spoke inaudibly to them a moment, called for a note
from the flute, then went through the orchestra asking for the
note from one instrument at a time. Patiently she brought each
one to the pitch. Once she dashed round to adjust the slide of a
trombone herself. He could hear the dissonances squeezed away to
a thin, resonant line.

The children in front, saxophones on the left over to flute and
piccolo on the right, were looking up at her with something new
in their faces. Anticipation? Humor? She wheeled around to face
the audience, quite dazzling of face even to him, and after a very
brief introduction of the first piece, nothing he'd ever heard of, she
turned back and stepped on her stand, drew up her arms (so slender,
so pale), and the concert began.

It was some sort of march, he thought; chosen to let the children
be bold, belted along by the drums, ruffles and beats in perfect
time. He imagined Julia pulling that would-be drummer out of
hiding, pursuing him on the basis of need, convincing him he
could do this. Then one by one all sections of the band had their
turn with the simple tune, and the harmonies came through, and
so did the dynamic changes she called for, without an
embarrassment, until a final satisfactory pounce at the end. She

turned and smiled, dodging the applause herself and from one side waving it on to the band, some of whom were laughing.

She asked Mrs Jones to come forward to conduct the next pieces. Mrs Jones stood up from the trumpet section, in back, and to everyone's applause came round to shake Julia's hand and take the baton. It was a slow piece, with deep, layered chords, which the orchestra played with surprising openness and sustainment. Monica led them in a way Mr Weller had never seen, with full-body movement, deep, knee-bending scoopings and drawings-up of her hands. He wished he could see her from in front. She looked remarkably good, considering the town's fears for her—that streaked blonde hair a new color. Was she feeling something she had missed for a long time, what an orchestra well-prepared could give you back? So encouraging for the kids, he imagined, to deliver this to her. Surely Julia had prepared them. The applause was a notch stronger, the audience realizing that something had happened to these children.

Other pieces followed, less interesting to Mr Weller, kids' favorites, the theme from some recent movie he knew not. He was waiting to loose his sentiment on *America, the Beautiful*, listed on the program. The arrangement, when it came, was too fancy, too indulgent for his taste—a straightforward rendition would have moved him more—and it was a little too brilliant for the kids, but mostly it went the way it was supposed to, with mounting beautifulness, Julia's every gesture calling up a clear new element, piling up complexity until at the end it all resolved back to an honest, plain *From sea to shining sea*. He was moved.

In the applause were whistles and shouts and stompings on the bleachers—almost like the applause after a basketball win. Without turning to accept it, the conductor, astonishingly, sank to her low platform, and curled up on her side, facing the band. Her face was away from the audience but the saxophones and clarinets were smiling and laughing at her, leaning toward her, speaking. They and other band-members put down their instruments and knelt around her, peeking at her face, caressing her arms; and two of them, girls, gently unfolded her and lifted her up, turned her around, and made her bow to the audience. She looked like one of them, smaller than many, bowing and laughing, holding hands with those beside her, while the applause, sustained all this while, died down. Leo put his fingers in his mouth and whistled.

After an intermission were the choruses, one conducted by Julia, all business again, in which the coach's younger son, with his short hair wetted down on his forehead like a Roman soldier's, earnestly and audibly sang a tenor solo (unheard of in other times). Julia accompanied, on the piano, the girls' choir directed by Mrs Higgins, ending in a Beatles medley, very up-to-date he presumed. Then a break, for setting up the jazz ensemble, the last section of the program. Missing Leo beside him, Mr Weller looked about, exchanged pleased smiles with Neva Day. He searched the exit doors, where the smokers had already come back inside. The gym lights dimmed. The ensemble was lit from overhead, the conductor in silhouette as she snapped her fingers. But of course: Leo was on stage.

Why not? He couldn't see over the first row of players, but between the legs and stands and chair-legs he found Leo's sneakers stretched out toward him, ankles crossed. He caught a narrow slice of him between other players' shoulders, his hands close together in first position, ready to begin; his lips being rolled and licked, then settled into the mouthpiece, dead-center.

Julia only got them started, then went back and played, one handed, some flat instrument he didn't recognize, electronic apparently. He couldn't make out what it did. The drummer was set up out of sight behind the piano, but he was clearly having the time of his life. The trumpet and saxophone soloists actually tried to improvise, rather dully; but the collective sound was confidently musical. Donkey-like hee-hawing from the trombones, Leo standing, much applauded when he sat down. It wasn't much to Mr Weller's taste but it was, still, unprecedentedly good. The applause rose in volume when Julia acknowledged Leo. Leo, red-lipped, red-eared, too serious, ducked away from it. She made the whole band stand and bow, which they did with flushed, happy faces.

Leo assured him as they walked home: "You see, Père? Everything's going to be all right."

"That was very nice indeed. She illuminates the sad fact that we have been short-changing our students for ten years or so, so far as music is concerned. As you've always known."

"Not I. I always loved Monica, hopeless as she was and is."

"How does she do it? I thought perhaps she was just young, and undiscouraged, and—

"She's got it."

"You think so? More than another person might."

"Way more."

This brought a worry to Mr Weller's mind. "It doesn't have anything to do with her relation to the town?" This was his secret burden.

"Oh no."

"They don't suspect it?"

"Oh heavens no."

"Well. That's good."

"They wouldn't believe it! She's a now-person, Père. So are they. History? They take her as she is. You have to admit, that was the best concert at SF Central in many a year."

"It was too. God bless her."

But he didn't sleep straightaway. A damned nuisance, this secret of his sister's, what he had just called (awkwardly, as if even he and Leo couldn't talk candidly about it!) Julia's relation to the town. It put him in a false position with the school board, the Shampines, the whole town. With Sarah too.

Yet it was a fact, and but for this relation Julia wouldn't be anywhere near this town. Wouldn't be at Moira's music school rather than another, wouldn't be practice-teaching here. She was related to people she shouldn't be related to, you might say— wouldn't be, if things happened as they should. To the Shampines, Clarence and his sisters. But she was unknown to them and for the time being her connection to them was secret, absurd as that might be, so decreed by her protectress, his own older sister. Who had pressed him and Neva Day into a scheme for the girl, involving not only her elderly antecedents but their land, a piece of the physical North Country itself, something he deeply felt it was a shame, somehow indecent, to finagle with.

The Shampines had had a younger sister, Milly, the baby, the daughter of the other siblings' young and much loved step-mother. Milly was everybody's darling. Mr Weller himself as a boy was in love with her. He remembered very well the summer she was taken from him—not but what his family had already told him that she was not for him. It was about 1925, and the hillsides along the shore of the lake were being stripped bare of the last accessible virgin timber in Olmstead County. That desecration, that rape and pillage (as he saw it now) was going on in full tear right in front of the Wellers' faces, across the lake from their cottages. The lake was so full of floating logs, waiting to be boomed down to the jackworks at the southeast end, that it was hardly safe to go out in a canoe. The scoundrels who were timbering it would go bankrupt before they were done and leave a million board feet of logs to sink to the bottom, where they still were now, no good to anyone.

That was when the gangly red-haired artist came up from Brooklyn and took his room and board at the little lodge, there at the end of the bay, just beyond the first few cottages. The three Shampine sisters were working at that lodge, the boy Clarence too, and the painter got Clarence to take him all over the woods, bull-heading at Mud Pond or trout fishing on the outlet. He seemed to have a great appetite for experiencing everything that was natural to the natives. He went everywhere, knew everybody, painted everything.

Anybody might have seen it coming—anybody older and wiser than Loyal Weller was then, a boy of thirteen who'd been given to understand that though Milly was a treasure, there was a difference of class, if not of quality, between their two families. Well, no such scruple troubled the painter. He took advantage of his age, his experience, and his charm. Against that romantic background of the slaughter of the lakeshore, he misbehaved with the innocent rustic girl who made his bed and put his pie in front of him every day.

Granted he was gentleman enough to marry the girl and take her away to Brooklyn. Granted it wasn't any fault of his that the childbirth was difficult, leaving the mother so frail. They had some sort of a life, hard as it was to imagine Milly in a tenement. They were certainly poor. The painter could have done perfectly well as a commercial artist, and sometimes did so for a spell, but he preferred to starve his family by selling original paintings on the street. Their daughter turned out to be glamorous, worldly, married a succession of slick fellows, an airline pilot, an Italian count, and whatnot, and the connection with the north attenuated until there wasn't any. The child of the count, if he was really a count (delBorgo, if that was really a name), was Julia.

Only Sarah, since she lived down there near the City, the wife of a Westchester County newspaper editor, had stayed in touch with Milly's husband and their daughter, and then their daughter's daughter. She'd insisted on her "rights" as a friend of Milly's family, to be informed, to advise, to supervise. She had some sort of relationship with the grandfather, the painter; and despite her distaste for the mother's way of life, and the child's growing rebelliousness, she demanded visitation, she had her say, sometimes she paid for what she thought the child should have—at some point a baby grand piano which she allowed the grandfather to pretend he bought for her. After the child and her mother effectively disowned each other, when the child was fourteen, and Julia went back to live (nominally) with her "Gramps," Sarah assumed the primary financial responsibility for her. Someone had to. She had to be given a chance to become what she could, "to show what she came from!" as Sarah put it. And now here was Milly Shampine's granddaughter, virtually an orphan, virtually impoverished but for Sarah's assistance, with very expensive ambitions and educational requirements; and here were the aged Shampine girls with all their land.

Sarah had had much to do with the child's coming to college in the North rather than elsewhere, despite the child's resistance. Sarah Bryant was paying the bill, and tuition anywhere else but a state college was frightful. The School of Music at State (once the Academy, which Sarah herself attended, before it was the Normal School, before it was the teachers' college and then just college) was the oldest music-education institution in the country, and that was good enough for anybody. The theory might have been that the North Country climate alone would teach her who she was, since she was still not allowed to meet her superior relations. She needed chastening first, for she'd been just as bad as her mother, an outrageous teen-ager, very nearly given up on. But now, once this period of practice-teaching was behind her, and Julia had (let us hope) acquired some appreciation of the salt with which she was salted, Sarah intended to introduce the child to her great-aunts. To Clarence too, in the course of things; but he was unimportant, no land in his name. His sisters thought him too foolish to be trusted with a deed. Neither of the girls, now in their 70s and 80s, had any children. They couldn't go on as they were, living by themselves, heating with wood, out on the sheepfarm forever. Sarah reasoned that when they went into a home, they'd be wards of the state. The state would take their land and auction it off to pay for their care. Nellie's sheepfarm along the river west of town, Bessie's woodlots in behind the home place—think of the value of that property today! Whereas . . .

Whereas—Sarah proposed to argue to the Shampine girls in due time, no later than the coming spring when Julia graduated—whereas, if they passed it on (cheap) to a certain somebody before they became infirm, (this the sisters need not know) it would put somebody through graduate school, start somebody off in her intended career.

Loyal Weller had once objected, "Seems a shame to let the sisters think it'll stay in the family."

"There are only two reasons to own land," Sarah Bryant declared. "Use, and redemptive value." That was that.

9

Blue Balls

Peter Hubbard had a kind of crude, Cajun style: lank hair, eagle nose, dihedral neck, starvation ribs, no abdomen. He still wore the same clothes he wore in high school: white carpenter's jeans over his skinny legs with a useless hammerloop on the thigh, a denim jacket open over a tie-died teeshirt. He carried a few things including finger-picks in a small suede bag tied to an empty beltloop though he no longer tried to play the guitar. He didn't use the roach-clip, either. He could have used a belt, but beltlessness had been part of his rebellion against his mother from age eight and was a habit by now. Hawk, they called him. He'd made All-Northern forward, could have had a scholarship somewhere, but the town had held him, the girl-friend pregnant in their senior year.

Every so often in the past, one of these ragamuffin Sabattis Falls Central basketball teams with a half-empty bench took fire and won the D Division of the Northern Zone championship. After all, the other towns in the division were much the same sorts of places, small towns on the borders of the woods and any boy the right age got drafted to play and you had a strange mixture of skills and body types and haircuts and facial expressions even if only one skin color. The team Peter played on two years back clawed and cliff-hung its way to the Division title and then actually embarrassed two of the bigger schools and drove all the way to the regional finals.

Not that this made Peter and his teammates heroes. Because as Leo Weller liked to say, this town didn't have any idea of Progress. As with present-day lumberjacks, axe-handlers, ladies' men and fiddlers, present-day basketball players could never be more than pale reflections of the ballplayers their fathers had been (gone now to belly and gimp), and their fathers' fathers before them, proof that the world runs nowhere but down as time rolls by. Even when he was playing, he'd felt himself an echo of something ineffable, connecting way back. Just like the crowd, Peter out there on the court was lost, thrown away in a sort of homage, aware of nothing else but the striving. Not the pain in his lungs, not the lactic acid in his thighs. He was so lost he'd sometimes miss the sudden changes, defense, offense, defense.

He was fast, he was all over the court, he made detailed invented breaks and drives from one end of the court to the other and sometimes all the way around under the basket along the baseline and out around the backcourt and in under the basket again and finally some gangling crazy levitation and fake and twist resulting in a feathery lay-up or a fallingaway pump that the laced net caught almost horizontally, while he crashed into the stands or against the orange mats roped up along the wall. Or he'd have shoveled off an unexpected pass in the middle of his spinning leap, which his teammate wouldn't even have seen, or couldn't handle. Out of bounds. Or he'd find that he hadn't had the ball for the last three moves and had laid up a fantasy.

He hardly knew what feats he did. He couldn't follow them, they were too fast. He wouldn't be aware that anything had happened until the building roared like the sea, drowning the selfless dream he was in. A foul. *A foul?* Who? *Me?* His mouth would fall open. He would run to the referee begging for belief. He hadn't done anything! *With the body? What body?* Huh? He would slam down the ball, which he wouldn't know he had torn from someone's arms, leaving a slick of sweat on the floor where they wrestled. He'd dig his fingers into his long hair so that the sweatband bunched it up in loops. The long ends of it would fly around his shoulders and slap his face from behind while he tried to find his man and he'd have to put the sweatband back on over it while running back into combat still denying, protesting, staring beseechingly at Coach for sympathy or explanation as he passed.

And South would be on his feet with his face knotted, yelling at him, pointing, with a yellow tablet in his hand, at the place on the court where his stupid, traitorous, criminal mistake had been enacted and white towels were now flashing.

He, Peter, wouldn't know what South was shouting about. He always did what South told him to do, didn't he? What's he mean? His face would be wrenched with self-pity, he'd seem about to cry, but everything would be swept away again in the silent dream of fluid violence until the next awful, aching moments of pause, technicality, stasis, thunder.

Or South would send in his replacement, yelling at him to get off the floor. He'd stare at South. "Huh? Who?" South would point at him, "You!" He'd point to his own skinny panting chest. "Me?" Then go out, unquestioningly obedient but grieving with frustration, and drop onto the bench as if his spinal column had been clipped.

That year, Peter's senior year when Patty was already pregnant, this little backwoods team, with nine players if nobody had the flu, raged through its division almost-losing every game, as if it could not stand a comfortable lead no matter how South wanted one and how they meant to give him everything he wanted—almost throwing away every game but winning them all the hard way, through tension so dense in the last minutes that they might have been played under water or in amber. Except in the regionals, at Moira in the college gym, brilliantly lit and colorful like an Olympic venue, when they had won their semifinal game against an A team and were leading Harrisville, a B team, a bigger school but another upcountry case, another pack of lumberjack's sons with a wholly different kind of muscle and discipline, for the overall championship. That game the Bearcats led throughout, by big leads, fifteen points with two minutes to go. And they couldn't stand it, they threw the game away with errors, turnovers, and unnecessary fouls in the final seconds, for the love, apparently, of South's passionate abuse, his furious scolding, his caring and belief and urgency; because that was the last of it they'd get. That was the last of Coach for them.

It was the same when Patty told him she was pregnant. He didn't know what he was doing when he did that either. What? Who? Me? But it was just the same, he had somebody telling him what he had to do and a crowd on the sidelines that demanded it too. Patty knew what he had to do, and she was right; she was in charge of that kind of stuff. Babies, what would he know about that? South would have said the same thing, Get in there and play the game. So he pushed up his hair and wanted to cry but he did what she said, okay, okay, with the same complete submission.

He didn't want the basketball scholarship anyway. Playing for some college—what would be the meaning of that? He had a much older uncle at Alcoa, his great fan; it was no problem getting in there as a fireman. That was the hardest, hottest job at the plant but he hadn't had to remain a fireman very long, his uncle fixed that too and now he worked on the steam system, traveled all over the plant reading gauges twice a shift. He could do them in an hour. He fixed himself a bed, in among some big dollies loaded with scrap metal, a pad of newspapers and an old sleeping bag on a shelf of angle iron. There he read, or slept. He always had a paperback in his hip pocket, one of Patty's romances that were being passed around, and a plastic coffee cup clipped to a belt loop. Francis, his buddy Frank, had picked up that habit as an Army cook and passed it on to him. The pay was good. He let himself acquire a pot. The uncle who loved basketball so much died and left him the very nice shingled house, just up Main Street beyond the school. Money, things, freedom. God's country. Excitement hanging out with his mother's younger brother, charismatic Ray.

He and Francis left the plant together to ride home in their car pool. In back, a wheel with a shock going bad thumping just behind them, they rocked against each other in the dark, mumbling so the others in front couldn't hear them. What they shared now, more than the loss of their friend, more even than JoAnn and the problem of avenging Ray, which she forced upon them, was that face turned toward them both, that hair, that bosom, those fingers in their belt-loops. They were talking about her even when they never mentioned her name.

The way she was to each of them, to both of them, was something they had never known before, either of them. She relieved them of their shame, their pain, their burdens, shame and pain and burdens that they didn't know they had. She made them think that everything could be so good. That they could be good, life could. She understood the way they felt about their lives as they actually were. Peter was married, but he hardly knew how that had happened to him or what marriage was supposed to be or why. He'd had children before he had grown up himself, before he had lived. She understood how that had happened and she showed him that it wasn't his fault. It was because of the way the "society" was that he was trying to grow up in, that Patty had been trying to grow up in, and their parents and their friends and everybody else. It was because this whole town was living with ideas and teaching them to its kids that were two hundred years out of date and weren't right in the first place because they were cooked up by people in power (men) to keep everybody else (women) in their places but what they did was screw up the lives of men worse than women. They could never remember all that she told them but that was the gist of it, something like that.

Of course the first thing was that she understood about Robert, what a creep, what a coward he was, sure, but that was his problem not theirs. It wasn't their job to do anything about him no matter what JoAnn said. She went one-on-one with his Ma, she wasn't afraid of her. She said she loved her but she was so wrong, they didn't have to screw up their own lives to do anything about Robert Sochia. Not only didn't have to, she said they must not. It would only ruin their own lives. Their lives were worth too much for that. They had to just leave him alone and let him deal with the thing that he had done, all by himself. If they didn't think he was paying for that, they were wrong. She guaranteed he was paying for it. "Maybe he'll grow up himself some day," she'd sing, "You never kno-ow!" The way she would finish a serious talk like that, suddenly smiling and singing her words with her head on its side and her eyebrows raised and her eyes closed. You just wanted to close your own eyes and taste her mouth when she did that. And they did taste her mouth. She kissed them all the time, right on the mouth with her arms around their shoulders and her tits against their chests. She'd climb up on them and do it with her legs around their waists, being like a little girl with them but it made them dizzy with what they wished.

She could be awfully serious. She rolled her lips together when she was going to say something serious and she looked upwards at them from a face that was tilted down. They would just be giving him what he wanted if they did anything to him, she told them. She rolled her lips together. "He *wants* to be hurt. Why do you think he has come back here? I know this without even knowing the person. His whole life, that you've told me about, stupid robberies, reform school, breaking the law, shows how self-destructive he is. He hates himself as much as you hate him, don't worry."

At first this seemed ridiculous to them, Robert Sochia hating himself. She didn't know. But anyway she was right when she said it wasn't their job to oblige JoAnn. "What does she expect you to do? I know what she wants to happen to him and she's crazy, man. That's crazy and you know it. Let him do it himself, ha-ha." She turned it into a joke, made them laugh about it. Then she said, "That's not funny though because I am afraid that he will. If he doesn't find a way to be happy, by which I mean a way to see that he is okay too."

Frank snorted at the idea. "A piss-yellow coward that shot his own cousin and then calls O'Neil and says come get me, I'm in trouble." But she rolled her lips together again and said, simply, in a dull voice as if they were hopeless, "That *is* okay, Francis. To be afraid of being hurt. That isn't inconsistent either. That is perfectly okay." As if she knew everything. Which she couldn't, she couldn't know these things about him, about everything. But Francis had to hang his head and accept it because if he didn't what then? What about her lips and all, and what they wished and she promised, sort of. In spring. In winter she didn't do any of that, she said. She slept a lot and got really well rested up, for spring, hint-hint.

Peter was sure Francis was the same as he, obsessed. Seeing images of her, the way her hair, so heavy, pulled her head back; how her big soft bosom pulled her shoulders forward. Little wrists and hands and ankles. Most of all her eyes. How could you describe them? You couldn't. They were green with sparkles of brown and gold, and they were deep but they were also prominent, the whites were very shiny. They moved a lot, back and forth to yours. She did things with them. He gave up. It all went straight to his balls, his cock felt the least thought of her and woke up, click click click, up up up. God how he wanted her, in his arms, naked against him, skin on skin. She knew. She let you know she wanted it too. She touched you. She touched your ass even. Nobody else ever did that. Your thighs. Rubbed them and patted them under tables. She even promised it. She'd say, "Just wait 'til spring, man." Wasn't that a promise? "Spring is my time of year, man." What did she mean by that if not that when it was warmer out, when you could lie on the grass, the warm rocks, the pine needles . . .?

His cock could get out of this cramped place, unfold, stand up in the warm air blowing over it, where she could appreciate it. It was a pretty amazing thing. Then up inside her, way up so she didn't need her legs and they'd shiver, loose; 'til she'd hook her heels behind him and pull him in farther. They'd be face to face; that face smiling into his about it being in there, up to her ribs, hers as much as his. Which it was! He wanted to share it so!

Francis beside him in the dark said something. He had to shake himself to bring his mind back up from his groin.

"Maybe I'll go on a fast," Frank said.

There was this idea of improving themselves. Both of them had it. They wanted to change themselves, make themselves better. Frank had bought a set of weights. He was building up his body. He was purifying himself, he said. That was all right for Frank, he had peace at home. He was single, he lived with his mother and sister now, had them waiting on him.

"Julia's been on fasts," Frank said. "She fasted with that comedian, Dick Gregory, against the war."

"Yeah, right." This kept happening. Frank would tell him something he thought she had told to him alone. Then they'd realize they were both there when she told it. Each of them just wanted to be the only one.

"Maybe I'll quit eating," Frank said. "I think I will." She had made it sound pretty good. She went without solid food for two weeks. In a day she might have a cup of broth, bouillon. Maybe she would have part of somebody's milkshake, in the cafeteria, she said. She was always eating some of your food, chips, drinking your beer, whatever. She said it made her feel great, fasting.

Frank said, "At first you have cramps, but after a while you feel clean and light, and you lose your baby fat. You shit these tiny little beads of shit like a rabbit's."

"Yeah, right," Peter said.

Their ride dropped them off by the town buildings. Dark, except for the young doctors from Saranac still holding their clinic, crosscountry skis on the roofs of their foreign cars parked outside. There would be kayaks on the cartops in the spring. They would go crashing down this river that he had lived by all his life without ever thinking of going down it in a boat. It was just rocks the whole way, for Christ's sake. But these rich doctors would be playing with it, in wetsuits that cost two hundred dollars, when it was all white rapids and freezing cold and you couldn't even fish it yet.

His own vehicle was over by the pumphouse for the water system, just across the road from The Rapids. They walked past it and across, side by side with their heads down and their hands in the pockets of their jackets, in the cold wet air swirling up from the open water below the dam. This was the routine, checking in here at his mother's. A habit, a duty. Later they would go up and watch the ball-game and they would see Julia at least from a distance because she was coaching the cheerleaders. She didn't know anything about cheerleading and she didn't even believe in it but the girls were so crazy about her they wanted her to do it and she did. Meanwhile it wasn't always great in here with his mother but he didn't want to go home right away, either. Patty would probably tell him that he shouldn't go to the ball game, that he ought to give Cheryl her bath and read her her story and put her to bed. Which was true, he should, and he would like to, but then he would be late and maybe not see Julia at all. He always looked in at Cheryl sleeping when he did come home. Could not walk past the door of her room without looking in at her sleeping. They'd see Julia at the game in pleated skirt and bobby-socks and a megaphone on her sweater like all her cheerleaders. They'd catch her eye, she'd blow them a big kiss in front of everybody.

Peter kicked the door and shoved it open with his shoulder, went behind the bar and pulled them up two Schaefers and came back around and sat down next to Frank in the usual place, near the door, away from his mother and her friend Harry. There was Ray's jaunty sun-tanned face in the best photograph, bushy brows under a sailor-hat tilted back, hello you poor sucker. He threw a crumpled bill on the counter. His mother turned around off the stool she kept back there when it was quiet and came and put it in the cash register and slid the change in front of him.

Always some sort of smile, meaning she knew something he didn't. Robert was making the rounds, crosslots. On foot. Haven't you heard? No shit, Ma. The DeSoto goes nowhere. No shit. Robert's got a doe hanging in Johnny's barn, some bullshit gossip like that, every time they came in. No shit, Ma.

"What's so funny, Ma?" he said now. "Give us some chips." He pushed the change back toward her. JoAnn leaned on the bar close in front of him. "Go on, Ma. The chips."

"You heard."

"Sure I heard. What?"

"You didn't hear."

"We didn't hear. What."

"O'Neil's found your friend some work. Actual, legal, paying work."

"Robert don't work for pay, you know that, Ma." Smiled with his teeth at Frank.

"It's not work, exactly. A job. A one-time job."

"He don't need money. He's got whatever Grogan got out of Social Services for him. The J. brings him supper. He's living the life of Reilly."

"Well," his mother said, "O'Neil's looking for him, to give him an assignment. Comes right in here and asks *me* where to find him, the fool. What kind of job could it be? A trip. To Montreal, for expenses plus fifty dollars. O'Neil can never find Bobby home, so I'm supposed to pass that on!"

Frank grabbed the chips. Peter grabbed them back. Frank grabbed at them again, missing. Peter jumped up and punched him in the shoulder and shoved the chips into his midsection and embraced him from the rear, furiously. Then he went away and looked out different windows. He slammed a couple of weights over the sensors of the bowling machine, against the cushion that bounced them partway back. He came back and took his stool again in front of his mother.

"Aren't you curious?"

"No. O'Neil's looking for him. For a job. So what?"

She dropped her hands and looked back along the bar at Harry, his big hands propped together over their shared ashtray. "Show him the story, Harry," she said. She took the newspaper out from under Harry's elbow and showed it to them herself.

"Remember that car that was stolen in Malone? Late model GM car? Back while Robert was still in jail?"

"No."

"Hew! Well, read this. It belonged to a woman dentist in Moira. The Quebec Provincial Police found it, way up near Hudson's Bay, with the serial numbers ground off the block. When they got done examining it they informed the New York State Troopers that they could come get it. The troopers had better things to do and informed the Olmstead County Sheriff, and our great lawman O'Neil thought it would be a kindness to pass Robert Sochia the job of going after it. Probably took him up to Cornwall himself and put him on the train. O'Neil's queer for Robert anyway."

"So what, Ma."

"Read the article. This isn't just a random incident of car theft. There's a syndicate doing it, spread out over all the northeastern border states, Maine to Lake Ontario. Stealing late-model GM cars, one here, one there. It says here, 'The police suspected they were all finding their way to the Province of Quebec.'"

Somebody down the bar said, "Them Pepsis'll do anything for a Body by Fisher."

"Well?" JoAnn said.

"What?"

"Don't you think that's kind of funny? Bobby going on an errand for the police to fetch a stolen car? He'll probably join that syndicate and steal the next one himself. Maybe he's already in it. It's just the sort of thing he'd do."

The boys had no idea what she was getting at. Follow him and find out? Help him get caught? "Ma, hey. I'm not messing with Bobby. He can come and go. If he doesn't cross me, I don't care. He isn't going to stay here. You know that."

She dug her fingers into her face and hair and made a sound that he had never heard. He almost went around inside the bar to her. She was like that for a minute. Then she was all right. She said, "You know what I thought he was?"

"No, what?"

She faked going limp at his not knowing.

Okay, he knew. "So?"

"Ha!"

"I ain't no coward, Ma. You know that."

"I wonder what anybody would have to do to make you prove it."

"Nothing. I don't have to prove it."

She said, "Oh."

"I can't explain it. I know somebody who could explain it."

"No, you explain it."

"I forget how it goes, Ma. Ask Frank. She told the same thing to Frank."

His mother just looked at them both. Now she seemed okay, very calm. She said, "Listen to me, boy of mine. My brother Ray was the meanest little shit that ever was."

"Yes, Ma."

"The meanest, best little shit that ever was. He was!"

"You're God-damned right he was," Francis said.

"All right. Your little slut of a music teacher doesn't know anything about it."

Frank got off his stool. He still wore his Army jacket with the dark green places where the patches and insignia had been. He said, "Don't give us this, JoAnn. Are you saying I'm afraid of that sack of shit?"

"Why is Robert a sack of shit? He had the guts to shoot somebody. Who was, I'm quite sure, going to smash that ugly nose of his, for once. He has the guts to come back here. Why is he a sack of shit and you two think you're men? This is my son, Francis. I'll call him what I please. I'm concerned with his becoming a man. This is still my role, to teach him how to be a man. *Who else will?*"

"We're going up to the game, Ma," Peter said. "We'll see ya."

They put on their coats unhurriedly and JoAnn, blowing the hair out of her face, turned away. Before they left they heard her say to Harry, "I don't expect anybody to kill anybody. But my God, does he need to live in this town where I have to look at him? Does he? Do I have to live in the same town with that filth?"

Peter paused in the door to see if Harry answered. He was a solid man. The biggest hands you ever saw. Ma ought to give him some, it would do her good.

Harry didn't speak. Harry knew it was a dumb question. Peter waited long enough to hear what she said next. She threw a damp towel on the bar and pushed it around in a circle. She said to Harry, "I'm thinking about making us some fried chicken." Harry didn't comment. "Or fried shrimp?" she asked.

Harry still didn't answer. Harry wouldn't answer a question you could answer yourself. He didn't give a shit, shrimp or chicken. JoAnn didn't *make* those dinners anyway, they were frozen dinners, right off the restaurant supply truck. She just heated them up.

"Which?" she asked him, impatiently; and Peter let the door click shut.

10

Sochia Sochia He's Our Man

Remembering that day when he came back from California, describing it to the jurywoman, he saw himself as if he were somebody else, as if he were the town looking on. That's how far he had reverted, changed back, shed whatever California had done to him. He'd been away more than a year and now in the spring he suddenly appeared in the town driving that well-preserved two-tone green DeSoto and coming into places with his long hair in a braid and with his beads and bell-bottoms and Buddhist shirts, but not only the outer signs, the other ones, the strange way of relating to people, of touching them male and female and looking into their eyes and smiling all the time—if she could imagine that. Oh, she could, she said. She'd changed for a while too in those years—and changed back too—it was mostly gone now, wasn't it? And look: bras were back long ago. She used to go without them, even to work! All her friends did too. For a while.

But that first day, bringing Carol back. Amazing to see himself as the town must have seen him, coming into Eugene's and giving her back to Ray, as they had agreed. Carol had missed it all, almost all, there in Rochester. She knew Robert was a stranger to her now. She was frightened coming back beside him to face her husband but at the same time eager to see Ray and happy to be going back to him if he would have her. She'd never wanted to change, or go all the way west in the first place. She'd stayed true to herself, only wanting to help him. Now she didn't know if she had helped him or not but it was over and she was ready to go back but afraid what Ray might do to her or to Robert; either or both.

They just drove around for a while, visiting places where woods roads crossed the river, a farm where he used to visit for gossip and doughnuts. They went up the Blue Mountain Road and the Cook's Lake Road and back and forth through town crossing the two bridges so that people would notice the psychedelic DeSoto with the California plates and pass the word that he was back, so that there would be plenty of people in the bars that night, expecting him to show up.

Carol was kind of excited, and scared, all this time, knees up and legs under her on the wide slippery seat beside him, leaning against him and playing with his braid, occasionally putting her face in his neck. They went to Chittenden and left most of her stuff at her mother's and then late in the evening he drove them back through town looking for Ray's car and found it in front of Eugene's, and they got out and went in, he sort of pushing her ahead of him because she was bashful about her extra weight. Robert then wasn't nervous at all but now, telling Marjorie about it, he saw himself as the town must have seen him, coming in there behind Carol with his black braids hanging down below his waist, his bloused shirt open on his brown and hairless chest where (in the town's eyes) some big symbolic sort of hood ornament hung on a thong around his neck, and every color of the rainbow patched into his flared and tattered jeans. Ray was sitting at the bar, his back toward them. To the others who turned to see them, Robert must have looked unbelievably insolent, insufferable, as he dropped her white plastic overnight bag on the floor behind Ray, and when Ray looked around, not even doubting Ray's reaction, smiling at him and putting his arms around him. He actually half-hugged him, face-to-face. Ray for a wonder let it happen, though his grin was always dangerous. Then keeping one hand on Ray's shoulder Robert opened up the circle and reached back for Carol's arm, and brought her into it, and, if she (Marjorie) could picture it, kind of married them back together, in a wordless ceremony, one arm around each. What was he thinking? Good-will, acceptance, hope, peace. In the historyless California fog he was still in.

Ray seemed smaller and wirier and older than Robert had expected. He showed all his teeth, gold and white. He pulled back his head, pushed Robert gently to arm's length and turned his attention to his blushing near-sighted wife, looking her over with high interest. He tugged appreciatively at those new handles of sweater-covered fat at her sides, grinning at her and shaking his head until she burst into tears and clasped his scarred, butch-cut head to her bosom. Ray could see she wasn't changed, the same old soft-hearted sweetie, sweet on them both as always and wanting them to love each other or at least be friends. Somebody made a place for Carol next to Ray and he helped her to the empty stool and began to chat with her, make much of her, that gnarled ropy forearm draped across her soft round back. Everybody welcomed her back, all the old fellows in Eugene's, and Eugene too, and Robert stepped away, surrounded in a few minutes by younger men asking him questions, how was it out there, did you like it? Trying hard not to state the obvious, that Robert had taken on the whole style, hook line and sinker, he'd gone over to freakdom with a vengeance. But that was cool, that was cool. They nodded at him, he looked pretty good, they had to admit.

So for a while it looked as if it was going to be okay. Carol went back to Ray and Robert moved his stuff into his sister's, though he didn't stay there much. Johnny Pelo had inherited this old out-of-the-way farm, and he had the fields, the manure pile, the barns, the space. Helen was eager too back then and all the younger people in town, the schoolkids and the young loggers and carpenters and hairdressers and the ones going to vocational school and State. The plantworkers too. It was as if they had all had just been waiting for him to get back with the stuff. *What's it like? What's it do? No fooling? Gee—*. It wasn't just the stuff itself, it was the Indian prints, the hair, the music, the dancing, the hand-painted cars and motorcycles, the rituals; the sharing, the trusting, the touching; so totally different from the old usual ways of behaving in the town. Swearing, fighting, insult, jealousy, unforgivingness—that was just habit. That was always half in jest, an act. They were ready to change. Robert told them what it was like at Big Sur and the kids wanted it that way right here, they made it that way themselves. Robert didn't have to do a thing but get them the stuff, the pipes, the sounds, set the example . . .

The kids. Not just the Pelos' children though they were right in the midst of it, with a dozen parents and a hundred uncles and aunts. The bigger kids, the high school kids and a few that had quit or just recently graduated and were still kids, who flocked out there and made something like a tribe around him and the Pelos. The kids who saw him with his long hair and gold ring and dark face and buttonless bolero and sharkteeth-and-shell jewelry. With Helen's help they slit their jeans up the seams and made them into wide bells with darts of colorful print. They grew their hair. They loved it all. They loved him.

It was better than California. A circulating all-day familylike community like the ones he had drifted through out there, that everybody drifted through, that made their shacks and shelters out of what drifted ashore or down the creeks in spring, but here it was different, without the interchangeableness of bodies and faces and hair and sunsets, without the fuzziness and serenity of beliefs and the simple dimwitted smiles about everything and nothing, and that four-letter word beginning with *l* that didn't mean much because you passed it out to anybody. This wasn't a swarm, this was more like a tribe, real and familiar and detailed, with the old vigor and sneers and shouts and flashing of eyes and teeth, the toughness and dangerousness that the blood and the ground and the climate and the history of the place gave to them. It was better than anything he ever saw in California. And the deer and the trout too, same as ever; Johnny and he were great hunting and fishing buddies, they were all over the woods, no matter whose.

"And you were the guru," the jurywoman suggested. He didn't like that. She tried other expressions. "You were king." He didn't like that either. "Chief. You had what you wanted."

He was stalled in the telling, just thinking of it. It seemed as if Marjorie saw it all clearer than he did.

"Am I not right? You were rich, without owning a thing. You had a permanent form of outrage, in that 'dope' that terrified everybody so. You could hunt and fish, trespass and poach all over this country, and I presume you could make yourself at home, as it were, in the bodies of different women and girls all over the country. You had the best of everything, didn't you?"

He was stalled, and she went on, saying she still couldn't quite see how it was possible, in this climate. "The first summer, okay, I can see that. In the summer generally. But I can't imagine all this in snowmobile boots. And there isn't room in here. I mean did this sort of commune you had actually *live* here? Was it a commune sort of thing?"

So he told about the normal farmhouse that was here then, built by the first Pelos to come here, from New Brunswick, shortly after the Civil War. It was small but then, the chicken-house, they turned that into a pad, with a big, white, claw-footed bathtub full of purple and orange pillows, a big color TV always on, with the sound off, a many-colored parachute draped from the ceiling and all around. There was also the barn, they built all sorts of spaces in the barn, lofts and things.

"But then there was a fire," she said. "Vigilantes, who didn't like this scene. Ray."

"No, not Ray."

"A disapproving faction not including Ray. Or including Ray peripherally?"

He allowed her to think that.

"But that wasn't enough. That didn't discourage you."

"We built this. The kids, the Pelos, all of us."

It was another thing he had wanted to bring back. He'd been to Canyon, out over the hills behind Berkeley, and up in the redwoods in San Mateo, and in Bolinas, he'd seen treehouses made of nothing but old window-sashes and planks, houses made of rocks and rammed earth, with wood cookstoves and open fireplaces, everything overgrown with plants of every description, where indoors and outdoors, tree branches rock gardens kitchens and beds were all mixed together. He'd brought the Dome Book back in the DeSoto too, and they had put this thing together out of it, all these pieces of two by four, cut to different lengths and angles, marked with colored tape to tell which from what. Half-naked kids swinging from the network as it went up and music blasting from the speakers out by the chicken-house, pickups and motorcycles coming and going, and the older guys, the plantworkers and loggers, coming by after work, bringing beer, sometimes by the keg. After the day's work maybe they would do a cookout, bass and pike in a beer batter, in fat, over a fire outdoors.

They raised pigs and slaughtered them by the book too.

"Not *The Foxfire Book!* I know professors who did that! Subsistence farming! But you were in business, no? Were these kids your customers?"

The kids didn't have any money but he didn't need it from them because after a while there were others from other places who came and moved into empty houses all over the North Country, looking for the cheapest remotest most godforsaken place they could find where they could live cheaply with nobody looking over their shoulders. They wanted some. They had money enough. And there were middle-class people in all the small towns who wanted to try it, and in the college towns there were students and professors. Even the white-collar types going into their father's insurance business or whatever. Robert told her she would be surprised who his customers were.

"No," she said, "as a matter of fact, I wouldn't. I know some of them. Your fame preceded your trial." But she noticed the one customer he'd left out.

"Did your cousin Ray ever . . . join the party?"

The answer wasn't simple. She answered herself before he finished thinking what to say.

"No. He couldn't have given you that much credit, could he? What about Carol?"

He shook his head.

"Ah yes, Carol is straight. I was too straight for that sort of thing too, though I tried. So Ray stayed apart from your . . . your thing here. His friends too?"

He shrugged."They checked it out."

"I'm trying to see how we get from the happy tribe, on this farm, to— Is it that it just made him madder and madder, seeing what you were doing, what you had?"

He didn't exactly accept that. He didn't offer any answer. He wouldn't explain it in the courtroom and he wouldn't explain it here either. She thought, "What then? You take the entire burden on yourself?"

After the first few days he didn't tell the jurywoman where he went, beyond a vague reference to visiting some friends at the Rez. She knew what that was, the Mohawk Indian reservation on the St. Lawrence. If she put it together that he'd had business relationships on the Rez back then, good for her, and if she didn't ask about them, good too. She knew he needed to think about money. He'd told her about Grogan giving him $400 out of his own pocket, to go to Florida, pissing and moaning that Social Services would have given him that much or more if he'd been getting out of prison, but since he was innocent they wouldn't give him anything. Grogan complained that he had been going to buy his wife a riding lawnmower with the money but here he was giving it to Robert instead to make sure he went where he intended to tell the press he was going and where he had better go because he, Grogan, was running for District Attorney after this trial, and when he was District Attorney, Robert Sochia had better not be in the North Country. So he was, he was visiting the Rez, seeing what was doing. His friend Lumen now had a new sawmill. His sister Ernestine was director of the new Museum. They were smiling ear to ear, there was money around; they were not telling him everything.

Returning from the big river one Tuesday night, coming down through the darkened town at about seven o'clock, he found the street lined with cars and pickups along both sides. He wondered first if it was a wake or funeral at Merrill Sochia's, across the road from the school. Who had died, Old Herman? He'd heard Old Herman had had a leg taken off while he was out west. Herman knew the old stories of the town. Old Herman was the authority, he was expected to keep the stories. What if he died? The secrets, the things that were never talked about, except you knew that Old Herman knew them. What if nobody knew them any more?

Some of these stories were important to Robert, they had to not be lost, like the story of his father and JoAnn Sochia and how that connected to the story of himself and Ray and of himself and JoAnn, secret and unspoken just as if it was unknown, but you counted on Old Herman to know it even so, because it had to be kept and known somewhere. And what about stories surely to come? What if there were no record anywhere, ever? If Old Herman, with only one leg, had died?

But then he saw that the lights were on behind the curtains in the big windows of the gym, and he saw, back around the side of the school, the clouds of vapor billowing up against the dark trees from the glistening orange buses. He slowed, and as he came to the corner of the street that led back beside the gym to the school parking lot, he stopped, hesitating over what he felt himself about to do, unusual for him. He turned in.

He never went to basketball games. From the time he was a kid he had wanted to be a woodsman, a hunter and fisher, an outlaw at those pursuits like the great ones of the past that he had heard about in his father's hunting camp. He didn't want to be a clean, obedient, disciplined basketball player or baseball player, half naked running around in front of a crowd. Even though in such a small school there was pressure on him to join the teams, because they needed every player they could get, he had refused. They said he was selfish but he didn't play those games after school, his father didn't practice with him, he didn't think he would be any good, he had a different kind of coordination, he'd be embarrassed. So he wasn't a fan, either. But here he felt himself moved to go into the gym, look in on that scene where the community was present and focused.

He didn't know why; he just felt to go in. He left the DeSoto across the fronts of three cars backed against the snowbank under the trees and walked toward the lighted entrance of the back wing. A sign told visitors to go around to the front entrance but the door was unlocked. He walked in past the cafeteria and the shop and the music room to the stairs up to the front entrance, and looked up the stairs. The gym was just down the hall from the main entrance at the top of these stairs, but now he decided to go back to the lower entrance and up the stairs there and walk past the kindergarten, first and second, third and fourth grade classrooms and the restrooms to the entrance, just to see the colors, the little chairs in the rooms, the kids' artwork on the tiled walls of the hall. He wasn't thinking anything, he was just following his nose, seeking these impressions of things forgotten. But he didn't find things forgotten, everything was newer, smaller, blonde, the brightly colored artwork of the kids and color photographs of them along the walls. In the classrooms the chalkboards were not black but green.

The front hall was empty, just the waxed tiles tracked up with snow and sand from people's boots, large and small, the plaque on the wall about who gave the money. The booming sounds drew him around a turn to the left. The school nurse he remembered, Mrs Boudreau, sat at a table with a cash box and a roll of tickets. A few men leaned against the tiled wall across from the gym door, smoking. He passed right by the nurse and turned his back to the smokers and looked into the gym over the heads of people crowding the doorway.

He didn't see himself walking in onto the overlit varnished wood, didn't see himself teetering, like others he saw now, into the bleachers, waving their arms for balance, dodging piles of coats, sitting down with his knees in somebody's back. He held himself there, looking upwards at the steel trusses of the roof, the lights in cages, the balls coming from all directions at the basket up out of sight. He could see the bottom zigzags of the net, torn open by ball after ball, one pounding another through. The rim bonged and rattled with other balls that flew away from it in all directions, to be snared by hands, banged on the floor, thrown up again. Around the brush-cut heads and ears of people in front of him he saw flashes of pale flesh and floating colors, hands held up, a wrist bent back, the ball spinning backwards on its arc. There was a seething sound of talk from the crowd, and the rumble of boots on the bleachers.

The press in the double doorway cleared out and then the door was guarded by a tall man and a red-haired woman, both wearing sportcoats, one on each side, and the men behind him pushed in past him, parted the sportcoats and went through, and three hollering little kids raced down the hall from the restrooms and burrowed through at a lower level at the same time as the men, and he got sucked into the doorway with them all. Vague muffled words were spoken up among the steel girders and tied-up climbing ropes. A space opened for him between the principals at each side and everybody stood up and quieted, and a harsh scratchy echoing male voice came on and stepped downwards and upwards through "Oh say can you see." A moan of singing arose that made no point of keeping up with the voice on the record but just went at its own rate and got further and further behind.

He didn't think of his hat until during the anthem he was bumped into from in front by somebody backing against him and then he couldn't get his hands out to take it off nor would there have been room for it in front of his heart. He backed up to make room for whoever wanted more space but then he was backed into again and it seemed he was being leaned into purposely. He tipped his head to look down: it was a girl, one of the cheerleaders, their green-and-gold sweater. Hair and sweater was all he could see. A lot of hair, kinky but long, parted in the middle to a thin line of colorless scalp. During the anthem a small hand came up in front of his face and the fingers waved at him and then it went back down and he thought it patted her heart a couple of times before resting there on the sweater, fingers splayed. They were all in a crowd touching together. He could hear her voice clearly over that murmur that came from some of the veterans and women in the crowd and the thin sopranos of the other cheerleaders who were bunched up in front of her. She was singing in time with the music, nodding with the rhythm to help people get the idea. But still leaning back against him. She must think he was somebody else. Then her other hand came around her side and in between them and patted him on the front of his thigh, at the speed of the music. Then the anthem was over and she gave a quick squeeze on his knee and ran forward while the other cheerleaders all ran out onto the court. They collected into a huddle around her as she squatted down on her ankles. Then they unwound into a line on the court and all side-stepped away from each other to spread out in front of the crowd and start a cheer, at the same moment as the two teams broke their huddles and drifted to their positions and the crowd started stamping and yelling, and there she was looking right into his face at ten feet, wide-eyed, mouthing something like *I don't believe this!* She rushed toward him, turned around and took an arm of each of the principals and pulled them close to her side in front of him, shutting him out. The crowd got up a thunder of stamping on the bleachers. The ball rose high in the air, the centers leaped together too early, missing it. Whistles blew. They had to start over. Robert turned and went out, past Mrs Boudreau who had been coming toward him to get him to pay. He felt like a target, like someone made fun of. Shouldn't have gone in there at all.

He was away overnight sometimes now, and Marjorie planned her visits around those nights. She would just bring a salad and good bread from the Co-op, and they would have deer meat with buttered toast and the salad, the meat broiled on a marshmallow fork in the open stove, the bread toasted in the Pelos' old Sunbeam toaster. He told her how they used to fill up a car with boys and girls, as many as seven or eight of them, and patrol the Fourteen Mile Woods road, looking for eyes; then when they shot a deer, go off together to some hunting camp or other and have a party that might last for two days, until that green venison, getting better all the time, was entirely gone.

She was getting to feel she had a picture. There was a context. The thing she was making for him was about the size she had in mind. The scraps, by pure chance, made something rather likeable. She brought some muslin and batting, and began to baste it all together.

"Now tell me what you've been avoiding. I don't blame you for avoiding it. We've both been. But why, in the end, do you think, did it happen? Was it what Mrs Day obviously thought, but the judge (and your feisty lawyer) wouldn't let her say?"

He didn't know what Neva Day and everybody thought it was.

So she had to say it. "Was it . . . drugs?"

She was being very prim, sewing away there with her elbows close to her sides, knees crossed, wearing glasses that she didn't usually wear. She was making great progress, a little blindly, winging the assemblage. "I don't mean the grass. Marijuana's benign, so far as I can tell. But you didn't, surely, limit yourselves to marijuana. Didn't you go on, to—?"

"Acid?"

"Why not? You'd had it in California. Didn't you bring that here too? Or if not you, somebody else? There was a market, I know that. Some perfectly straight people, like my husband, felt that they had to check out LSD."

She was being manipulative, or coy, not to mention his friend, who was it, Frenette? One of the tribe, she gathered. That was the one time Marjorie had laughed aloud in the trial. Buddy Frenette had sworn, when asked, that no, he'd never taken acid. Then he'd said no, he'd never taken acid with Robert Sochia. Then when he was asked whether he'd taken acid with Robert Sochia on the night of September 16th of the previous year, he refused to answer on the grounds of the Fifth Amendment! Her chirp had brought the judge's face around to her, a stern look in which she sought in vain for a wink. The old judge had more practice at keeping a straight face than she had.

Robert didn't answer right away. She added, "*I* was afraid of it, of course. Should I have been?"

Finally he said, "I had enough of it out west."

"Meaning?"

"It was cool, without Ray around."

"Oh Golly. I'm always going to be in the dark about this, aren't I?"

11

Whatcha Looking For?

He had other plans for the less tender parts of that doe, now that she had been hanging ten days or more. He wanted some jerky that he could carry with him wherever he went, a paper bag full of the salty, smoky chunks. And he wanted some meat boiled and canned, to put away in a place that he knew, where he could get it any time later, for instance if he was driven away from the town or for some other reason was living on the loose, in the woods. A feeling was coming to him, of what could happen, if he chose, or of what was going to happen whether he chose it or not. When he looked at the woods, at the mountains to the south, from any high place, it felt to him as if he ought to be out there, or wanted to be out there, or would be, regardless. Somewhere in those folds of blue and dark green, in those dark trees in the snow. Houses, roads seemed not his places. He had missed a whole year in the woods.

On a morning when there was a low overcast and the beginning of a January thaw and he knew that the carcass of the doe would be softening, easier to take apart, he walked down through the pasture and the woods to the river, and across on the ice and up through back lots to the street and then by the shoveled sidewalks over to Arquit's, to get some salt for smoking and canning the meat.

He heard the klaxon sound from up the street just before he reached the store, the call to school. On the step he saw through the glass in Arquit's door the young people rushing toward him. The door opened in but he had to step back while they came crowding out with their gum or candy. He watched them run across, zig-zagging into each other, one of them touching another's hand and the two stopping to look back at him.

Maybe because of the kids startling him, or because of the darkness inside, he had to remind himself what he was looking for. Salt. Not in a cardboard cylinder, not that kind, but a larger quantity, in a paper package. He went to looking for it, for the thing he came for, but he became confused again and momentarily he couldn't name the thing. Somebody was behind him in the aisle. He found the sugar and flour and thought that the thing he had come for would be somewhere near those things, but now he couldn't see them or name them either. Labels and names jumped out at him but they were just pieces of color, meaningless and jagged. He couldn't see things for all the bits of color clamoring at him, getting in front of what he was trying to see, and he felt a flash of anger at this when all he wanted was a name, the name of the thing, not all these colors competing for his attention.

The other shopper moved, blocking the light from the street. That didn't help. He was trying to make his eyes distinguish among the packages and now all these colors and shapes that he was trying to see the meaning of were in shadow. He was trying to say to himself what he was looking for but the word wouldn't come to him.

The person blocking the light had on a dark coat and now came closer. He couldn't stop all the colors and letters from moving toward him and away from him. He would look like a fool if she offered to help him find what he wanted and he couldn't remember what it was. The hem of her coat was touching his wool pants. For a minute they both just stood still and he forgot to look for anything, wondering why she stood so close. Then he heard her voice, talking to somebody near. "You can't feel me? Can't you feel me right here beside you?" She was talking to him. He didn't look. Couldn't feel her? He didn't want to say anything in answer to that. "Whatcha looking for?" she said in a normal tone.

"Salt." He said it without thinking, what he had been trying to think of.

"Tst!" She touched his arm, reached with her other hand, brought it in front of him. Salt. He took it. It was the cylindrical package but he didn't put it back. He looked where it came from and tried to see the larger kind of package, paper, like a package of sugar.

"You felt me," she said, low-voiced, like a warning. Then somebody else came in the store and he was in the light from the street again, alone with the salt in his hand. She was gone and he thought, *Who says I felt you? Why would I feel you? I haven't even seen you.* There was nobody in the aisle with him. He put away the table salt and picked up a package of canning salt.

She wasn't in the other aisles. He paid for his salt and went outside. He pulled the heavy door closed and stepped off the concrete step and turned to go down the hill. She elbowed herself away from the building and blocked him with her feet apart, her mouth open, her eyes flicking from one of his to the other. She said, "I never come in there at this time of day! I never come in there."

He couldn't think what that was supposed to mean but it had, the second time she said it, that lowness, like a warning to them both.

She said, "You're supposed to say, 'So don't I ever come to basketball games.'"

"I don't."

"That's right!" She gave a click of pleasure in her throat and turned and skipped away toward the school, and he was just mad again, as he had been coming out of the school. This was the same person. They each did something they never do and both times they ran into each other. So what? Why the big smile and the wide-open eyes? He still didn't know what she looked like. He tried to remember her mouth but it was always moving too fast. He couldn't pick one of her eyes to look into with them skipping back and forth between his. He couldn't have said if her voice was low or high; it was up and down too fast, too.

Back at the Pelos' he got out a pan and laid some newspapers on the counter, and then he went back out to the barn. He had already taken the hide away from one of the hind legs to get the meat they had been eating. Now he cut the hide around the forelegs and slit up the legs to the brisket, and up to the neck and around that, and peeled the hide off the legs and then, from the neck, rolled it in his fingers and hauled it down off the shoulders, running his knife-blade along the crease between it and the dark flesh every inch or so to cut the transparent icy membrane that made it pull hard, and sometimes hanging by his whole weight from the rolled skin and fur held in his fists. His hands became so cold that he had to stop and put them between his legs to warm them up. When he had the hide off her shoulders he left it hanging like a coat half off, and cutting and prying between the still half-frozen muscles he took the shoulders and forelegs off.

All the time he was doing this work, he felt as if she was watching him, looking over his shoulder, saying *Whatcha doin'?* He tried to do the work quickly, with as few motions as possible, no clumsiness, so that she wouldn't say *Tst!* and show him how easy it was.

What did you want the salt for? Inside the spherical house he laid the shoulders and forelegs on the newspaper on the counter and took them apart muscle by muscle. He cut the meat into chunks and layered them into the dishpan with plenty of salt over every layer. Then he looked for a place to put the dishpan out of the way where it would be cool but not freeze, for a couple of weeks, or only a week or a few days if he didn't have that long to wait. He didn't know how long he might have.

There wasn't any particular threat that would drive him into the woods. There had been threats, they'd been reported to him in jail, by his mother among others, the last time she was up north. She loved to tell him what they were saying about him in the bars. That was his mother, thrilled by stuff like that. She lived on it, believed it all, exaggerated it, tried to scare him with it. He was just as glad she'd gone south and stayed, this time. No particular threat, nothing. Only that shooting the first night, and his tires deflated, pitiful gestures. But JoAnn was seething. He knew JoAnn. She would never forgive, or soften. Maybe it was JoAnn, in a way, that was keeping him here. Except for her judgment on him, maybe he wouldn't feel any need to stay. Unfinished business with her.

Marjorie pressed a little on this. She didn't understand. "Unfinished business?" Did he mean, could he ever redeem himself with her?

He didn't want to talk about JoAnn but he thought about her, a lot. He was close to her, he told Marjorie. She was important to him. They would always be enemies but he wanted to have her respect.

"Is she your closest family? I mean, that's here, not gone away?"

"You could say that," he admitted. The only way to redeem himself with her, or something like that, to gain any kind of respect from her, was to show her he didn't care if she hated him and he wasn't scared of anything she might do to him.

"But you are, I hope. You won't do anything to aggravate her, at least. I don't think that's what you should do. I think you should stay here, live here, make a life. That's your right and I think you should claim it. But what's wrong with remorse? Have you ever showed her that? What would be wrong with an apology? Mrs Hubbard lost her brother. I mean, look at it from her point of view." He hadn't replied to that, and Marjorie had returned to her sewing, saying, "Don't mind me."

It was quiet. No one was saying or doing anything to him. They were just waiting for him to go. He'd been expecting himself to go, too. But he was held. He felt on the verge of something. The country was, as if, pregnant with something for him. Snow, the woods, the landscape sparkled with some kind of invitation, potential. It always had, for him; there was always an agony of stasis in the landscape, as if it offered itself, begged for you to make something happen in it. Fishing and hunting were like that, ways to get inside it, tickle the heart of it. He was waiting to know what it was going to be now. It doesn't make any difference what you plan, or what you think ahead of time. Something tells you. You do it and there you are, the ache is gone.

He put clean newspaper over the salted meat, climbed the ladder and put the pan off to the edge of the loft where the roof slanted over it, and all the time he was doing that, it was just as if those eyes were watching him, those lips were saying *Good thing I found you the salt, isn't it?*

He stood on the bed and pushed up the tarp over the opening and looked out to the south, where the hills obscured the country he was thinking of, Blue Mountain and the huge space around and beyond, which the mountain presided over, the heart of the country he knew. But the person's face interfered with this vision. All he could remember was parts of it. The eyes were like the eyes in a magazine advertisement for eye makeup and the lips were like the lips in an advertisement for lipstick. Except that there wasn't any makeup or lipstick. The teeth were like teeth in an advertisement for toothpaste. They were all moving so fast he couldn't put them together, like the insides of a clock where you can't figure out what is moving what.

The chunks layered in salt were for the jerky. He would smoke them when they were ready. Now he went back to the barn and took off the hind legs of the deer, to cook and can. There was a box of Mason jars in the cellar. Helen had a canner.

He knew where he was going to put the canned meat, where it would keep: in the mud spring back in behind the Shampines' home place on the lake road. That was a rare thing, he knew of no other: the ice-cold seep of an underground spring, close to the brook that was the outlet of the lake. How he had learned of it he could not have said. It came down to him in the lore of the woods and he had found it once while fishing that brook. He had put his arm down in it as far as he could reach, in several places, and felt something finally and got ahold of it: a jar of spaghetti-sauce. He didn't look for any more but that was good sauce, perfectly preserved as anything would be in such cold.

In the house again he got out the book. It was still there on Helen's shelf, the same book they had used to slaughter pigs, to geld the colt, to make brine and smoke the hams and bacon.

Whatcha looking up? Whatcha need to know that you don't already know? I don't believe it. Robert Sochia, looking at a book to learn how to do something!

On second thought he was not going to do this. He never had canned venison himself. Helen or somebody else had always done this part of it. He would smoke the jerky on another cloudy day like this when the smoke wouldn't be so obvious, but he wasn't going to do something he had never done, especially with somebody looking over his shoulder, ready to make fun of him. Grace would do it for him. She'd have plenty of jars too. She and Millard liked canned venison as much as frying-meat. He would take her one of the hind quarters and she'd do it, she had a real pressure canner like they called for in the book. He would just ask for a couple of jars for himself, to put down in Shampine's spring, in case he needed them. He closed the book.

Whatsamatter? the watcher said. *Give up?*

Whatcha gonna do now?

I'll see you!

12

Farm Girl

Nellie and Bessie lived a life hardly different from the last century's; born in it, brought up with values older still, preferring not to change. Nellie's husband Rob, the sheep-farmer, had been a die-hard too, progressive only in letting Cornell show him how to grow alfalfa on his sandy soil; but the girls had outlasted him and the sheep. They wrapped themselves up against the penetrating wind and went out with pails of hot water to pour into the radiator of the old Allis-Chalmers, and one of them helped the battery crank it over, with the hand-crank, while the other one, up on the cold seat, worked the spark and gas.

They drew the rubber-tired wagon across the road and out through the meadow to the long, long woodpile, and loaded it up with the split and seasoned maple, and hauled it back to their woodshed door. They went inside, flushing in the house-heat like children just in from sledding, and made their lunch, canned soup, crackers, tea, not taking off their snowmobile-boots and layered socks; then put the dishes in the sink, wrapped themselves in their men's coats and feminine scarves again, went out and drained the tractor, and covered the motor of it with burlap again. They threw the firewood into the shed and piled it; and one stayed out there and split some of the straight-grained pieces smaller, to feed the cookstove, which, even if they did their cooking on the electric range, still kept the kitchen warm.

Clarence could have lived with them and eaten that good cooking every day. They regularly told him what a fool he was that he didn't. But that was just the trouble. They would call him a fool if he did, too, if not about where he boarded, everything else. So his answer was, "Thanks, sooner live in a hollow log." He used to board himself and his horses with a farmer here and there, bartering their labor. Now he couldn't afford horses at all, and made his winter deal with Arquit. For horses, he depended on the team Millard Frary kept to sugar with. He quit his town job to gather sap with Millard every spring.

The Frarys being another set of these stubborn and unchanging old-timers. Grace, her kitchen always superheated with her baking, the sleeves of her light dress pushed up on bare arms while she rolled or kneaded, or fished the doughnuts out of the fat, her ancient, doddering father asleep in the Boston rocker by the old Estate Heatrola in the parlor; in her refrigerator the jars of fresh milk, carried up from the barn in a shining steel jug with a bail, the cream coming slowly to the top; conceding only the black telephone that rested between her hunched shoulder and her cheek as she worked. Millard as frugal of speech as she was generous of it, frugal of gesture too, comfortable and perfectly reiterant in every chore in every season, shoveling a narrow path down to the horse- and cow•stables half underground in that hillside barn, to clean the stalls, shake up the straw bedding, throw lime on the wet places on the walk, and grain and milk his few Guernseys. Not by hand: the quiet catch and sigh of his DeLaval milking machines accompanied his attentions, all the morning news he cared to hear. While the milk cooled in the milkhouse, he climbed the narrow stairs to the mow to throw down hay for the cows, and over the other part of the barn, for the team. Then up the path again with the bailed steel jug, filled with milk still warm and foamy, to his breakfast, always the same. Grace would pass on to him everything he might not have heard from Radio DeLaval.

After breakfast the team let out in the sunshine, to go down to the brook to drink, their bay and chestnut coats standing out like fur, absorbing and refracting light, and their breath freezing in clouds against the pastured hill behind them. They would stay out all day, stamp holes in the ice of the brook to drink, patrol the fences in deepening paths in the snow.

In the evening, after his visit with Amos and the others at Eugene's, Millard would come back in the pickup, and down to the barn without going into the house but with no loss of intimacy, knowing she heard his truck, saw lights in the barn. They could be no closer to each other if they were holding hands. The horses picked up their heads at the sound of the sliding stable door, which meant not warmth so much as oats, and ran in muttering to him as they passed him, delicately turning into their separate stalls.

When this season ended, they would learn to work again, in maple sugaring, the only excuse for feeding them all year. No better power in the world for this, the horses would pull the sap-sled around the maze of ways among the maples, no-one driving them, the gatherers coming with full pails to the side of the road and just saying, "Come up, Dick," and when the team had brought the tank abreast of them, "Whoa." Or hopping on to catch a little ride, murmuring "Gee" or "Haw" at the forks. Clarence Shampine would start nagging any week now, saying they ought to hitch those horses up and start to break the roads. And it was true, Millard and Grace conceded in advance: if they waited too long, the way the snow kept falling, it would be as much as the team could do.

January was gone, they were right into February then, the deepest part of a winter already notable for snowfall. It sifted down out of a light gray sky day after day, no more than two days in seven with any blue sky to speak of. The snow not blowing, not drifting, just piling up, to the delight of people like Farnan Day and Leo Weller, to whom it was an opportunity for virtue, Northmanship, sculpture in the most metaphysically interesting of materials. Infinitely clean, pure, renewable like the potential energy of Sisyphus's stone, but ephemeral too, subject to all kinds of changes of form before vanishing. Dirtiable, but, for now, sparkling fresh every day to carve in. Covering all mess and negligence, beautifying everything, repaving even the pot-holed streets. Offering them all, the town at large and all its fallible citizens, an infinity of absolution, even before they had to know they were going to need it.

Clarence shoveled too: a space had been paved in the Project, with some of the state's Youth Conservation Corps money, for summer flea-markets, outdoor dancing, basketball and bluegrass. In the winter this little square of asphalt was sided with low boards, and the water department flooded it from the hydrant by the gate, to make a skating rink. Clarence walked stolidly round in his high-laced boots and jodhpur-like hunting pants behind his hollow-bladed shovel, head down in oppression, while children swept around him on their skates, got in his way, hid from each other behind him, caught on to him for support. No shovel-artist he, a grumbler, never more conscious of indignity. This was the teamster's time of year, when the lumber camps had been full of men and the barns full of Belgians and Shires, any two of which might weigh forty hundred pounds yet looked tiny next to the towering loads of logs they hauled, on roads watered and frozen like this rink.

Those days were gone forever but the heroic feats of horses, of axe-men and teamsters still rang in Clarence's head. When he finished going round and round behind his blade on behalf of children who repaid him in litter on the ice, in jeering laughter, who would lose their hockey pucks in two inches of snow rather than lift a shovel for themselves—when he stumbled into his cabin and made his tea and sat by his woodstove in his rocking chair, he dreamed of the smell of those horses and their blowing breaths and the jingle of their harness bells, the foamy sweat between their rubbing buttocks and the outward bow of their hocks as they lay into the tugs. He mouthed the old songs to himself, "*Ou sont aller tous les raftsmen,*" "The Ballad of Blue Mountain Lake."

This weekend, though, Clarence and Millard hitched up Millard's team for some actual old-style log-hauling. The boss, Duke Arquit, had decided that the town should apply some more state economic development money to hire some more teen-agers next summer and build another log cabin on the Project, to be rented in the summer, thereby bringing a little more business into the boss's grocery store. The logs had been cut the preceding spring, in a patch of woods up along the river to the south, accessible by the River Road. They'd been left piled to dry out through the summer and fall. Now, some time or other they had to be brought to the new cabin-site on the Project.

The boss had let out that some civic-minded logger would be welcome to offer his loader and log-truck to bring them to town, but otherwise the town crew would do it with the backhoe and dump-truck. Clarence had bearded the boss in his den, told him Millard Frary had a perfectly good team, and a double-bunked sled, so what ailed him? Couldn't he add that up? "State where you want them logs, then stay out of the way."

"Well," said Duke, "we ain't insured for such a thing, I don't suppose. But as long as the logs get to where we want 'em, I don't know nothing about it. Go a-lumbering, damn it. Be my guest." He offered to send out the backhoe, at least to lift the logs onto Millard's rig. But Clarence said if he couldn't load them spindles all alone, with nothing a block and tackle and cant-hook, he would go out in the woods and shoot himself.

The sun broke through on Saturday, shone on an overnight dusting of newest white, and warmed the air up into the higher twenties. Grace togged herself up to come along, and up along the river where the logs were piled, she built a fire to warm their drinks and muffins while the old boys worked, without hurry, hitched the horses to single-trees, ran long ropes to blocks at the bases of standing pines, rolled the logs up a ramp and onto the bunks.

She rode the log-loads with them, back and forth to town all day, slowly, peacefully, rolling the logs off in the snow on the Project, going back light to fetch another ten, Millard at the other end, sitting low on the back edge of the rack, watching the polished tracks emerge from under the runners, fascinating as the wakes of boats. Then in the mid-afternoon Grace stayed at home to cook, and another rider took her place, dressed in Grace's boots and overpants because she had nothing warm enough herself, her hair caught inside Grace's scarves and woolen toque, two sweaters under her peacoat. Clarence's special friend because she was interested in the weather, just like Clarence, interested in learning what it was like before they took the horses out of the lumber-woods. She sat on the log-ends behind the driver, with her legs splayed out like

any boy's, Clarence standing, with the reins in two hands, just
giving a kind of a kissing sound when the tired horses slackened
their pace; thinking, as they passed onlookers at the turn by The
Rapids, *You didn't know I took girls for sleigh rides? Well, hnn, I don't
tell everybody everything.*

Now on the last run in to town, carrying the last ten logs, still
back along the River Road, riding backwards close to the snow
and watching the country flow away behind them, Millard heard
the sudden slap of reins on rumps, Clarence's sudden "Get up,
Dick!" He rocked back against the ends of the logs as the sled
jerked ahead. What was the captain up to now, he wondered, who're
we racing, anyway?

He heard the slap of reins again, more clucking, and then the
captain's voice droning unduly loud, monotonous, over the bells of
the hames now ringing continually, as the horses settled in a lugging
trot, too fast, Millard thought, too hard on them after their
unaccustomed work. He turned his head and shoulders to protest.
But he couldn't see over the logs, and he turned the wrong way to
see the cause of Clarence's haste, until, perplexed, he turned back to
ease the strain on his stiff shoulders. There, already past him, standing
on the snowbank, on snowshoes, in a different, many-colored wool
coat, was Robert Sochia. Their eyes met, and Millard lifted a hand
from the edge of the rack beside him, hello and good-bye.

The dirt-floored horse stable was dark and the dirt was covered
with hay and straw that had accumulated all winter. Robert felt
his way in the soft darkness, against the horse-worn ends of the
stall partitions, the mangers made of maple rounds that tilted out
to be filled with tossed hay. He felt along the boarded wall, the
pegs where the harnesses, gone now like the horses, were hung.
Light getting in at the edges outlined the door to the sloping
pasture beyond, where they went down to drink, and showed the
pine board door of the stairway to the mow.

The cows must have heard him, listening for the smallest sound
of Millard coming to milk; they began to moan. Or they had

heard, as he did now, Millard's old truck, the tailgate chains clanging, one loose fender thrumming hollowly. He started up the mow stairs, turning in the confined space on the steep short steps to pull the door to, behind him.

The one window, high in the gable end, was a square of blank late-afternoon sky, the blue gone gray. It made the darkness around it absolute. He felt his way up and across the tiered bales and down the stepped cavity, completely dark, where bales had been quarried so far this winter to feed the team. On a little patch of hay-polished floor, against the slope of the gambrel roof, he felt for the hatchway, and slid it open. Warm fragrant air rose to his face. He turned and sat beside the opening, in the loose hay from broken bales, his back against a beam.

He hadn't seen her at first. He'd stopped on the snowbank and watched the horses approach, their heads bobbing, bells continuously jingling, old Shampine standing at the front with the reins, a picture out of a history book. There was somebody beside him, a kid. Clarence approached without even looking at him, slapping the reins and clucking to the team while talking straight ahead about how this used to be a sugarbush, along there, "pastured to cows in the summertime. You could drive a car in it anywhere." And then the kid had suddenly hung out from the side of the sled, from one hand on the corner-stake, and reached the other mittened hand to pass it over the breast of his wool jacket as the sled went by, smiling right in his face and mouthing *You're It!*

"All cut off for furniture wood, cut off chest-high, so's not to hit any spouts and dull their met-al. Looked just like a wooden cemetery." The person pulled herself back and disappeared down in front of the logs, except that one booted foot rose up straight in the air and wiggled. Then there was Millard, seated facing backwards with his legs dangling, boot-heels plowing snow, nodding to him.

Now here he was, doing just what she wanted him to do, come looking for her to tag her back. He didn't like this childishness. All he wanted was to catch her still for a second, see her clearly one time.

Suddenly the light in the mow, from the gable window, had turned purple. In the warm updraft from the hay-hole, listening to the quiet soughing of the distant milking machines, he might have dozed. He'd heard sounds of Millard clanging the covers on milk cans. Now he heard the sled thumping and gliding on the packed snow outside, grating on a stone, the clock-like sound of two horses trotting in step.

The barn door rumbled open, the light-string rang against the bulb and light came up through the hole, around him. One horse was being led in at a trot or came in by itself, in a tambourinelike jangle of bells. It swung into the stall beneath him and the big hooves knocked wood, stirred the straw. The voice which came to him in short gruff sounds was Millard's, from around by the cow stable door. He heard the girl's voice, clear and sing-song, right under him, with the horse, he missed the words. He heard the snap-ring clipped into the halter, the horse's flapping breath through nostrils. Then the other horse, brought in more slowly, turning into the other stall and the barn door sliding closed.

Now old Shampine was in the stall beneath him too, across the horse from her, telling her what to undo. Shaking the hames out of the collar with the reins looped on them, drawing the britching off the rump onto his shoulder. He would carry it to the wall that way and hang it up, hames first and then britching, as Robert had seen Millard do.

Then telling her where the grain was and how much of it to feed each horse, after they cooled off, how much water. Finally he told her to give them half a bale each from overhead, like she did this morning. "You're the helper, that's your job," he said, "the team-ster heads for the tavern, ha-ha." No humor in his tone, gruff and in a hurry. Then more of that continuous rapid riffling voice that he heard like a brook without distinguishing the words. Was she talking for his benefit? The barn door rolled two ways and banged against the stops. It was quiet.

Was she still standing in the stall down there? Did she notice the open hatch? The cover clanged on the oildrum where Millard kept the grain, and the scoop chucked into the grain. Then not her steps, she was soundless on the dirt floor, but one of the horses moving over and the grain rattling into the feedbox.

Clarence's truck now, an airplane sound, the fan roaring.

He didn't know whether she was below him now or not but he seemed to smell her there, the way he could smell deer, or fox. He smelled her hair, a clean smell, in the midst of all that other soft rich smell of the stable with the sweat of the team drying. The horses muzzled the grain, their lips brushed wood, they ground away with their molars. They shook their loose coats, cooling, and blew.

Then the trigger latch of the mow stairway door. A change in him, from level to level of attention. The stairtreads creaking. A thump, then steps on hay. They quickly stopped.

She would be waiting for her eyes to adjust. He could have been right there beside her, seen her while she was blinded, spoken first. Instead all at once she was standing above him, herself black against the purplish glow of the rafters. Her voice was low and dull.

"You terrified my friend, you know. He's worried about me. He cares about me." She had picked up a sniffle, outdoors half the day. "And you come here ahead of us and leave the hay-hole open, really! Do you think Clarence wouldn't notice that? I had to get him out of here as fast as I could!"

She was just an outline still.

"Robert, we have to be secret. You have to respect my needs. I mean this seriously. You have to be careful for my sake. I am risking a lot for you and I need you to be careful."

She held a hand toward him to stop him from answering. She seemed to be listening for something. Then she looked down at him again. "Listen to me, please? I have to say these things to you and then you have to go away, so listen to them, please. We are going to spend some time together. The gods want us to do this, look at the miracles that have already happened to us. We can see that it is going to happen, I'm going to give you a little bit of my precious one-and-only life but I need you to realize what that means to me, how important that is. Because I am very different from you, Robert. My life is more precious to me than you can imagine, because I live in the present moment all the time, it isn't a dream, I am made of earth and water barely held together and made out of a tiny few of the same eentsie teentsie molecules and atoms that were in the first cloud of dust and gas that this earth and hay and horses and woods were made of and every minute of my life is important to me. And every other speck of human life and plant life and animal life is important to me too. You have to try to understand me and wish me well in my life. Okay? And you have to understand how much I care about everybody else's life too. Because this will be a little bit dangerous, Robert. If we do this it will be dangerous."

Millard's voice up the hay-hole. "That you up there, miss?"

"Yes, it's me! Talking to myself. Mister Shampine this is a neat place! I want to sleep up here sometime!" She made a face to Robert, that he couldn't see. *With you*, she might have mouthed. Or *Don't move!*

"Well you're letting a lot of heat out of the stable," Millard said, his voice already turning away. He was talking to himself when he added, "Clarence just took off and left you with the chores, looks like."

Robert got up quickly and climbed the tiers away from the opening, so that she could roll a bale down from the edge into the space where he'd been, and then another that partly covered the hay-hole. She climbed down after them onto the bare floor where he had been sitting and dragged the second bale away from the hole. She pulled off the strings and hung them on a nail in a rafter where others were. She kicked the bale apart and shoved the flakes down the hole.

"You didn't know I was a farm girl, did you?" she said, dangerously loud, not being careful herself. "That's the second time I ever did that in my life. My friend Clarence showed me how this morning."

He still wasn't that sure that Millard had gone back into the cow stable. But she climbed up to him and suddenly threw the loops of baling twine from the second bale over him and tugged him toward her. "Where do you get all that money?"

"What money?"

"The money you have. To buy such a coat."

"Grogan gave me it to go to Florida."

"Liar. Where?"

"It's true."

"Liar. That was a long time ago. I heard about that money. You've spent that by now. How come you didn't go to Florida?"

"I was going to."

"Why didn't you?"

"I wasn't as scared as I thought."

"That's good. Why not?"

"I don't know."

"Tell me the truth. You get money smuggling something to Canada, right?"

He didn't answer.

"What? Grass?"

"No."

"I know. Don't worry, I've heard all about it. Cars."

"No."

"Everybody knows. Late model GM cars. That's dumb. It's very stupid for you to be smuggling cars to Canada."

"I'm not."

"You're not?"

"No."

"All right, then what?"

She pulled him against her and put her arms around him and rotated the two of them left, right, left.

"Tell me," she said. "What are you smuggling?"

"Chinamen," he said.

"Oh, come on!" She pushed herself away and turned all the way around on one foot and nearly fell off the top tier of hay.

"Haitians," he added.

"Robert Sochia, be serious."

"Haitians. Some Chinamen." This was all in the future. It might never happen. His friends on the Rez were working on it.

"I'm not going to kiss you if you tell me a thing like that. Is that true, Robert? Why Chinesey-people? I don't know whether to believe you. My God." She stepped back and cried out, too loud, "You're smuggling Chinesey-people into Canada?" She slanted her eyes with her fingertips, then came back against him with her face up. But that instant they heard the barn door rolling open. She seemed to count to ten, then let go the twine and climbed down the tiers. She crouched by the hole a moment, listening. Then dropped her legs through. She piped up to him, "Don't get lost in the dark." Then he saw only her head and shoulders. She must have been standing on the manger below. She ducked her head down for a moment, looking around. Then it popped up again. "Hey, Bobby!" She kissed her mittened hand and blew over it toward him. "Didja get it?"

The slide closed and he was for a moment blind. Then it slid open again. She half-whispered, "Hey, you want to know how you could kiss me right in the middle of the street and we could still be secret as could be? And we could take a shower together and go to bed together and sleep like spoons together and when we get up have a croissant and cafay oh lay and read the Sunday papers together, *in bed*? Wanta know how we could do that?"

He still didn't say anything. He hadn't heard that he wanted to do those things together with her.

"You could take me to Montreal with you, one of these times, hint-hint," she said. Then, differently, mock-sweetly, mock-innocently, "By-ye. I'll be seeing you!"

13

Small Comfort

Nowadays it seemed to Peter and Francis as if all the girl did was sleep. She didn't come out. "It's winter, man," she'd say. "This is what I do in the winter, get lotsa sleep. Don't you?" If they wanted to see her they had to come in and sit in Neva's living room with her and Neva and Farnan and their daughters and hear about everybody's frigging *day*, before she went up to bed. They hadn't believed that Neva would let them in the house, but Julia said of course she would, come in and sit with us before I go to bed. They had tried it, once, but Neva was so hostile. Julia must have made her let them in against her will. She didn't say anything but she was so hostile and it was so stupid that they didn't go back.

So now every day another shift at the plant, car pool, beer at The Rapids before going home, where Peter didn't want to be, but he couldn't stand it at The Rapids after a while either. His mother's disgust with him—you could cut it with a knife. When they were at the bar, JoAnn always had some new report about Sochia to pass on. How he was smoking venison out there at Johnny's, where anybody could see the smoke and report him but nobody did. How he wasn't just walking all over the place, he was driving, you wondered where the old De Soto was carrying him, to be gone so long, so often. North, mostly. JoAnn humming, smirking, grabbing some addict's ashtray and emptying it into her trashbin under the sink and slinging it spinning back along the bar so the addict would lose the ash off his cigarette to grab it before it flew off or broke a glass or something. She was getting a little crazy, his Ma.

This Saturday night they went to The Rapids, what else was there to do? But it was worse than ever, JoAnn comes smiling along the bar telling them that somebody who looked a lot like Robert Sochia, and somebody else they knew, had been seen together at some frigging bar in another town over in St. Lawrence County. "Sitting in a booth, in plain sight," his mother said, right in front of him, right in his face, with her phony smile. He didn't like to see her smile that way.

"Oh yeah? Sochia and somebody else."

"So Murdock says. In Norwood. In Dick's. You know Dick's?"

"No, I don't know Dick's. What's Dick's?"

"A bar. Near the fire station. The Norwood firemen favor it. Don't you go there when you play Norwood?" Coming from behind, Peter understood she meant softball. She meant when the Falls firemen played the Norwood firemen in softball. That was summer, when there'd be some *heat* in this life. But shit, Peter thought, he was just trying to make it to *spring*.

"Oh yeah, Dick's."

"Murdock says somebody saw him there. In the fancy sheepskin collared coat."

"Why Murdock, Ma?" Murdock, the telephone company lineman, the great visitor.

"Because Murdock saw them, or knows whoever saw them."

"Sochia and his coat, sitting at a table."

"Ha ha."

"Okay, Sochia and who?"

"Would it make any difference who?"

Frank grabbed the chips. Peter grabbed them back. "No," Peter said. "Why should it?"

"It'd make a lot of difference," Frank said.

Peter said, "Look, Ma. Murdock comes into here with some story. He don't even buy a drink, I bet. He's so cheap he makes his own wine. So who believes anything he tells you? He doesn't care what he says. He got it from one of his women friends who has a lot of phone trouble."

"Oh? Do you know someone with phone trouble?"

"You can drop this Murdock, Ma."

"He's a popular man."

"He's a gossip."

"You hope that's all he is."

"He's the phone company's problem."

"Apparently he gets his work done."

"He's got seniority. He doesn't do no work. He's all over the country in that van."

She took a toothpick from a glass beside the salt in front of him and used it, smiling, teeth together edge to edge.

"Drinking coffee all day, talking," Peter said. "They can't get him out of their houses. That's all he does, talk."

Murdock was an opportunist, not serious. Didn't care what trouble he sowed, just interested in everybody else's business. Available to every woman, a hairy shoulder to cry on. No threat to any man, gone without fuss if caught with someone's wife, no need to yell. Yes, the telephone company van was often parked up the street from Peter's house, yes he was in there, consoling Patty, or whatever you call it. Peter didn't worry about Murdock. He was just browsing, looking for an easy lay, whatever. Patty wasn't any easy lay. Fucking Murdock. Peter hated him.

But JoAnn had something else on her mind. With that phony smile, hiding her bitterness, pretending to be just curious. "I was wondering, though. What you would do if it was her."

"Her."

"Your Julia. In Dick's, in Norwood with RS."

"I ain't supposing."

"Well do suppose, Peter! Imagine her! Reaching under the table, right in front of anybody who wanted to watch. Rubbing his knees, patting them, just like she does yours in here."

Peter looked at Frank and laughed. JoAnn pressed her lips together and closed and opened her eyes. "Don't you think that's an interesting development? I do. I think it gives you an opportunity, Peter."

"What. What opportunity?" He looked at Frank and shrugged.

She smiled at them. She didn't say what opportunity. They weren't alone, it wasn't like this was closing time. She shouldn't talk in front of some of these assholes along the bar.

"I don't get it, Ma."

"You don't want to do anything to *him*. Well then, don't."

She waited. His mother had such a pretty face when she truly smiled. He loved her, wished she could be at peace. He repeated, "Don't. Okay."

"Don't harm a hair on his head." She was still smiling.

"What are you talking about?"

She sighed, and went along the counter, wiping, toward Harry, who frowned at her. She turned back, changing hands on her cloth. She let her hair partially hide her face.

"Oh . . . . There is a good old way men have of getting even with each other. Perhaps you wouldn't know about it, but I do." Shaking her hair away from her face she looked right at him no longer smiling. "I'm very familiar with it. It makes the other man very mad, usually. I would like to see our cousin be upset."

Peter asked his friend, "Do you know what she's talking about?" But Frank was watching JoAnn. Peter looked back at his mother, who was waiting for him.

"You might kill two birds with one stone, in a manner of speaking," she said.

"Huh? How, Ma? What two birds?"

"By doing something that you have been dying to do anyway."

"What?" Peter looked at her open mouthed but Frank beside him started to stiffen up, straighten his back.

"Whether she wants to or not."

"Oh wait a minute, wait a minute," Frank began.

"Dying to do." Peter didn't get it.

"Wait a minute," Frank said.

"What?" Peter said.

Frank looked at him.

"You don't see it," she said. "Do you."

"What, Ma?"

"Holy shit," Frank said.

JoAnn said to Frank, with her smile, "She'd never tell."

The two young men looked at each other and away. Frank moved back and forth on his elbows and turned his head left and right as if he had a tight collar on. Peter stood off his stool and walked to the Seeburg and back, and back to it again. It had come to him now.

He couldn't believe his mother was suggesting a thing like she was. In front of people too. Of what kind of people.

"When's the last time you had any, Ma? You're going crazy."

"You'll never get it any other way, boy of mine."

"Jesus, Ma. Jesus. We ain't even sure it was her. At fuckin' Dick's. In Norwood? What bullshit. Even if it was. All that, touching his legs, playing around. That's how she is. She does that stuff."

His mother laughed in his face.

"She might be trying to change him too. To teach him." He hunched his shoulders. "That he doesn't have to . . . you know. Doesn't have to do that with her to be her friend. To. To have her . . . love him."

She hissed. "Do you believe that?"

Peter said, "Yes, I believe that."

She covered her eyes and shook her head. He wished she wouldn't humiliate him in front of people. She turned her look on Francis, who at least defended him a little. Frank said, "It's true, we ain't sure she done anything with him."

"Well why don't you *make* sure?"

"How?"

"Why don't you follow that little white car some night? Mmm? She's not at Neva's sleeping all the time. *That car is gone.* A lot. Just like his."

"What do you know?" Peter threw in.

"I've got a very observant sister on that street, remember? Nothing, nothing, does Marlene not see, that goes up and down that street."

Francis hesitated. She spat out, "Find it, tonight! Where is it? It hasn't been there all weekend. Find it, tonight, tomorrow night,

some night! And when you discover that Robert's all this time
been getting what you don't have to get to have her love you—"

"Yeah? What, Ma?"

"Help yourself to sloppy seconds!" Peter's arms flung out and up
and he turned on his heel and strode back and forth, grimacing
the way he used to appeal to South when a foul had been called
against him. *What? Who? Me?* But he stopped suddenly. This was
ridiculous. He just said, "I gotta go home, Ma."

"Fine! You can get them there too!" She was climbing up onto
her stool behind the bar, going to stand right up on the little
round top of it.

"Get what, Ma?" Peter wasn't thinking. He'd shut off thought,
he was worried about his mother trying to stand up on the top of
that little stool.

"Sloppy seconds!" she yelled.

On tip-toe on top of the stool now with her back to the room,
reaching as high as she could to the high shelf along above the
mirrors. She had her ceramic collection up there all along the shelf,
shiny, brightly colored ceramic cars and ships and roosters and
things, to decorate the bar. She got ahold of a red and black
locomotive with gold numbering, bell and headlight, a favorite of
his, and she twisted around half off balance not even bringing it
down but just pushed it at him, with like a girl's two-handed
set-shot. It tumbled over Frank's head and crashed on the dull tiles
at Peter's feet, tiny shards streaking out in all directions. When he
looked back up to see her falling, she wasn't falling, but another
one of her things, something he couldn't recognize during its arc,
caught the edge of the bar and landed on a stool and then fell off
the stool before he could catch it, and broke on the floor. She still
hadn't fallen, she'd wrung herself around again and caught the
shelf and saved her balance. She was breathing hard up there, her
face hidden, even in the mirror her hair all down in front of it.
Once he was sure she wasn't going to fall, Peter went to the door.
Then he stopped, hesitating over whether to go out or go back
behind the bar and help her down the last bit and give her a hug.
But now she was okay, on her knees on the stool, then down to the

floor, turning, not looking at him. Suddenly she grabbed a bottle
of some green crap, liqueur, to threaten him with, and he went
out. Francis came out a moment later.

Peter waited for him. "I'll give you a ride," he said.

Francis said, "What the fuck was *that* about?"

"I know what that's about. Robert's fuckin' father."

"Hanh?"

Silver-haired uncle Royal, when JoAnn was fifteen. That was
rape. Statutory rape. That was what she was talking about. Peter's
father, Souver Hubbard, had told him the story, after he and JoAnn
got divorced, so Peter might understand his mother better. People
didn't talk about it nowadays but everybody knew back then. And
that was about Royal and *her* father, Lucas Sochia, which were
cousins too. Anything they could do to insult each other, they
did. But he shouldn't be passing it on; he'd promised his father,
for JoAnn's sake.

"Hanh?"

"Never mind. Let's go."

Frank was on his own topic anyway. "But I mean God damn
it, Hawk! Think of the bullshit she has told us! Think of the fucking
lies! Hanh?"

Peter shook his head sadly, once in the truck. Wiped the inside
of the windshield with a leather glove while Francis slammed his
door, then drove them up the street to their sleeping families.

Marjorie'd made up her mind to hurry along this folly she was
making for him, not big enough for a bed, nicer to throw over
your legs in a rocking chair, or two pairs of legs in two rocking
chairs side by side. Finish it, give it to him, and remove herself.
Her husband had been patient but when she passed on the latest
news, her suspicions about what Robert was doing (professionally
and socially), he said she could be called an accomplice to the
smuggling, and there might be violence about the other. He wanted
her out of that town. She'd done her bit and then some, he said.
Which was true, she freely agreed.

So now, wasn't it amazing, as she was finishing the quilting and preparing to find a way to say good-bye (she'd thought of saying, "Sure enough, just as I thought: You're innocent"), she was overcome with reluctance to part from him. She felt an odd mixture of maternal and sisterly concern for him. Would he be all right? Plus, she had to admit, a frivolous, unambitious sexual interest, a desire to be desired, perfectly trite, perfectly well under control. He was beautiful, after all, good of his type. She hadn't come to feel she knew him but she liked him.

She really felt like crying. She didn't want to say good-bye at all. Hopeless! There they were, toe to toe, a few tufts to go, and she could hardly stand it, could hardly force her needle through, up and down, hardly had the strength or will to pull the thread out arm's length. She slowed almost to a stop.

"Robert."

They hadn't yet really spoken about his future and now she was about to leave him to it, she had some information that might be of use to him. She knew a little bit about this girl, this college student who was pitching herself at him. When she asked herself whether it was her place to say anything, utter any word of warning, she answered, No, no, it wasn't.

"Oh, never mind."

But then she asked herself again. No, and it wasn't jealousy either. She had to inspect herself on that score too. Anyway, suddenly the last of the quilting was done, she couldn't drag it out any farther. She slipped the quilt out of her hoop, stood up from her rocker and showed it to him, suspended from her outstretched hands, the center of it caught under her chin. She studied it herself, rolling her head left and right. "It's just a patchwork," she said. "It doesn't have any clear purpose. It's not a piece of art."

"It's nice."

"But I thought about every piece. I thought about them all as if I were putting together a puzzle. And I thought about what looked interesting next to what. I thought if I did that, it would all look interesting. Chance would take care of it. In a sense, I think chance did take care of it. In fact I rather like it."

"I like it too."

She still had her chin down, holding the middle of the top edge. She carried one corner down with one hand to draw her finger along the line between a pattern of *fleur de lis* on a blue background and an adjacent bit of plaid mostly green. She wondered if he recognized any of these pieces. Maybe some of the same fabric that Helen had patched into Johnny's or even Robert's shirts, or their hippy jeans. In her mind all these different pieces were like all those different young people, and Helen and Johnny, and their kids, and the horses and pigs and chickens. They all fit together jaggedly and were interesting next to each other individually. She could imagine this quilt with the pieces all forever changing places and yet it being the same always. He reached out for the workpiece now and she let him take it into his hands.

Free of it, she was over the precipice, beyond hesitation. She said, "I don't know if I ought to tell you this, Robert. You haven't asked, and perhaps you would rather not know anything anybody else might know. About your new friend." She looked up from the fabric to his face. He continued moving the comforter through his hands, looking at its parts.

He said nothing, of course. He never took bait of this kind.

"Well, listen to me for a minute anyway. You've never asked me what I do and that's all right but as it happens I work in the college library, in Moira. She, your new friend, is a student at the college. At the music school part of the college, but still, music students have to darken the doors of the library from time to time. Actually they tend to be very good students. So I have seen her. I've noticed her, known her by sight, and by sound, since she is not one to whisper, for years."

He looked up from the comforter to its maker, who dropped her eyes and sat down again across from him, put her stocking feet back up on the ottoman and frankly pushed them against his to get her rocker tilted back. She held it there. "Many faculty wives, which I am not, also work at the library and are my friends. We talk. They talk. And I have to warn you, Robert. Julia is much talked about. She is . . . notorious."

She let some time pass. He was listening, of course.

"For just the same sort of thing she is doing here, with your 'enemies,' if that's the right word, and now with you." A little chirp of amusement, amazement. "She does this, Robert. She puts herself right in the middle of everything. The visit of Governor Rockefeller to the campus. Guess who took hold of his arm and led him around! The refusal of tenure to a good teacher who neglected to get his doctorate. Guess who led the student protests. She's in the homes, virtually in the families, of three or four of the smartest, most artistic, or politically the most leftist professors; and she's all over some of these men physically, like a child without inhibitions. She seems to have very great powers of charming and manipulating people, men especially, and she uses them, some of my friends think, shamelessly, for her own selfish ends."

She was not liking herself for this, but having started, she went on. "For some reason, men tend to become obsessed with her. Men who shouldn't, more often than not. Her own classmates seem to be able to resist her, but her professors don't. I don't know whether they get what they want from her, but they certainly follow her around hopefully, whether or not. She pretends to be a feminist, but among other women she leaves a trail of unhappiness. She pretends to love children, and perhaps she really does, but at the same time she callously, or perhaps I should be kinder and say 'carelessly,' threatens their parents' marriages. For all her undeniable intelligence and her undeniable charm, my friends (granted I am talking about the women) consider her an obnoxious, homewrecking *brat*. To be succinct. And *I* think you'd be *crazy* to trust her."

He looked up from the patchwork in his hands, across their pressing toes, at her face. She closed her eyes. She knew just what she looked like. Her knee-socks, her pleated skirt, belt, sweater; her chin tensed into dimples, her eyes squeezed shut and a glint of liquid from under her lashes, damn it, which she wiped away with a bitter "Oh, shit!" She took away her feet from his, tilted her rocker upright and composed herself. "I thought I owed you that, but now I feel small. I shouldn't worry, I suppose. She's the *last* sort of woman you'd be interested in. *She's* throwing herself at *you*. You're not throwing yourself at her."

She stood up. "Well. Stand up and be hugged good-bye, please. I'm going."

He did stand up. "Good luck," she said, putting her arms around him for once.

"Take care." She was frankly crying now.

And he kissed her! A lovely, heartwarming kiss. "Thank you for this," he said, about the comforter, with a very nice smile.

"You're very welcome," she said. She never did say "You're innocent." It would have been silly, or literary, or something.

14

Towards Polaris

Looking north from the higher ground on the road to Moira, that river that you see on edge in the blue haze of the horizon is the great St. Lawrence, and the land beyond is Canada. The river is the international boundary southwestward toward Lake Ontario, but eastward the boundary soon leaves the river and runs due east, a land border dividing Northern New York and Vermont from French-speaking Canada, from what Leo calls the "sub-flumenal" part of Quebec. In the business of getting somebody named Bazille to Montreal, Robert and Julia were weaving back and forth across that landscape and that border (between three nations, counting Akwesasne, the Mohawk one, and two tongues), all day and night.

The river-boundary, with the Mohawk Nation straddling it with land on both sides of the river and a long island in the middle of it, a stepping stone for the international bridge, is a natural for smuggling nowadays, as it was for rum-running during Prohibition. The land border to the east is a natural for smuggling too, the remote farms of the northernmost part of the state backing up against similarly scattered farms in Quebec.

First over the bridge near Massena. In the countryside along the river, you pass between the entrances to the Reynolds plant (aluminum) and GM (engine blocks and cylinder heads made of same) and then the road rises in woods and it feels like a hill but the trees fall away and you are riding up over the St. Lawrence Seaway ship-channel as if you were on a Ferris wheel. Underneath, the wind drags the river along, left to right. The Seaway is closed at that time of year but the channel was open down the middle, where it looked to Julia as if an icebreaker had been through. That made her think of the ships of another season, other waters. Right there on the crest of the span, she said, "Hey Bobby did I tell you I'm going to Greece?"

She said that on the spur of the moment, excited by this international travel, the sense of the great world's traffic underneath their arching flight. But not without a half-dozen swift calculations too. It would serve as part of her time-teaching. Robert Sochia needed, more than anything, a new and healthy concept of time, eternity, forever. The one he had was bad news for them both. She was going to teach him, 1), that this that was going on between them was real and would last forever and ever. But, 2), forever-and-ever isn't what you think it is. The trip to Greece wasn't that definite, it depended on a lot of things (like graduating!) but never mind. It was good to have planted in his mind a *terminus ad quo* (if that was the phrase) for the merely chronological aspect of the relationship.

He was cool, as she knew he'd be; showed no surprise, only said, "When?"

"This summer!" She went on chattering about how her Gramps and this old lady who's kind of like her guardian were going to help her go to Europe as soon as she graduated; on a shoestring of course. She and a boy they knew, she knew, an old family-and-school friend, a great friend, *not* a boy-friend ("*he* thinks he may be gay, he's working that out"), she and this old friend would travel together, for mutual benefit. "He's a brilliant oboist. Anyway Aunt Sarah insists on a companion. My Aunt Sarah (not really my aunt) says, 'I don't want you getting mixed up with any of those *gypsies* over there!' *Waitaminnit is this Canada?*"

"No. The Rez."

They were descending onto the island now; there, ahead on the left, was U.S. Customs. She was intrigued, she had had no idea this was the *Rez!* "No kidding, Akwesasne?" She knew the names, there was a newspaper, *Akwesasne Notes*, naturally she had great political sympathy for Native Americans.

"The Indians just call it the Rez."

They passed a duty-free liquor store and turned onto a small road to the right that she sensed paralleled the river though she couldn't see it, through country that really did feel different from the mainland. It seemed stripped, worn, scaled-down. The road was paved but narrow, and not so well-paved—pot-holed and bumpy. The houses were small, far apart and mostly far back from the road, at the ends of dirt driveways, and there were not necessarily barns with them, these were not necessarily farms. All the dirt cross-roads sloped down to the right, toward a line of trees beyond which must have been (down a steep wooded bank, she guessed) the river, the American channel which they had just crossed. Up to the left were big old trees but those woods must have been a narrow strip along the ridge of the island because she could see right through them to the space of air over the river on the other side.

Julia was looking, commenting, everything was interesting to her. Where were the people? They weren't outside, not even the kids. Where was everybody? Robert told her that you didn't see many people outside even in summer. The kids, bunches of them, all ages, were inside a lot. With the women. Sisters, mothers, sisters-in-law, neighbors. They were always washing, baking, boiling that corn of theirs, the kids watching television cartoons from one foreign country or the other.

"What's your friend's name?"

"Lumen Sinohese."

"*Lumen! Lumen?*" Even such a thing as the name delighted her. She was up. This was going to be a fabulous day. They found Lumen Sinohese outside his father's little house working on a brand-new, orange bandsaw mill, in the mud and snow, a few muddy small logs scattered about. He was brawny, short, in brown overhauls, round-faced, his dark hair sticking out like a brush from beneath his watch-cap. Robert said Lumen was getting ready to build a radio station on a hill near the foot of the island. A grant, money from somewhere, like the money he got to buy the sawmill. This was his sister Ernestine's shiny black sports coupe pulled up right to the door of the little house. They went inside under the low ceilings, and Mrs Sinohese and Ernestine took Julia into the small living room to look at their sweetgrass baskets and bead jewelry.

They were very friendly, hospitable women and Julia won them over easily by paying close attention to their crafts and asking questions and praising the work and the smell of the sweetgrass, which she loved. She only kept an eye a little on Robert and Louie and Lumen sitting together at the kitchen table just through the archway there, though she would have loved to hear them too, planning their interesting crime. Louie so short and bowlegged as she'd noticed, with his long grey hair in a ponytail, his string tie, his western shirt tight across his big chest, always showing his gold tooth—she saw him tilt his head toward the living room and smile, nodding. That was about her, she guessed. Approval. And Ernestine might be jealous but Julia would ignore that and show her interest and make her tell her things. Robert would take care of Louie's doubts. She saw Louie get a wad of money out of one of the tight pockets of that Western shirt and flatten it on the table between them.

This was so neat! This was going to be such a great day!

The women didn't ask her about herself and she was glad because what could she say? She was nothing, a mere college student and Ernestine was the director of a whole museum and her mother the wife of a chief and they were both the great basketmakers of the world. She heard Louie ask something and Robert say "Over near Trout River," and Louie, no answer. Nadine was leading her back into the kitchen to serve some juice and store-made cookies. She went around Robert touching his collar and took the red chair beside him, facing Louie.

"Way over there," Louie observed, doubtfully. But apparently whatever they were talking about was Robert's part to decide. Louie smiled, mostly wrinkles around the gold-rimmed spectacles. "What time?"

"Eleven o'clock."

Louie squeezed his forehead, pretending to complain. Was that too late? Too early? But the time too must have been Robert's to say. Louie broke out in another grin. "Quebec farmers go to bed at eight," he agreed. Then he opened the wad of money, counted it, folded it shut, laid it down again and nudged it, moving his whole arm, not just his thick brown fingers. *Heavy*, that ring, and that bracelet! Robert put the money in his breast pocket just like Louie: men and their chests. It looked like a lot of money; a pretty good business you're in, Bobby.

Then they were out in the sun again, shaking hands with everybody, Julia hugging Ernestine and her mother, both slipping in mud to the car; driving back to the bridge, past the little houses that meant much more to Julia now. She was enthusiastic about the women. This was a matriarchy, did he know? A woman was the Long House chief. They had the great idea that the earth was like a turtle and we were all riding on its back. She was having fun. They turned onto the bridge highway again, north away from U.S. Customs where they didn't have to stop.

"So what about this Bazille?" she asked.

"Wants to go to Canada."

She licked and rolled her lips, looking out the windshield. Then fell over with her head on his lap, laughing. After a moment he pulled her up. "Customs," he said.

She looked ahead. Oh! Canada Customs. These people are police-like people! Is this scary? Robert was smiling at her, calm. She guessed it wasn't scary. Douannes! Who was a *Douannier?* Some great French writer. Hawthorne and Melville were customs guys to make a living but who French? Balzac? She thought it was Stendahl. *Le Rouge et Le Noir, La Chartreuse de Parme.* She didn't know.

Stop. *Arrêt.* The slender, mustachioed official shaded his face with his clipboard, looking in. "Where were you born?" The question was directed at Robert.

"Moira."

"Purpose of the trip?"

"Pleasure."

Julia was sitting Indian fashion, crossways, on the seat beside him. She ducked her head so the man could see her face and told him that she was born in Brooklyn New York and she was going to Montreal for the first time in her life, for a whole day and a night.

As they drove on toward the toll gate, Robert said, "Just let them ask."

"What do you mean?"

"He didn't ask you anything."

"Ah, I get it."

"They're trained."

"Ah-h-h." She nodded. Privately she thought, "Phooey, I didn't do any harm." But she got his point. He was a smart man. "Hey, another bridge."

The Canadian span over to Cornwall was steeper, older, its paving rougher. It was two narrow lanes with close guard-rails that interfered with her seeing the river, and it curved unevenly to the left as it came down over some old locks and a canal in front of the huge paper mill with high smokestacks, a mountain of pulpwood beyond. The paper mill smell filled the car. Wetted ashes and sulfur? It must simply permeate those tenements and asphalt-sided houses, the whole city. Robert told her that when the wind was in the north you could smell that in the Falls.

She knew that. She did know some things. But her good will was great, and she said, "Yeah, so if you smell it, you know which way the wind is blowing, right?"

She looked at the rows and streets of houses almost under them as they came down. "They're used to it, they live here," she said. Then, almost at ground level, "We're in a foreign country!" She turned around on the seat, knelt backwards beside him, put her face in front of his. Lips to lips. Not too long, lest he have trouble finding the right turn. "Our First Kiss in a Foreign Country," she said. "Good, huh? Just you wait."

It was a sort of childlike kiss and she knew that as they went into the traffic circle at the foot of the ramp he was stirred. They were together. This was the way they would feel all day. Dual, together, neither alone. She could make him feel like that, and he'd be happy.

Outside Cornwall, he drove fast, like the Canadians, with her touching him and talking all the time. In that country along the river, the road signs pointed off to one town after another with the name of a saint or a church and everybody drove fast.

In open country they passed the border between Ontario and Quebec and she said, "Ah, now we're in a *more* foreign country." They left the divided highway and stayed near the river and the flavor of the country changed, the towns were like resort towns, there were night clubs, with tropical themes, she realized this was the sunny south of Canada, Canada's Florida! There were all kinds of restaurants, Italian, Mexican, Chinese. She asked him what kinds of food he liked. She listed the cuisines that she would introduce him to, in Montreal. "I saw that wad of money, man." They could spend a little of that, right? They were staying in somebody's apartment that night and all day Sunday and going back late Sunday night. The apartment of somebody named Ness. Who was not going to be there, yay.

"Oo ees eet, zees Ness? Ee's Nice! Never mind, I know, he's the Underground Railway!"

Oh, it was such a relief to be in a foreign land, going to Montreal, a great cosmopolitan city, a *French* city, with this very cool *garçon* her own age! She had gotten herself into a false position with Michael, and not only Michael but Bernie, Paul, too, other teacher-friends. It wasn't her fault. She was such friends with their wives, with their kids, she never wanted this sense that developed in this senior year when she would soon be (supposedly) all grown up: a *graduate*, that she and they were going to have—that she had promised them—some Big Thing? But they had taken her that way and she admitted she hadn't been clear, she'd been self-indulgently dreaming too (in Michael's case). She couldn't help it. She was human. It was unfair to leave all the self-discipline to her. *They* were supposed to be wise, not she. But here, now, was Bobby. He needed her worse than they did. He was an emergency, and she was glad of it because what would be so good for him would also be so fine, for her.

He was going to be a good student, she could tell. He was going to be her best pupil ever. He had a wrong idea about life and maybe wrong ideas about men and women and a wrong idea about

what happened to him when he kissed her. It was good, not great.
Nice, not tragic. Normal, common, standard! He'd know better
when they were making love. She was going to be in love with him
for a while, because he was her own age, for one thing, and perfect
for her right now, and he needed her, badly. She'd help him to be
happier, no problem, and it would be sweet loving, nice for her
lonely little body, and after it she'd get busy on the things she
ought to be doing for her own life's sake. Finish her practice
teaching, easy. Then her recital, Oh God she should be practicing
for that right now. Classes, papers, exams if she couldn't talk her
way out of them. But she wouldn't think about that, today. She
needed this, first. She was taking a chance that those other boys
would find out, no it was almost a sure thing they would find out
but that would be good for them too. They would have to get
around it and see that she had a right to do this and Robert had a
right and nobody had a right to deny it. Really that's what
everybody had to learn! No jealousy allowed! Then her practice-
teaching would be over, and back in Moira, she'd put on a spurt
and amaze everybody, finish everything just in time.

They had crossed back over the river before coming even close to
Montreal, a thing she didn't know you could do. There was no
map of Quebec in her car. Bobby didn't seem to need one. There
was water left and right and she was confused where it was flowing.
Then there was a city, Salaberry de Valleyfield, which they toured
to familiarize her with it because she was going to come back to
this same town or city and sit in a restaurant, eat something, buy
a paper and read—kill time inconspicuously. She couldn't picture
it. She never killed time. He stuffed some Canadian money in her
pea-coat pocket. Were they getting close? She needed to pee a
little bit but she could wait. Out in the darkening country again
she said, "I don't believe I'm doing this! There's a whole branch of
the government devoted to catching us."

"Two governments," he said.

"Two governments!"

"Two branches of each."

"Of each!"

"At least."

"I don't believe I'm doing this with you! When you don't have me, who do you have? Lumen? Ernestine-with-the-hot-car? Who is this Bazille, really? Really, Bobby, don't you want to know the politics of this Bazille? What if he's a Tonton Macoute? Maybe he's been cutting people's hands off down there. Oh never mind, we're out of our *trees* to be doing this!" But she still didn't let the happiness go out of her voice, her face. He often looked at her. He was still checking her out. Wondering who in the world this was, next to him. Just me!

Out in the country the farmhouses were farther back from the roads and they were smaller and had steeper roofs than the houses in the North Country. The little towns had big churches and houses were right against the streets and were painted a lot of pastel and bright colors. Robert thought it was because these people were cheap, or poor. They bought any color that was on sale. But she said, "*Non, non, I* know about that, that's the French being French, man. *Amour couleur!* Aren't you French? Don't you know French? Stop! There's a patisserie!"

He got out and followed her and listened while she parlayed. It was hot and smelled sweet inside and the walls were orange. She thought she did pretty well, making her voice go up and down, relishing the pronunciations she had learned, the tenses and genders probably wrong but surely intelligible? The bakery woman looked as if she didn't understand a word. Then she said a lot of short fast things, pointing at different trays in the case and at hand-printed signs on the wall. Julia turned her head to Robert with her mouth open and her eyes gaga. But finally they got a loaf of bread and a few pastries and a hunk of cheese. She came out laughing. "Dose Quebeckurr, dey talk like ducks! What kind of a name is Sochia if it isn't French?"

"It is French."

"How come we're going around in circles?" She tore off a hunk of the baguette for him and fed him pieces of cheese while he drove.

The road followed the bends in a smaller river instead of going straight. It followed the edges of fields. It would go along beside a field and when it got to the end of the field, turn ninety degrees. That interested Julia, a country where the farms pushed the roads around. A killer curve, just to avoid crossing over the corner of a field! No guard rails on the 90 degree curve, either, just a row of maple trees with their trunks painted white. Julia whistled as these white tree-trunks flashed past. "Hey, you could run right into those trees if you were drunk a little. These people don't get drunk, I guess."

"They get drunk."

He told her how he used to come up across the border on Saturday nights. There were cover charges but the beer was cheap because of the good exchange-rate. The bands were good. They'd give a bottle of whiskey for a door prize.

"You came up here? Looking for women, I bet. Yeah, and finding them too. Little Catholic Canucks with bobby-sox. I bet they wouldn't give you anything, though. Not a bit. Right?"

She saw him trying to remember why he came up, as if it were more complicated. He admitted there had been the idea of picking out some girl, the most beautiful one in the place, and trying to get her away from her boyfriend. That was part of it. The danger. He and his buddies were raiders.

"What about the dancing? I bet you're a good dancer. Do you dance?" He didn't answer but he sort of blushed.

"I liked coming up here."

"Yeah, what's a border for?"

"I like the different talk that I can't understand."

"Yeah, what made everybody think that if you went away it would be to Florida?"

"It wouldn't."

"Of course not. *Á bas Florida!* So who were these buddies who came up here with you? Your Indian buddies? Do they call themselves Indians, not Native Americans? What about Ernestine, huh? Was she your girl?"

"That would be a good way to get killed."

"And you're not that dumb, good! That was her car, you know. That black Firebird or Thunderbird or some kind of bird. How can she afford a car like that?"

"You never know."

"So how do you smuggle people anyway? Is this your first time?"

"Carry them if they won't walk."

"Come on! How? What's it like?"

"It's like being a guide. Or a scout. In the olden days."

"Right, the French and Indian War!"

She was driving now. Montreal was way behind and they were going away from it but that would come after they did this thing in which she would be alone, driving, nervous and out-of-place. What if she got lost? If she was stopped and questioned what could she say? But why would she be? Also she needed to pee. She would do that after she dropped him off.

They went through another town, Huntington, and turned to the right at its main intersection, where a sign said *Frontière 23*. Bobby told her to remember the turn, the numbers of the routes. Why shouldn't she wait in Huntington instead of going back to Salaberry de V.? Too small, she guessed. No anonymity for *étrangères*.

They were getting close, *Frontière 9* (kilometres, shorter than miles), and suddenly he told her to turn where she didn't even see a road. It was a much narrower narrow road, though paved, and plowed. She thought it must parallel the border. She was seriously paying attention but she could hardly see. Sometimes the road was squeezed between woods on both sides, and sometimes there were fields or at least open space. The snow-banks were low compared to home and the road was icy. It was dark now and this, the road, the low clean snow-banks, occasional woods close-by, the sudden driveways of the farms, dim lights in the infrequent small houses and long rows of windows of the barns were all she could see and hard to see and yet she was supposed to remember them.

Off beyond these plowed fields, to the south, there was rough pasture and scrub woods, and in this, he told her, was a cleared strip or scar running exactly east and west like a power-line right-of-way with no power-line. Every so often there was a numbered concrete post. There was a well-worn path in the strip, worn by the Border Patrol riding on dirt-bikes or snowmobiles.

"With dogs?" Her nose was running, suddenly, for no reason.

He shook that off, but why wouldn't there be dogs, and what if there were?

"Slow," he said. "Open your window." From the car, in the dark under stars, she could more sense than see the crowned field disappearing to her left under a snow horizon, a ragged line of fenceposts drifted halfway to their tops. Robert's flashlight, held across in front of her, showed a rutted lane turned brown by manure that had dripped from a spreader. Then woods. "Slower." She was not to stop. She was not to touch the brake. He had fixed the dome light so it wouldn't go on. He opened the door and got out running beside the car and closed it just enough to make it click, and then he stopped and vanished and she looked for him in the rear-view mirror, to see him lit red, or an edge of him lit red, but she didn't. She just heard the crunch of the tires on frozen slush and imagined him waiting for that sound to dwindle and the sounds of the cold clear night to take its place.

Did he feel as alone as she suddenly did? She didn't like this, at *all*, without him. There was no reason, no excuse, for her to be here on this road. At the first place she could, she was to turn right, away from the border, and then left, and the next right would be the route from the next border-crossing to Huntingdon. She was scared, and it made her angry to be scared. She'd been the sweetie of a gang-leader at *fourteen*, but that was in a city, *her* city, *the* City. What if she slid on some ice and got stuck in a snowbank? What if she ran out of gas? But Robert had thought of that, he'd filled the tank, good.

She didn't come to an intersection; what happened instead was, she thought, that this road turned sharply to the right. She thought she was going north now but she didn't really know. She stopped and got out to see if she could see any stars. And she could. She saw the Big Dipper, upside down overhead, and pointed to the two stars of the dipper opposite the handle, and marched off seven times their distance, and found Polaris, and thought, *Is that what he is navigating by?*

If she were on her own, she would go all the way into Montreal, find the Bohemian part, get rid of the car, eat deli food, dig some music. She was a city girl, she'd get right into Montreal. But she wasn't free to do that. Back in the car, relieved, she held her wristwatch near the speedometer to read it. She would see how long it took to get back to the bright lights and her supposed diner. Subtract that from twelve o'clock. That's when she would start back. She would *really* be freaked then, driving slowly back along that border road, looking for the lane turned dark with manure, waiting for the sudden clatter of ice-chunks thrown against the car as it passed. For the moment, she couldn't even think of the night ahead of them, at this Ness's apartment, and the reasons she was doing this at all.

Delinquent boys! None of these bad-boys would believe her if she told them how clearly she understood them, how perfectly they fit the type. She did not dare to let Bobby know; he'd hate it. But she could even just about *see* them when they were younger, kids, pale, nervous, often tearful in their pain. By the time they were Bobby's age they had learned to cover a lot of it up, but she could see it. They looked at the world, the stupid world of everybody else who has a house and a car and a wife and kids and a job, and who is going to die of boredom and old age in equal measure, as if they were looking at one of the world's great promises. They'd never admit that they even wanted that world, of course, that was the last thing they would admit, even to themselves, but that was just because they felt so far outside of it. And that was because one way or another their parents had cut them off.

You could just bet that they had been neglected by their fathers. And sure enough, Bobby was. Leo had told her about him, she hadn't needed to pry it out of him. First his father indulged him and introduced him to grown men's things before he was old enough, and then when he *was* old enough, he wasn't *good* enough, wasn't exactly like his father (probably had some of his *mother* in him, for shame), his father dropped him. He couldn't stand him. Bobby was just a child, his tears made everything worse—she could just imagine how he was hurt!

Just like Tony, her gangleader boyfriend in the City who was probably dead by now. Talk about delinquent boys! One of the things he said still echoed in her mind. "They can't forget me." That was a funny way to put it, she had thought at the time. In the first place she was pretty sure he meant his parents or his family, the people he came from. But then did he mean he wouldn't let them forget him, or he begged God not to let them forget him, or he was going to make sure they didn't, by doing—something? Maybe it meant all of those things but she thought it meant most of all, he couldn't stand it if they did. And they already had.

But she'd said, "They won't forget you."

And he'd said, he wasn't so dumb: "They will, and that makes me want to kill somebody."

It sent a chill through her even now. He was such a good brave kid and she hoped he was okay but she doubted it. They broke up, naturally, she had a life to live, even before her mother and Aunt Sarah banished her to the Frozen North because she didn't get accepted much less a scholarship at Juilliard. Her nose was trickling. She took a deep breath through her mouth and concentrated on driving, on watching her rear-view mirror, on not missing a route sign. 132.

Bobby had even been sent to special schools, boarding schools for delinquents. Tony had too. They hated being away from the world. They couldn't bear the thought of it passing them by. She'd tried to tell him that they weren't out of the world, they were somewhere. But Tony had said, "No we weren't. We were forgotten! I hated it! Other people being remembered and spoken about and us forgotten there. No better than a jail!"

They were bugged by questions of reputation, those boys, all of them. Tony would say, "Do people know who I am? Do they know what I did?" He was worse off than Bobby, she thought. Tony was obsessed with that problem because he really had no past to speak about! How *would* anybody know who he was? He

would talk about being photographed and written about or even
drawn by court artists—anything to bring him into the picture.

But Bobby had a past, at least, didn't he? Anyway, it was just
plain child development and how families fuck you up. The point
was, she had a really terrible insight into what that next level of
recognition meant for Robert Sochia. The opposite of cowardice.
Did anybody around here know anything about the death-wish?
Did anybody around here take Psych 101 for Pete's sake? Her work
was cut out for her. Here was Huntingdon.

He turned and walked back to the lane, the edge of the woods.
Across the dark field, the farm buildings were illumined, one side
each, by a pole light. Silos, otherwise black against the sky, shone
on one edge, and a long barn that might be turquoise in daylight
stretched in black silhouette. He didn't hear dogs. A moment's
thought of the girl, her light dress, her legs under the steering
wheel, her face turned toward him lit only by the instrument lights.
Behind him the noise of her tires on the road diminished, ceased.

He was aware of her always now, as if she watched him. He
took quick steps along the iced pavement and dived to the side
over the snowbank, to leave no mark that could be seen from a car,
rolling over his shoulders into the brush of the hedgerow, at the
edge of the woods. He lay amazed at the stars, his own sense of
time in his mind, an old vigor in his chest.

The vague loom of Chateaugay, seven miles away, served for a
bearing. He made a rapid march, passing the length of two long
narrow sections of tall maples, bordered either side by cultivated
ground. Then the maple orchards ended square and the country
opened up to pasture, rough walking between the clumps of low
brush without any limit ahead or to the sides as far as he could see.
The starlight was almost like moonlight to him now. There was a
half-mile of soft footing amid small birches and small cherry trees,
woodcock feeding grounds, and small dark cedars that seemed to
reach out to him like children in a playground, or stand and watch
him pass. She might have been one of them and then another.

The frontier itself was a treeless strip twenty feet wide, clear-cut and poisoned fifteen years before, now grown up to brush, with the paths of the Border Patrol's and farm kids' dirt-bikes rutted and frozen hard. He slipped from nation to nation, following the paths of deer and dogs, trails of blackness under the starlight. This was the States now but still the same Quebecker's farm until he crossed a low barbed-wire fence. Then the stony, hummocky ground of some American's back pasture, same but different.

"What'll I do with myself while I'm *waiting*?" she'd said, stretching out the word to make it mean more than waiting for him to get back with Bazille. "Shall I go ahead to Ness's and take a nice long bath? Want me to shave my legs? And my arm pits? I don't, usually, but I would, for you. Look!" She'd showed him, there in the car, surprisingly long curly dark hair under her arm, which he wasn't ready for. But now, as he thought of it, he liked it.

She seemed to be beside him as he came out from the woods behind the little crossroads bar. He was briefly lit by the lights of the Customs stations two hundred feet along. He noted the single pickup truck parked in front and entered by the front door. The place was a sort of roadside aquarium, full of tropical fish in tanks, a fetish of the owner's wife. Behind the bar and along the walls and in the window on the road, all these green-lighted tanks of fish. She would have had to look into all of them. At the counter he joined a man with a ponytail, not Indian. The man nodded and ordered a beer "for Johnny here," in a New Jersey accent. They shot a game of pool and then the two of them left in the New Jersey man's pickup truck. It was a small Japanese pickup and she wouldn't have fit on the seat, she'd have had to sit on his lap.

They went south, then east to Chauteaugay, then north, then northeast again to the New Jersey man's homestead, in what was once a gravel pit. Two old Mercedes cars rotted in the snow. Behind the unfinished log house, under a succession of tarps, was an unfinished ferro-cement sailboat in which the other man and his wife planned to go around the world. These people lived temporarily windowless in the basement made of concrete blocks, where the carbon-faced Bazille, brawny, shadowy, foolishly dressed, shook his arm and hand together, bent over sideways left and right, with a wide yellow-teethed smile, looking around behind Robert as if he knew he had her with him and wanted a look at her.

Bazille either had a big chest or was carrying a lot of sweaters, under a farmer's padded workcoat, but he wore light slacks on his thin legs, and small black shoes of thin leather, nothing for his hands. He had a newspaper to hold over his head and a flimsy box to carry, tied with string. His enthusiasm waned in wet pasture and he stopped to smoke, talking to himself some sort of shifty song. Robert closed his eyes and noticed his own breath, smooth and deep. Bazille was like his own shadow, touching him in fear. They crossed the border which was like a beam of moonlight and Robert moved more easily and faster, following Polaris, leaving Bazille to keep up on his own.

Then in the car, they heard him, in the back seat, opening his package. Then the sounds of his little drum and his songs in French, his voice husky, gravelly, full of liquid clicks and gutterals. Julia looked across the seatback to him, smiling. "It's for us," she said to Robert.

They took him east of the *centre-ville*, to the French part of town, to the broad Avenue St. Denis running north over the plateau between rows of houses either side with iron stairways from the street to their second floors, a long boulevard which finally leveled and then turned down toward a distant plain where chains of streetlights laced through dark industrial suburbs. The avenue became more residential, lined with large trees behind which the houses were still of two and three stories with outside iron stairways to the second floors and the streets were completely lined with the cars that belonged to the houses. It went on and on like that maybe getting poorer but still the same, and then the wide avenue narrowed to a street lined with trucks and cars and they found the block they were looking for, and the house, no parking space near it so Robert turned the car around and parked across the street, half of the car overlapping the interdicted zone near the corner. The house was dark. He threw cinders from the sidewalk against a basement window, black.

And then, too soon for her, they were on their way across town again, toward the Côte de Neige, and he had a terrible feeling in his chest, an awful sense of loss. She'd wanted to hang out with them. She really dug Bazille, his smile, the bones of his face, those long-fingered black hands tan on the undersides, the music in his voice and all the others', and the Caribbean sounds all around them coming from half a dozen hidden sources. The cellar of that house that looked from the street just like all its neighbors was a complete surprise, all divided up with quick cheap carpentry from odds and ends of materials like 2 by 4s and plywood and tin, into a dozen or more sleeping places, two-high sometimes, built in around the furnace and the coal-bin and the stairway, the support posts. Sleeping-places that the people had to stay in even when they weren't sleeping because there was so little room left, around the little crates that served as tables and some actual chairs and stools. She had wanted to hang out and Bazille had given her his beads, a long string of green beads he had fished from his pants pocket. Bazille—that shiny black face so lined, so carved. She had those beads in her fingers now as Robert drove, back down St. Denis toward the river. She was supposed to watch for their turn, for Sherbrooke.

But he'd had to park *Stationnement Interdit*, he couldn't take a chance on lingering. But also he just wanted to *go*. To get to Ness's. She said but they had all night for that and tomorrow too. She gave him a sort of a lecture about it. When was she ever going to be right in the middle of a bunch of Haitian refugees who had risked everything to come to Montreal, where, great for them, they could go right on speaking French? They were so beautiful, so happy to see Henrique safe among them, they touched so freely, all shaking hands and kissing, so grateful to her and Bobby, *they* wanted them to stay. That was where it was at, man! But she understood him, it was okay. She gave Henrique a big hug and kiss and some of the

other women and men too. She breathed in deeply, the smell of
them and their skin and what they were drinking, and the *smoke*,
cough-cough! She tried to get Bazille to keep his beads, for luck,
didn't he need them for luck? but he laughed and put them round
her neck, and his lady (Julia assured him that tall one with the
short kinky hair was his lady) agreed with him and laughingly
fingered them either side of her neck and with her wonderful mouth
kissed Julia's cheeks. Well. She left them with regret but turned
herself at once back to him, didn't she? She knew, she said, that it
would be terribly easy to spoil things. Jealousy would spoil things.
No jealousy, please, jealousy was a bad feeling, forbidden between
them. She'd make sure he didn't have anything to be jealous about,
tonight. He was probably not as comfortable with blacks as she
was, but no, he was right. They shouldn't have lingered. What had
she been thinking of? They were going to Ness's! She whistled to
get him to look at her, and smiled with her excitement. Leaned
against him, humming. Under his coat, inside his shirt, three light
flute-player finger-taps.

When they got out of the car on the steep hillside above the
Côte de Neige she bumped against him. She held her face up to
him happily, with her eyes closed.

He didn't kiss her, he just looked. The light mostly came from
below, farther down the north slope, because right across from the
apartment was a dark cemetery, and here was this face, held still
for him at last. Brows, lids, lashes, cheeks, nose, lips. He had a very
clear perception that such a being would surely reject him. He
knew that that was part of what this was. But it didn't matter.
What mattered was how he felt.

She opened her eyes and said, "Wanta brush your teeth first?
Wanta gargle? Need some mouthwash? I've got some mouthwash
right here in my mouth for you."

She unbuttoned her peacoat and unzipped his jacket and stood
inside it against him in her light dress. She raised her arms around
his neck and herself on tiptoe while his hands went under her coat
around her small waist and felt the indentation of her spine. Their
noses touched. Each eye had another eye to look into. She turned

her head just a little and her lips touched his. They were soft, cushioning. A warmth, a flavor came into him from them. He just felt them, for a long time. He couldn't breathe. She was breathing warmly and deeply through her nose while she was kissing him but he couldn't breathe. When he couldn't hold his breath any more he turned his mouth away but then he couldn't exhale smoothly either. His breath shook him when he let it out. He took another breath and they were kissing again for a long time and he was just feeling it and she was breathing warmly but he couldn't breathe again because when he did, it jerked him too much. So he held his breath again as long as he could, and felt the cushioning and took in the thing that wasn't a taste or a smell but was like them.

When he had to breathe and took his lips away and let it come out slowly, trying not to shake, she said, "It's good," and hugged him with her face down against his chest and swayed him, bashfully. What was it? It was amazing to him that she was there where she was, in the circle of his arms. What could come of this? How could it be a humiliation? But what else?

Inside Ness's door, a wooden floor shining, all the way to a wall of glass overlooking the northern slopes of the mount. White walls, wooden floors, sparse Danish furniture. In the bedroom one wall of glass covered by drapes, a balcony outside, one wall a mirror, a black metal machine like a sculpture, for exercise; the bed a wide field, very low, only a futon on wooden slats. A poster of nude bodies, male and female, black and white, thronged together, beautiful dancers, Chicago. He opened the drapes and slid the glass: a balcony and across the Côte de Neige the cemetery going up the hill to the horizon. Northward beyond the top there was a shining dome, and far beyond that, he knew, the Laurentians, the same ancient rock as at home, the oldest in the world.

She came up on her tiptoes in the flannel nightshirt that she said she wanted to wear for a little while, at first, because she was embarrassed, and the same thing happened, she could breathe deeply and easily and slowly and warmly, through her nose, he felt it on his cheek; but he couldn't breathe. He held his breath the whole time. When his breath had to go out he let it out carefully and unevenly through his nose but it still shook him. When he inhaled it jerked his whole body and he had to take his lips away from her mouth. He couldn't conceal it.

She said, somberly, "I always knew that we would be like that. Didn't you?"

He did not know but he wondered what he had expected, how he had gotten here at all.

"Third try and if you don't understand it, you have to give up and just accept it. That's the way it's going to be."

He could not breathe and couldn't hold his breath either, and she was humming smoothly along, and twining their fingers together, and he held his breath as long as he could and then he broke away and let it out and it caught and caught, shaking him.

When they knelt facing each other on the wide hard bed, at first he couldn't move his body smoothly either. His hands. His legs. His whole body caught and jerked when it touched hers. But she was amazed that he could just take off his shirts, both at once over his head—that he could just do that, which she couldn't. She was scared about him seeing her breasts which she hated, which she said weren't her. He knew before he uncovered them that they were not what women wanted, probably a bother. Not what men wanted either, usually, too big and low and too soft and the aureoles too large and dark and the nipples thick and not standing out; but he shook when he touched them. He brought them to his eyes, his ears. With his face between them, his mouth against her breast-bone, he couldn't breathe.

He was ashamed of what he had imagined, in jail. He had imagined how what he had saved up after so long would astonish some girl, whoever she was, that there would be so much she would have to drink it, and even then it would come out the corners of her mouth and she would scoop it off her cheeks and lips with her fingers and lick them too, and still have to wipe them on her breasts. But now he was ashamed of that fantasy because this wasn't like his imaginings and he only wanted her to feel this way too, being so shaken, so moved, like a tall tree by wind. But the end kept coming closer and closer, she was pulling it closer and closer, and it became right to let it come, or at least he couldn't stop it. But it became not the end after all, the end stayed at a little distance and something else happened that he had not known could happen. He had not known even that he could have hoped for it to happen. This was the proof, for him. This:

When she had pulled him in and her legs were wrapped around him and her ankles hooked together behind him and they were rocking together, slowly, slowly, and then less and less slowly, he found himself breathing easily. The shaking had stopped and he breathed easily and smoothly, like her, right in time with her. Deeper and deeper, with her. Exactly in time with her breathing. Deeper and deeper. Freely! Easily! Deeper and deeper. In unison with her, without trying. Always a little bit deeper and a little bit faster, until they were both almost out of breath, taking in complete lungfuls all at once, expelling them all at once, together, with a ringing sound that made him think of a tank being filled and emptied, as if they were two pipes to one tank. He heard them, together, taking these deep, hard breaths. The sound of the air rushing in, then the air rushing out. One sound for the two of them. He breathed and listened. A ringing, a higher and higher pitch, an echo, something larger than they were, resounding, like two pipes to one tank. And when it could get no deeper, when no amount of air could fill them, something else did, both of them, together, and they stopped breathing together and let it fill them and spill over them and roll through their veins and ease them down to rest, very slowly, and to breathing again still interlocked and holding each other tightly, for his part as tightly as he could without hurting her.

This was the proof, for him. You could go your whole life without this. With it you would do something exceptional. To express it you'd have to. He would want it to be known, someday, he knew. Whatever happened they couldn't take this away.

15

She'll Never Tell

They had just left the tiny little U.S. Customs at Churubusco, a pool of light, and were back in the dark in New York State, which was a sort of a letdown. No starlight, no moonlight, hardly any house or barnyard lights. They hadn't been talking. They hadn't talked, really, since leaving Ness's, they'd just been feeling—she felt, at least—completely fine and together. The customs officer had broken a nice silence.

The officer was a smart-looking young woman and she had asked Bobby a quick series of questions not in the most predictable form or order and he answered them all without any confusion. So cool, the officer bent down to look across at Julia.

Did he notice she remembered her lesson? She watched his profile, in the light of the dash. He was thinking other thoughts. Maybe they had better start coming down, talking. She said, "Wasn't I good?"

He didn't get it.

"The Customs person didn't ask me anything and I didn't tell her anything." He got it now, and nodded and glanced at her. She raised her eyebrows and blinked at him innocently. He had the sadness in his eyes again. That was okay, their time together was over. There had been quite a lot of sadness in his eyes earlier, before they left Ness's, but that had had to be, too. They had gotten over it and they had been happy together on the drive, and before the sadness part, they had been happy all day. That morning, whoo-ee. The night before, whooo-eee, after his little bit of jealousness because she had showed kindness to Bazille and let him give her those beads. Which were, where? In her pea-coat pocket. She wasn't wearing the peacoat now, it was warm in the car and she had thrown it in back and she was in a dress, still, her Sunday-in-the-City dress. Flowery and pretty and a real bra underneath, white! And she had her hair piled up, she had a neck, she looked grown-up.

She had surprised him, being such a lady. She had opened his eyes in lots of ways to what she was: *no ordinary gift, man, me giving my sweet little self to you. Does that tell you anything about* your *self?*

She had run out early in the morning, throwing her bell-bottoms on and her pea-coat over her nightie, and had searched northward in her car on the Côte until she found a *depanneur*, and they had had a great breakfast-in-bed, *croissants* and *café au lait* from Ness's fancy coffee-machinery, with the English Sunday paper, and then a lot of loving, and then all day doing city things. Bobby was in sync with her, they were touching all the time, he let her make all the decisions, and she knew how to find things in a city and she found them, the great delicatessen on Sherbrooke where the intellectuals and artists and McGill students met, the upstairs place where the little sign said *ici on chant, ici on mange.* They hung out in the *vielle cité* and came back there for dinner at a tiny table next to another tiny table where a very young gorgeous rich girl was being taken out to this scandalous counterculture place by her grandmother and listening to separatist and anti-US songs, sung by their very own FLQ songwriters. It was a great city day and he was gallant and beautiful the whole day, in clothes she didn't know he owned, that he said he had gotten out of storage in a room that he kept over all these years, upstairs somewhere in The Rapids of all places! Fine shoes and twill pants and a sportjacket with patches on the elbows, it was like a costume of a perfect Montreal dude, plus his shaggy hair and the daring ring in his ear. That was good for him, to be happy and unlonely for a whole day. He looked great all day and she stopped him in the middle of the street crossings and climbed right up on him and kissed him like a Parisienne. He stood back while she parlayed with people, related with them, touched palms, learned stuff. He was cool. Even in a bookstore, where she would have loved to just take up residence.

(Michael gave her James Joyce's *Pomes Pennyeach* for her birthday. That was a sort of thing that Bobby couldn't do.)

The little contretemps in the evening made him sad but that was inevitable and it was corrective and good for him. He had to know she loved him but also what love wasn't that he thought it was. He had a bad case of not knowing what love wasn't. That love was still there when what you thought it was wasn't there, for a while. He wanted to make love even more, after that whole long day which started with making love. It was really ridiculously important to him. But she didn't feel that way and she refused. She just let him lump it for a while. How could he be so amazed at that? How could he forget what she had given him already?

But he just couldn't understand and so then finally she told him that whenever she made love a lot, this happened to her, she got to feeling lost and lonely and afraid that nobody really loved her or understood her or appreciated what she loved about herself, which wasn't what a great bed-mate she was. She said it sullenly and coldly and didn't help him understand it at all, because she really did not like anybody being upset about that, he did not have any right to be hurt about that. She didn't help him but he helped himself. He got it and they had been fine and together on the whole trip back.

Maybe that was what he was thinking about now that put the sadness back in his eyes or maybe he was thinking about what she had said the last time they crossed the border, about going to Greece. Whichever, it was okay. He was getting things straight.

He knows, she thought. *He's a great pupil.*

Now they were going west, south of the border; the landscape was darker and emptier even than Canada. She didn't break the sweet-sad spell of the end of the trip to ask nonsense questions. Pretty soon they would come to the town with the herringbone parking down the middle where they had left the DeSoto. She hadn't liked that, leaving the DeSoto right in the middle of that little town for two whole nights and almost three whole days. But *she* wasn't the shrewd outlaw, *she* didn't know where better to leave it.

She had sure made up for a lot of not being touched by human hands. She would sure sleep when she finally got home to Neva's.

They came into sleepy midnight Fort Covington and turned right this time on the street with two rows of old stores and businesses and houses so wide apart, with parking places in two interwoven rows down the middle. Robert's funky old car sat all alone in the middle of the space. She didn't like this. She thought they ought to have stopped somewhere else, on another street, and cased the scene before going to his car. *Why isn't he being more careful about this?* But here they were, he pulled up beside the DeSoto and got out. She scooched over behind the wheel, rolling her lips together in her worry. They had better not kiss good-bye in this street. He opened the trunks of both cars and threw his stuff from one to the other. *Mine too? Did you switch mine?* But this might be good-bye for quite a while, so she did get out and gave him a warm long kiss and hung onto it until he breathed a couple of times, and then she slipped back into the warm car and cranked open the window to say, "I love you. Gabye."

Faint shake of the head. Not a worry in the world. She had the weirdest sense that he had capped the whole experience. It was all done, for him. He'd done something fatal with it. Permanent. He didn't need another thing from her.

She didn't like to drive and she didn't like her stupid car. *Some* day, when she was a conductor of, say, the Boston Symphony Orchestra, she would be whisked about by limousine and not have to drive and not have to teach school and deal with Francis and Peter and not have to go back to State and finish her classes and write papers and give her recital. Now, her time of giving herself up to Sabattis Falls was over. She had done what she could for all those people and maybe she had put a little bit of hope in Robert Sochia's heart and she had had her little city holiday and now she had to do everything at once and, of course, she felt a cold coming on.

Bobby was going some different route but she would go straight through Moira and so she could truly say that's where she'd been, if anybody asked. Francis and Peter ought to know better than to ask, but they would. They might even be parked by Neva's waiting for her, to get her into their car with them and maul her, tell her the latest news from JoAnn about Robert, and task her and task her. She had dug herself into a hole with them and she would just have to lie and brazen her way out of it. She took a deep breath, blew out, fluttered her fingers on the wheel, fingers that didn't want to be holding anything but a baton. She almost cried for the difficulty ahead of her, between her and her awful scary ambition. How easy and tempting it was to put off working really directly toward that dream! How little she needed all these obstacles and distractions! But she had needed this weekend and Bobby had needed it and she was glad that she had done it.

She was, that is, if everything was okay. Now that she was alone and didn't have to be just fine for Bobby she had time to think about it. She had to think about It. The *real* reason for the contretemps, the *real-real* reason. She knew she might have been pushing her luck the night before. And that morning. Earlier tonight *would* have been pushing her luck. She never, never did that, she knew her body, she was pretty regular, and she *planned*, usually, the rare occasions when she did that stuff. She thought it would be okay. But now she was a little bit scared and she needed to watch herself and feel herself, she needed to take careful note.

Her body was sacred to her and she loved it and cared for it in her way. Not by exercising well and eating well, but in her way. She didn't take The Pill. She didn't shave her legs and armpits. She didn't eat junk food except a little. She washed and washed and brushed and brushed her hair. It was one of the few things about her physical self that she liked. She could do anything with it, hang it over her ears, braid it, put it in a bun, pile it up, let it down all around her like a house. Her body was like no other body, in the way it healed when it was cut, with a raised white weal; in the way it could go forever without solid food and she could still hand out energy by her little fistfuls. She might not like her big old-ladies' boobs but she loved her super-fine ankles and wrists. But this wasn't the point. What she had to think about now was the *z-z-zing*. That was what her mother called it. Her mother had so many bullshit theories and they didn't get along but her mother was in touch with her body, if there was one good thing about her, and her mother could feel herself ovulate. She could feel her egg slowly-slowly going up the tube, up her abdomen, it was like a snake swallowing a toad, she said. She showed Julia, with the nail of her finger, slowly going up to a spot on the side of her flatter-than-Julia's belly, up to the ovary, z-z-z-zing.

A very weird thrilling scary sensation, z-z-z-zing. Julia thought she had felt it sometimes too. Just last night in fact, sitting on the john when they had just come into Ness's apartment from the long evening of music and wine at *ici on chant ici on mange* she was not even worrying about it, she was just feeling the pressure of Robert's wanting more and more and feeling lost and lonely and un-understood, and feeling that nobody, not Michael and not Robert, nobody was the perfect mate for her and maybe she shouldn't have one, in other words just feeling sorry for herself and lost the way she always did when she had been fucking too much, all at once she thought she felt something, to one side of her tummy, a slow-moving phantom wave in a hidden muscle.

So *think*. If she was ovulating tonight, right now, on her right side, which she thought she was, then she was okay for last night and this morning, whew. And she didn't screw tonight thank god, though Bobby just couldn't understand for the longest longest time and she did not give him a hint about this because if Bobby Sochia ever got the idea that he had made her pregnant oh my God—

But was she really okay from last night and this morning? What if she'd had an egg in place on the other side? Or what if one or a zillion of Robert's little swimmers got up there and lived this long? He could have falooshed it halfway up there just by how hard he came and how much of the swimmerstuff there was. She could feel it now, in her physical memory: over and over! What if the little swimmers stayed alive in the warm dark waiting, all day, while she and Bobby were bopping around Montreal? Could it live that long? One or a million of them?

Well, if something had happened, she would just have to take care of it. Go back to Montreal and undo it. Gramps would have to come through with the money. She knew how to set such things up, she had just done it for one of her cheerleaders. In Brooklyn, she'd driven Claire down there herself in her own car, instead of practicing in Moira where she told everybody she was going. She had promised herself she would never never have to do that to herself, her sacred body. Never. But if she had to, she would.

She was sniffling now. Shit. She *so* wanted to be in bed. This part of the North Country even in the dark seemed like the badlands, scrub and empty, mostly level but not farmed much. She passed one church turned into a bar, still lit, on a little mound of the ground with all the vehicles nose up toward the steps to the door. Did she remember that? She had to pay attention to remember the turns, the bridges; she had no sense of direction. She heaved a sigh and closed her eyes a moment when she found herself coming across the tracks, past the Agway, then past the campus on the northern outskirts of Moira, through the snowy well-lit empty downtown and out to the south. It was late! She was paying now for all the energy she had given to Bobby all day, to keep him in good cheer, to show him all her attention and respect, to share everything, all the city, with him. That was what love was, to her: wanting to share, feeling like a fellow-creature, really feeling that way with somebody.

From Moira through Chittenden and on south to the Falls the ground rises gradually and though you don't directly perceive the incline, especially in the dark, the engine sounds louder and you have to press the accelerator farther down and so you awaken to the effort of reaching a higher level. And it is colder, and you have to turn up the heat, or perhaps it is all the way up and you can't do anything about the increasing chill. The windshield fogs, you have to look through a smaller part of it. And if the roads are snow-packed or icy you have to be more careful not to let your wheels slip on the curves. Julia had stopped to put on her pea-coat in Chittenden and she was in this state of alert, tense single-mindedness when she reached the height of land, came over the crest of the main street into Sabattis Falls and saw the red-orange light of the house-fire reflected on the underside of low, hitherto invisible clouds straight ahead across the valley of the river.

Was it across the river? She couldn't see well enough through the pitted and frosted windshield, even by looking from under the rim of the steering wheel. She pulled off by the Catholic church and got out, to look more carefully: between the houses, through the trees. She couldn't see the fire itself. The orange-red light on the clouds moved and changed and sometimes dimmed as if in the shadow of smoke. She listened hard but heard no sound of anything she might have expected, the fire siren, trucks racing. No sound at all. The town was, as she'd wanted it to be on her return, asleep. But *shit!* That was the Pelodome burning. *Jesus, shit.* That was the Pelosphere burning.

She got into the car again and moved down Main Street, past the sheriff's dark house. She opened her side window so she could look left up the side street toward Neva's house. No car in front of Neva's, where she wanted to go, please, but couldn't. No cars on the streets at all. She passed Peter Hubbard's house on the right, then the school and the gas station and the restaurant, all dark. She closed her window and went cautiously down through town, past Arquit's, the Seniors', the Bank, the drugstore, then The Rapids on one side and the town buildings on the other, all dark. Behind the medical offices and the town offices, the fire station faced the river and she couldn't see whether the doors were open, but in the light of an ever-burning blue light there she saw no firemen's vehicles. The firemen were home in their beds sleeping as if nothing was happening.

But that was the dome burning. *Jesus. Shit. Where's Bobby?* She continued across the bridge and up French Hill. The lit sky went out of sight until she reached the higher ground on the south and then it seemed much closer

She turned onto the Gokey Road. She was only creeping now. She still didn't see the flames, only the fluctuating reflection of them on the low clouds and occasionally a billow of smoke, or steam, shading them. The clouds were right down over her head, lumpy, pink, mobile, very low. *I do not believe this. Things people talk of doing, threaten to do, practice doing, they also actually do. They did it. I do not believe this.*

She gripped the wheel tighter, licked her lips and rolled them together. *I shouldn't go here, I shouldn't be doing this.* But where was Bobby? Did he get here first? Did they do anything to him? The headlights found only empty black distance between the converging snowbanks, as far ahead as she could see. She needed to get to the space where the snowbank in front of the dome was cut away, where he parked. There, the fire would be right beside her, it might burn the side of her car. If his car was there it would be ruined. Where was he?

But it wasn't there. The firelight flooded across the road in front of her, through the gap in the snowbank. It lit the opposite bank and etched the small scraggly limbs of trees in the pasture beyond. She drove abreast of the opening ready to shield her eyes, to perceive the heat and noise even through the door and window of the car, ready to accelerate and get away from it. But already the dome was down in a flaming heap smaller than she'd have said the building had been, with black lacunae where something, the stove maybe, wouldn't burn. The car was filled with the not-bad smell of a bonfire or a camp-fire, and the crackling of a million little firecrackers. Momentarily she seemed to see a person half-rising in flames, with black beams and smoking roofing holding him down. But it was the old wringer-washer that stood on the cement pad by the door, next to the firewood. Something, some water source, kept sending up billows of white steam into the smoke. To the right, the windows of the chicken-house shone orange, and beyond the chicken-house the barn stood dimly red. She wondered how long it would have taken the fire to burn down this far. Not very long, she guessed. *He couldn't have been here yet? Could he?* He went a different way but he drove so much faster than she.

She took her car a little further, out of the hot one-sided light. She stuffed her hair inside the collar of her peacoat and pulled on her wool cap and folded up the collar and put on her wool gloves. She was wearing the only boots she had, not high enough but no matter. She got out and put her hands in her pockets and looked up and down the road. Nothing to the right, toward the woods where the plowing ended. The other way there was a light that could be a car on the highway. It moved very slowly, disappeared, reappeared, staying distant: a car on the main road. She looked at the clouds overhead, so low, the pinkness reflected some of the firelight back down so that she could see a little into the shadows behind banks and waves of snow.

Was his car not being here proof that he wasn't here? She hoped it was. But—"Bobby?" Her voice was a croak.

"Bobby!" She tried again but her voice was still feeble. She pulled off her right glove and put two fingers in the corners of her mouth and whistled, loud. But the sound was sucked away into a deadness that left her aware only of the crackling, which lessened every moment. Chilled, she walked tensely back to the opening and the one-sided warmth. She stood looking at all she could see from the mouth of the space. The steam came from somewhere black, in front, pulsing and hissing. It made her wonder if something was about to explode.

She walked past it and set out to walk all around the building if she could and look for anything, tracks. Just to be sure. There might be tracks. Robert could have gone, for instance, to the barn, taken whatever he needed out there; or to the chicken-house, which had a stove-pipe, a little one, so maybe a heater. But. *Florida would be better. This place isn't worth it. Florida would be brilliant right now, Bobby.* She hopped from leg to leg in the snow, balancing on each foot for a moment. A lot of heat came from that pile, dark as it was getting. There was a dark hole in the middle, the cellar. She could not see well enough. She found the path to the barn but she couldn't tell whether there were any new footprints in it. Her bare legs were wet to the knee. She had snow in her boots, melting fast and freezing her ankles.

Turning around back she caught a flash of light from the road again. Oh shit. She'd been wrong, the car was coming along the Gokey Road. And here she was, not in her car, and her car blocking the road. Maybe it was Bobby, just getting home and going so slowly because— Yes. That was probably Bobby, yes! She hopped on around the fire and reached the front just as the car came up beside the space in the snowbank and stopped. But it wasn't

Bobby's car and the face of the driver was low in the side window, looking at the remains of the dome, and then, since she stood there stupidly, at her. She didn't know the face, the long hair, the mustache, but she'd seen it. He must be very short, his chin was hardly higher than the bare elbow stuck out at her on the windowsill.

She had an image of two short, very short men, obviously brothers, built just alike, moving alike, with long hair but no beards, wearing caps something like engineer's caps that farmers sometimes wore. She'd seen them at The Rapids, somebody had told her something about them. Hippy farmers, very good with cows, their cows had the highest herd-average in several counties. Eighteen thousand pounds, whatever that meant. Who told her that! Leo Weller, full of funny information. The head turned away from her and there was the other beyond it, dimly lit by the instruments in the car. Looking at her. And somebody bigger leaning over to look at her from the back seat? Also long-haired, oh a woman. People who had heard about the fire, at The Rapids probably, and who had come out to see it. There was probably a parade of them earlier.

All this had to have happened because they knew that she had been with Bobby in Canada this weekend.

She had to get out of here. She would have to get these people to back up and let her back up until she could turn into this parking place and then they could go past and she could back out and leave. She went to the window of the car to explain what they had to do, for some reason thinking it would be hard to make them understand. She smelled beer. And grass. Leo had told her, they got stoned and went out to milk with Grace Slick and the Jefferson Airplane on the radio and the cows gave and gave, eighteen thousand pounds a year! The elbow stayed put, pale and gnarly, the military shirt rolled up on the little bump of a bicep.

The driver had a beer bottle in the hand, and tapped it on the wheel while she spoke. He said, "No', no', guess we'd rather no'." A glottal stop at every opportunity, followed by a little pushed-out *nnh*.

"Please. Or you turn around first and go, and then I will."

"No'. No'. You just go on there t' the end of the road, there's room to turn araound. I ain't pu'in' my tire-tracks in here. Go on ahead there, t' th' end of plowin'. We'll folly ye."

She hadn't liked the North Country accent at first. She had gotten used to it. But this was stronger, stranger, it made her cringe. The driver had a face she could have admired for bones, for lines, though it was both feral and blank and the dark brows were tied together over the good nose and the eyes seemed unlinked, which frightened her. Julia stooped to appeal to the woman, whose arms she could see, plump in a thin white sweater. But oh, she recognized her too. In Eugene's one time when she was coming with Michael and Bernie and their wives to check out this town, they wanted to play shuffleboard, and started to since the table wasn't in use, and this same woman had put herself in their way, in that same white sweater, with her black bra under it cutting into the flesh behind her arms. She'd said without the littlest bit of friendliness to strangers that she and her partner "had the board." She wouldn't let them play. If Julia's group wanted to play at all, she said, they had to put up their money and challenge her and Lefty. Michael, so Jewish, said, "But nobody is playing." And so on and so on until her team-mate, the one-armed guy, Lefty, told her to let it go. Julia had felt sorry for her, an unhappy, unlucky person, poor, neither smart nor attractive, middle-aged, apparently unattached. She didn't think the woman would be on her side now. This was one of the repeat tragedies of her life: other women didn't know that she was on *their* side and so they weren't on hers. They were dupes of the system she was struggling to reform, wherever she was, as much as she could.

Then the one on the right reached across in front of his brother to hold his cupped hand toward her. A big, fat joint, held between a stained, black-capped thumb and finger.

This was really scary. Normally she should have been friendly and taken a toke but this was too scary, somebody had just burned down somebody's house and she was alone and she had to get away from these people. She ran ahead to her car and got in and started it and drove ahead toward where her high beams showed a line of gray trees and treetops that seemed solid right across the road and the road disappeared, dropping downward out of sight. Somewhere, the plow turned around, so certainly she could. They would have to come after her to turn around too, so she could drive out then; they said they would. Or else get off to the side more so she could get by? Maybe she could go fast and take a little chance and drive by them cutting into the snowbank and hoping she didn't scrape them, or get stuck. But no. No no no.

She kept on going, into the woods, the road still narrower here because it was cut down into the ground and there was no place for the snow to go, so it spilled back in behind the plow from both sides. She knew there were no more houses until the road turned downward beside that one forlorn camp with the tire-swing still hanging from a maple limb, where somebody must have raised a kid, once. She put her lights down to follow the down-curving road to see ahead better and then she was being pulled by gravity. She wanted to stop, knew that she shouldn't be doing this, the road dropped away, her lights just shining ahead into the dark treetops overarching from both sides for a moment. When they came down, shit! there was another car, facing her, its headlights off but gleaming opaquely like the eyes of a dead animal.

Merde! But naturally. Everybody knew about this fire, don't kid me, lots of bodies knew about it, in this town that pretended to be sleeping when she came through. So sure, here's somebody else with their booze and their lay for the night; they drove out to see the sparks, say fuck you to Robert Sochia, then park and screw. She put on the brakes, carefully.

She felt her car slide a little before it stopped but it did stop. She hadn't been going very fast. She put it in reverse and tried to back up, fearful of that little slide, and sure enough, her wheels spun. She was pointing downhill and she had no traction, zero traction, man. The other car was in the way of her turning. She dared not go ahead, she'd already gone too far.

And then in her rear view mirror a flash of light, the other car. As she watched in her mirror, the headlights turned orange and went out. They were coming into the turnaround behind her with their lights off. They passed her very close on her right and turned in beside the other dark unlighted car.

She didn't recognize the other car and she did not want to have to do with these people, but they would have to help her, that was all. She sniffed. She needed only a little push to go backwards and turn and then she could drive ahead turning the rest of the way. She would get up that little incline all right with the least bit of a start and there were these people who could push. She reached across the front seat and rolled down the window.

The first one to get out of the brothers' car was the blonde woman. When she described this to Leo Weller, months later, Julia said it made her lose all hope immediately: the woman floundering uphill into her headlights, flapping her thin, tan overcoat, yelling, "What do you think of these little shits? They said they was taking me home. I didn't know I lived on this misable road!"

Then the two brothers, short-short triangular men, skinny-legged but broad-shouldered, walking as if they were on a ship that was rolling from side to side. Their pants were tucked inside high black rubber boots. They walked slowly, both the same way, cowboy-like, dipping one shoulder and then the other, their arms bent and held away from their bodies at the elbows. She wouldn't ever forget them.

They were good farmers, nice to their cows, right? They were going to push on her fenders. But no, not for a minute, they didn't even look at the wheels. Her right-side window was still open and she didn't lock the doors against them because she didn't want to seem too scared and give them any idea and then it was too late because there were four doors and she couldn't reach all of them that fast. On her side she saw a thin chiseled French-Irish face with eyebrows tangled together over the sharp fine nose. "Evenin'," that one said, cowboymoviestyle, he was a kid like her but he pushed her across the seat and the other one was already there and she was between them with no room, and the woman already in back, thrashing around wheezing as if she were trying to pound the car into a different-shaped nest.

Julia started to talk, she was talking a mile a minute trying to cajole and kid them because what good would it do to say hey get out of my car? But suddenly the woman grabbed her around the head in her harsh smelly sleeve and snarled at her. "Jesus Christ I could break your neck!" Then just as suddenly she let go. Julia felt the car rock as the woman threw herself against the back of the back seat. These men were in a hurry, there was no time, she got a whack of somebody's elbow on her jaw and a yank on her hair and a hand over her mouth, and the woman pulled on the seatback over and over and her head was right behind Julia's. She was saying, "You fools! It took two of you sorry little shits to get up the nerve to feel me up, didn't it? Now look what you're gonna do." There was no time and no room and all these pains, she couldn't get her arms free, they were hurting her, everywhere, and hurting her clothes which hurt her as they pulled on them and she heard the woman commenting close to her neck and all their tobaccoey breaths and hard breathing, the woman's voice gravelly, so mean: "Oh I remember you. Don't I. From the first time you was ever seen in this town. No bra then. (The snap is in back, you fools!) You was asking for it. She was asking for it, wasn't she, boys? Honey if I was you I'd wear a real brassiere, all the time, with those tits. They're almost the same size as mine! But not so nice-shaped." ("That hurt my feelings, Leo. That was mean.") She was being *skinned,* that's how it felt. "You think you can do anything you like. We know where you've been. This won't be nothing new. My land, no more hair on your pussy than a baby's got on its head." ("Wasn't that mean?") "Does he like that? Most men wouldn't like that, honey. Men like a nice big bush like what I have." ("Wasn't that mean, Leo?") She was wondering, Didn't they see the other car? Would *those* people get out and come and rape her too? She had been crying "Wait wait wait wait wait" all the while trying to fight but she couldn't use her legs, she couldn't use her arms. She couldn't use her face, her smiles, her voice, her conducting fingers and arms, any of her things, man, her various *means.* There was no wait-wait-waiting, they were not listening, none of her powers was any good. She couldn't do *anything* about this, she'd never not been able to *do* anything about anything before! The woman had her around the neck, her rings and bracelets against her throat, the soft fleshy arm clamped her chin and she could only see the tree limbs, lit by her headlights still on, ahead over the other car.

She never stopped fighting, she told Leo. She never gave up. She didn't know if he did it or didn't do it, exactly. It was only the first one, anyway. The second one never even— The woman in back was bawling, "On Christ I hate this place. Jesus if the sun would shine, but it won't." Julia had a hold of something and was squeezing as hard as she dared but she was afraid she would only make him madder, but anyway he started to tremble and he said, "Okay, okay" and opened the driver's door and the light went on and she let go and he got out and she instantly squirmed completely around and hugged herself, kneeling, her head right under the dome light, looking down at herself in the dark.

She didn't know what had happened, exactly. She felt wet stuff on her when she pulled her panties back up. She pushed at the other one to get out too but he just hunched there saying "no', no'," with his revolting glottal stop. She tried to put her bra back on but one arm hurt when she reached up to hook it, she couldn't. Before she got herself organized the first one got back in and closed the door, it was cold outside, but not all the way, the light stayed on. The woman pulled herself up by the seat-back and said, close to her, "Are you all right, dear? Look at this hair. She didn't fight, did she? She didn't fight at all, remember that. Lindsey, you fool, wait till Robert Sochia finds out what you done. Wait till I tell Robert Sochia." Somebody rolled down a window and spat.

Then the two triangular men sat there beside her saying things that were not real, while she was sniffling and trying to get her bra back around her. Her arm hurt but she just did it, hooked her bra with it hurting and got her arm through the sleeve of her dress hurting. If she had to she could do things against hurt: let them hurt and still do them. They went on saying unreal things while she put her peacoat on. She thought she could come into this town and make fools of everybody. Well now maybe she knew that that didn't go with them. Maybe they had made their point, eh?

She needn't to think she would get any sympathy for it, neither. Or that anybody would blame them for what they done. If it hadn't of been them it would of been somebody else. They knew she wouldn't tell the law. She could tell anybody else she wanted to. Tell Robert Slushy. Give him their greetings.

Then they all got out of her car as if *they* were disgusted by *her*. They got into theirs and without even turning on their lights zoomed out past and up the little slope and away. And she knelt there amazed, leaning on her forearms with her bottom against the dash and her head against the seatback. They hadn't managed to do it, but they were going to *claim* it! She wanted to just lean there a long while. She thought it would be all right just to be still and feel sorry for herself for a while. But she had to get home before it got any later because Neva might even be waiting up. She'd at least be listening for her in her sleep. And she had to keep Neva from seeing anything wrong! Neva would have waited up and waited and waited but by now maybe she had gone to bed and she could go up to her room without being seen. She wouldn't be able to wash though because the bathroom was everybody's, on the second floor, she couldn't go in there and draw a bath or take a shower, the plumbing was so noisy she'd wake everybody up! So did she have to stay unclean all night? Not fair! That was so unfair but she could do it. Nothing had touched her. They violated her just as badly as if they had gotten inside her but even then they would not have touched her real self. No way could those people really touch her. She hated what she had had to do just as badly as to have been passive but she had won. But she would have won the other way too. Sniff. Sniff.

Sniffling, she turned herself around on the seat and got her feet down on the wrong side of the transmission hump. She didn't even want to open them enough to slide her left leg under the steering wheel first; she slid them under it together, awkwardly, her heels getting caught on the hump and her knees under the wheel, but she did it. She wanted her thighs tight together, forever. The engine had been running this whole time. She got her hands on the wheel and shook off a shudder that came up her back. She put the car in reverse.

All these North Country types kept telling her to take it easy, not to spin. She tried to take it easy but she spun anyway. She shifted into first and went a little further ahead, downhill, to get her tires in a new place. She tried backing again, taking it easy again, and she did back up a little way and was getting it and starting to turn but her back wheels spun again, the car stopped and actually slid ahead downhill even after she stepped on the brakes. It slid with all four wheels locked. *Shit!* But she was very calm. Sniffle. She would have to go to the other car and wake them up or break them up. The guy in there would have to pull his pants up and give her a push, that's all.

Which the person did very cordially in his happy state. With a little push and care not to spin she backed and he kept pushing while she turned, and backed away from him into the driveway of the place with the tire swing, and then she went ahead and climbed right out of the woods just like that. When she went by the dome she didn't even look. She was done. She had already made up her mind to leave. Just go. Go back to Moira, but that wouldn't be far enough. Go home to New York, to her mother or her Gramps. Go somewhere.

16

Come Again?

At nine in the morning, Leo was still performing his ablutions. He bathed, singing; he shaved, applied his cologne and combed his hair, testing debonair and heroic facial expressions in the mirror. His lips were red and swollen from an impromptu practice session on the Olds trombone, undertaken in pajamas, soon after he had heard his father stirring. Then, with a wool cardigan over a V-necked teeshirt exposing a bestial swirl of chest hair, the suspenders to his Malone pants hanging around his legs, he went down the former servants' stairway to the kitchen. There while the oatmeal cooked he made up, with great attention to his method, a bowl of tuna-fish salad, by way of a hearty lunch for a working man. He skimmed *Downbeat* with his breakfast, and then—neither he nor his father having said a word—suspenders up, coat and galoshes on, ear-flaps down, scarf flung thrice about the neck, went shoveling.

The town was still. No one hailed him as he crossed Main Street and went up as far as the drugstore. There, he turned right. He was singing, "I got a woman/Way 'cross town/She's good to me!"

He went two blocks, turned left, passed two houses and came to the Beckmans' walk, which was to be shoveled every snowfall, if there was only an inch. Was there an inch? Oh, there was always an inch, this winter. Mrs B. was a retired teacher, Mr B. a retired lawyer. Europeans with great stories of loss and survival, escape and love. Leo would be invited in for a kuchel and a buzzing black small cup of coffee in their kitchen when they no longer heard the coughing of his blade.

Leo loved their story. Mr Beckman had been separated from his first wife in the death camps. He had been told that she had died. After the war he found his way to Montreal. There he met and fell in love with another refugee and married her. They moved to this obscure American town on the edge of the woods, ignored its shallow habitual antisemitism, served everybody fairly and in time became revered members of the community. But! (What makes a story? Ands, Buts, and Therefores.) But! Mr B's first wife had not died after all. After years of searching for him, through some miracle of the grapevine she found people who knew that he had gone to Montreal. She came to Montreal. In Montreal she learned that he had married again, and where the couple had moved. She found him here. She told him her story. He told her his. He told her that he had thought her dead, had fallen in love, and was now happy. And she went away.

It made Leo sigh. You never know the tales behind quiet people and scenes. *Ya nevva know.* He made his first pass north to south, flinging the snow toward the street; turned and made his second pass south to north. Swing, step, lift and throw. Paused at the flagstone walk to the Beckmans' door. From here the top of the white compact car at Days', half a block away, was visible over the walls of its fox-hole. Good, he thought, she's back from her weekend, she's in school. He'd go find her this afternoon. They'd go to the drugstore and he'd buy a sundae and she'd mooch from it, they'd gab. He'd be nosy. Where'd you go, what'd you do? She'd scold him for it, tease him. Lie, no doubt, making it obvious. Mystery!

He got into his rhythm again. Swaying from right foot to left with the sweep of the shovel, loading it. Left to right with it lifted, right to left again tossing the diamond dust into the empyrean. Looking up at each toss, to watch the sparkling drift, then swaying back down to recharge the pendulum. Did he hear Neva's door, see the flash of its glass? He looked over the snowbanks toward Days' again. Somebody came out of the house, in a hurry. Neva, impatiently stamping down the steps, while her car, hers and Farnan's, was backing from the garage in a steam-cloud. It stopped, she got in, the door shut with a thump, and the car backed into the street. It turned, turned the corner toward him, and came along, very swiftly for Farnan. Leo raised his shovel high in greeting.

The car stopped. Neva from her side-window ordered him to get in. With his shovel, he slid in the back. "Where's your father?" she demanded. He told her he was at the office. What was the matter? "You wait. I'll tell the two of you at once." But Neva couldn't wait a second more herself. "She's gone!" she said as the car moved along.

"Gone?"

"Abducted!"

"What?"

"Stolen!"

"By whom?"

"By Robert Sochia, that's who! Who else would do such a thing!"

"When? Where?"

"Just now! From her very room! She only got back in the middle of the night and I don't think she slept a bit! He folded her up like a valise! Punched her in the chest, if you please! And carried her off in his awful old car. We just had time to get her some warm clothes and boots, didn't we Farnan, he'd have taken her naked, the savage! And he had the nerve to say to me, 'Wait ten minutes, Neva Day, and think, before you get on the telephone.' Hmph! As if I would tell anybody, but your father, *this!*"

She wouldn't go to the office of the Feed & Coal to tell him, either. Wouldn't go near the place where Loyal Weller kept his hidden bottle, where anybody might come in and interrupt them in this private conversation, take note of such an unusual visit, go away and tell the world. No, she had Farnan drive to the Weller house, ushered herself right into Mr Weller's little study with the fieldstone fireplace, which was cold. She sent Leo to call his father at the office, telling him nothing (did he hear? not one thing!) but that Loyal Weller must come back across the river at once, as fast as he could walk. Farnan lit the fire, always laid up, shavings of cherry and dry slabwood that would go at the touch of a match. Neva sat primly down on a needlepoint chair-seat with her coat and hat on, to wait, and would tell Leo no more until his father, summoned by telephone, arrived.

"All a damn waste of time," Mr Weller said, when he'd heard the bare fact, "if we're going to get the police after them."

"Well, we're not!" Neva said. And this shut him up, coming from her, who would, now that Leo thought about it, normally have been on the phone to O'Neil herself, before Robert and his victim were out of the yard. "And don't you swear at me!" she added.

She had another surprise. Even before Robert burst into her house and up the stairs to that garret room, the girl had been packing! Getting ready to leave! Taking down her posters, everything! When she didn't come down for breakfast Neva went up, and she found her standing half dressed in the middle of the room with boxes, clothing, books, blankets all around her, in jersey and jeans, hair down in front of her face, fists shaking in the air. And all she would say was, "I have to go away," in a voice of the dead. Would not tell Neva why. *Would not.* Where she was going? What had happened? She would not tell! Just in the voice of the dead told Neva it was all right. Nothing was wrong. Nothing had happened. "I've finished what I was doing here, that's all," she said. And she warned, "Neva, don't come in."

Neva did go in, sat on the bed. The girl said in the lifeless voice, "I don't want to be seen. I need to pack. I love you. Go away." But Neva would not go away of course, so she said, "Then help. Don't ask questions. I've got to do something with all this, this *shit!*"

She was jamming things into her little beat-up suitcase, a pitiful thing. Books into boxes, other stuff into paper bags. Neva was beside herself and still puffing from her climb and something made her want to look at the girl more closely, did she see splotches on her arms and neck? but she couldn't help trying to save things from ruin, roll up the posters together and tape them, see that the clothes were at least folded. Then without dressing for outdoors Julia suddenly took an armload down the stairs. Neva started after her, telling her it was zero outside! From the first landing she heard her hoarsely murmuring to Farnan from the front hall. Farnan would do anything for her, of course, without asking why. The door opened, didn't close. Farnan's chair creaked in the parlor. Neva had just reached the bottom flight when Julia came back in, avoiding her eyes, holding her arms across her breast for warmth, and brushed by her going up again. Farnan was putting on his scarf and overcoat. He took the shovel from the vestibule and went out. And Neva started up again, hand spread open on her chest.

When she reached the garret room she was short of breath but had regained her sense of duty. She called the girl's attention to her benefactors, to her grandfather and Mrs Bryant, who were paying her tuition, her rent. She needed to finish her practice teaching, in order to finish school and get her diploma. Heavens, she mustn't waste all this that people had done for her and that she had accomplished. What about herself, her ambitions, the plans and hopes that she had confided to Neva? The girl just said, dully, "I know all that. I've thought about all of that. Don't make a federal case of it. I'll be back. I'll graduate, don't worry. When I have the energy I'll explain."

Neva wanted to get boxes from her storage room and fill them properly but as she began to say so, Julia opened her eyes wide, ran to her window. She looked out and instantly turned around, open-mouthed. Then she sagged against the dormer-side in sudden despair and frustration. Neva dropped her boxes and went to the window beside her. That ugly green car was actually at that moment sliding into the back bumper of Julia's car, banging it ahead as it stopped, and of all the horrible, obscene creatures to see at this moment, Robert Sochia jumped out of it and vanished under the porch roof. Coming into her house!

Neva bustled out of the room to barricade the stairway against the brute. But incredibly he was already swinging around the last newel-post and leaping up toward her three steps at a time. She found herself flat against the wall with her tummy sucked in rather than be so much as touched as he passed. So she turned to the room again, just in time to see the girl blow out every last ounce of her breath and fold up over his hand. He lifted her under one arm. Neva did barricade him now, blocked the narrow door with her poor self. But he turned his shoulder to her and drove her back onto the landing, pulled the girl through and rumbled down the stairs like thunder. Neva had no choice but to follow as fast as she dared, calling to Farnan to stop him. She had to pause for breath at the bottom and then, her heart forgotten, flew to the door.

Robert Sochia was coming back from his car asking almost politely for the girl's coat and scarf and boots and mittens, which Neva was already automatically turning to gather up. She pushed them at him. Peacoat! Toque! What about her legs? Blankets! She commanded him to hold his horses long enough for her to throw in everything she could think of from the vestibule. Sweater! Umbrella! She was swept away by fear of the cold, trying to take care of that before even thinking of stopping the crime! She had another armload of she knew not what, carried it out, got right into his filthy car, because he had thrown her into the back seat; dropped her armload and took the poor thing in her arms. Julia couldn't speak! She couldn't breathe! There were two sharp lines in her forehead, between the lovely tapered brows. The car rocked, Robert jumping in the front seat. His door slammed, the car started backing into the street. Neva yelled at him. He stopped and let her get out. They had some words at his window, she told Loyal Weller he could believe that. The beast drove away, not toward Main Street. Not toward anyplace civilized. Away out of town to the east, toward no town. Nowhere.

She sniffled into her hanky. Put it away. Suddenly herself, she said, "I wish't I'd been a man."

Leo smiled at her approvingly.

"I don't know what anybody'd have done," her husband stolidly said.

Loyal Weller might have wondered at Neva's momentary quiet then. But forgetting that Neva had already stopped him once, he did what Sarah would do, and would expect him to do. He got to his feet, saying, "You did well to tell me first, Neva. But I'll call Terence O'Neil this minute."

Almost simultaneously she burst out, *"You'll do no such thing!"*

Mr Weller stared at her, pipe out of his mouth. She'd sounded for all the world like Sarah herself, though the words were surely not what Sarah's would have been. Neva knew this as well as he. She needed a second to force herself to go on. She pursed her lips. "Unless you want it all over the television and the papers."

Then to his further amazement, still more flustered at her newest words, she blurted out, "Unless you want the helicopters and the bloodhounds, too!"

"What, Neva? What's this?"

She was puffed up now. "You heard me. You know how it is when the law gets up a manhunt!"

Mr Weller looked at her, his expression like an eagle's, which might be either stupefied or shrewd. For a moment he did not understand her at all. What you got if you called in Terence O'Neil was, first, usually, muddle and ineffectuality while O'Neil kept the problem from his superiors and tried to smooth things over on his own, without harm to all concerned. That was the town's particular cross-to-bear of a law officer. Then, true, if it went to the state troopers out of Moira, you'd get . . . you'd get what Neva said: television, the papers; and then the Air Force from Plattsburgh, the DEC with its dogs.

But that assumed he was taking her somewhere near. Mr Weller had automatically thought of Florida. "Where d'you think he's gone with her then?"

Neva's mouth was clamped shut.

Leo, in the pause, said, conversationally, "I've got an idea. Remember the guy that jumped out of the hospital window in a bathrobe and socks?"

"What?" his father said.

"Remember that story in the news, a couple of years ago? That patient at the research wing at Ogdensburg, who jumped out a third story window, in his hospital robe and socks, and ran off into the brush? Into the badlands, they called it. It was all the news for days. Television, papers, radio. You remember. The Border Patrol, the State Police, the DEC, everybody was in on it. Volunteers from all over. The swamps were already frozen, it was in November. Don't you remember?"

"Of course I do," Neva said. Her husband nodded.

"No amount of troopers and deputies and volunteers could find that fellow," Leo said.

"That's right."

"He wasn't a native, or anything. Just a screwloose from the hospital, in pajamas, in the frozen badlands. But they couldn't find him. Not until they brought in the helicopters and dogs. Then they found him quick enough. His toes were frostbit. Otherwise he felt great!"

"What're you getting at, you!"

Leo put on his worst North Country accent. "Ain't no Florida abeout it! He ain't going anywheres. He's hit for the hills and timber with her."

"Why d'you say that?"

"Hunch!"

Neva was all out of patience but Leo's father was careful. He said, "You mean you think he's taken her into the woods?"

"Yes, sir."

"In all this snow? At these temperatures?"

Leo turned to Neva. "You got all that stuff from Robert, didn't you, Neva? You didn't make that up. About the helicopters and the bloodhounds." She was tight-lipped, undenying.

"Good Lord," his father was saying, "what for?"

"I'd have to work on that. Maybe he couldn't help it. Maybe it just come to him what he was put on earth for. Maybe he just couldn't stand the dailiness of days anymore. Maybe because that's the only way he can hope to be up to it. Only way he can equal her. Because no woman amounts to just quite so much against a man if he's in the country he knows and she isn't. Ain't that what Old Herman said? Maybe he's finally found the one way he could get them to make him pay up for what he did to Ray."

Mr Weller stared carefully at his son. Not with scorn for these ideas. If Leo had his problems, he had insight into things like this, earned by a lifetime study of this town, and paid for with his own self-knowledge and suffering. But if there were any such motives in Robert Sochia's act, especially such as that last one, the more reason to bring in the law without delay. If the law were the ideal of the law. But Terence O'Neil would surely blunder and confuse the issue, perhaps creating deadly havoc too, instead of doing his job regardless, like an ordinary policeman. Which could be worse yet.

"Besides which," Leo said now, "Robert isn't the only one who told Neva to think twice before she called the cops."

"Oh?"

"Is he, Neva?"

Mr Weller turned to Neva again. Her face, cross, clamped. But she shook her head. "She couldn't breathe! Couldn't speak!"

"But she could hear," Leo insisted. "She could shake her head. She could wave her hand. You got into the car with her. You told her, didn't you? 'Don't you worry, Julia, I'll have the law after him so fast it'll make his head swim!' Didn't you? You aren't Neva Day if you didn't. And what did she say? She made the shapes for 'No no no. Don't! I can handle this!' She commanded you *not* to call the police, Neva Day. Didn't she? It was Robert who mentioned the bloodhounds and whirlybirds but it was Julia herself who turned you upside down. You're taking your orders from her!"

"Is he right, Neva?" Mr Weller asked.

She sniffled, got out her hanky again. "There, there, Neva," Mr Weller said.

"If the law was any good," Neva said, "that filth wouldn't be on the loose!"

"Yes, Neva. Well. But good heavens—"

Neva burst out: "She said she would call! First chance she gets."

"Dear, dear." Mr Weller covered his eyes with his hands.

"She may not be near a phone," Leo said, with a certain excitement. "But she can handle him. You'll see, Father. She'll fix him. Don't worry about a thing!"

"Then Neva," Mr Weller said, "you misspoke. She wasn't abducted at all. She went with him willingly."

"I said no such thing. But we are not to tell O'Neil. That's what I said."

"What I mean is, they may not be going anywhere. A personal matter between the two of them, and nobody else's business—? Still, he hit her, you said."

"Solar plexus! He hit her in the solar plexus! I saw it with my own eyes!"

Mr Weller shook his head, as if to escape the image. "Farnan, what d'*you* think?"

Farnan turned his hands up in his lap and looked to his wife. Whose face was firmly set.

"*Come again?* What did you say that sonofabitch thought up to do now? Come again?" Thus Billy Atkin. Robert had sent in a note.

Amos Cheney had found it attached to his snowmobile, up on Massawepie Pond Club. Or rather, his wife's. Millard had hired somebody to milk his cows and he and Amos and their wives had gone up to hunting camp, in two pickups, with bags of hay pellets and corn piled in all around the snowmobiles, to cook a steak and feed the deer. They took along half a quart of Hiram Walker and spent the night in what they call Dan's Camp, on the railroad bed where it skirts the pond. Amos had awoken in the early morning to the sound of his brand new Pantera howling away down the railroad bed. Got his pants on and outdoors just in time to see the last twinkles of its taillight as it went into the trees. Whoever it was took a five gallon can of gas too.

He'd found the note stuck over the brake lever on the handlebar of the older snowmobile, his wife's. So they had loaded up their pickups and come back to town early, minus that one sled. Amos put the torn, penciled note down on the bar and turned it around with two fingers for Eugene to read.

> *Looking for somebody, Amos?*
> *If she'd been a bear she'd have bit you.*

Rumor had it the girl was gone. Rumor had it Robert Sochia had taken her away by force. Rumor supposed he took her somewhere warm. So this was a surprise.

"Come again?" says Billy. "He's stolen her off and tooken her to *the woods?* In the middle of *winter?*"

And Leo, on the way home along the river, thrilled to his toes, already composing:

So it had finally gotten around to it and happened; what when he came out of jail that day in early January he didn't even have to think to realize he was surely going to stick around until it did. Until it came to him what exactly it was going to be. Maybe he still hadn't had to think, to realize it. Maybe it just happened, and he, like the town itself, was saying, like Billy Atkin, "Come again?"

Because stated in so many words it was something that even the town had to hear twice before it realized what it was, too. Let alone realize that it was going to be able to look back at it and tell it like a story, eventually; some day a long way ahead. What meanwhile it had its work cut out for it just to understand, let alone believe. Let alone do anything about. Because it had to do something now. There was no getting out of it now.

He hummed. He threw a hunk of ice into the river. He could simply wait on events for events, which would surely come, thus provoked, without his in the least needing to think them up. This book was going to be great.

17

Go Fish

JoAnn, presented with that note by Lenny LaBounty, who walked it down the street from Eugene's, picked it up by the least little bit of one corner, with the tip of her thumb and long-nailed forefinger. She held it at arm's length, her head over on one side to read it while she turned with it, moving her smiling, moistened lips. With her other hand, and without looking, she pulled a tack out of a cardboard she kept handy by the cash register. Then, where to tack it? Both the walnut columns that framed her bar mirror were still covered with the generous scraps of buffalo-plaid wool she had tacked up there during the hunting season, cut with her big scissors from the shirt-tails of hunters who had missed their bucks. She pinned Robert's note to the middle of the left row of shirt-tail scraps, at eye-level. She stood back and judged. Smudged white note against checkered black-and-green, black-and-red. "Will that catch everybody's attention?" she asked aloud. "I think it will."

The rest of that afternoon and evening, when any man came into her bar, she would drill him with her eyes until he took good note of her, which any man would; and then she would flick her eyes in the general direction of that note up behind her shoulder, until he saw it, grubby piece of paper with a tear in the middle and some smeared writing done with a dull pencil, tacked over her collection of shirt-tails, possibly including a snip of his. The man would maybe stand up on the rungs of his stool and lean over the counter and squint at it, read it aloud with difficulty, the others at the bar grinning at each other. He'd sit back down, finally beginning to get the point. "This from Sochie?" Nobody along the bar would seem to have heard the question, but the fellow next to him would growl out the side of his mouth, "Fire station. Nine o'clock." A smiling JoAnn would be wiping up around his already-sweating beer. And if he was dense enough to be about to say, "What? We goin' after him?" the fellow next to him would jab him with an elbow and add, "There's big ears in here and everywhere."

Leo Weller, of course; mouse-in-the-corner.

The fire station because a bunch of cars over there most any time of day would not attract attention, from, say, Terence O'Neil. Car-poolers left their pickups there for all three shifts at Massena, and firemen met there, as did the Trail-Blazers (snowmobile club), not to mention the Red Cross blood collectors and civic groups of all kinds, though these not in the middle of the night.

So that the heretofore unscheduled 11:00 P.M. meeting of the S.F.V.F.D. was thronged with the young and early middle-aged men of the town, virtually the same group as the Trailblazers, all abnormally infused with civic virtue. The old-timers who'd found Sochia's note had driven the Brighton Road far enough to see where he had cut onto it from the railroad bed. The track was then lost in the tracks of the loggers coming in to their landings that morning, but the old-timers had followed anyway, studying the snowbanks until they found where the same machine (possibly; presumably) cut over the snowbank onto Rockefeller land. There was no discussion what to do. They had lots of people, lots of trucks and sleds. Obviously, divide up the territory. Get out on every road and trail, follow every track, figure out what section of the country RS was in by then, since he probably wasn't still on Rockefeller, if he ever was. "Surround the sonofabitch!" Billy cried. "Then close in. We'll have his ass in no time."

Harry LaFleur was the foreman by common assumption, a big, big-handed, deep-voiced man and a man of few words, pock-marked and serious. He was closest to JoAnn Hubbard, and it was JoAnn, after all, who had held her little brother in her arms while he coughed up the last of his blood, which was what it all came back to, music teacher or no music teacher. So Harry divvied them

up by the clubs they belonged to or the areas they'd logged or
hunted, east and southeast to the Franklin County line, south to
Lake Clear and Long Pond, southwest and west to Hopkinton and
Parishville. And the next day no plowed road in all that area went
un-studied by half-a-dozen Falls men's trucks, no woods-road un-
run by half-a-dozen snowmobiles; while Harry with Peter and
Francis in a couple of squads of trucks and snow-machines cased
the heart of that territory via the Brighton Road and the old Tupper
Lake-to-Ottawa railroad bed, looking for another crossing track or
signature. They covered the fringes of Rocky, but didn't follow the
day-old spoor. They dared not go on watched land yet, with
anything that left a track, for fear of the caretakers, just as they
dared not go on Forever Wild for fear of the DEC, or the rangers.
The rangers were tenacious woodsmen, always out there in their
zones, seldom missing anything. Sochia himself, they figured,
probably got off of Rockefeller quick, and never went on state land
with Amos's machine.

Billy Atkin said if he had any principles, he wouldn't have
taken that thing. Scoffed at snowmobiles, said he'd never own one
himself—which was true, he'd never work hard enough to buy
one or pay for the gas. Ridiculed them all his life and then here he
goes and steals one to make his getaway, make it easy on himself to
cart the girl around. Just like him; slimy.

Slimy or not, they assumed they had a simple deal with Robert
Sochia, proffered with the note: that he was there, somewhere, in
these woods. Not the entire North Woods of the state; not the six
million acres of the whole Park; only their own South Woods, these
woods that hereditarily, you might say, pertained to the Falls, drained
by the Sabattis River. Sochia would stretch that territory, probably,
honor unknown to scum such as that. But, the point was, he didn't
have the whole world to run around in. He had to stay within certain
limits. They'd find him, sooner or later, if he did. And if he didn't,
he was chicken-shit and there wasn't any dealing with him. You
couldn't chase the sucker all the way to Florida.

For Harry's group the thing to check above all was camps—
hunting camps, private camps along the river, summer places on

the Blue Mountain Road. It wasn't enough to look at these places from the roads; you had to tramp all around in back of the camps to see if they'd been broken into. Surely that was Robert's game, break and enter, turn on the propane or kerosene heater or fire up the wood-stove. He had to keep her warm. Second, feed the two of them. They might get by on whatever crackers and canned goods he found in the pantries; green venison or snowshoe bunny if he had a gun. They assumed he did. That was about all he had to do except be somewhere else when they came looking. What he would do with the gun when caught was a question. What they would do in that case, either. That was a bridge to cross when they came to it.

He hadn't even been where they came looking that first day, except Benz Bond Club, across the creek from Massawepie. That was where he'd evidently slept the night before he stole Amos's sled. Back-tracking him in only one day's snowfall they reconstructed that affair. It looked as it he'd come up the railroad bed to Massawepie Pond himself, and found the Cheneys and Frarys there in that little camp on the shore. Maybe he'd been planning to overnight there himself; but finding it occupied, he led his companion on along the north side of the outlet brook to Benz Pond Club's camp and broke in there to eat and sleep.

"Separate bunks, by Jesus," Billy noted. And just to be sure of the back-story and eliminate the idea of him traveling by car, Harry sent a couple of machines home by way of the railroad bed. Sure enough, they found the old DeSoto, abandoned, right on top of the trestle over the Sabattis six miles in from Stark's Mill. It looked like he had run it as fast and as far as he could on that steep-sided, rail-less, tie-less mole, used as an access road to several hunting clubs but unplowed in winter, the snow on it irregularly packed by snowmobiles. They hated to give him the credit, but that was kind of a miracle of driving, to get that far, with any rear-drive car especially that old tub. It wasn't going anywhere now, until spring. That bridge is narrow, supported by wooden trusses either side, with long steel bolts from the peaks of the trusses down to the beams, and there wasn't room either side of the DeSoto for these boys to get their sleds by. They had to run up the river to find a place that looked safe to cross, and then go like hell in case there wasn't any solid ice under the snow.

The second day there was already some attrition, certain people having to show up at their jobs. That was accepted from the first, because this wasn't the project of a day, or even a week, and one need was a semblance of normalcy. Retired men in general, like the old-boys' chorus in Eugene's, didn't feel the call. An occasional man in his fifties, a few in their forties, most between twenty and thirty-five, the pursuers quickly settled into going out part-time, each when he could, with whoever else could go at the same time, all checking in at The Rapids before and after, or the fire-station at night if they saw a light there, careful not to arouse O'Neil's curiosity. They kept in touch about what was covered and what wasn't and how recently. If he moved he'd make tracks, the theory was. If he didn't move he'd make smoke. Either way they'd find him, sooner or later.

Just past the Rockefeller gate-house the Brighton Road turns sharply left and a little further on, the east line of Bay Pond Park cuts up over the shoulder of St. Regis Mountain. The line trail, geometrically straight, is cleared out as wide as a one-lane road. Peter Hubbard left his truck with the sled on the back and floundered up that line trail on foot.

It was his assignment to follow that trail, keeping the state land on his left and Rocky on his right, over the mountain and down to the shore of Big Fish Pond. There he would turn west and follow Rockefeller's south line until he met up with Francis coming the other way. Theoretically one of them might come upon the trail of Amos's sled going off the private land and into the state wilderness reserved to canoeists, where snowmobiles were banned.

Peter's machine wouldn't have done well on this trail anyway. It would have been harder horsing it out of the holes it would dig for itself than this walking. But walking in this stuff was for the birds. He couldn't believe that Robert Sochia would be doing it. He'd steal snowshoes, or skis, you could bet; for Julia too.

He had trouble thinking of them together. He just couldn't picture it. Out here? He couldn't see it. After half an hour he reached the height of land. Going downhill was easier. He overheated quickly and unzipped his jacket. He could feel the open space over Big Fish Pond though he couldn't see it. He checked his map. The corner was practically at the edge of the pond; he couldn't miss it.

Like any Falls man he was a hunter, an outdoorsman. He thought of himself that way. He'd just never had so much time to play outdoors. But he'd shot deer, he liked to fish and all that. The only reason Robert Sochia might be a better woodsman was that he never played basketball. So.

When he could see the pond he realized the corner was on a bluff overlooking it. There was no sense climbing up there. He thought he might as well cut across to the south line by a lower draw. It would mean trespassing on Rocky. But he would feel ashamed of himself if he scrambling around on the rocky slope on the Pond side just for fear of trespassing. Besides, he'd be in plain sight out there.

Sochia could be anywhere around here. You had to remember that.

People used to have so-called platform camps over there, across the pond. The Canoe Area. The camps had to be temporary, like a tent, a canvas building; but people brought in refrigerators and stoves and docks and everything, made themselves right to home. They had a lease, for so many years, for just a few bucks. They could hunt and fish on state just as if they owned the place. But now it was *wilderness*, so-called. The state came and burned their tent platforms and took their boats and refrigerators out to some dump, dangling from a helicopter.

Rocky's south line was rougher because once he got off the mountain it went straight over everything in lower, rougher country. He could see the pond down to his left from the higher places. The shadows of the trees, skinny or thick, fell across him from the side and he felt the dazzling flicker, a very slow version of it, that you felt when you drove along a winter road perpendicular to the sun. Frank was supposed to be coming the other way but they didn't know where they would meet, which of them had farther to hike. This was just what Harry told them to do.

He was comfortable, at least. If you were comfortable, this wasn't bad. If Julia was comfortable like this, he didn't have to worry about her so much. What the hell. He didn't rape anybody. He didn't necessarily believe anything he heard, either. He hoped she was warm enough, that's all. And if she wasn't exhausted, getting from place to place. She didn't eat very much, she wasn't very strong, he didn't think. She always needed a lot of rest.

Snow, trees, rocks, up and down, wet cold feet; it wasn't bad but it was boring. That would be the hard part for Julia. The whole woods was just like this, wherever you were. Except swamps and mountaintops. About three different kinds of places in the whole zillions of acres.

He could see the land bridge that showed on the map between the west end of Big Fish and the east end of Little Fish. Once in a while there were sharp, fresh deer tracks. They kind of startled him. He never saw the deer but the tracks looked so fresh he supposed he had jumped the deer out of the trail ahead of him. The tracks made him realize, imagine: other life, here, *just now!*

Now these here were bigger tracks, and way older. Bear? No, bears were asleep. They had better be asleep, because he had just come through rocky places where there had been caves, like, in the boulders. He hadn't thought about bears and had gone right past them, maybe. He wouldn't want to wake one up.

Wait a minute. These were not deer tracks. He had been following in a line of shallow depressions in the snow. Very shallow depressions in the top surface of the snow. The snow was about twenty inches deep, mostly soft powder.

He looked at his old tracks behind him. They might look the same if they were snowed over. They'd be filled up and just be these sort of saucer-like depressions in the powder, so you couldn't tell which way they were going, like these.

These were a couple of days old. One person. Or maybe two: she would put her feet down in the same places. *Holy shit. This was them!* he thought. *Who the hell else would it be? It wouldn't be anybody else.* Christ Almighty he had found them. He grinned and then he stopped grinning.

He didn't step in the tracks any farther. He punched his own track beside them, looking for some way to read them. The direction, the number of walkers. It could have been a watchman. Oh sure. It was probably a watchman, a long time ago. Rich people's watchmen would patrol in the middle of winter. Waste of time but that's what they're paid for.

He had been looking down so long that now he was nervous about looking up, ahead. He looked out of the corner of his eye first. He thought he saw something, and almost ducked as he took it in. A black shape more solid and rectilinear than the trunks and boulders around it. A shack? That was a shack. The line was low and close to the shore of the pond in this stretch and the dinky little shack was right on the line.

He went nearer. It was no bigger than an outhouse. What the hell was this doing here? The stuff to build it must have been dragged in on toboggans, some winter fifteen or twenty years back. Tarpaper, a few boards. The rafters of it, hanging out at the sides, were just cut saplings. They stuck out to different lengths from the roof boards and tarpaper.

Some lazy fart's idea of a deer-stand? It was barely big enough for a monkey-stove and a man sitting or standing, looking out the little panes of glass framed into the walls, at least the one facing Peter. No, no, right on the line: this was a watchman's shack. Watching for hunters sneaking over onto Rocky from state.

It was where the footprints were going, sure. It was just the watchman. The adrenalin drained out of the back of his neck, left him shivering.

He wasn't ready to find them, this quick, without warning like this. He didn't have a pistol or anything.

He wasn't anybody's enemy. Didn't everybody know that?

The watchman would be long gone but just the same, continuing, he left the trail. He'd go above the shack. He'd circle it and see if these old prints came out anywhere on the other side.

He tried not to make a sound. He took cover from the irregular ground, from great hunks of rock broken by frost from the mountain, trees of all sizes, at all angles and fallen.

As he came up higher, above the shack, he saw that it had a wood-pile, built up man-high between two black cherry trees, two steps from the wood-framed, canvas door, which had a piece of glass in it. Against the gray sky, he couldn't tell if the stovepipe coming out of the slanted roof was carrying heat or not. Heat wouldn't have to make smoke. It could just make a vibration.

He edged his snowmobile boots for footing, pulled himself up by the trunks of small trees.

He kept high until he was a rifle-shot beyond the shack and then scrambled and slid down again, catching a tree on the line with both arms to stop himself. He hugged the tree, startled, taking a deep breath and letting it out, *whoooo*, trying to do it silently. Scatterings of pure whiteness leapt into close-up, with their own shadows, beside sharp-edged dark pits in the snow. These were fresh, human bootprints, just made. They were pointing straight back to the shack.

His heart was pounding. It was like buck fever, which he always got when he saw a deer, any deer, buck or doe. He seemed to see him (no watchman now), RS with a bag of groceries, going back to the shack. Actually, a bag of groceries under his arm, as if he'd walked out to Paul Smith's for food. He was in the shack! Jesus!

There was no sound from there. He'd gone far enough past, he hadn't been heard. He decided to go on around his circle, out of sight. Make sure that RS was still in there, before anything else, while getting back on the safer side, the side toward his truck, his haven. That was the thing to do. Maybe he wouldn't be there. Maybe they had already left the shack and cut down to the outlet and crossed that ridge he'd seen between the ponds. He couldn't worry about Frank. Frank was on his own. Frank probably came on those fresh tracks already and headed back. He wouldn't want to find Sochia yet any more than Peter did. He left Peter to bump into him alone.

This time he was in even rougher ground, thicker growth of small trees, nearer the jumbled rocks at shore. In his haste he forgot to watch for tracks. Then he remembered, but assured himself that he would have noticed them if he had crossed them. When he was sure he had gone back far enough to be well east of the shack he edged upward again and soon he saw above him a poster, and right and left more posters, saying POSTED, warning, all persons warned blah-blah-blah. The Rockefeller line, good.

But before he came up to it, still down in a ravine where he felt hidden and exposed at once, there they were again! The bright, fresh, hard-edged tracks! They didn't go to the shack? What the hell? He followed them with his eyes, imagining. They passed in front of him going to his right. They were turning up toward the line. He crouched, listened. Impatiently then he stood up and walked beside them, feeling them like a companion, unseen, silent, but odorous like himself, warm with exertion.

He stopped and made himself think. *These tracks were circling the line shack too. For what reason? Is he sneaking around his own hide-out? Well shit, sure. He wouldn't just walk straight back to it. Anybody as cute as he thinks he is.*

What am I supposed to do now? Coach would say, 'Get in there and do your job! South would have his clipboard, his diagram hastily drawn on the yellow tablet, two circles around the shack's square. Seeing that, he felt clearer. *Well, he isn't going to find my track. He's inside of my circle.*

He began to move up the ravine toward the one yellow steel poster he could see now. He looked ahead and sideways and behind him every step, moving slower and slower. The further he went, the nearer the yellow sign, the surer he felt what was coming. He imagined himself taking the bullet before he heard the shot. Lying in the snow, not hurting at all. Surprised but peaceful.

He'd be famous for his bravery.

Well, it would be true. He wasn't afraid. That would be just fucking justice for a change. He knew that about himself at least. He wasn't any fucking coward.

He was almost on the line now and nothing had happened to him. The old filled-in tracks were just above him, the height of his head. East, it couldn't be far, were his own fresh tracks, leading back to the corner and back over the hill to his truck. He'd go back and report. That's what Harry would want them to do. Go in again with a plan, tomorrow. Christ Almighty he'd found him!

"Hey!"

Somebody had said "Hey!" Peter's mouth fell open. Where did that come from? Who the hell was that? He didn't want to look around, look stupid. He had no idea where to look. He almost lost his balance, panning back along the line of posted trees.

"Hey, Dumb-ass!"

He knew the voice but still didn't see the man. Or make sense of this. His own voice came out of him unexpected, "Where?" His mouth stayed open

A crunch. Steps as near as his own. Then a leg, black, a snowmobile boot ticked the base of a maple. That outward-swinging style of walking: a moment of confusion, because it was Frank's. It was Frank.

Peter shook his head to clear it. He was glad to see his friend. Hey, why not? Just embarrassed that he hadn't seen him first. Now in relief, smiling open-mouthed, he held a finger to his lips. Though it seemed wrong. There was something wrong with it but he didn't know what except they'd better be quiet. He pointed in along the line, mouthed to Francis, *In the shack!*

"You tracking somebody, are ye?" Francis was talking too loud, like indoors you'd talk. But Francis stamped his boot in the snow and pointed to the print and said, "His tracks look anything like that, shit-for-brains?"

"Oh," Peter said. "It was you."

"Oh."

Peter turned around, kicked a tree. Took ahold of it and tried to move it, frozen roots and all. Then just as suddenly, he laughed.

Frank laughed too, briefly. He said, "You bring anything to eat?" Sat down, lay back. In the snow against a rock. Jerked out his tin of snuff. Peter remembered the sandwich zipped in the pouch in the back of his jacket.

Peter never had a problem about being kidded for something like that. The best thing to do was take it, laugh along with them. It could happen to anybody. So they told the story on themselves and everybody laughed and they laughed along with them, and it was okay.

But Harry's voice cut like a drum through the laughter. "What about those old tracks?"

"What?"

Then his mother's, condescendingly. "Those old tracks. Where did they go from that shack?"

Peter looked at Frank. Frank hadn't seen them either. But there was only one direction likely. What was Sochia doing on the south side of Rocky if he wasn't going to cross into the Canoe Area, where they couldn't go with machines any more than they could on Rockefeller? And sure enough the next day, when they took a chance and ran in on Rocky as far as they could on machines, and then slid and clambered along the ledges down to that line shack and broke the padlocked door, they found, in pencil, on the inside of a label peeled off a rusty can, one word. Sochia's second missive. "Fish."

"Like in the card game," Peter said without thinking. "Go fish."

"Fish Pond," Harry said.

"Or—yeah."

There were lean-tos on Fish Pond. Lean-tos, the traditional wilderness shelter. DEC builds them for the canoeists. They are log sheds with overhanging roofs on the front, facing a stone fireplace with a log fire-back. They are chinked with sphagnum moss, their floors are up off the ground. They have out-houses. You make a bed of evergreen boughs—balsam, by choice, for the smell. Usually there is a spring of water near-by; or you fetch it from the pond.

Rupp, the ranger from Lake Clear, patrolled the canoe area diligently and hated anything with a motor, but Frank said, "Let's get back to the machines and go around west where it ain't so fucking steep and get them down to the other pond, there. Fuck it, run the ponds. In and out. Fucking Rupp won't hear us. Come on!"

Harry wiped his big hand down his coarse, strong face. "After dark," he said. It wasn't just Rupp. You didn't know what went on in those state woods any more. Cross-country skiers, with companion dogs the size of elk. Winter campers. People from the city mushing Alaskan sled-dogs. They'd all of them report anybody riding a sled.

They took their time getting around to the outlet, quietly. They waited for the last of the light. Then under the stars they rode as fast as they dared. From the fish-control dam on the river, up Lydia pond and Little Fish, over the esker and onto the blue-white spookiness of Big Fish. They ran four close abreast the length of Big Fish with the St. Regis Mountain like a conscience, cold and clear up beside them, masking the Dipper, with Orion rising over the lower southern hills with his scabbard dripping gems.

The lean-tos are on the east end, one on a low point, the other on a shelf of the steep southern shore. Even from the lake they could see that the low front logs of the overhanging roof of the lean-to were charred. They left the machines on the ice and ran up to it, with powerful flashlights. They looked at the bed of hemlock boughs heaped in the back of the shelter and thought how high the fire had to have been, how it must have been blazing, to scorch the overhang of the roof. How warm it must have been back in there, way against the logs of the back wall . . .

So they couldn't help imagining it—as Leo, learning of it, imagined it himself—*couldn't help making it into almost-myth.* A picture that would madden them, drive them onward in their hunt, but give them no help, no clue to where he was or how he was traveling, surely no release: *Robert Sochia reclining back in there behind the blazing fire like some wild warrior on a pile of furs, his hair longer, his beard curlier now, the golden ear-ring glinting, a necklace of bear-claws and the teeth of catamounts underneath the red neckerchief at his throat—a net sling of chewed rawhide, full of venison jerky, hanging on a peg behind him by the leaning rifle. So warm in the firelight that his hairless chest is bare and that damned old ank of his, peace symbol*

*or whatever it stands for, hanging there again. Not to mention, ta-da!
the face of the girl, glowing like amber against his boney shoulder, her
shiny hair rippling like a river down past his insolent nipple,* or, well,
check nipple, *down past his navel*—check that—*down his side—*

18

Centerfold

Somebody would see a day-old or two-day-old snowed-in track, of man or skis or machine; or they'd see some hut somebody'd broken into and slept in, in this part of the territory or that. Then next day, or the same one, somebody else would find a track or break-in twenty-five miles' arrow-flight away. It began to seem the theory was wrong, and he wasn't making tracks at all, but flying. The weather handed him a cover-up every night, new snow, the way it will, some winters. But who really knew? Any of these sets of sign might be anybody else's, too, out for a hike or a ski or a ride or one-night shack-up. "Sochia ain't the only outlaw ever roamed the woods," as Billy Atkin said. You'd get on a track and it would be rabbit hunters, or some old geezer's trap-line. Fisher were bringing good money, otter too, beaver less, but still . . .

So that they might have gotten discouraged, or thought they were fools to chase at all, thought he was probably gone to Florida, laughing all the way. But just about then they'd find another note. The third one was an old post-card, an antique card, never sent, with what looked like a hand-tinted picture of an orange rowboat at the shore of a lake, other boats out on the water. Found weighted down with a bullet-casing on the breakfast table of somebody's summer camp at Joe Indian Pond. In the address space, "To the S.F. Rescue Squad." The message scrawled on the back was, "Help help. Trackers on my tail."

Which way from here? Joe Indian Pond was about as far west as the hunters felt he had a right to go, in woods pertaining more to Parishville or Risdonville than the Falls. Did this mean they had to rope in still more territory? They couldn't hunt all the way over to Colton, for Christ's sake!

He even called in by radio one day. That had to be much nearer the Falls. Who knows where he found a short-wave radio to call from, he didn't say. He called Terwilliger, in the business office of the SF Central School. Everybody knew that Terwilliger had a short-wave in his office, along with his big stereo and personal water-fountain. Robert called Terwilliger from somewhere out there, not too far away, and passed the time of day. It wasn't to boast or taunt, Terwilliger said. He seemed to want to hear a friendly voice. Talked about the weather, how beautiful it had been in the woods, and only at the end of the conversation he wanted to know, Terwilliger being the town's great Emergency Medical Technician, how long a person could keep going on a cup of bouillon a day. When that came in, Francis Prentice swore violently and pounded the bar, complaining, "Now is that fair? Is that fair?"

It seemed as if he must still be using that stolen snow-machine. They hadn't found it. They came across all kinds of snowmobile tracks, of course, tracks that could be anybody's including their own. Amos's sled had a big logo molded into its rubber track and would press into the snow a panther's head and the name Arctic Cat every foot or so but in this cold dry powder snow the imprints didn't hold. Or maybe he had somebody helping, one of his Mohawk buddies picking them up along some road and carting them to somewhere else. They thought of watching the roads by night, sitting silent with their motors shut off, and listening; but surprising to many, the woods were positively honeycombed with trails and paths and roads, too many to begin to cover, where it was supposed to be "wild forest." Except on state. They had to give him credit, he wasn't sticking only to state.

"And you have to give him credit," Billy Atkin insisted, "for doing it with a passenger. I mean, I ain't surprised *he* can cover the ground. But her—what's her name?—I kindly presume she ain't really *willing*. Does he *carry* her?"

For that matter who knew if she wasn't helping him? No one wanted to say it, but how could he keep her with him unless she was cooperating? With all this country to shake him in, couldn't she escape, if she tried? Couldn't she at least get to a phone or a mail-box or leave them some message, somewhere? As Billy said, "Couldn't she at least weigh the fucker down so he made footprints, like an ordinary human being?"

One morning the second week they got a new hand. He was there in the parking lot in front of the fire-station before any of the rest of them, before the first intimation of daylight, sitting in his truck with the engine roaring, headlights on, tailgate stuck into the snowbank behind him so firmly that at the end of the day, when they all came back, the young partner assigned to him would have to get behind the truck and wedge him out of there by main force, while he spun the wheels to no effect.

You couldn't tell Clarence Shampine anything about driving. Couldn't tell him how to use his choke, either. The engine was racing because the choke was out, forgotten, though by now the truck was warm. Lenny LaBounty had told him, putting in that manual choke at Clarence's insistence, "You shouldn't have this thing in no vehicle of yours, Clarence. Just like you ought to have a automatic transmission, because that way you wouldn't be forever burning out your clutch. You'll thin your oil, Clarence, if you leave out your manual choke too long." But Clarence knew what he wanted. *Huh, automatic*, Clarence thought. *That's just what nobody needs. Something complicated in the place of something simple.*

He was here now because he was sent here. *Ordered, by the kind of a boss that you wouldn't trust with a team of horses. So why would you trust him to run a town?* Sitting here hunched over his steering wheel running over that conversation and many another, real and imaginary. Duke Arquit, the town supervisor, said to him the afternoon before, "Clarence, I'm sick of your damn muttering.'What do them young fools know about the woods?' I ain't listening to that no more. 'Them young galoots will never save that girl.' I ain't listening no more. Forget the skating rink, forget the dump. You report to Harry LaFleur tomorrow morning. Tell him you're the Big Heap Guide I promised him."

Well, that was more than Clarence expected. Those fellows searching for Mister Murder Man and the girl could certainly use somebody who wasn't born yesterday, somebody that had lumbered in those woods since he was knee-high to a grasshopper, had hunted and fished in them all his life and knew the ways of the animals. But he went back to his cabin and sat by the stove the rest of the day, only getting up to clean up the mess when he let go the tea-mug he'd been holding on his knee. And to let Leo in.

Leo Weller had got wind of this assignment and come down to his cabin on the Project to talk him out of going. "Clarence, you know what your sisters'll think—"

Yes, 't I ought to be kept in the house under a loc-k.

"And my old Aunt Sarah. Sarah Weller Bryant'll have your neck." Clarence jerked his head aside at that threat, even now. "Father said to tell you Arquit's got no business sending you on a deal like this."

Hnnn. Don't I know it. I would just as soon be on a river drive, with the logs jammed up tight's a puzzle, and have the boss tell me I had to go out on the jam and prize out the key log. Dangerous business."

"Yes," Weller had said.

If they told you to do it, you was what they called a volunteer. No social security. No insurance. Two or three volunteers caught by the logs every spring. You know that old song, Weller,

> *Some of the men were willing,*
> *And others they were not.*
> *To break log jams on a Sunday morn*
> *They didn't think they ought.*

Well, just like that, today. If I claimed I was a expert on this kind of a feature, it would be just like a fellow saying he could teach school, and come to find out he can't write his own name. It would be the same principle.

Another pickup truck drove into the parking area now, tires creaking on the snow. It swung around, parked a little way along, and the fellow turned out his headlights. Clarence remembered to push in the choke now and pushed in his light-switch too. *Should have done that before. Forgot: we're here on the sly.*

I told Leo Weller, it's just like those waterlogged hemlock rafters on the deluxe cabin we built for the Project, last year. Middle of winter, five degrees of temperature, and you had to work bare-handed. Fifteen feet up in the air with nothing but a log wall to stand on. I am ascared of high places and always was, just the same as water. Heights and water, them two things. I have worked on both because I was tolt to, but I never liked to climb and I can't swim no more'n an anvil. Well it's the same principle.

Other trucks swung in around his now, men getting out of them and clumping together in twos and threes, and Clarence thought, *Here's the rest of the dogs. About time* but he went on imagining a better conversation with the boss. *I told Arquit, "That boy can shoot like a pirate. Any five or ten of this party is likely to get hurt. 'twould suit me just as well if you give me one man that can walk, and leave the case to me.* Opening his door now and stepping down, he said aloud, "But no deal, I have to go with the rest of them. You want to know why I am angry, mister, that's why. To have a boss that would send you somewhere with a pitch-fork, to cart water."

In his high-laced boots and jodphur-like hunting pants he came up to the nearest bunch of fellows, most of them wearing thick snowmobile suits and carrying helmets in their gloved hands. He managed a chuckle and said, "Look at all the manpower, hnn. That old buck don't have no more chance than a snake has got hips." Somebody gripped his elbow and moved him slightly. He took it as an introduction to the crew and went on, "You want to know where we are going, all right, something different today, not where he was yesterday. Maybe where he's got to go for food tomorrow. I've got a few tricks up my sleeve." Somebody said, "Clarence used to be a member of Camp Luck Club, didn't you, Clarence?" Somebody else said, "All right, let him go with Clarkie, then."

Doors were slamming, engines starting again. A very young man stood next to him, saying, "I'm your partner, Clarence You might's well leave your truck and come in mine."

The fellow led him to a little yellow pickup, Japanese. His hat didn't fit on his head inside it but it was warm."We're going out the Blue Mountain Road," the fellow said.

"Who says."

"LaFleur," the boy said. "You got a helmet? You ever ride a skidoo?"

Clarence answered, "When I want to scare everything in the woods, I let out a Injun yell."

He hadn't been up this road in a long time, and it was unfamiliar to him, much wider than it used to be, curved and graded like a highway. More houses, without barns, houses he'd never seen before. Old houses and barns that he last saw lived-in and well kept were gone entirely, or empty. He didn't see where the road to Dexter Lake turned off. Likewise that other old track in to the far end of Cook's Lake. *Used to be right next to Dexter's driveway, where'd they put it? I used to know that road as good's I know my name.* He told the boy, "I drove a team on that road for Harold Purryer Senior, sixty years ago, when I was scarcely old enough to hold the reins. Leave Center Camp before day light, get back to camp after dark. Loaded both ways, every day. Hauled a big load of pulp out, come back in with hay and grain and other supplies. It took a lot to feed so many men and horses."

He would have liked to tell him more, how they iced the roads to make the going easy, how they lit the way with kerosene lights on poles stuck in the ground, but he was lost again in puzzlement. Beside the road a white bathtub, water falling into it from a pipe— was that where the old barrel-spring had been? The road in to the ranger's cabin at the foot of Blue Mountain used to be trimmed and mowed, grass growing along both sides and down the middle, a flower-box by the sign. No sign now, the lane unused, almost choked by the growth of fat young pines.

A mile more of the big, wide gravel road winding, climbing; then the pickups ahead swerved and stopped, and he saw they were in a cleared space, the end of the big road, a wide turning and parking area. Off down to the left where the old road continued, narrow, unplowed, he saw the bridge over the Sabattis, the ironwork loaded with snow.

He knew where they were now. This was the Intersection, he told the boy, busy as the middle of a town all winter in the old days, logging going on in all directions. In the present the hunters' pickups were backing up to the snowbanks and the men were pulling their snowmobiles off them, then starting them up and turning them sideways and revving up their engines, skinning down the snowbanks onto the level. They dismounted and gathered around LaFleur.

Clarence knew LaFleur, worked with him years ago in Wilfred Gonyea's sugarbush. That was when he owned a team of work-horses and would hire himself out with the team wherever he could board them. That year the sap didn't run much and Gonyea used him and the horses to skid hemlock logs when there wasn't any sap to gather. He'd formed a good opinion of LaFleur, strong as a ox, appetite to match and not afraid of work. Cold didn't bother him any. *Hand on him just like Paul Bunyan.* Today, short zippered jacket and overshoes that were unfastened, the buckles rattling when he walked. With those big hands LaFleur touched the other men the way you would a horse, patted them into bunches and shoved them back toward their machines.

"I guess Harry thinks Sochia's back in this area," Clarkie said beside him. "Some logger found a gas-can missing." *That all?* Clarence wondered. *I know something better than that.* But then the air was ringing with the rattle and jingle of the sleds. Helmets were looked into, pulled on, face-shields lowered. Suddenly it was a crowd that looked to Clarence as if they just stepped off a space ship. In clouds of blueish smoke the sleds jerked ahead, stopped. Men got off, lifted their sleds' rear ends around and raced their tracks, then dropped them and jumped back on. His partner put something in his hands. While he was holding the pumpkin-like thing in front of his nose trying to see what was frontwards, a sled swept almost over his toes. In the clatter and stink he squeezed his head into the padding. Another world in there: his ears were shut off, all the faculties of a hunter dulled. He couldn't see out the corners of his eyes, didn't feel as if he could even turn his head.

The point of one line of sleds fed out of the area onto the road toward the bridge. Another went over the plowed bank under a gate with a set of antlers on the top bar. He sat down behind his partner and felt for something to take hold of, but there was nothing. The sled whined faintly outside the close padding around his ears and the seat shot forward under him. He lay back under the streaming treetops, rigid. He could not sit back up. He hung on with his legs, dizzy, until they caught up with the pack, and then he flew up against the boy's back. He said, "Excuse me, it will take me a minute to get used to this." The boy reached back for his hands one at a time and put them around his middle. Clarence said, "Well, I never. All right if you don't mind." He looked at a blur of trees.

He was lost, except for an unconscious bearing on the sun and a notion of the time of day as it passed. They turned and turned, whenever they came to another trail or path wide enough for the sleds, sometimes so many turns in one direction it seemed to him they must be going around in circles. The boy told him why: they had to follow what roads there were because the snow in the woods was too deep, too soft for the snow-machines. They would dig themselves a hole and fall in. So, what good were they? Snow machines that couldn't go in the snow. It would make just as much sense to have a boat that couldn't go in the water. When they did get mired, Clarence stood off and the boy lifted the back end around like nothing. Clarence muttered congratulations, "anybody that can lift like that."

They stopped for lunch. Clarence took off the helmet, took out of his inner pockets the bread and baloney he had brought, and sat on a fallen tree to eat. "No deer today. Maybe the deer don't stick to the highways, ha ha. I have heard that on Sunbeam Club they take the watchers to their stands in a school bus."

The boy said, "No shit?" with a laugh. Interested, was he? Well then might as well go on. "Mister Murder Man has a lot of territory to hide in, and plenty of accommodations easy to get into, plenty of kerosene and stove-wood to keep warm. Ven'son and pa'ridge to eat, and rabbit if he likes it. Me, I had too much snowshoe bunny as a boy to ever need to smell that kind of meat cooking again. No one likely to stumble on him, not even watchmen on the gates this time of year. I could think of worse deals," he said, suddenly the jester. "Out here with a good looking girl, nothing to do but steer clear of this posse."

He went on, since the boy had his mouth full, smiling at him.

"If 'twas me, when I got caught, it would be b'cause I couldn't take it no more. Paradise."

The kid was choking, but Clarence forgot the joke just as suddenly. "Pulp cutters, that's the only people in the woods steady now-days, and few of them, in and out by truck every day, no matter how much gasoline you burn. Nothing like it used to be. No such thing as a lumber camp no more, with a cook and bunkhouse and barn, where you lived two-three months to a time. Not to mention no horses. My line of work, teamster." He pronounced it teamuster. "Sad day for me, the day they took the horses out of the lumber woods."

Breakdown. Up ahead somebody pulled a shoe, as a horseman might say. Sleds piled up into one another's smoke, overlapped herringbone-style, stopped. Keys were turned off; a sudden peace and sunlight. The men got up, taking the chance to light up a cigarette and talk, take a leak, waiting while somebody fixed a drive-belt, jury-rigged a broken ski or spring, changed the wet, blackened plugs.

Clarence stood apart, embarrassed. He would have felt sympathy for the fellow down in the snow freezing his fingers while he worked, but for him swearing, blaming everything, the winter, the snow, the storms, the woods, of course that God-damn Slushy. *Good for you if you can fix a machine, but no need to misuse a whole family's name.*

Then one day they drove into the yard of Alder Stream Club and looked all about them amazed, the whole area tracked up with bootprints, fresh bootprints going everywhere around the camp, the gas-tanks out back, the wood-pile, the out-house, in and out the door. They could only be from Robert Sochia's boots and his companion's. Their coming to the camp, Sochia's bustling about to turn the heat on. And their going? Quickly the hunters cast about to see, and yes, the last prints on the log steps came out the door and led straight among all the others out to the road, the Brighton road again. Where of course, as always, they were lost in the churned up snow of logging trucks, rabbit-hunters, whoever, whatever. All they'd have had to do was happen to come here yesterday instead of today and they'd have caught him.

Except for the lean-to at Big Fish and the camp on Joe Indian, this was the first time they had found a place he'd been so recently, and this was in the middle of the territory, this was where he belonged, pretty close to town, and as somebody said, "too fucking obvious." So with a kind of presentiment of disgust, Roger Cascanette stepped up to the door, going to look in. Suddenly there was a sound like a big fly-rod whipped through the air and Roger turned upside down, his feet swept up over his head and his head thumping the top log of the steps. Then he levitated, pulled upward by one foot, four or five feet higher, the edge of the eave gently untucking his shirts. He hung there, bobbing and rotating, the other foot scrabbling for a foothold on air. He grabbed the little wobbly railing of the steps, pushed up his red face and yelled, *"That skinny puke-colored dope addict! God-damn him to hell!"*

"Jest a minute, Roger," Francis Prentice said, and the others stood still too. They had to get it right in their minds. What had happened here? The young birch tree that had raised him up there, growing near the corner of the attached bunkhouse, was still hooped over at the top and trembling with his weight. "Roger, you asshole," Francis said, "you put your foot into a snare!"

Cascanette bellowed, *"I know it!"* then saved his breath, what with his inwards weighing on his lungs.

Francis warned him under his breath, "You could have a heart attack if you don't be calm, Roger. Look here, boys: he hit the trigger when he pulled the screen door. How the fuck did Sochia bend that tree down, though, if it's strong enough to lift Roger here? How much you weigh, Roger?"

Peter Hubbard stepped around Francis on the little platform, jerked open the screen door against Roger's back and kicked the inner door open and stepped in. There he halted, mouth-breathing. The room was a gallery of female flesh, pictures torn from skin magazines stuck on every nail and coat-hook, deer antler and drawer-knob in sight. Straight ahead of him, impaled on the wire handle of the stove-pipe damper, a two-page *Playboy* or *Penthouse* centerfold smiled at him frontally (perfect teeth) from one page, showed him her back and bottom from the other, kneeling on tumbled lilac sheets in a white lace chemise, open. In each picture, her left hand dangled a champagne bottle and in each, light came between her legs making a narrow little aura of blonde hairs. Peter was momentarily fascinated, comparing the simultaneous back and front views. How'd they do that?

But Francis brushed him aside, he lost the connection. They both looked around the camp, kitchen, washroom, poker-parlor and lounge all in one with a bunkroom off one end. Left, right, all around them, shiny color pictures of naked women, breasts and legs and buttocks, pierced by whatever protruding thing they were stuck on. When he turned all the way around Peter's eyes went willy-nilly up over the door: another page out of *Hustler*, to judge from the pink, somebody with her knees up and long-nailed fingers spreading the labia, the black toes of the deer-foot gunrack bursting through her belly. "Hey guys," he said out the door. "Hey guys."

Outside Cascanette was trying to hold himself by the railing, to keep the blood out of his head. Clarkie Tharrett managed to reach high enough, standing on the backs of two others and leaning on the building, to pull on the rope above his foot. Harry took the heft of the man while Clarkie undid the slip knot and they let him down to the steps and the snow, where he lay holding his hands over his face. One after another the men caught each other's looks and went inside. Five men in snowmobile suits and thick boots, moving around the camp, shifting places, to see it all. The magazines, ripped up and thrown a bout anywhere, had come from a pile on the home-made coffee table in front of a sort of bed-sofa built into one corner of the room.

Somebody said, "Look there." Over the archway to the bunkroom was a wooden plaque, shield-shaped, such as deer-horns are often mounted on, only this one had a bulging pair of plastic breasts on it in place of antlers. Billy Atkin said, "You can't blame Robert for that one. That was there before. So were these fuckin' skin-magazines. He didn't bring 'em here. What club is this? Alder Stream. Tchk tchk."

People shook their heads. Someone said to his neighbor, chuckling quietly, "You know who'd like to see this."

"Who?"

"Old Shampine. He pretends he can't stand working out at the dump, because of all the pin-ups Armand likes to insulate the shack with. But Lenny LaBounty says he carries a stash of his own skin-magazines, behind the seat of his truck."

So they called out for Clarence, and he came in casting his eyes around the floor, suspecting something from the first. When he looked up and saw the two images of the cutie with the champagne on offer he snapped his head away, closing his eyes. In a moment he opened them, avoiding looking in that first azimuth. But now, similar sights leaped to his eye from every direction, bosom and bottom, hair nobody but their husbands should see. There was no place to look to avoid them, and he staggered backward, turned and stumbled, banged against the door-jamb going out.

Harry brought out the torn pages crushed in his hands. "Wait, Harry, let Roger see," somebody said, but he carried them out and shoved them down into a steel barrel the club used for an incinerator. He felt in his breast pocket for his lighter and set them afire.

The men stood around the incinerator watching the pictures turn to ash. Over beyond the incinerator, a pole lashed horizontally between two trees was where Alder Stream hung their bucks. It was deduced that he had used the block and tackle from the buck-pole to bend the birch tree down.

"What's he getting at?" the kid asked Clarence, back at the sled, waiting for the column to start back toward the Intersection. "I mean what's the point of it. Do you get it, Clarence?" But the old man was mum. "You lost respect for him, huh," the kid said. But that wasn't worthy of an answer, either. Clarence had his own thoughts, not like everyone's. "Anyways," the kid said, "I think anybody who says he doesn't like them kind of pictures is bullshitting theirselfs. Don't you? I think he's just trying to get us mad. But this don't make me any madder, particularly. I weren't mad in the first place. I'm just along for the ride. My Daddy, he said I had to go. He has to work, and I'm out of school. So."

19

Almost Myth

Along in here, a lull, no sightings, no tracks, cold snap, Robert
Sochia apparently holed up somewhere or traveling by air. Leo was
reading a book that Julia had pressed on him in lieu of "a whole
long rap about Love" that she "didn't have time" to give him directly.
It would tell him a lot about "where she was coming from." She
had added, "But you would have to read all of Doris Lessing and
Anaïs Nin, and Berkeley and Hume and a lot of other people to
know me really-really, like I mean *know* me, Leo."

"And not just me, Leo. This book will tell you a whole long lot
about you-know-who, too."

Anybody but himself would be irritated by such an assignment,
he knew, and would never read any of those books. But Leo wasn't
irritated. He read this one. It was a pop-psychology book but it
was by one of those geniuses who have read all the great literatures
of the world and know everything about every culture and its
myths, and he had it all at his fingertips, and pulled evidence from
here, there, and everywhere, showing the way love was different in
different cultures, and how peoples' lives and relationships were
shaped by these ideas of love their cultures gave them.

Leo could see that this guy's analysis and his world-wide multi-
cultural and historical perspective would be very useful for a young
woman constantly under pressure from boys and men, a young
woman sympathetic and responsive to them yet who dreaded being
tied down, who was in no way looking for a long-term mate, who
had scary artistic ambitions and who wanted the whole world,
wanted to experience *everything*. Who was humbled and frightened

by these ambitions and also committed to living every year of her life at the age and place she was in, too. But without giving up hostages to the future.

Anyway, reading the thing he was seeing her everywhere in it, picking up the useful bits she could then try to teach to her suitors for the sake of their improvement and her freedom. He loved her all the more her intellectual opportunism, sucking up everything handy to her needs from this sparkling compendium. He tried to imagine her out there in the woods with Robert, trying to educate him in love and thus save herself and him from whatever he thought he was doing. But this was too difficult, this imagining. He drew a blank on it, mostly. He knew he would have to get the story from her own lips, in the end. Meanwhile he was bubbling over with mental activity sparked by this book. He'd been holding it all inside as he read, but when he was finished he was bursting to share, to show off.

And so one night in the office of the Feed & Coal, after sitting with his father for a good long time in silence, Leo slid down and leaned back in his chair, stuck his boots out toward the heater, wove his fingers together over his sweatered tummy, and became a non-silent Sphinx:

"'Every man wants to experience certain perilous situations, to confront exceptional ordeals, to make his way into the Other World.'"

He let a good bit of silence elapse. No comment from Père. He said, "He seeks 'a metaphoric death of an old, inadequate self, in order to be reborn on a higher plane of existence.'"

He smiled, watchfully. His father's small, thin-stemmed pipe hung against his lower lip, levered by his upper front teeth, his mouth in a familiar grimace around it. Finally Mr Weller said, with a sort of tremulous vehemence, "Robert Sochia might well want to be reborn on a higher plane of existence."

Encouraged, at least enough to raise his eyebrows, after another interval Leo continued, "'His hope has taken on her shape, and he can no longer wish it to have another.'"

"'Hope,'" his father said, taking the pipe in hand and moving it to the side of his mouth. "That's a big word. Robert's Catholic, of course," he admitted. "Any Sochia."

Leo gave him one more: "'He loves redemption in this maiden.'"

His father took the pipe out of his mouth completely. "Redemption! That's a bigger word yet. Stealing the girl and carrying her off into the woods redeems him?"

Leo simply beamed at him, repeating, "He loves it."

His father had his eagle look now, sharp-eyed and unamused. "Loves what?"

"This chance. What he's doing." Leo batted his eyes in a charming, dismissive way and said again, with relish, "'He loves redemption in this maiden.' That's good. I think that's the one." To his father's blank look he said, "For the epigraph."

Mr Weller grumbled, "Where are you getting these quotes? I guess you're using someone else's words. Whose are they?"

"Mircea Eliade's (whoever he is). Bruno Bettelheim's (heard of him). Thomas Mann's. Not bad, eh? I've got 'em on cards. Others from Dostoevsky, James Joyce and D. H. Lawrence, all very juicy. I found them conveniently gathered together in a book about Love, that I dug up at Julia's insistence. She's quite the expert on that subject, you know. Wants me to be able to talk her language. Especially since I'm the one who's writing it up."

Another pause while his father decided not to follow that lead. Instead he asked—and Leo could have asked it for him, was mouthing the words as he spoke—"Are you taking your pills?"

"Threw them away. They make me sleepy. It's between 'He loves redemption in this maiden' and 'His hope has taken on her shape.' That's the Thomas Mann one."

But his father was ignoring these perfect phrases. "You're joshing me about the pills, aren't you?"

"'course I am. For now. Who she really needs to read this book is Robert. I doubt she has it with her, but she has it in her head. She can do a spiel on Love, and a spiel on Time, and between the two of them, his goose will be cooked. I believe that will be her project: educate Robert Sochia on those two things. That will be his education, and hers."

Here he looked closely at his father. "Get the pun?"

"Hmm? What?"

"I don't like these witty things of mine to go unnoticed. Education, his and hers. It's a pun, rather nice, I thought."

"I did not get it."

"I have not forgotten my little Latin, Father. Educate is *ex* and *duco, ducere*, to lead. The *ex* is from, of course. So, to lead from. To be educated is to be led out of—something. The dark of ignorance, wrong thinking, in his case. In her case, the woods!

"His education—"

"Oh never mind. She's quite a teacher, so they say. But I almost think she might be up against it with RS. Don't you?"

A nod from Père but a blank expression. Leo hung his head. He had been feeling a brilliant paragraph coming up in him. Such a waste. He started it anyway. "Oh, I just mean I think he'll be a tough nut to crack. He'll resist. He will prove to have no weakness for that kid-stuff common banal love of hers: 'Come on, people-now, smile on your brother, everybody get together try to love one another right now.' He may be too vain to succumb, whatever the temptation. He might have too much invested in blood and passion to take the easy way out. He don't want mere Time. He's after Eternity, and quick. She'll have her work cut out for her, that's all I mean, Father."

During this his father had put a hand up to his face, fingers spread on his brow, the finest thin pale skin over smooth bone. Leo knew he was giving his father exacerbated doubts about his mental health. He would have liked to tell his father his thoughts on how she might do it, but they were perhaps over the line.

There never had been a January thaw, and there was none in February, to settle that deep snow and make a base for riding. In late February what they got was cold, the tree-popping, house-cracking kind of cold you do get in February, with week on week in which the mercury never rose above ten, and one whole week it never rose above zero and fell to thirty-two below for several days around the fullness of the moon. More clear weather than usual, as

Clarence Shampine would observe; still showing up in his roaring
pickup before daylight every morning, as ordered, and going
hunting with anybody who did go; no longer expecting to lead or
even making suggestions, though now, in smaller groups, he
probably could have. He'd gone sullen, kept any good ideas he
might have had under his hat. If nobody showed, or nobody wanted
to take him on behind, he drove back to the Project and shoveled
the skating rink. He never ventured into the grocery store and said
to Duke, "Well, no hunting today, so here I am, what's my next
assignment?" Instead, without orders, he went out to the dump
and bluffed at a little work there, hardly passing a word to Armand.
Then disappeared on up the Cook's Lake road to the "home place,"
as he called it—not the log house he had been born in; that was
mouldered down out of sight; but the little frame two-story house
across the road, at the bottom of the hill, by the brook, built by
his older brother (deceased) with his help. He would go up there,
light a fire in the kitchen stove and be miserable by himself, on the
town payroll.

By rights, that place ought to have been his, not Bessie's. It
ought to have been put in his name, so that he could live there and
cut his firewood on the property and if he wished to, keep a team
of horses in the shed. It would be nobody's business but his if they
earned their keep or not, as long as he could afford the hay. Instead
his sisters had everything, every piece of land his father ever owned.
They didn't think him capable of taking care of property, paying
taxes. Always treated him just like a baby. Little did they know.

Little did anybody know what he came up there for, either.
How he was keeping an eye out for someone that would come by
here sooner or later, and when he did—

There was a certain place back up the brook behind the home
place that he would walk back to and check, for reasons of his own.
A place he used to salt deer in an old stump, once upon a time, as
his father had before him. He had a shrewd suspicion he would see
the sign of Mister Murder Man there some day. He felt that he
was sticking his neck out a long, long way, when he went back
there, lest he actually catch the fellow there. He proceeded very

carefully when he got close, silent as an Indian. Something you won't find everywhere, a mud spring.

That was a very special thing, if you had one on your property you kept it to yourself. The Shampines might have been poor but they had a very good refrigerator long before electricity. Even without his present motivation, every so often Clarence would go back there, the better part of a mile, and make himself a bed of evergreen boughs to protect his woolened knees from the mud underneath the snow, and roll up his sleeve to the shoulder, and plunge his bare arm down into the ice-cold mud, and feel around down there at arm's length for the glass jars of venison or spaghetti-sauce which his sisters had canned for him and which he had pushed down there for safe-keeping. That food would keep any length of time down there, forever if you left it that long. That's where he went for a taste of his sisters' cooking; better than going out to the sheep-farm and be told he was a fool not to come and live there with them. *Live with them two, hnn.*

He had not thought that any other person in the world but himself and his sisters, the last of the family, knew about that mud spring, back up the brook by a well-worn trail most of the way but off the trail and over next to the brook, at a crossing-place where they used to put out apples or salt for the deer. The brook was the outlet of Cook's Lake, come way around behind the hills from the further end of the lake.

Well, very certainly no member of his family ever told anyone about that mud spring. But one day not very long before Robert Sochia disappeared with that school teacher Clarence liked so much, that liked to talk about the weather same as he did, Clarence had happened to go to the spring. Nearly to it, was making his way quietly along the crest of the ridge beside the brook, approaching with a hunter's stealth as he always did, to see if a deer happened to be there at the salt. And so the other fellow had not known that he was seen. But there he was, kneeling there. He had done just what Clarence always did, fetched himself a few cedar boughs to float on and exposed his arm clear to the shoulder; because the jars were down deep as a man could reach.

Clarence had felt a great violation of his family and birthright. He wished for the courage to shout, to march down there and strike the fellow on the side of the head. But the fellow was not taking jars away. His arm wasn't muddy yet but one jar gleamed beside him full of something pale, and he set another one by it and took a third from inside his shirt. Clarence could see perfectly well what it was, with the aid of a shrewd guess. The fellow was a known poacher. It wouldn't matter to him that the season was closed. That was venison, sure, cut up and boiled and canned boiling hot, so a vacuum would form inside the jars when they cooled and seal the cap. Venison put up that way was just as good as new, a year or two years later. Clarence's family had lived on little else, certain times in his childhood.

He watched the boy push his three cans down in the spring and wash off his arm with snow and let down his wool sleeve and button the cuff. He watched him put on the tall black hat. He felt a sort of jealous affinity at the sight of that hat, for he wore a wide-brimmed felt hat himself, no matter if he was mocked for it. That kind of hat was good enough for the Rangers and the troopers. This other fellow's one had a band of beadwork around the base of the crown, made the boy look like an Indian, which he wasn't, but good as one in the woods.

While Clarence watched from cover, the outlaw left the scene, crossing the shallow gravel ford as if water was no different from snow, and Clarence spoke to himself inwardly and perhaps aloud though softly, *Wellsir, you know about my secret spring, do you. You are a slippery one, to know that. I guess you expect to come back here some day and get that ven'son. I guess you think you will want it, maybe next summer, and you don't have no refrigerator. But you are trespassing, Mister. My sister owns this place, wants me to ask for permission to cut stovewood on it myself, what do you think she'd say to you? I don't guarantee but what that deer meat might be gone, when you come back for it. I might not know that meat from some of my own, put down in the same Mason jars.*

And now, sitting at the little oil-cloth-covered table by the window in the home place, in that tiny kitchen where he could feed the firebox of the cookstove without getting up from the painted chair, he could see the road, too. He was sticking his neck out even being there, but he did so deliberately, conscious of his unfamiliar daring. Ever since Duke Arquit set him to this hunt, he had had that spring in mind, that one thing he knew that Mister Murder Man didn't know he knew. More, he knew other scenes where Mister Murder Man would go, as sure as shooting. Center Camp, for one, where Clarence used to drive a team for Harold Purryer Senior. Purryer's big log camp down at the far end of the lake. He had rowed supplies down there many a time while yet a boy, not knowing how to swim. He had done things he was afraid of before. When the pirate came for that meat, Clarence would know pretty well he was holed up in one place or the other.

Or Dexter Lake, a third good hideaway, not far away either if you knew the route. Remembering now the story he'd been told about his father, a poor man but a famous talker, especially when in liquor. The rich man that owned Dexter Lake, Orrando Dexter, hated for closing his woods, had been shot, riding out from his house on Dexter Lake to the Blue Mountain Road to get his mail. Killed with one ball. The judge at the hearing asked Clarence's father, looking at the map, *"Mr Shampine, here's Dexter Lake, and here's your home place on the Cook's Lake Road, how long would it take a man to walk from your place to Dexter's?"* And his father answered, *"That, Sir, would depend on how fast he walked."* Well, in either of those last two places, Purryer Camp or the Dexter Lake House (more like a castle), a man could make himself comfortable as a king, safe as in a fort. Neither one of those places was more than six or seven miles away by crow-flight from that mud spring. *When he hits one of them places, come crosslots not too far and fetch some good eating, for himself and his partner.* When Mister Murder Man did that, Clarence would know right where to look for them. *I wouldn't need no posse to surround you, my boy. Come catch you red-handed at your feast, solo.* Though what he might be required to do then, by the ballad that would be sung about his life, Clarence feared to think.

Millard Frary had been avoiding the question of breaking the roads in the sugarbush. This could be one of those years when there would be too much snow by the end of March for the team to get through, pulling the sap sled. Normally Clarence would be at him to break roads about now, but Clarence was assigned to the hunt. Millard thought maybe this would be the year he didn't sugar at all. Such a year must come.

At least he might have waited a bit longer, left to himself. But Grace kept bringing it up, and the horses did need exercise. "Do it!" Grace had urged. "Come March you'll be glad you did." So one morning after breakfast he went down to the barn and brushed down the animals, aware of having been just a little bit pushed to do it.

While he was still at his patient brushing the barn door opened and closed with a flash of outdoor light and Grace appeared in the dark stable dressed in a pair of his wool pants and a thick jacket, and toting a hamper which she held up with a smile. It looked as if they were going to have a picnic up at the sugar-shanty. She was quite flushed by her decision to come along. Very young in face, his wife; very like the girl she had been. But he looked at her with suspicion.

They harnessed both horses there in the stable, on the dirt floor between the stalls, she handing him the parts of the harness just as they came off the pegs on the wall, each side. Then she slid the door open and he led them out and up the ramp to the level of the yard, to back them up to the hay-wagon in the machinery-shed. They needed the hay-wagon for the trip to the bush, because the sap-sled was stored up there, in the woodshed of the sugar-shanty.

The horses knew where they were going, paused for the gates to be opened and turned by themselves along the fence at the edge of the woods. They followed an invisible way along the fence to the sagging old shanty, a very cartoon of dilapidation. The big flue was down inside, lying on the overturned pans of the evaporator, and the shutters of the raised roof, where the steam would billow out in another month and a half, were closed. The place so silent now would hiss, then, with the seething sap, and the fire in the arch would rumble.

With a load of sap Millard would drive the team up the ramp on the up-hill side of the shanty, to halt on top and lower the big spout and let the clear sap run into the storage pans by gravity. But now they passed on the downhill side, along by the windows, to the open-sided farther end, the wood-shed, stacked almost full of three-foot wood. The sap-sled didn't come into view when it should have. It had been pushed to the far side, and in its place was Amos's black and purple Arctic Cat.

"Whoa," Millard said to the horses, and they stopped. "Wonder how long that's been there."

Gracie said brightly, "I knew it! I knew he'd give that back."

They both looked around, as they dismounted the hay-wagon. But there were no tracks, only the vague depression made by the snow-machine itself, coming under the eave onto a bare ground of bark and chips. "Been here some time," Millard said.

"Oh, I wish he'd have come in, for a doughnut and a glass of milk! He was right here, so close! I could have given him a few things for her, you know?"

Millard looked a little sharply at his wife.

"I wouldn't tell on him! He knows that!"

No, he thought. *You wouldn't tell your husband, to start with.*

They rode the sap-sled standing, either side of the big upright spout, trying not to grab it for balance when the sled thumped and tilted suddenly over hidden rocks and roots. The lazy horses paused to listen to the birds now and again, then blew and shook their bells and agreed to push on. As they looped and looped through the familiar ways among the leafless maples, Millard said, "I guess you got me to break roads today just so's to show me Amos's machine."

"But isn't this nice? Aren't you glad you did?"

"That little basket of things for the girl, I'm surprised you mentioned it. I noticed when it disappeared."

"Well anyway. Vi will be relieved. You know that sled was supposed to have been Violet's, but she just didn't like it. Too fast, too powerful for me, she said; so Amos had traded with her. She wanted him to put in an insurance claim on it, but Amos wouldn't."

She stopped, aware of chattering. They rode along, letting the horses rest when they wanted to but not as long as they wanted.

Millard said, 'The girl must be all right, I take it. You'd have told me, if anything was wrong."

"As far as anybody knows," she said. "But I'm ashamed to tell you how little I learned. He made me promise to wait to tell you."

"Well. You can tell me now, I guess."

So she described the visit, little by little, as she remembered it:

The sun had gone around the west end of the house and she didn't have any direct sunlight in her kitchen. Millard was almost due home for his chores, and when her summer-kitchen door suddenly opened and light poured in around somebody's silhouette she half thought she had failed to hear his loose-fendered truck drive into the hard. But, Land sakes, it was Robert Sochia. She knew it even though there was no face, no tall wide-brimmed hat, no red-and-black hunter's woolens, just the halo of the sunlight from behind him firing up the fur fringe of a white hood, within which his face was a dark blank. The rest of him was all white, a voluminous white parka, down to below his knees.

Sure enough, Robert Sochia, in an old war-surplus ski-soldier's parka. That was lynx-fur, around his face. She knew those parkas, people had them right after the War, two layers of cotton, reversible, white one way out and olive drab the other. Long and loose; you had to wear sweaters and longjohns under them but they were warm, and they were good camouflage against snow. She wanted to hug him, but didn't, somehow intimidated, conscious of her short, round self, the flour on her arms as usual. The kitchen was too hot, the ceiling too low for him, as large and wild as he looked. She passed around him and closed the door on that force of light from behind him.

But she didn't get anything out of him. He wasn't there to convey information. He filled himself up on her hot oatmeal cookies and cold raw milk and gave a backward, upwards nod of the head, toward the hills out back. "Mr Cheney's sled," he said, his mouth full. And then he stood to leave. Already! He wasn't in a talking mood, or a listening one, either. He wasn't in this world!

But she could hardly argue, because Millard might turn in at any moment. She didn't want to force her husband into a secret he didn't want to keep. All she'd managed to do was give Robert the basket of things—socks, mittens, a knit cap with ear-flaps—she'd set aside in case she had the chance to send them. She went out behind him with her broom and swept the path down to the barn, to destroy his tracks. She could have lain down full length between his footprints, which were more like bomb-bursts. She followed through the horse-stable. Out back of the barn, she couldn't even see how he'd gone, but she imagined him taking huge strides, zig-zag, stepping in the horses' brown hoofprints, then in the water to cross the book. She caught a dash of movement up toward the woods, disappearing in a depression, appearing further along and higher up. Up in the air, it seemed. Or was that a crow?

He'd been hot. He'd been in mid-flight. But he did look wonderful, so dark, with the hood pulled back off his shiny black hair, the gold hoop shaded by the lynx-fur at his ear.

During that cold snap the thinking was, RS and his charge would be indoors. They were nice and cozy somewhere, don't worry. The boys would be fools to be out there freezing their toes and fingers searching for a track. He'd given up moving and was hunkered down deep under the snow, with plenty of heat and plenty to eat. For that matter he might be down in Lake Placid, or back up in Montreal for the season. He might be lying on a towel beside her on some beach in Florida. "Never forget Florida. He'll get there eventually!" Billy said with a laugh.

JoAnn smiled at all of this with what almost seemed like tolerance, surprisingly. She herself seemed to be relaxing into this passage of time. They all did. Winter was like that. A lot of time. You keep warm, and everything else just keeps. One day in March she asked Harry if he had ever seen the movie *The Hustler*. "Piper Laurie, George C. Scott. Jackie Gleason? And that little shit with the blue eyes, what's his name everybody thinks is so cute?"

No, What about it, unspoken. Harry was not a moviegoer, nor a supplier of obligatory lines.

"Oh, there was a thing in that movie that I always remembered. About losers."

She looked around the bar, smiling. "Paul Newman and Jackie Gleason are having a serious game of pool: the brilliant, cocky young kid, the old champ, past his prime. The kid's winning. He can do no wrong. He's making terrific shots one after the other, jumping balls over each other, spinning then off the cushions. He's hot. Jackie Gleason's beat. He's fat, you know, he's soaked with sweat. He goes in the lavatory, takes off his shirt and washes up. He puts on his shirt, his tie, his jacket. The kid's laughing at him, gloating. It looks like he's going home. But unh-uh. All refreshed, tidied up, Minnesota Fats shoots his cuffs, picks up his cue. Minnesota Fats, that's his name. Chalks his cue, sinks a ball. Walks around the table, sinks another. Makes every shot. He turns the match right around. The kid's too drunk to shoot well now, and Minnesota runs right over him."

She looked around the bar again, and back to Harry, waiting. "Well," she said, "Next day George C. Scott tells the kid, 'I wouldn't bet on you, you know why? You're a loser. Know what a loser is? A loser is a guy who always gives himself an excuse to lose.'"

Her son Peter, at his usual place along the bar, in front of those sunny pictures of young Raymond the sailor-boy, was supposed to hear that and did hear it. "So? What's the point, Ma?"

She hunched her shoulders, unconcernedly.

"I ain't no loser, Ma. I don't get drunk when I'm trying to do something."

"Good. I'm proud of you."

"Why don't *you* go out there and find him, Ma?"

"Oh, I'll think of some excuse."

Such bits of dialogue, actually heard or reported to him, Leo happily noted down. Others that should have been spoken, must have been spoken, but that he and his sources had missed actually

hearing, he made up quite confidently. The difference between
the two kinds of information didn't amount to much, to one so
attuned to the talk of the town.

For now, he couldn't do Julia at all. It seemed to be beyond
his ear, memory, and imagination, to get her onto paper. She was
way too alive, way too foreign to these women he really knew and
knew he could do. When he tried to imitate her, she came off
silly, childish, an embarrassment to his love for her. And he just
did not know what was going on up in the woods. But never fear!
Authors have ways of making up their deficits. Research, for
instance. In this case, he would find a way to get it all out of her
at the end. Somehow, when this ended, she would come out of
the woods. Needing protection, maybe; needing rest. Needing
isolation from the curious. Needing, call it, nursing. Who better
than Leo himself, to provide such things? And where better than
the Wellers' inviolate house?

And whatever the outcome with Robert, she had to confront
her benefactress. Aunt Sarah still had to introduce her to her secret
old great-aunties, in the hope that they would leave her their farm.
There would have to be a certain amount time for that to happen
in, and Leo would be there, her servant, her confidant, possibly
her only true, forgiving and understanding friend in this world.

Meanwhile those quotations from the Love book haunted him.
There was more where they came from. Mircea Eliade, such a
name. He persuaded his father to accompany him to Moira, to the
library at the College. (He still had his license, but Père didn't like
him driving with his medications.) And lo what a title Marjorie
found for him, under Eliade, M.: *The Myth of the Eternal Return*!
Wasn't Robert the exile, the outlier, trying to come back home?
Did Leo Weller have a great universal theme on his hands, or what?
Did he know it all along?

Back in his room, he curled up with his dry, difficult, eye-
popping reading, and lo, what he found therein! Mircea Eliade
was another of those incredible scholars who seem to have read
everything, from all parts of the world, in all literatures, through
all historical time. Sabattis Falls was clearly what Eliade called an

archaic society, in which the people do not live in history, in regular historical time, but in some other kind of time, where they see themselves as merely reiterating the deeds of their ancestors, the Titans who performed the only truly great deeds far in the past. "That's us!" he cried. He found that the people of archaic societies tell and re-tell the stories of these great forbears, hoping only to regenerate and reiterate their myths, never thinking of themselves as new, as creating a future, making Progress. "That's us! That's us!" He had his handle on Robert, trying to make a story for the town to tell that would match him up with Jean St. Jean Baptiste: an archaic man.

As for Robert's voice, he had always known better than to spill his assets in talk. Think of his testimony: *"Did you shoot to warn him?" "No." "Did you shoot to wound him?" "No." "Did you shoot to kill him?" "No." Then why on earth did you shoot him, Mr Sochia?" "I just pulled up the rifle and fired."* So far as RS was concerned, less was more. Robert Sochia was going to be a being created by hearsay and gossip; because that was what he really was, to the town. To himself, too, perhaps! Robert Sochia was already almost-myth. Modest Leo didn't think he could handle full-blown myth-making, anyway. Nor could his subject. Sabattis Falls was not Troy! Nor was Olmstead County Yoknapatawpha. But Robert was almost almost-myth already.

20

I'm Here

She walked. She was a good walker. She took his hand for balance or a pull up when she needed to. She looked about her. She went ahead sometimes. If she was ahead she didn't worry about the saplings and branches she bent whipping back into his face. They were his problem. When she crossed a brook on the snow-capped stones and climbed a bank on the other side she didn't turn back and offer him a hand. She took care of herself.

She didn't speak. That was clear from the start. He wouldn't get a word from her. He could interpret her silence any way he liked. It could mean many things. Her anger. His being beyond the pale. It could mean just what it was, that she wasn't talking. He wouldn't know for sure.

That was all right with him apparently. He didn't talk either. When he did say anything it was as a teacher. "Spruce." "Balsam." White pine, red pine. Rabbit. Spruce grouse. He was in his own world and time.

She didn't talk and she didn't eat, either. Not eating came to her just as clearly, as naturally. Let him cope with that too. He found food, offered her food, brought her things from his forays, wherever he went, sometimes very tempting. She'd fasted before, she knew how her body reacted. She took a little liquid, cheated a little. She spared herself completely when they weren't traveling, only got out of her blankets to pee.

This was just one more outrage. This wasn't the end of the world. She needed to get away from everything anyway; and think, and wait. But she was a city girl and a good walker and she walked when she had to. When he found a place where apparently he thought it was safe to stay for a day or two, where he could leave her and know that she was truly lost and would still be there when he came back, she slept. She practically went into hibernation.

She was cold, of course she was cold, and her boots until he brought her some really good ones from somewhere were no good, but she was not a baby and she could stand it and the walking kept her warm enough and if her toes got cold she forgot about them, until they were holed up somewhere and she could warm them up. Then they hurt terribly for a while and she learned to warm them up with the cold water he offered her for it. When they were traveling her hands with two pairs of mittens stayed warm from her warm blood. She imagined people were pitying her if they were thinking about her but she was soon used to the cold and walked and kept warm and coped with it and soon enough it was nothing. Most of the time they were down in the woods near streams and it was very rough and rocky under the snow and no trails, no roads, and thick evergreen woods, or thick willow-like bushes, so thick and hard to get through sometimes that she would have asked him what was the point, if she had been talking. Like, was this really necessary? But she grew to like the swamps. The low, flat places, wet sometimes down under the snow. They were springy underfoot, and they were warmer and sheltered. She could see how they were like homes to the deer, full of hideaways from the wind and the deer made these deep deep trails in them, scattered with their droppings; little round beds that looked blissfully comfortable, under low boughs.

Robert was so good at seeing the deer. He'd make a minimum gesture for her eyes to follow and at first she wouldn't see them even then. All he'd be seeing was some half of a hind leg or something, that looked just like a part of a sapling until you got the idea. She made up her mind to learn to see them first. Point one out to him some day, that he didn't already know about.

At first the woods were just a mess to her. Really, Nature? Everything falling and leaning and rotting and broken everywhichway. Trees were supposed to be so beautiful but she just saw deformity everywhere and was irritated at it, until she got used to it. This was nature's system, make a lot more than you need and then it doesn't matter if millions die. These poor dumb things, trees. Individually just trying to grow up, toward the sun, but all kinds of bad things happen to them. Ice storms, windstorms. Animals trample them, eat them, they fall down and hurt each other, bend each other over, break off each other's limbs. No such thing as a nice neat old plain old tree that grew up undamaged. Really! She searched the forest for one undamaged tree. Cripples! All cripples! Just like (guess what?) us!

Bobby told her that the nice innocent deer were the worst thing for the trees. Nibble away at any sapling that even just barely makes it up through the leaves and snow. If there are many deer, the little trees never escape! Never survive sapling-hood. Except beech, she knows beech now. They leave the beech saplings alone, because they want them to grow up and have beech-nuts. So then there's just the little beeches and all the big tall trees, and big trees' branches mushroom together way up and block out the sky. So then there isn't any sunlight down there in the rotten leaves where the little saplings have to grow anyway, so they don't even get up through the snow in the first place.

Bobby showed her what happened when a big old tree got rotten and fell down dead: there's a hole in the canopy overhead, and now the sunlight does get down to the ground in a little area, and the leaf-duff is rich and ready to go, so there's an *explosion* of saplings growing. Explosion of *beech* saplings, that is, because the hungry deer eat everything else, maple, birch, cherry, but they don't eat beech. They eat the twigs, buds. So pretty soon the woods are all beech, and nobody wants beech trees including the deer. So the *deer* all starve. Jeesis!

She didn't know deer ate wood in the first place. In the winter they'll eat cedar and hemlock needles. Around the edges of ponds, they eat the cedars up as high as they can reach, standing on their hind legs, on the ice, and it makes a level line as if the gardener went around with a clipper and clipped the underside of all the cedar trees.

The trees came to be something else to her. Every tree was a hard column of strength. They might be beat-up and broken up high but at her level every one was a pillar.

In the beginning when she and Robert moved every day or night they sometimes followed roads some of which were plowed and used and some deep in unmoved snow. Mostly they followed lines of marked trees. Ah, she'd thought, *Blazed trails, Natty Bumppo and all.* She was inclined to be impressed with men's woodcraft since this was something she didn't know anything about. But weren't you supposed to cut a piece out of the bark of a tree every so often? With a hatchet? That's what you call a blaze, right? These bozos walked through the woods with a pail of paint and a brush and just swiped a big up-and-down swipe of paint on practically every tree along the trail. It was crude. Ugly. Disrespectful to the trees. Or else they did it with a spray-can, psst-psst, so lazy. Day-glo orange. Yellow. Red, her least favorite color, truly ugly in the woods.

These new nowadays white-men didn't keep the trails clear, either. On the trails there were always fallen trees to go over or under or around or through. The hunters just made a detour around them, through brush that would trip you (deer-hobble) and saplings that would whip you in the eyes. When she was stumbling after Robert in the dark she felt like cursing those men for their laziness. Didn't the Indians use to pick up every twig in their paths so they could go quiet-quiet? I thought these white men were trying to be like Indians, like Deerslayer.

Sometimes they would be on a trail with no paint drips all over the trees and only old-old hatchet-blazes, almost grown over, far apart and only on very big old trees, and she guessed that they were on an ancient path that most men nowadays didn't even know about, though Bobby did, in some part of the woods that really was a wilderness. These places were spooky and magical to her. And she and Robert really did sleep out under the roots of a fallen tree! In those forests the biggest trees were huge old things, with rough reddish bark, hemlocks, hanging in there, man, two hundred years old. Too old, some of them, huge pines woodpeckered to death, or in other places old old maples and cherries, lots of recent

crashes giving a break to the young. Great deer feed but no deer.
So it goes. The Vonnegut phrase came to her a lot.

She preferred to stay low, in what he called swamps but were
not what she thought of as swamps, sheltered, warm, springy
underfoot, and more colorful, or less chiaroscuro, with the flaxen
and gold colors of the grasses making you see the dark dark greens
better. But Robert sometimes led them up high. He hauled her
up many hills. He seemed to like the higher places and though the
hills were round-topped and forest-covered there were always rocky
bluffs and faces where they could see over the country below and
she guessed that he was thinking out his moves though nothing
she could see helped her to know where she was. Maybe he could
hear things better from high places. Sometimes you could hear the
loggers' machines, or chainsaws or whatever. See smoke.

She didn't know what was the point of climbing this mountain.
She didn't want to climb it but she wasn't talking and so she didn't
complain or ask why. She wasn't yet even looking him in the eye. He
hardly gave her the chance. It didn't look like a very big mountain
but it was steep even at the bottom and she saw that there was a trail
up it, a trail that seemed to go almost straight up the slope along
what she supposed was a telephone line, some kind of a wire going
up from tree to tree beside the trail. Of course he didn't lead her up
the trail, somebody might find their tracks; he led her diagonally up
the shady side where the snow was deeper but there were small bare
trees with smooth greenish bark, he called them popples, closely
spaced so you could pull yourself up from one to the next. They
were so pure and hard and clean and such a nice color, gray-green
with black triangles where little low branches had been.

She didn't get the point until they were finally up there, by
the old fire tower. She couldn't see to the north because of the trees
but the south side of the top of the mountain was bare rock, curving
down steeply, dizzyingly, into a void, out of sight, and over that
scary void she could see far in that direction, south, all the way to
another real mountain a long way south, and higher peaks way
beyond that. From the fire tower she'd be able to see that far all
around. Now she wanted to be up here, she wanted to see.

He told her the state abandoned these old fire towers long ago. The first two stages of the stairs that zigzagged up the tower had been removed and wire fencing wrapped around the bottom of the angle-iron legs, signs hung on it, KEEP OFF. But this fencing had been torn open where it overlapped, probably by summer hikers, and she could see by the way the metal was worn that they climbed up the angle-iron bracing to the remaining flights of steps suspended above. He offered her his hand, but she went inside the fencing and started up on the diagonal bracing by herself. She felt him guiding her boots and keeping them from slipping. She pulled herself up with her hands just as much. Above the wire fencing she switched around to the outside. It was colder the higher they went but she took off her mittens for a better grip on the rusted steel and put them in her mouth. When she was high enough she straddled the rail and swung over to the suspended landing and ran up, zig-zag up and up, because it was really cold in the wind. At the top the trap-door was open, she crawled onto the floor of the cab and stood up.

Not much shelter, because the windows were gone, but the view was tremendous and the height was dizzying and she was already looking around at the whole three hundred sixty degree panorama when he blocked out part of it. Between them was a circular map under glass, on a pedestal, where a swiveling liner-upper-thing had held a telescope, probably. There was a transparent ruler under it that swung around with it so you could tell the direction and distance to whatever you were looking at.

Where are we? That wasn't a question for him. She'd have to look him in the eye to communicate that way. She answered herself, rolling her lips and looking. *We're in the middle of this map.* It said Azure Mountain near the missing worn-out center of the map, where the ruler pivoted. So this fire tower was on Azure Mountain. She'd never heard of Azure Mountain. But azure was blue and she knew about Blue Mountain. There was the Blue Mountain Road, just out the Stark's Mill Road a few miles past the infamous Gokey Road. And Leo had told her about Blue Mountain. No, he had *showed* her Blue Mountain. You could see Blue Mountain, she had seen it, from Cooks' Lake, where the Wellers and Mrs Bryant had their summer camps. Leo had paddled her down that lake in a canoe and he had pointed it out to her, bubbling over to tell her his naughty idea about it. It didn't look very big from there, it looked like just a little mound from there, between long low hills on either side like legs and knees, and Leo said it was the *mons veneris* of a supine giantess, a sweet round-topped mound right in the crotch. So in paddling down to the far end of the lake to show her that old lumber baron's camp, they were penetrating the wilderness, a titanic lady on her back. Leo, what a kook.

So she was on top of the *mons*. So where was that lake? She and Leo had been paddling east, she thought. Or, southeast. So the lake should be west, or northwest. She got the bearings from the map and looked out. West and northwest from the tower there were two lakes, one beyond the other, not in a line. She looked back to the map. The nearer one was . . . Dexter Lake, not it. But the farther one, beyond and to the left, was Cook's Lake. It didn't look long and skinny like on the map. It was foreshortened, extremely. But she could interpret it, un-foreshorten it in her mind: the bigger bay at the other end where little black squares represented buildings—most of the cottages were at that end, and those two islands, one big, one little, almost touching—they were right out in front of the Wellers' camp. She could see them, like a mother duck and her duckling. How far? Swing the ruler over. Fourteen miles.

He was watching her figure it out. Well, what else? She could see from here, surely, the whole territory they had been in, were in, would be in. Robert didn't point anything out to her but he let her look, and surmise, and consider where the sun had been today and yesterday as they moved. She could see several ponds to the southeast and south, and right down in front of her, as if at her feet, the winding river (check: Sabattis, but of course!) where the alders had been so thick. Beyond the broad plain of the river, that other bigger mountain was . . . St. Regis. Off the east side of the plain there were glimpses of white road. Just one road in all this view? The Brighton Road. To the east another big long high-backed hill, DeBar Mountain, that she couldn't see beyond. The limit, she supposed, in that direction.

She turned slowly, counter-clockwise, looking for the Falls, to place all this in relation to the town. She couldn't see any town to the north but she could see civilization, that way, bits of paved road, houses, barns, open fields among the lower hills. There was maybe Risdonville or Chittenden or the farms between. The Falls was hidden by hills *but sure, that figures, you can't see Blue Mountain from the Falls, either.* And then the descending, dishing, whiter landscape to the north, toward the St. Lawrence River and Canada. You could see the plants near Massena, the smoke of the paper mill at Cornwall, and, turning clockwise again, Montreal, Mount Royal itself! rising from the plain and far beyond it, faintly, even the Laurentians. Finishing her turn she licked her lips and then looked right at him for a second, bravely. Almost sent him a message by telepathy, *How come you're showing me this?* Maybe he didn't think they were enemies.

Then sniffed. Her teeth were chattering.

Cold up here in the wind with the windows out.

Not me, he seemed to say. *I'm perfect.*

She hadn't imagined there were so many camps. She hadn't imagined what hunting camps were like, either. They were not necessarily old or rustic or woodsy. They didn't smell of pipe-tobacco and whiskey and wool and gunpowder, as she would have sort of liked, upside-downly, if she'd thought about it, which she hadn't. They were made out of junky little trailers or Quonset huts or re-used lumber and old storm windows and tarpaper and linoleum. Some of them had been patched together by klutzes, like little boys' forts or clubhouses. Once in a while Robert broke into one that was like a regular house (boring), with a cellar and imitation-wood walls and plastic kitchen counters and a furnace, and a telephone yet.

Weirdly, they were *clean*. She felt that she and Robert ought to sweep off their boots before they set foot in them. The hunters did, apparently. Swept every little bit of twigs and dirt off their

overlapping scraps of leftover carpet. Ashes and cinders from the
stove. Kept the broom beside the door. She pictured grownup
men like little old housewives, in red-topped stocking-feet, shuffling
around sweeping all the time. Each of them must have a wife inside
his head, like an internalized parent, telling him, "Tidy-tidy!"

Except for being clean the places were frugal and negligent.
We came to hunt, man. Hunt and play cards. Flake out, eat, sleep.
What the hunters made surest of was heat. Stoves in the main
camps, stoves in the sleeping rooms. Piles of good dry firewood
under cover, tanks of kerosene. Old iron bedsprings hung from the
rafters over the stoves, to dry things on, exactly what she needed.

She would be following the fuzzy blackness of Robert's
footprints in the snow, and she would hear him, ahead somewhere
in the dark, rap a hollow-sounding propane tank. Then she would
hear a window break, and when she could make out the shape of
the camp she would search around it for the outhouse and she
would bare her warm bottom and sit on the cold ring of wood,
trying to see, through the open door, if there were any stars. She
liked to know where the Big Bear was, so she could find Polaris,
north, or Orion in his arc. But usually the night was so black that
the whiteness of the roll of paper on a nail beside her would be her
only company. That and the quiet and her body-warmth and the
sprinkle-sound of her pee splashing a frozen like sand-castle under
her, and her tiny hard b.m. giving a little pat when it hit, amid the
click and creak of bare frozen trees. A dim yellow glow would
appear, from a window in the camp, Robert finding the gaslight.
She'd be greeted inside by the smell of sheet-metal warming up,
dust on the stove-top smoldering.

There would be something for him to eat—nuts, instant coffee,
stale crackers, dried soup, a frozen can of ravioli or beans. If he
found Bisquick he'd make pancakes, and have them with sugar if
he had to, but there was usually Aunt Jemima or even real maple
syrup. There might be jam or jelly and peanut butter and he'd
make biscuits instead. She watched him, snitched his crumbs. She
watched him splitting firewood, cooking, bathing, washing his
socks. He did everything so economically. He was so formal. He

was trying so hard, to control everything that he did and that happened and make it fit a standard, a style. Her silence fit his style, and his style was Spartan and pure and that is the way she needed to be too, while she gathered herself and figured him out and figured her body out.

You'd think they would both be disgusting. They were the homeless. But his hair shone in the gas light. There was great color in his face. When he finished washing himself she would step into the same space, where the hunters washed dishes and shaved. There was maybe a little peeling mirror tilted down from under a shelf. She looked in the mirror and saw herself. There was color in her cheeks too. The light from the frosted globe of the gas lamp behind her gave her hair a halo. She backed up and looked down, and there were her very own sockfeet on this specific wet, worn linoleum, and she'd sing to herself, "I'm here."

She'd think, "Bobby thinks he's carrying me all over the woods but I am carrying myself. He thinks he's taking care of me but I'm taking care of me. I'm going to take care of you, too, Bobby," she thought. She didn't know how. She had to figure that out.

Then he led her on a long southwesterly hike through country where there had been no human travel in many snows and left her alone in a place he called Center Camp. It had been a large clearing, now grown up with pretty birches, healthy trees that grew in the open, that she thought must be thirty or forty years old. Children of the Depression. There was an old, clapboarded, two-storey house, empty but intact, and there were barns, and ways went off in the woods in different directions. He left her in an old hewed-log cabin that seemed older than the house and barns, along one edge of the clearing, half hidden between the mole of a railroad bed and the evergreens. The cabin might have been there before the railroad too. He said he had some places to go but he didn't want her to walk any more for a while. He was probably going to bring something back that he thought would tempt her to eat, but it wouldn't. She was into her fast.

She was just as glad to be left alone. She had all she needed. There was a stove and wood and a bed and blankets and water, and a calendar about fifteen years old on the log wall chinked with old newspaper. Even a white porcelain chamber-pot, the luxury! She paid no attention to what he'd left for her to eat. She was into her fast, she was okay, she felt so thin and clean. She could explore the house and barns, if she got bored, or tame a chipmunk with some crackers. She'd move like a zombie, slow herself down to the metabolism of the deer. She'd let time flow around her, light, dark, light, dark. Because what she had to do most of all, all she had to do besides think, was let time pass. How much had passed already? Two weeks? More? She hadn't counted carefully at first, and now she didn't have any idea of the date. She'd better establish a guess and count carefully from now. Wait and find out, if she was or wasn't—blank. She didn't like to say the word even to herself, an ugly word in English. It was better in French. If she ever said it she'd say it in French. If she was or wasn't *that*.

He would only be gone two days and two nights but without him and his rituals the days themselves lost their form. She didn't explore. She stayed in bed. She didn't take the chamber-pot very far outside to empty it. There wasn't much to pour out, anyway, and the snow hid it. She was undisciplined, she sort of fell apart.

She had time to think, but it was as if time almost prevented her from thinking. Thinking is split-second fast; how do you do it slowly? She hardly could. She would make herself be methodical and try to think consequentially but after the first baby-steps she got no further, she just said the stupidest obvious things to herself over and over. *The first important fact is, I was raped. That was rape, whether they got anything into me or not.* She had been violated by cretins by force. That was one simple fact. And maybe this was the second, she had to put it in here every time: it didn't touch her. Not the real her. It wasn't going to damage her or her life or her mind, and she wasn't going to cry about it or demand justice or anything like that. Because that would be to give those cretins and the value-system that let them think they were doing a community service too much credit. That would be giving them a victory of sorts. Lots of women are raped, that's what she was fighting about, that's what she was trying to teach about. It's nasty but she was untouched, intact. That's what intact means and she was. That's fact number two.

Number three? If she could write it down—but she wasn't a writer-downer and she had nothing to write with or on. She was a letter-writer. If she could write it in letters to somebody she could have put her thoughts down more consecutively. So she tried to think as if she were writing. To whom? To Leo, maybe. To Michael. To Gramps best. *Hi Gramps. I'm at Center Camp! Didya ever hear of Center Camp when you were up around here, chasing the lumber-boys' little sister?* There was probably a center camp in every logging company's territory in the olden days. They had so many camps, Bobby had told her, that they numbered them. She'd stayed with him in a place called Number Four.

Dear Gramps, I was raped, but I'm intact. She had made herself a virgin again more than once. *You might think that's funny, Gramps, but no kidding, I have.*

But I am afraid I might be dot dot dot, but not necessarily by the rapers. But maybe by them. Here was the third fact: not a fact but a determination, a fixed resolve; a fact as far as anybody else was concerned: whatever did or didn't get inside of her in that rape, in a crazy, crazy way, if she turned out to be blank (*enceinte),* it was the rape that got her that way. Period. She didn't get pregnant some other way. Fact Number Three was going to help her get out of this, some way or other. She was going to need it. She didn't know how, but she had a sort of fore-sense that she was going to need it. And she had a right to it.

She had been a fool that night in Montreal, she had made a little human mistake, the mistake she promised herself never never to make but she made it, out of kindness, not need. It was a measure of Bobby's awful need, not hers. She made it for him and it wouldn't be fair if she had to pay for it, it was so rare a slip. He was so stricken at the idea that she didn't want to fuck, it was such a blow to him, incomprehensible, that finally she was touched. She had given him some good loving, as good as she knew how, and she did know how and she was not selfish and she could fake anything, to make a person happy. But she had gone immediately into the *salle de bain* and let it drip out. And she douched and douched and she promised she'd never do it again. Anyway she didn't think the timing was *that* bad, at the time. With any luck it wasn't. Because the little swimmers would have had to live . . . how long? Until she felt the egg move, the z-z-z-zing in her side, and that was when she was driving home alone in her own little white stupid car. Two hours later? But did she really feel that? Neva didn't believe she could feel that. Maybe Neva was right and she couldn't have and she didn't and there was just nothing to worry about. But she'd thought she felt it then and she hadn't felt it later and women *know* these things about their bodies. She was afraid and she wasn't afraid for nothing. But the point, the point, the point was, for sure there was no reason to allow anybody, especially Bobby, to get the idea that Robert Sochia's sperm ever got near any egg. The father was a malformed triangular dwarf with one eyebrow over both eyes and a long down-pointy nose.

But then what? She had to think new thoughts, think through the hard stuff, the stuff she always avoided even though she had nothing but time to think now, and other times when he'd left her alone. Think what to do, if. If various ifs came to pass. If she was, then what. There was Bobby, and what he knew or didn't know, and what he guessed, and what he thought he was doing, abducting her. And then there was the town, and what it knew or didn't know, and what it thought Bobby was trying to do, and what it thought it was doing. Think think think! Neva Day might have been keeping closer track of her periods than she did herself. That would be just like her. What if she knew how ripe Julia had been just then? If she found out about the rape, she'd have been doubly, triply horrified, and then what if she told somebody her fears?

She had to *think* about this! If the town jumped to conclusions, were those people who were trying to find them thinking of *her* needs? That's a Catholic town, mostly! Wouldn't they be trying to rescue her in order to help her go away somewhere and have the baby and give it up for adoption and keep the rape a secret and keep their town from disgrace?

Nobody could know, nobody could understand, how much she couldn't have a baby! If she was pregnant, then the little baby wasn't going to get to be born and live a life and that was terribly terribly sad and too bad but it wasn't a baby yet and it wasn't going to be, that was all. She never wanted that to happen and she tried to make sure to never let it happen and maybe it hadn't happened but maybe it had, but she had made up her mind a long long time ago what she would do if it ever did happen because she had ambitions! Hard hard scary ones! She couldn't have a baby! Not now. Not *ever*, probably. She loved babies and little children so much but she had to give her baby-love to other people's babies. Some people, serious artists especially, had to do that.

At least she was pretty sure that *that* wasn't why Bobby abducted her. It wasn't because he thought she might be *enceinte*, and that she was getting ready to go away to do it harm. *That* wasn't why he abducted her. *Let's say we're sure of that.* Because if he knew, and knew they knew, wouldn't this be just what he would be taunting them with, trying to get them to try to do and admit that they were trying to do? Save the town from disgrace?

The rape was addressed to him, not her. He did know that. They must have told him, bragged about it to him. *That's* why he abducted her. The abduction, likewise, was not addressed to her, it was addressed to them. She wasn't even really involved! Anybody could read Susan Brownmiller if they didn't get it. *He wants them to come after me. And they have to do it. And they are. And he is making fools of them. So then what? Think think think. What's it prove? How does he see it ending? What do I have to do to get it to end?*

Go back to the abduction. It's more than just to shame the town with the rape that was done in its name. Why? Why does he want them to come after me, after us, after him? To show them that he isn't afraid? Yes, but that isn't all. To make them admit their own cowardly acts? Yes, but that isn't it either. There's more. It's ultimately to make them kill him and thus pay up for killing Raymond, and be famous forever and ever for being cuckoo. Stupid stupid stupid but that is it. He may not even know

*it himself but that's why. And the foolish wrong stupid idea he has about
how he feels about me is what gives him the courage to do it.*

He didn't come along the railroad bed, he came out of the dark
woods behind the cabin and alongside it under the eaves. She
heard him scraping past the logs behind her bed. That wouldn't
be anybody else but him, contriving to make tracks nobody would
notice from ten feet away. Now he blocked the light from the pane
in the door, and she listened as he stamped his feet. With a sudden
eagerness she imagined him shrugging off the pack and holding
out a milkshake for her. *She wanted a strawberry milkshake.* She
wouldn't even try to resist temptation if he brought her a milkshake.
If he had enough imagination he could do it. He could think of it,
if he tried at all.

He pushed the door in and came and looked at her, carefully.
No, he hadn't had that much imagination. Too much to expect.
But he was awfully vivid, dark face, snow sparkling on his beard.
She wondered what she looked like. Messy old lazy old frau under
a heap of rugs. He opened his coat and showed her a big bag of
unsalted peanuts, with raisins and chocolate chips mixed into them.
They swept milkshake out of her mind. *You've been to a health-food
store, huh?* That would make her vomit, probably, but how would
she keep her fingers out of it? She shook her head at him and kept
her hands under the covers and telegraphed him one word, *broth.*

He pulled up a can of chicken noodle soup.

Pretty good at code, Bobby, she sent.

21

Cold Cow

Nowadays JoAnn kept a fancy, multi-colored ceramic biplane from her ceramics collection right down on the bar. Whenever Peter came in she slid it in front of him. Pointed it at him, turned it, took it for a little flight and landed it in front of him again. When he paid for his and Francis's beer she flew the airplane up over the taps and around by the cash register and put the money in the drawer and flew it back to a landing in front of Harry, gave him a gay smile, and taxied it on around the bar to a stop against Peter's bottle. The red-and-gold ceramic biplane, shiny, a pert little artifact, seemed very heads-up, resting on the scarred and burned mahogany.

It was obvious what she was getting at. Peter knew it. Harry knew it. It was Billy Atkin who finally said, not quite under his breath, to his neighbor, with a wink, "Say, don't Souver Hubbard have a airplane?"

Souver Hubbard, Peter's father, had several businesses, up on the flat, west of town, all in ostensible confusion. Truck wash, septic systems, hauling. A log truck. This and that for sale, a half finished house in one end of which his present wife did hair. And among his many machines Souver actually did have an airplane. They couldn't remember when Souver had last flown the thing, maybe a couple of years ago

It's what you might call badlands up there west of town. It's flat, but it's all scrub brush. On the way toward Risdonville you go under three orange balls strung over the road and the power lines, and you look around and see that odd-shaped shed, sided in vertical slabwood, that would be T-shaped if you looked down on it, and a narrow swath cut through the brush, going away to the edge of the woods.

Billy said, "I don't think Souver owned no airplane all by hisself. Owned it in a partnership, didn't he? With that insurance fellow up to the lake?"

Other voices were found. "One of them little twin-tailed airplanes. Little thing. Aluminum color. Didn't look safe, to me."

"That ain't aluminum color, that's aluminum. You rather be in an airplane made of aluminum or made of cloth?"

Somebody down the bar cleared his throat and said, "Had skis on that plane once."

After a pause, Billy said, "Be just the thing, you know it? Cover a lot of ground. See a lot from a airplane."

A laugh somewhere. "If you could get Souver to take time off." Souver was a notoriously busy man, dawn to dark. Called his activities, collectively, Spry Company.

So now JoAnn stood in front of Peter, the ceramic biplane between them, and finally said it herself. "Ask him, Peter."

"I don't want to," Peter said.

"Tell him it was my idea."

"Nah, Ma, leave him out of it."

"Tell him I ask him myself! Tell him to quit his God-frustrating work, and forget his hairdressing shrew, and shovel out his runway and *help me!*"

The town plow crew was in there, resting with their coffees at a table. Another cold snowy night. One of the crew yelled out, "Hubbard! Does that thing of your father's still fly? I ain't seen it up in the air in two years or better."

"It flies," Peter said.

"Can he fly it?"

"Yes, he can fly it." Peter said.

To his shotgun the plowman said, "I always thought it was that DeLong's, from up t' the lake. Had some deal with Souver to keep it, make him a runway so he didn't have to go all the way to Malone to fly. But it don't matter, what's the difference?" At large he said, "It ain't ennathin' to scrape the runway. He still got his

license? If he'll do it, I'll plow 'er out with the grader, 'fore day
light. The boss don't have to know."

"Arquit? He wouldn't care."

Peter got out his handkerchief and blew his nose. "My father's
got his own bulldozer."

"Yeah, well. Is it running, is the question. I'd want an airplane
to run better'n some of his other junk."

"My father's stuff is old, but it runs. He takes good care of it."

"All right, let him plow her out himself," the town plowman said.

JoAnn was still in front of Peter. "Something wrong with that?"
she asked.

"Huh?"

"Something wrong with getting your father's help here?"

He looked at her, hesitating.

"What are you going to say?" she said. "It's cheating?"

"No," he said, reluctantly.

"Good. You know you could use a little of your father's
gumption here, Peter. Tell the stingy stinker that he can perfectly
well afford the gas, too."

"I don't know if he has any airplane gas," Peter said.

"No. You don't. But I imagine it can be found."

Peter looked away.

"You're embarrassed. Aw. At bringing woman trouble to your
father. Ha? He's got enough of it!"

"He don't have woman trouble," Peter said.

"What?" his mother said. "He used to, is that what you were
going to say?"

"No, that ain't what I was going to say."

"Listen, sweetie, he will love it. One more thing to cram in
between sunup and sundown. He will eat it up." She took Peter
by the ear. "Ask him!" she said. "Or shall I twist this off?"

Peter rose, wincing. "Okay, okay, Ma!" She let go, smiling.
Peter pressed his ear to his head. "Jesus, Ma! Are you crazy?"

"You said okay. Everybody heard you. Did you mean it?"

Peter circled around and straddled his stool again with his
head down, still holding his ear.

"I don't know why he doesn't want to ask him," she said to the company at large. "If I'm not ashamed to, what's his problem?"

Nobody took this up. Everyone knew that if Peter was ever going to call on his father for help, he'd have to come to it his own way. Even JoAnn accepted this, rather to Leo Weller's surprise, and flew the airplane over to Harry LaFleur, with a pretty smile, and landed it in front of him.

"You know who'd be the man to find Robert Sochia," Billy said quietly to his neighbor. "Hate to say it. Johnny Pelo. No shit. He'd find him. I dunno what side he'd be on, anymore. I mean Robert's brought enough shit down on the Peloses' heads. But Johnny could lead you to him if anybody could. You know it? He prob'ly could." Then with a laugh, slapping the bar: "Helen should thank her lucky stars he's still in jail!"

Meanwhile the town had other things than RS & Co to think about, openly civic and important. One morning while the school-buses were still out on their routes, gathering up the students, the school had called all over to tell the parents the kids were coming right back, or to find out where to take the children whose parents had already left home. The school had no water.

Nothing new about that. Presumably the water system had frozen and busted again, a more or less comforting perennial event which showed that some things stayed the same, if you were careful with your tax dollars. Once every winter or spring there would be a day when at least the school and the Catholic church and that whole higher north end of town would lose pressure because the mains heaved and broke, usually under the streets. Down by the Feed and Coal, or The Rapids, water would come up through the potholes and freeze and make the streets a good place for sleds, not cars, and the kids would have a holiday until they got the problem fixed.

So naturally this time too the town started by digging up the old holes, searching for the underground stream of escaping water. Soon there were piles of ripped-up asphalt and brown dirt and stones blocking the streets all over the lower town. Nobody paid much attention to Skunky Wilson soliloquizing down at the end of Eugene's bar about the olden times when that water system was put in.

"Why don't they ask somebody who was there, for Christ's sake? I can't figure that out. Can you?"

Usually he'd get a head-shake meaning "No, Skunky, I can't," just to soothe him; because if anybody really challenged him, asked him what, exactly, he would do if it was up to him, Skunky would wail, "God-damn it, was I the engineer? I wasn't the engineer, God-damn it, Joe Augustine was the engineer. I was just his assistant!"

"All right, then." The challenger would turn away, and Skunky would yell after him, "But wouldn't you think they would be interested in my opinion?"

There was plenty of water. Nobody doubted that. The pond was full, up there on French Hill, out past Shaheen's. The pond was iced over and deep under snow, but higher than every house in town that wasn't on a well, and spring-fed, and it was always full, only got a little bit low in a dry August. The water was obviously getting loose, underground somewhere, rushing out of a busted main. It sometimes came out on the surface but this year it must have made itself a vein underground all the way into the river. That made no difference. They just had to find the break and put in a patch, as always.

Cones of gravel as tall as a man, with orange sawhorses and sandwich-boards, made a slalom course for the traffic up and down Main Street. Shortage of water-pressure in the houses was good for business in the bars. The first day a busy logger working up south, in the middle of maneuvering his rig up through town, stopped in front of Eugene's house, left his big diesel rattling there and stepped into the restaurant to holler, "Anybody belong to a red Ford pickup that's stuck in the snowbank, on the hill out past Pete's?"

That would be Pete Shaheen's, on the road to Stark's Mill. Nobody present did belong to such a truck, or showed much interest in it. Somebody said, "Did you look at the plates?"

"New York, is all I know. I'd noticed if it was anything else."

The crowd in Eugene's was ready for diversion, airing of grievance, deploring all change. You couldn't tell anything from the license plates anymore, anyway. "You get any damn set of numbers and letters the state wants you to have. Unless you go in in person, early, and ask for the few that has OLM on it. They still gets a few to hand out. Arquit always gets one, I see."

"Well," the logger said, "it's stuck there good, ass-end out in the road. Still got a rifle in the rack in the window. I done my bit." He went back to his rig and pulled away, toward Cornwall.

Duly noted: some poor fool went off the road and didn't get hurt. "A kid, prob'ly, or one of these newcomers that don't know how to drive." A lot of people were showing up in the North Country that weren't born knowing how to drive on snow and ice like everybody present. City people, southerners, all kinds of people, from anyplace you might name, were lately turning up owning little bits of land that you wouldn't even know had been for sale unless you read the tax sale lists in the paper.

Amos pointed out that it wasn't only land that had gone up for back-taxes that was being sold out of the country. Lyle White, a realtor just down in Chittenden, ran a boxed, outlined ad in the classifieds every week: "Wanted to buy, farms, woodlots, land, good prices given," and his box number. "He's got customers lined up, evidently," Amos said.

"Lyle White," somebody said. "Yes, well, he makes a living too."

"Somebody must be answering those ads," said Amos.

"I don't care," Lenny said. "I don't like that. You thinking of selling your place, Millard?"

"Not I."

"So, what's the matter with anybody else holdin' on to their land? God damn it, pay the taxes on it and keep it."

"Easy to say if you ain't got any land. But anybody could get tired of paying one or two hundred dollars a year on some little brushgrown parcel they had already sold the stumpage off of. That's what's happening. One thing that's happening, ennaways."

"Well, don't sell the trees, in the first place! Make syrup, like Millard."

"Lyle White's one of our own. Paul Trussell's one of our own too."

"Yes," Lenny admitted, getting hotter. "And he'll buy anything with wood on it, cut the wood off, and let it go back on the tax-sale list without ever paying no taxes at all. Thanks to him, pretty soon you got another neighbor that lives in New Jersey. It's the truth. You feel as if your country was coming down with the chicken pox, all these New Jersey holes in it."

"You got a problem with New Jerseys, Lenny?"

"Yes I do," he said forthrightly. "I'll a'mit I ain't nice about it. It makes me want to tear my hair out just to hear one of them people talk. They're all nice. Oh Jesus they're nice. They'll tell you how nice and generous and neighborly they are till it makes you sick. Where the hell do they get them people?"

"New Jersey."

"That's right!" He laughed.

Another voice put in, "I tell you what, though, boys. Some of these new folks we're getting are the best people you have, anymore. Put us natives to shame, some of them. About the time you get sick of your rotting Jim Daniel wood furnace in the cellar under one big register for the whole house, about the time you decide to join the world and put in automatic heat, here these new folks come telling you you're wasting the world's supply of oil, ain't you got a wood-lot? They're all buying firewood contracts off the county forest. You got to get a firewood contract by lottery now, they's so many of them back-to-the-landers around. Wood stoves so God-damn air-tight they could tar the roads with the creosote they make! Kerosene lamps. Square dancing, fiddle music, cotton dresses. Next thing you know they'll be plowing their gardens with horses, like old Millard here."

After a sharp glance to see how Millard took that, he went on. "Who, besides Indians, got all het up over that high tension power line going through, here back a while?"

"That was the college people, wasn't it?"

"Some. College longhairs, hippies, Indians, and a few old farmer women up Fort Covington, that it was going right through their yards, Jesus Christ. The rest was these new folks. They ain't all New Jerseys."

"Jest the same, I wouldn't live under one of them high voltage lines, either. It ain't safe."

"Neither would I, by the Jesus."

"Not if I hadn't got my children yet. Cows don't procreate, you know, that graze under them things."

"You know what that damn thing is for? Nothing in the world but air conditioning in New York City."

"Shit," Lenny said. "Let 'em have the power. Maybe they'll stay there."

Skunky Wilson tugged his neighbor's sleeve. "You'd think they'd ask somebody that was there when that water system was put in. I was there, God damn it."

Billy Atkin said, "Then, of course, if we're talking about change. You know one more thing? Eh? If we're talking about places getting sold to strangers that don't quite fit in?"

"Eh?"

"Old Herman's place. Eh?" Billy chuckled.

"Oh. Oh." Chuckles, shared looks. "Oh yeah."

On this subject, though, they didn't know each other's mind that well. He meant the mixed-race couple from Massachusetts that bought Old Herman's. At least the man was from Massachusetts. He had appeared the year before, a real down-to-earth person, near-sighted, energetic, overweight, sociable, glasses thick as your finger; with a tow-headed kid about nine. It turned out he'd bought Old Herman's place before he even came to see it. "Prob'ly from Lyle White!" Billy cried. "That was when Herman lost the first leg and went into the boarding house. The state took care of that quick, ho ho. State social services slapped his house on the market just like that."

The fellow had been hired to teach high school English in the school. He didn't say anything about having a black wife. Just said he had a wife, and after she finished up some degree she was getting, she'd come too. Well, he taught last year, and the kid went to the school, and everybody liked them fine. And this year the wife came, and she must have been his second wife because she certainly wasn't the mother of that tow-headed kid. She was from South Carolina, had a kinky black Afro, wore a kerchief over it just like they'd seen in old pictures of Negroes in the cotton fields. The town was just a bit surprised.

But they couldn't help but like her too. Beardsley was their name, and hers was Marcia, with the accent on the *i,* Mar-*see*-a. "She's a nice person," they would say. Because she was nice. But they weren't saying exactly what they thought. She was a nice person, smiling and gregarious, with a charming voice, but she was so appealing of eyes and lips and teeth and skin and shape that she started fantasies in men's minds. She made confusion of any prejudice they might have acquired, in their ignorance and isolation.

Marcia Beardsley came equipped with a brand new graduate degree in biology, and the school needed a biology teacher too. But there the town, through its school board, or through the school board's domineering president, drew the line. The school board president not only ran a dairy farm and the school but drove the bulk milk truck too; he had no doubt of his own virtue. He said what those two did was their own business up to a point but the town wasn't ready for both of them employed at the school and then having children that wouldn't be either black or white, wouldn't rightly belong to either one parent's world or the other's. So she didn't get the job, she went over to Malone and got a better one, teaching at the nursing school. And even when she began to appear to be pregnant, and then when she certainly was, she was still so attractive and pleasant to see and talk to that maybe they were wrong there too and could just forget about it, in her case. Her husband's too. You had to hand it to him, to have a woman like that attached to him. They built a barn and raised their own pigs. There wasn't a particle of pretense or superiority in either one of them. Good neighbors, the best.

So much for sticking to the subject of the water system, or even that Ford truck that was found out by Pete Shaheen's. Next day, Murdock, the telephone lineman, came in for his lunch and mentioned the pickup again. It was gone now, he said, somebody with a car-carrier hauled it away, with Deputy Sheriff O'Neil standing by to direct traffic. But did they want to know where it came from? Murdock had this from O'Neil himself. It had been abstracted from right outside Charlie's Inn, near Lake Clear Junction, forty miles south, while the owner was standing in a throng of people, outdoors, just the other side of the old depot there, watching the dogsled races.

"Oh yeah?" Lenny LaBounty cried, interested. "I seen them races on the television at my grandfather's last night. North Country Sportsman. I never knew they had such of a thing here, dog-sled races."

Amos said to Murdock, "Stolen, was it, that truck?"

"Borrowed," Murdock said innocently. "O'Neil said the owner was getting it back, no damage, so no theft."

"That's O'Neil for you," Billy said, disgusted.

"You mean somebody took it from Charley's Inn, got it stuck way up here, and decided just to leave it?"

"Some kids on a lark, is what it sounds like to me," Lenny said. "Some of 'em in another vehicle, mebbe. Racin'. One vehicle spins out, gets stuck, they all just pile into the other and skedaddle. Anybody seriously stole it would have taken the gun. Which is another thing you didn't use to see, guns in the back window. They all do it now, picked it up from television. They do it all year long!"

Eugene sputtered out some syllables and Amos Cheney nodded at him, blinking.

"I say," Eugene repeated, "Kinda like your Cat."

"That's what I thought you said." Amos looked at him, impassive across the bar.

"Sochia," Eugene said, sudden like a sneeze. "I say, Sochia. Think so?"

Amos hunched his shoulders, didn't say.

During these emergencies, the south side of town usually had water right along, even if at lower pressure. Now one of the town workers came in for a bite and said the other side of town was dried out too. Skunky Wilson suddenly flung out what he'd been keeping to himself, bitterly, afraid of ridicule: "It's an air-lock, God-damn it!" He waited for a few heads to turn down his way, mumbling something the others couldn't make out.

"Air lock, what the fuck is that? Get the marbles out of your mouth."

Skunky said, "Don't you know what an air lock is? Air lock's an air lock. Air in the pipe, don't ask me. You got to tap that pipe on the top of the bulge! Out by Shaheen's."

"What the hell do you mean, 'bulge'?" Billy Atkin cried.

"A bulge is a bulge! Where the pipe comes up a little before it goes down again. You think she slopes the same, all the way?"

"Yas, I do. Jesus Christ, look at that hill!"

"Well, she don't. She's got a bulge." He weakened again, softened his voice. "Maybe she's got an air lock there. I ain't saying she has, but she might."

"You don't mean a bulge. You mean a rise. Anyways, so what? You telling me water ain't going to push air ahead of it? How do you think a siphon works?"

"I was there, God-damn it, when that was put in. Was you there, Billy? I didn't think so."

Millard Frary remembered that day. That was a historic day in Sabattis Falls, the day the water was turned on. That very day, while they were getting ready to have the celebration, the blacksmith shop on the west side of Main Street caught fire. The blacksmith shop stood close beside a solid block of three story wood-frame buildings all built together side to side—the general store, newspaper, something else—milliner's shop, Millard thought. Shop ablaze, the clapboards on the general store already getting charred, and there lay the brand-new water-main, in an open ditch, with a brand-new hydrant sticking up from it. So they thought they would turn the water on without waiting for the speeches. They hooked a fire-hose onto the hydrant and Joe Augustine took Skunky down to the brand-new water building, and the two of them spun the big valve. But nothing happened, and the blacksmith shop and that whole other block of buildings burned right down to the ground.

"Why?" Skunky cried. "Air lock!"

"Air lock, by God," Joe Augustine said, and he took Skunky and a set of tools and a horse and wagon and galloped across the river and up French Hill, and off across a field to where the line was newly laid, and they dug down to the highest point in that buried water main, where it followed a bulge on the hillside, and tapped a hole in it right there.

"Yeah? And what happened?" Billy demanded.

"What the hell do you think? The air blew out of that tap like a banshee!"

"No shit," said Billy Atkin.

"Yes, shit," Skunky said. "And once the air stopped hooshing out, the water ran, sixty pounds of pressure down to that hydrant, threw Art Livermore that had aholt of the hose right off his feet, under a horse that stepped on him and broke a rib. Too late to save the general store but put the fire down, saved that other block."

"What a fuckin' story. You're so full of shit, Wilson—"

"Sure there was air in it that time, Skunky," Lenny said. "Naturally. It was just turned on. But how would you get air into it in the middle of the winter?"

"I don't know! How come it does it every year?"

"That ain't what happens every year! A pipe breaks in the ground. And it don't happen every year!"

"Ennaways," Billy said, "how could a little bit of air stop the water from running when all that air has got to do is run out in front of it?"

But Skunky shouted out one last time. "I don't know! Don't ask me! You got to tap into the line at the top of that rise by Pete's, that's all. You'll see! She'll whistle, oh she'll whistle!"

Duke Arquit wouldn't have anything to do with it but he let Pete Shaheen himself, a member of the water crew, take what Pete called the definding rods and some shovels, the hole-saw and a patch kit and five hundred feet of extension cord up there and try it if he wanted to. He wouldn't send the back-hoe, said they'd break the line with it. Pete led the water crew out back of his house. Out where he thought he was approaching the line, he began to douse for it. The definding rods were two three-foot brazing rods bent 90 degrees near one end, with the short ends stuck through handles of half-inch copper pipe. He held the handles in front of him, tilted a little, so the rods extended forward, parallel and nearly level, and he waded through the snow.

"It's right about here somewhere," one of the crew members said, sighting up and down the hill. "Ain't it?"

"Keep your pants on," Pete said. "We'll find her." He went ahead a little, turned around and waded back, holding the rods very carefully, wading in the snow. The rods swung apart, wider and wider, lining up with the underground pipe. "There. You're right, George. Runs right down through here, like that." He showed the direction, uphill and down, the way the rods had lined up.

"I thought so," George said. "I hope this ground ain't froze under here."

In the end they had to persuade Duke to send up the machine, but they did find the pipe in the vicinity. With a man stationed in Shaheen's cellar to replace fuses, they tapped it with a hole-cutting tool on a half-inch drill turning rather slowly at the end of that long connection. Towards the end they stood back, and Shaheen averted his face. But the circle of iron pipe came free and spun inside the hole-saw, quite dry. Tentatively, Shaheen approached his ear to the hole. If anything, the air was sucking in. "Hear a banshee in there, Pete?" Pete raised his head without answering and whacked the pipe with his tool, and they all heard a hollow ping going away underground.

In Eugene's, Skunky ducked his head and defended himself with his elbows flying over him like wings. He hadn't guaranteed it was air-locked, had he? But now they knew damn sure it wasn't. "Oh that's a big help, Skunky. It ain't air-locked. So what?"

"So it's something else! I don't know! Am I an engineer? Maybe the intake's clogged. I ain't saying it is. But maybe it's clogged. I ain't the one to say."

"How the hell could it get clogged, in the middle of the winter, with ice on top of the pond. Hah? Hah?"

And Lenny said, "Jesus H. Christ, ain't nobody ben up there and *looked?*"

It was after dark now, but finally the water crew did just that, went back into the scrub on snowshoes, to the storage pond on a spring-fed brook, with an axe and an emergency light. They shoveled off the snow at the intake and found the forehead, ears, and frosted

eyebrows of a yearling Holstein heifer, just above the level of the
ice. She was standing there under the ice with her side sucked
halfway into the intake hole. She'd been shot in the ear and slid in
there from the highway on the snow, and a hole in the ice chopped
out for her, apparently, frozen over now. You could kind of see a
track where she had been dragged. It led up about to where that
borrowed pickup truck from Charley's Inn had been stuck. There
wasn't any doubt about the pickup now. Robert Sochia had reached
a new low.

22

Bone in a Chowder

This O'Neil is a worrier. A tall thin man with a face like Lincoln's, big-featured and warty, he squints away from you and holds one elbow with one hand and puts his chin in the other, or pinches the top of his nose, moving the wire-rim glasses down on the tip of it. He seems absentminded even in the way he walks; his legs kick out straight long before the shined shoes land, as if he never learned how far away the ground was.

Olmstead County long ago gave up stationing a deputy sheriff in the Falls, but O'Neil became a deputy sheriff seven years ago, and he bought a house there. He is busy elsewhere about the county most of the time, presumably pulling over speeders and delivering summonses and answering reports of drug transactions and spousal abuse, hard as it is for the town to imagine him in action as a real law enforcement officer. His house, on a shaded corner lot up Main Street from the school, is just a house like any other, painted not recently, cream-colored with reddish-brown trim, the colors dimmed in the shade of its verandah and the old trees. One light is often on, inside, late at night, and it is not the flickering light of a television.

He hasn't found his way into the society of the town, being so unlike it. He has no informants. He's last to know the talk, the rumors. When he's investigating some incident or infraction he starts from so far behind the common knowledge that he becomes a bit of a laughingstock. Nobody has any malice toward him, unless it's for his indulgence of Robert Sochia. He is said to have been clumsy with certain evidence that might have convicted Robert.

Generally though, the town is content with him, with his ineffectualness, with the law's neglect. When something really needs doing in the law enforcement line, he's more or less helped to do his job, by the Supervisor or other leaders in the town.

No one knows better than himself his shortcomings. He is well read and thinks the ideal lawman in this town ought to be like one of those fictional Southern sheriffs who wear their towns like an old shoe, and carry their towns with them, when they have to, the way a foot carries a shoe. He thinks he's more like an aging, alcoholic priest, a cross for his poor, powerless congregation to bear, tolerated just so long as he doesn't spill the wine or fondle the little girls. He shines his shoes, he keeps his uniform pressed sharp. He's a bone, wrapped in cloth, stuck in a chowder.

He became a law officer after failing as a teacher. At least he thinks, and thought at the time, that he failed as a teacher. He wanted some sort of mantle to fall on him. In the Episcopalian military school he taught in, near Syracuse, he wore a brown wool uniform—an Ike jacket—and wool pants the same color, and a MacArthur-like hat, also brown wool. The cadets were required to salute him, and he to answer their salutes. They thought him ridiculous when he meant to be most serious and generous, saying, for instance, "Splitting an infinitive is the privilege of professional writers." That was intended as an encouragement to a bright student whom he believed to have a future in writing. It was his way of admitting that the rule could (in another setting, at another level) be broken. But he heard the remark repeated mockingly in imitation of a stuffy manner he didn't know was his, by that cadet and others, for years afterward.

Other mantles, too, had not fit him easily. He is content no longer to be married to the somewhat too vivid younger woman ("Raggedy Ann" to the cadets) who accompanied his life as a housemaster or Company Commandant at school. That was a mismatch that's past and not brooded over, though it has, he supposes, some relation to his present celibacy.

This morning it seems as if he has to deal with as much femaleness as if he were married. He is looking for Robert Sochia or for somebody who can get a message to him, but everywhere he goes he finds only women. So he's had to risk their ridicule for not knowing whatever it is they know and don't tell him. Until this very morning, he was ignorant even of the fire that destroyed the Pelos' geodesic dome on the Gokey road. He'd been amazed to see the ruins, in the course of a routine patrol. No such fire had been mentioned in the *Tribune*, where every car-wreck or house-fire is front-page news. If that fire was never reported to the sheriff's office in Moira, where he would have learned of it, then there hadn't even been an official call to the fire department. Standing on the snowbank and looking at a sort of crater of snow, the wind soughing over the landscape, he'd felt the awful bleakness of community-less life in such a place. What had happened here? Where was Robert living now?

Robert's case is personal to O'Neil. It's an indictment of his failure, in spite of interest, even a sort of avidity rather like erotic love, to know what went on beneath the surface of the town. After the accident in which Raymond Sochia was killed he had investigated a lead about a locked room which Robert Sochia reportedly rented, a store-room upstairs in Mrs Hubbard's hotel. He made a professional mistake there, asking Mrs Hubbard's daughter (typically, he had not been aware she had a daughter) to open the room for him, although he didn't have a warrant. And because he didn't have a warrant, what he had found there was inadmissible in Robert's trials.

He is aware, from various half-veiled accusations, that this had ballooned in rumor into a pile of hypodermic syringes and other "drug paraphernalia," which would, but for his stupidity or his softness on the criminal, have put Robert away for a long while. But what he'd really found was only more mystery, more implication, the kind of thing that couldn't be brought up in court anyway, unless every trial of fact were to become an exploding universe of inference, possibility, uncertainty. He had been prepared for that "room," in a hotel that wasn't a hotel, to be a plain, unfurnished closet where Robert, a transient, a nomad, and a cousin of the owner, was allowed to keep things he couldn't carry with him on his travels. But the large old-fashioned key had opened the paneled door to a clean and feminine Victorian bedroom, with a canopied bed and a carved and painted dresser, a fine braided rug. There was a lace doily on the dresser, an antimacassar on the rocking chair, framed, hand-tinted nature-pictures and mirrors on the walls, and on the flowery papered wall by the bed an ornate brass mantle lamp in a reflector sconce. The bed itself was a mahogany four-poster, with turned pins atop the corner-posts above the framework of the canopy, a skirt that brushed the floor, an extra folded quilt, embroidered pillow slips.

He thought perhaps the daughter had made a mistake and shown him the wrong room. But under the skirt of the bed was Robert's sad little duffel. A sort of travel kit, ready to go, containing, as to evidentiary interest, only a little plastic device for cooling and aerating smoke, and, of course, a plastic bag, rolled to the shape of a cigar, with about one cigar's worth of greenish leaves and pallid buds. A "lid" of marijuana—a term and a substance he knew quite well, from his occasional duties in the college dorms and fraternities.

He has already been to see Grace Frary, somehow touching in her contradictory youth and age, her flustered concern about the boy, by whom, uniquely in this town as it seems to him, she clearly means well. Mrs Frary has been kind to O'Neil too, kinder than others. She sent him cookies and doughnuts when he first came, and she occasionally asks him if he could use her extra milk, or some of the dairy spread she makes with a separator from the rich milk of her husband's Guernseys, or brings him some of the overabundant asparagus from her garden in the spring. She would know the talk, and he thought that she might tell him what she knew.

But she didn't. There was surely something she knew—she was so girlish and confused in her pretense. She offered him milk and muffins in apology. And of course he was too delicate or gallant to press her. He believes she really did not know where he could find the boy, and perhaps she was right in saying no one did.

After that he's stopped at Mrs Day's, a visit he'd have preferred to skip. He'd thought she'd certainly tell him what she knew, but probably too much more than she knew, and scold him all the while she told it. But she met him at the door as if she'd been warned of his approach, and sent him packing. "Oh, don't bother me about that scum! Go, do your job! If you had done your job last year he wouldn't be out among civilized people. Go! Get, sir! I won't talk to you!"

So then it has to be the bars. He finds himself passing Eugene's without stopping, reluctant to go asking stupid questions where that Atkin's truck is parked. He can't stand the loud mouth, the bluster of the man, foreseeing ridicule. He continues down the street and parks by the pumping station across from The Rapids and gets out. He notes a few cars parked by the fire hall, car-poolers probably. Only two cars of people presumably at The Rapids, parked around the corner. Inside, their owners are not in evidence. Mrs Hubbard sits alone on a high stool by the outside corner of her bar, reading a newspaper and stirring her coffee. He sits two stools away from her. She raises her head slowly from the paper, then drags her eyes from it slowly to stare at him.

"Quiet, today," his clever opening, meant as a reference to recent days when the streets were dug up and Mrs Hubbard appeared to have much more business.

"Well, there's you." She moves off the stool and turns her back to him to go around the bar and lift up the pot.

"Yes, please. Black," he says. Incurious, she serves him, puts away his coins. He holds the mug in both hands up to his chin, lets the steam fog his glasses and warm his face. He asks her his question, transparent even to him.

"I seldom lay eyes on him," she says.

When he has drunk a few sips and his glasses have cleared she is back on her stool at the bend, filing her nails. She says, "He'll be around for a little while, and then for a period of weeks you'll miss him. You wonder what the boy is getting into."

This is more than she usually volunteers. The sarcasm warns him not to comment, suggests that more will be coming.

It does. "I do happen to know one ambition of Robert Sochia's."

She pauses long enough to make him turn his head. Then with a nice smile: "To pan gold in Alaska and smuggle the gold in person to Paris France. When I haven't seen Robert Sochia for a few weeks I always expect that's where he's gone."

So he is in the car again. Unmarked, dark, antennaed. It's queer. It feels, this coyness, stasis, everything, a little the way it felt last year when things were getting ready to happen, and he failed to know what happened even after he didn't fail to not prevent it. He could be about to do that again.

The split infinitive. The double negative. Privileges of the professional writer, nonsense. He didn't fail to not prevent. It's exactly right. He would like to be the kind of sheriff who actually did fail to not prevent. Who, in fact, prevented—what? Not the bewildering passions and doings under the surface of things, of which he knew so little. What then? Suffering and death. Meaningless destructive misunderstanding and hatred. He would like to prevent meaningless destructive misunderstanding and hatred leading to suffering and death, this time, if he could. But he probably wouldn't fail to not. If, with better luck this time, those things were prevented, it would probably be not by him.

He feels the need of a woman. To know what he needs to know, it seems to him he would have to be the lover, nothing less, of a woman like JoAnn Hubbard, who is, to him, a sleepy-eyed giantess of knowledge. From whose secret room, from whose deep, soft bed, run, as he imagines, genetic and pulmonary and vascular lines which web the whole town and countryside. If he were JoAnn Hubbard's lover, he would either know everything he needed to know, or have no need of knowing.

Knowledge exists, he believes. It's all around him. Why is it so hard for him to find? He'd known about the drugs, the threats, that lifelong hatred of inseparable cousins. He hadn't known the generational history of this hatred, but at least he'd known that it existed. For "drugs," read marijuana, relatively harmless to O'Neil who'd tried it, carefully, without alarm. If people needed something illegal to do, by way of self-image, perhaps it was as well that using marijuana was illegal. Priest-like, he'd tried to warn and thus protect the young man even then. But that was not knowing as he wanted to know.

That little job he'd arranged for Robert months ago—he thought the favor might have built a little confidence between them. Driving him up to the train he learned little of the boy's plans, or his feelings. And that was the last he'd seen of him. But what did he expect?

North of town he turns left on a gravel road, then on another of stonier gravel under the snow. Stops at an old farm where the middle section of the long, ancient barn has fallen in. The weathered little house is overgrown with vines which are leafless now, and the shades are all drawn except at the one kitchen window on the porch, where the woman watches the road. Another woman. This is the home of Helen Pelo's mother, Mrs Chase, and it's where Helen Pelo is living, without her children, while John Pelo remains in jail. Not much longer.

What kind of reception he will receive here he doesn't try to guess. He had to bear a hand in arresting John not once but twice, with consequences horribly disproportionate to his offenses. Worse, now, he supposes, after he didn't fail to not prevent the combustion of John and Helen's house.

He does not necessarily believe what Murdock, the telephone lineman, particularly told him about Lila Chase: how when Robert came to this driveway with his old DeSoto the day of his release (to get Helen to go to Florida with him, Murdock had thought, just to crook his finger at her and say come on), that tiny white-haired woman stopped him cold, with a shotgun. Poked it through the ventilation slot in the bottom of the wooden storm window, having propped the inner sash up on a stick, and supposedly even fired it.

Murdock claimed to have been inside playing pedro with Helen's invalid father at the time. He said old Lila, hunched down over that gun lying right on her kitchen table, put three twelve gauge slugs from Newell's pump-gun into that elm tree beside the driveway, head-high, right beside Robert where he stood waiting for Helen to come out. Robert stood up to the first two, but true to reputation, about the same time as the third he'd ducked back into his car, backed out the driveway and fled fish-tailing down the road.

But he got control of himself, Murdock said, with some wonderment. Stopped at the next place, Crinklaws', and came back, got out of the car and hollered for Helen again, right in the face of that gun, though trembling. And when Helen came out, hugging herself in the cold, he didn't ask her to go to Florida at all. He just asked her if he could hole up in that "thing of her and Johnny's" out on the Gokey road. And she said, bitterly, "You can *have* it!"

So Murdock said. O'Neil knows how stories grow. Robert himself had told him, on their drive to Cornwall, that he had permission to use the dome.

O'Neil parks in the Chases' drive, well back from the house, and gets out. He measures the distance to the elm as he passes it himself, thinking, *Head high on him. That would be shoulder high on me.* He sees no marks in the rough, ribbed bark, but they might not show clearly and he doesn't want to be seen studying the elm. He makes his way onto the porch. The old woman doesn't answer or get out of her chair to let him in, but through the light in the kitchen door he sees her staring impatiently at him, so he enters by himself. The kitchen is unlighted. She sits not right beside the window but just beyond it, where she can see the road and not be seen; even though, he thinks, there might be only six vehicles to come down that road in a day.

He asks her his question, and she just says, "Pish!" So he asks her, "Has your daughter?" and she just snarls it back at him in a mockery of his cultured accent. He knows he will have to give her something, to break her puny static anger. He'll have to be as stupid as she thinks him. In her ridicule there may be information. "I think he may be in trouble," he says, hoping he gives an impression that there's more to it.

"Huh!" she says. "You're a great lawman. You prob'ly want to warn him. Before you have to go after him too."

This is it, then. But he remains obtuse. "What for? What's he done?"

"For stealin'! Hasn't anybody broke in anywheres?"

"Who's gone after him? Where?"

"Nobody nowhere. He's about done here, don't you think, and finally he's gone to someplace! Florida, I hope. Where all the old fools go and try to get me to go with them too. I haven't got a friend left up here, wintertime, damn them all and him in there and his stupidity." O'Neil knows that long ago Mr Chase had put his arm in a corn blower and had it whisked up into the silo. They have lived on his Social Security and her antique-dealing ever since. "He didn't take Helen, by Gollys," she says.

"May I see her?"

The woman bawls it, "She's at Dannemora, where do you think? Standing by her husband!"

O'Neil puts a hand to forehead, pinches the bridge of his nose. What is this? John's in the prison, yes, caught carrying on Robert's business in the aftermath of the mess last year and then walking off from a work detail. But he's been a model prisoner. He's nearly due for parole already. No reason for Helen to move over there now.

"He'll be out next month, maybe," O'Neil says. "Even sooner."

And now he's shocked, he doesn't understand this, the woman is coming at him, flailing something in her hand, saying, "He don't need to be out!"

It's a slotted spoon. O'Neil is trying to think and protect his face at the same time. Helen's over there, maybe, to help John keep the good behavior up, so she can bring him back. With him home (although now in what home?) she'll get the children back, if O'Neil has any influence. But the mother is driving him from her kitchen with her flashing spoon. "Let him set right where he is, the fool!"

"Why?" he asks, pained at having to ask.

"Hunch!" she cries. It rings as if he'd said it himself. He has his hat back on, his hand on the knob. She is actually pushing him out onto the sagging porch.

"'Robert may be in trouble', may he? You don't know anything! What use are you?" As he gets into his car, she shouts, "If anything happens to my son-in-law, Mister, it's on your head!"

This is it, he knows. But what is it? Along the road back, toward town, he has to stop. He tilts his head back, eyes closed.

He feels a parting, like a blood vessel pierced, in the back of his neck. It is the same feeling he used to get as a child when he would throw a baseball high toward the crowns of the elm trees in the yard. Throw it hard from way back near the ground and almost fall, facing the ground again, following through; then turn back up and find the ball still climbing, white ball with red stitches turning, against the sun-tattered foliage. Stopping, starting down. Watching it he would feel the same precious secret rupture, the sensation of some warm dark liquid released at the base of his skull and spreading and cleaning and warming his scalp, his neck and shoulders. He would drop his head and let the sensation run through him, with mixed curiosity and fear because he didn't know what it was. Spinal fluid, maybe. Blood. Maybe he should run and tell his mother. Maybe he was going to die. The ball would hit somewhere near him in the sod.

An airplane's shadow passes over the car, the loud flat noise following it, and O'Neil surprises himself as he starts again, by spinning the right tire until the lugs cut the packed snow down to the pavement. His usual way is to use second gear and a light foot, and he did not know that he was feeling this angry at himself, or this reckless. There's the airplane, visible now, a silver airplane, twin-tailed but tiny, heading low over the woods west of the town, apparently to land.

The reasoning isn't clear, why that airplane should mean Robert Sochia. Nor is it clear what point there is in going to Dannemora now. Find Helen Pelo; see what he can learn from her, who has always feared and mistrusted him, foolishly for he wanted nothing so much as to be helpful to her, a lovely child.

Hunch, as Mrs Chase had said. Who'd also said, "Let him set right where he is!" Yes, then, Dannemora. Try to fail to not prevent, this one time.

The day is bright, clear. Between snows, this has been a cold and sunny winter. The country seems shabby, depressed under the sun, in the unforgiving clarity. He is driving through farmland more and more marginal the further east he goes, most of the fields small, irregular, hilly. Many old farms idle and overgrown.

The country, he knows, is actually depopulated, like the English countryside of Oliver Goldsmith. Can it have been as pleasant as he thinks it must have been, when these small Greek revival farmhouses and their barns were freshly built, filled with the warmth of humans and livestock, this road a dirt track busy with horse-drawn vehicles? The tilled fields and pastures fitted among ridges, outcrops of granite, hedgerows, woodlots, but the road running straight while rising and falling, linking neighbor to neighbor in one familiar and settled culture? The only people he sees out in this brightness are farmers spreading manure, ear-flaps down on red or green tractors at the heads of lengthening paths of bright brown, spattered and dripped on the glaring snow-meadows. He swings left around a bulk-milk truck backing into a blind driveway.

Beyond Malone he heads southerly toward Lyon Mountain, through that empty iron-mining company town, the hills long ago denuded to make charcoal for the furnaces but clothed again in softwoods now, serene, cold; then east, moving against the clear day coming west. He is going backwards in time, he thinks. He still doesn't know what really happened behind that killing over a year ago, much less what is happening now. Going toward another woman who does know, who could tell him if she would, but won't.

He's remembering Helen around the courthouse during the trials, her breasts softly tendered in the bodice of her homemade dress. A mother-child, appealing to him in her plainness and innocence. Innocent even in perjuring herself, O'Neil remembers: to protect her family, calling her husband a liar. What is innocence if it isn't the dumb following of instinct? They were both so simple, so transparent. A hope, a family, could be built on such simplicity.

O'Neil is a familiar of the prison. He imagines they will know, in the prison, where she stays. He will ask her to lunch; the timing is good. She will demur, saying she has already eaten, perhaps lying, but she'll come and sit across from him, in the dark high-ceilinged restaurant, run by thick-accented Greeks, right across from the prison wall, where he goes. He can taste in advance,

pleasurably, the hot pork sandwich. Her answers, murmured while
he eats, will taste like the gravy spooned over mashed potatoes,
luscious, golden, rich. Like the light on thighs and breasts. Like
that transfer he dreams of, of knowledge from within the sumptuous
thighs and arms of . . . .

His whole body tenses, his hands bend the steering wheel.

It was nothing, an imaginary hazard, nothing.

He wonders when, someday, he is going to yank the wheel like
that, on a perfectly straight clear road, to avoid some thing that isn't
there, that he didn't even imagine clearly, and go crashing off over
the ditch, into the woods, wreck the cruiser, kill or maim himself.
But this has always bewildered Terence O'Neil, since he was a child
and other children seemed so confident in their knowingness. How
do other people know what they know? Do they really know it at
all? Last year, did they all just guess, brave it, bluff it, assume they
knew, for fear of admitting they didn't know anything really? Because
everybody else (guessing, assuming, bluffing too) seemed to know?
Does this assuming, intuiting, done by whole townfuls of people,
constitute knowing? Does hunch upon hunch, guess on top of guess
become truth? Because the guessers have the Gestalt right, in the
first place? Because they know the pattern?

Now he is coming down into the prison town from the west,
the landscape spreading out southward on his right all the way to
the distant cold high peaks, a cruel Siberian beauty for the urban
inmates to gaze upon. The tan sandstone walls blank out half the
sky above his sloping tinted windshield. On the one-sided main
street his parked car is alone. He walks in at the prison gate opposite
the single stop-light. A guard repeats the name and turns to open
a file drawer. Another looks into the room and asks, "Who?" and
when he hears the name, studies the deputy a moment and takes a
sip of the coffee in his hand before starting to speak and then
frowning downward instead, deciding something. With a finger
up he gestures *wait* while he thinks and then with the rest of his
hand *come with me*.

So the deputy is led beyond the walls into the open yard under
the parapets, then up a long wide stair. The guard stops halfway

and blocks his view, takes his arm, leads him aside while the doors at the top are opening, closing. The guard pretends to talk to him, with arm gestures, but says nothing. Over his shoulders O'Neil sees her in a long coat, only a kerchief over her hair. She comes quickly down past them. She slows for the ice at the bottom, trips across it with little steps, raises her hand at the far side to the other guard. The guard is watching O'Neil to see whether he wants to overtake her there or follow her outside. The guards are conspiratorial with him but he doesn't know what it's about.

Now the one who has led him up the stairs interprets his hesitation. "You want to see him," and leads on up the stairs. He is shown down a shining hall and into a small room with a table and two chairs. In the ashtray there's lipstick on a cigarette hardly smoked.

It is no wait. He hears a loud husky voice in the hall, inarticulate, and running steps. A guard's shout, "Walk, peon!" A hand grabs the doorjamb, saving the runner from sliding on past the room, and Pelo bangs in against the jamb. Flushed through his pallor, short-haired and clean-shaven, he looks plucked of his famed strength but he still has size and energy. He ignores the departing guard's tired plea, "Keep one foot on the floor, will you, Pelo? Here's your arresting officer come to see you too."

He's pleading already, "O'Neil! God-damn this! Is it you? Are you behind it?" He's leaning at O'Neil across the cigarette-burned table. O'Neil in his surprise doesn't need to figure out a noncommittal reply because Pelo goes right on, "It's Bobby, isn't it? Huh? Come on, O'Neil!" He inhales. "He never went to no Florida. That little bitch can't tell the truth."

He lifts the table by its top, drops it, pounds on it.

O'Neil feels a thrill almost athletic, like the anticipation of a tennis game he can win—an analogy from afar. He needs only to pretend to know what is going on, at the same time he's finding out. Place his shots, and Pelo will blunder. He can begin by seeming not to want to call John's wife a liar, simply demurring. He moves a chair. "Sit down, John." Points at the cigarette, which he supposes was Helen's, though, on second thought, her lips wouldn't have colored it. "We're not together. That's a coincidence."

Pelo sits, slightly calmer. Shakes his head by habit, the way he used to throw the brown locks off his forehead, but there are no locks. "He's out there, ain't he? He needs me. Right? Right? He didn't go to no Florida and they've chased him out of town. He's in the woods!"

O'Neil holds his chin in his hand. Raises his eyebrows in a way that could mean anything. But sees no harm in telling the man, "I don't know where he is."

Pelo grips his own fist, squeezes. "They're after him. I knew it! He's in the woods. If you don't know that, I do. I'm getting out of here, O'Neil. You're not gonna stop me, right? So I can help my friend. Right? Right? Come on, O'Neil!"

O'Neil feels a blush come up his neck, to his face. This is a temptation really new to him, a door opening on an unconsidered view. A pit, or moat. It would require a leap which he probably won't take in the end. But he wants to think about it.

"You ought to close the door, John," he says, "and you oughtn't to shout."

"Okay!" Pelo gets up and slams the door, sits down again.

"So you know your friend is in the woods. How? What makes you think he needs you?"

"I know from Helen's lies. She's a woman. *You* know, O'Neil. She don't care what happens to him."

"She cares more, certainly, about what happens to you. And the children."

"We'll get the kids back. They can't keep the kids away from us."

"I think that's true, if you don't—" he decides to use the vernacular—"screw up." He let that sink in. "You'll be sent right back here for the least breach of parole. This doesn't concern you, John."

It doesn't penetrate. Pelo groans and writhes as if in pain. "Get me out of here, O'Neil. Help me get my parole. I've got it coming. I'm the warden's cleaner, that's how good I've been. You don't know anything about Robert. You don't know what I'll do. I'm not telling you anything. I got my parole coming to me and you haven't got any business interfering with it. Neither of you."

O'Neil is unsure of his footing, what Pelo is referring to. He
temporizes. "Where'll you live? What about your job? The money
to live on?"

"They have to give it back. Worry about something real, O'Neil!
Jesus! Just let me get out. Don't let her do this."

"What can she do? She isn't going to the warden to get you held
back. That's up to you. If you miss this parole, you're in for another
year before you get conditional release. You know how that works."

"Yeah but she's the boss, O'Neil. I do what she says. That's
how we are. She was just here telling me I've got to stay in a little
bit longer, no parole, and she won't say why! I'm going crazy!"

A pause. It's occurring to O'Neil that this is his chance.

"*You* could talk to her, O'Neil."

He leverages Pelo's cooperation in return for persuading Helen
to drop this attempt to keep her husband out of trouble. It would
be dishonest, but he's already started. What he has just said about
parole is not exactly true. There's nothing anybody could do to
keep him in. Parole is virtually automatic after a year of a one-to-
three. He says, "John, your wife might have good reason to keep
you in for a bit, and I do too. I want you back together with your
family just as soon as possible. But like her I don't want you right
back here again."

"Get me out, that's all. I've gotta get out!"

O'Neil sits back and lets another pause elapse. "Tell me this.
What makes you think you can get to him? Nobody else can find
him." Surprised by this discovery, which came from nowhere
conscious, he's so audacious as to say, "They've got an airplane
searching now and can't. Do you think you know where he is?"

"Are you kidding, O'Neil? I'm not telling you anything." Then,
more calmly, "I gotta be able to—you know—"

"To go out there yourself and search, yourself?"

"Well . . . yes!"

"By hunch? By smell?"

"I could find him. That's all."

"Because you have some idea what he'd do. From hunting
with him. Or you know some of his secret places, routes."

"What are you after? You're the law, O'Neil. I ain't telling you."

"I'm after some reason to believe that we could find him before the others do."

"I could," Pelo corrects him. "Holy shit, not you. I can't take you, O'Neil. In the woods? Come on."

"Supposing I prevented Helen keeping you in." This lying is rather exciting, he has to pretend calm. "I couldn't let you go alone."

"All I need is to be out of here, and I'm after him. But forget that, that shits, you couldn't keep up."

This is probably true, O'Neil admits. But there's a good reason Helen doesn't want him out. He's got to assume she's right. John's record of stupid old-fashioned loyalty— He reasons, "John, I don't want anybody to get hurt. If you aren't going to help me, then there's nothing to talk about. I can't go to Helen with that. You know it. If I'm with you, maybe she says yes. Otherwise, Robert takes what he gets, without a friend's help."

Pelo is wincing with frustration. O'Neil watches, wondering what's so hard for him about surrendering some of his independence in this. He suddenly blurts out, "Okay! Ask her! She decides." O'Neil waits for more. "I do what she tells me," Pelo says, humbled.

O'Neil suspects they both think O'Neil himself has power to keep him in. But they're confused. Sure, Helen could write a letter to the board, but whatever she thought up to keep Johnny in, it wouldn't wash. John could ask to stay, he can stay his whole sentence if he wants to, but they'd know better than to believe he wants to. That wouldn't wash either. So that's his power over Helen. He can tell her this: John's as good as out. If she wants her man kept halfway safe, she has to send him with the law.

His scalp crawls. He looks up, way up. He seems to feel that burst of a blood vessel at the back of his head, warming him dangerously. But he shakes the feeling off, saying "You sit tight, John. I'll talk to her."

"What're you gonna say?" The face is contorted with anxiety.

"I'll tell her she's right. You get out and run off into the woods on your own to find Robert, you violate parole day one. You end up back in here for the full three and *no* parole. If you help me, you have protection from all that. That's the deal. She'll buy it."

"All right."

"Shake hands."

John extends his hand, numbly, rising as O'Neil rises. O'Neil goes out, his knees clicking loosely to full extension. In the hall behind him Pelo calls out, "But you'll never keep up with me! O'Neil! You'll never keep up!"

O'Neil's too new to this sort of thing, being subtle. He wants to think it through, imagine the encounter with Helen, in whatever cheap apartment Lila Chase is paying for. Should he come again another day? Deception, manipulation, these things take a kind of courage O'Neil has never had. But he is learning. He has learned just now a little something of where that kind of courage comes from: If you're doing something, if you're acting secretly, then you know something nobody else knows. And this gives you the confidence to do more.

Could this be the way other people sweep away the despair of ignorance? He suspects it is. They do it with creativity. Honesty too strict will stop you cold. He tells the guard who led him in, "I'll go talk sense to Pelo's wife. You know where she's staying, I assume."

23

Mow Him Down with the Schuman

They were moving again, fast, far, every day.

They didn't break into camps. They stayed away from them. They slept deep in the snow in down sleeping bags Robert had stolen. Robert hung his outer clothes in the boughs of hemlocks or spruces and threw his bare arm over her back.

For a long time they did not cross a single road except woods roads. They traveled south and east, south, south and west, west. She knew this from stars and sun. This was like a sea and his rudder was stuck. Robert told her rabbits ran in circles. He said deer would do it too. He was doing it himself.

She still wasn't talking to him, or eating. They were still enemies but physically chums. Arms-around, when they were sleeping. Piggy-back, when she pooped out. Now and then a collapsing, hold-me-up sort of hug. "It wasn't that old captee's love for captor," she told Leo, at the end, when no one knew where Robert was. "That's a myth. But I was runnin' on fat, and I didn't have much fat. Besides, I know what a circle is for. A circle is for getting back where you started, ta-ta! Two dots. Da capo, Right? Right."

He was almost-fasting too, not quite as almost as she was but almost. When he needed to rest from carrying her she held him tight around the shoulders and let her legs down from his waist and stood on the webbing of the snowshoes. She looked about, and it was always a new scene of intricate wilderness, exquisite as she saw it now, in deer time. A waterfall frozen in place. Tall hats of snow on the stones of a brook, with black water trickling among them over perfect autumn leaves on the bottom if you looked close.

Death was there. They walked across it every day. Geological time. A glade of birches among huge plane-sided boulders. A clearing of deep snow with young pines springing up like kids that have just stood up from hiding to surprise you.

Often they were on some avenue of white, a trail or a summer road, untouched by any step or print unless a little finger-path of mice, or the ditto marks of squirrels, once leading to a little crater in the snow and a drop of blood and the wide-apart paired strokes of spread wing feathers. She knew what had happened there. Several times she had sensed a difference in the silent woods, seen a moving shadow out of the corner of her eye, felt sudden fear, and an owl glided over her head on still wings.

Speaking of little live things did Leo know what partridges did in the snow? They dove right into it and squooshed along under it and slept, because it was safe and warm in there, and if you came walking close they would burst right up out of the snow and scare you with the whuppawhuppawhuppa of their wings. Then you could hunt around for the hole where they dove in and see how far they had tunneled.

"Dived, I was taught," Leo would say.

"I wasn't taught 'dived'," she'd answer. "You have to put it in the way I say it. And you know what happens in spring, like last night and this morning, when it sleets on top of the powder snow like it did last night? Do you know what happens to the partridges then, Leo? Bobby taught me. It's pretty sad. They dive down into the snow to sleep, like I said, and then next morning when they wake up and try to rocket up and away, wham. Roof. Ice, crust, no exit. They're dead. Bobby said they digest their food and overheat and cook to death in there."

This was at the end when Robert had disappeared and Clarence was missing and when Leo, in seventh heaven, nursing her in his own bed, had his heart's desire of her, the story, from her lips; and when until at least Clarence was found she had time to color everything the way she wanted it colored.

"I have to give you my lecture on the death-wish now, Leo," she said. She needed to make sure that Leo understood why she

had made the effort that she had made, why she took the trouble
with these boys. Because that was what Robert's trouble was: death-
wish. "And don't say you don't believe in any such thing because
that's just ignorance."

She had absorbed a lot more from her psychology classes than
most people do. More than was taught. More than the teachers
could have possibly conveyed by themselves, because she read. She
read a lot, read hard. So patterns such as Robert's made perfect
sense to her. For instance, he had told her that he could not
remember when he wasn't angry. She had wanted to explain to him
right then, Of course you can't! Life *begins* in anger, Bobby! Think of
the red-faced furious baby the instant it is born! The analysis that
she had learned by reading and modified by talking and ultimately
worked out for herself, by insight, really, said that a child in that
initial anger knows that it is right to inflict pain. That is the form his
instinct to survive must take. And because the infliction of pain
brings punishment, and pain is real and good, the child seeks
punishment. And so the little Robert did bad things. Sure, all little
boys do. It's a way to salvation to be punished. "This is a sort of
shorthand, Leo; have faith and keep with me, please."

It's a way to salvation to be punished, right, but it ought to be
constructively repressed by about *age two*. She remembered
Menninger on this. Menninger was writing during the Second
World War, and she was reading him in another war. He said that
in war-time, with all the violence the adults are doing and suffering,
the self-destructive tendency to seek good in punishment, those
"primitive and atrocious wishes" (death wishes actually) could not
be "estranged and overcome." They never got constructively
repressed at all, and grown-ups walked around loose with them.
In Sabattis Falls, in peace or war, the way the sexes fought
subconsciously, it would be a wonder if they ever were repressed.
And this was what was wrong with Robert Sochia, basically. Just
this. She understood him perfectly, don't worry. If anybody knew
about his death-wish, didn't she?

West, north-west. The circle was turning northward now. "I
had to beat it out of him some way, pretty soon," she said. "I had

to make him want to be a normal person for a change and want to live a little while longer, pretty soon. Because he wasn't going to let them not-find us forever. I knew that. And I didn't know about this circle."

They heard rabbit-hunters once, with beagles circling around them, in the scattered small spruce and pines and poplars of a place that Robert called a burn. The trees were loaded with the night's new snow, and she and Robert were suddenly in the middle of this crazy yelping, these little hound-dogs going all over the place, close but invisible. There was space between the trees and overhead but you couldn't see very far at all, snow-covered pine trees everywhere and the yapping of these dogs in this direction, that direction, all around.

Robert stopped. She stumbled against his back. And the way her head was turned, there was a hunter, roly-poly, in red-and-black check, just his shoulder and hat and the barrel of a gun, between puffs of snow on boughs, she saw him. And then he wasn't there.

He was *so close!* How far was he? Maybe she could have called out, run to him, hid behind him. Made him make Bobby stop. With his shotgun? This was the closest she'd been to another human being since Bobby'd stolen her away. He'd have her by the shirt-tail in a flash (since her shirt-tails were out), and then what? She could yell, Hey! Or the hunters and dogs could discover them right now, even if she didn't say Hey! And then what? Bobby had a gun. Sometimes had a gun and sometimes not. Maybe they weren't always the same gun. She didn't like it. When she had the chance she packed snow in it and over it. He really didn't like that. He went without a gun sometimes but she knew when he left her he probably went and got it. Now he had it and she couldn't see any point in calling out. This couldn't end with little sad-eyed wrinkled yelping insane beagles and their roly-poly red-clad owners with guns, so why bother, but it was strange to see a fat, out-of-shape hunter-human, who shaved his fat chin. They just froze and the hunter or hunters and their dogs faded away in the wind and snow and silence.

Day after day, walking a few miles, ten or twelve he told her, easy, sleeping, having a fire, not-talking, curling up in their bags side by side in a shelter, in no shelter, it didn't matter. It was so beautiful. But it was a circle, Orion up there rotating. She was tending to get tearful when it was most beautiful. Was this—? What was this? The end of something. She thought the end of her childhood. Maybe, maybe, the end of her sex-life. She'd had enough of that. She'd always faked it sort-of anyway. A very rich husband someday was almost a necessary part of her future, but that was far away and in the natural course of things, not cynically planned. She was here now. She was really here.

Sometimes he'd tell her, "Eat." She'd tell him, by telepathy, *You eat. You're the hungry one. Shoot a deer.* He had been carrying the rifle on a sling, its worn walnut with the varnish peeling and the black metal worn silvery and the leather sling with brass hook-things on it. It was like a shepherd's crook, he needed it to look right. Anyway he wouldn't ever use it.

C'mon, shoot yourself some meat. Why don't you?

"I don't want to waste the shell."

What? How many shells do you have?

He showed her two clips and one loose bullet from his left pants pocket.

How many in a clip?

"Four."

Nine bullets. So what's the problem? Can'tchya shoot good?

He shook his head. "Not nine." Then he made four fast noises with his gun and four more shiny brass cartridges flew out into the snow. They dug down for the cartridges, their hands were digging right around in the same place together. She gave him the ones she found. Robert put each one in his mouth, bullet end first, and licked it clean. Then he dropped them in his shirt pocket.

"Eat."

She didn't like this emphasis on her eating.

"Why are you counting days?"

I am not.

"You move your lips. You use your fingers like a kid."

She tried to telepathy him, *This is the way I always protest. By not eating.* But he didn't get it. *You're supposed to say "Protest what?" Then I say, Being powerless. Being oppressed.*

But he didn't get it. So she telepathied him *Aren't I doing pretty good? Aren't I keeping up with you okay? You are the one that isn't getting enough to eat. You're skin and bones, man.*

They came upon a gravel pit. They were on a smooth graded road some rich people had on their preserve for horse and buggy travel, and beside it, dug into a bank, was this little private gravel pit. And the snow had blown over it from behind the bank. And down in the bottom there was a slope of soft pure powder, deep-deep. It was all pure and blinding white. They stood at the top and they both got the same idea, or maybe she got it and gave it to him like a present, *Let's jump.* They took turns throwing themselves off the top, making a scallop in the lip of snow, dropping through air and plunging up to their arms into the powder. Then they rolled and tumbled the rest of the way to the bottom where the winds had scoured the gravel almost bare and the sun made it almost warm.

She plunged so deep she lost daylight. She couldn't hear anything. She felt his bare hand grappling for her. Then he pulled her up, and he fell over backwards, with her mitten, and she fell over him to get it back. And they were laughing with cold snow on their warm faces. But then he suddenly got up out of the snow and went to the old rusted steam-shovel sitting on its tracks across the pit. She hadn't even noticed it, it was so piled with snow. It didn't have any glass in its windows. He was in there, just sitting on the old driver's seat, with levers by his knees. She went to it and climbed up on the track and peered in at him, squeezed in there alone. Doing nothing. She said *Whatsamatta* with her eyes. He looked at her with no expression. *Whatsammata Bobby?* He wouldn't say.

"He was mad at me. I hadn't said a word to him, man. I was still waiting to find out for sure myself so how could he know about it? But he was mad at me. He sat there accusing me. For not eating and not eating and walking and walking and then running and jumping and playing like a kid like that. And I thought, Uh-oh."

A day later she saw, across a snow-covered lake, a vision, something from another time and world. A castle. Or a chalet.

No, not a castle or a chalet. See straight, she told herself.

A big house anyway. But a funny-book, fairytale house, somebody's idea of some kind of European-style, Bavarian maybe, but built like a block-house too, for fighting Indians, because the second-floor part was bigger than the bottom-floor part, it overhung it a little. The whole place was taller than it was wide because it also had a steep, steep, green copper roof with three tiers, no less, of funny-shaped little dormer windows in it, with little curved rooflets over them like eyelids. And a huge granite chimney coming out of its peak with a green copper roof of its own.

She wanted to make Leo see this image: on the far shore of this wide white lake—dark green shore, white sea, blue sky—this *castle*. Nothing else in sight except a mountain to the east that maybe she recognized but she hadn't seen it from this side before, maybe the one he first took her up to look around, Blue Mountain. If so they had circled back pretty close to the town. This was a big deal. Coming here was a big deal.

She knew that this was something big for Robert and so she jerked his arm and made him look at her. She licked her lips and rolled them together and went "erk-erk-erk" in her throat and opened her mouth and said right out loud, "Bobby, what is this place? Where have you brought me?" Her voice came out low and husky.

He didn't bat an eye, exactly. They were still in the edge of the balsams along a hummocky low shore, a long way across from the house. "It's Dexter Lake," he said. He told her to take off her snowshoes. He took the bindings off both of their snowshoes and put them back on the snowshoes, backwards. Was this going to work? Staring at him, she kicked her boots into her bindings and let him tighten them up again. There wasn't any hole in the rawhide webbing for her toes to pivot down into. Wouldn't the stick-ends of the snowshoes stick in the snow? Weren't they going to stay in the shelter of the woods and go around the pond, like usual? But she followed him straight out onto the pond and over the pond toward the fairytale house with their snowshoes on backwards. She had to sort of slide each shoe ahead of the other in his track. Their toes couldn't pivot down though the holes in the webbing and the tails of the snowshoes didn't carry little crescents of snow like the toes did and throw them ahead at each step which was so hypnotic and neat. This was awkward, not neat. What were they doing this for?

Out in the middle she fell over. Weak, but also, she'd used her larynx, didn't he notice? She made an angel, sort of. Half an angel, the wings but not the skirts. She hoped he'd look back, she needed to hitch a ride though it might be too hard with his feet on backwards. But he marched on straight away from her. So she stuck her snowshoes up in the air, rolled on her side and tried to push herself up. Her hand went right down through the snow into water! She pulled it up, got up and followed, scared, making backwards tracks over his and trying to catch up. She knew that there could be snow and then water on top of the ice but it always scared her, out on a lake or a pond, to go through the snow into water.

They came up on a terrace in front of the house and while he walked around to the entrance she looked through the tall French doors into the living room. It wasn't that fancy inside. Nice wood floors and nice wood trim and paneling but cheap modern furniture, not much of it. No drapes. Nobody lived here. She could see all the way to the front door, opposite, which opened, Bobby coming in. After all the places he had broken into, to this castle-y one he had a key!

She kept her nose to the French door glass and her mittens around her eyes and watched him come toward her and turn and go up the stairs. He looked good in there with his tall beaded hat and his beard, he should own the place. She scuffed around to the entrance and got her snowshoes off and took them inside as he had done. It was colder inside than out but the main room was bright with sunlight from the lake and the sky through fanlights over the French doors and beveled glass in a rose window over the landing of the stairs, with mullions that twined in curves.

The floor snapped above. She was sure the house was from another time but it was new-looking as if there was just the first coat of varnish on the woodwork. The stair-treads weren't worn. She followed up the square-turning stairs, to a sunny hall. Just outside the window was a pine tree, the reddish roughness of its bark very close, so clean and clear and rough, its boughs moving in the breeze that had helped her across the lake. Long yellow-green brushes of its needles stroked against the house; she could hear them through the walls.

Four doors stood ajar to four corner rooms with large un-draped windows. She looked in at each of them. A fireplace in each, all different. She went into the sunniest room where the fireplace was a tall, tapering hood of copper, over a tiled hearth with a tiled wall behind it. Weird. Neat. She told Leo she chose that room before she'd turned around and saw what else was in it. There was a plain single bed and pine needles clicking against the west window and signs of squirrels, exploded pine-cones on the wooden floor and she was thinking that with braided rugs it would be great and maybe they could find one to lie on in front of the fire when she turned further around and her chest filled to bursting in surprise. Momentarily she denied what she saw. A baby grand piano. Black, a silhouette so eloquent to her against the sunlight off the hardwood floor, the legs, the curved lid, curved side shining. A piano! Baldwin? No, a Chickering! A *good* piano! Unworn, unscratched, un-beat-up, unlike the practice ones at school. The keyboard was closed. When she lifted the cover there were pine seeds on the keys. She lifted the lid and propped it up and looked at the golden frame, the gleaming strings and green felts. Seeds in there too. Hiding place of squirrels.

What was a piano doing here, in this room with a homely chair, a motel bed, and dead insects on the floor? In this un-used, un-old old house? A baby Chickering, no less, why was it here? She was spreading and stretching her fingers without thinking. "Can we get it really warm in here?" she said, to no one. Then turning, searching for him, to show him her excitement, "Did you know about this? Did you bring me here because of this?"

He had been in every room before her and was gone. Where? Out in the hall there was another stairway, down to the kitchen probably. A door was ajar to a narrow stairway up. But then he stood beside her.

"What is this place?"

"Dexter Lake."

"What?"

"Dexter's place."

"Who's Dexter?"

"The man that was shot in the back for fencing the woods. You heard that story."

"Maybe, but I forget."

"Orrando Dexter. He built this."

"Wait. Who is this? Where are we?"

"We're right under their noses. You could walk to the Falls in three hours."

"*What?* I couldn't walk an inch. *Why?*"

He wouldn't answer. He went up the attic stairs and she followed, biting her tongue. On the third floor under the steep roof he slid the top off a huge metal-lined bin. She saw what it was, storage for bedding, and dug for blankets, pillows. She carried them down. He was gone again, probably to get firewood. In a great big closet off the hall there were brooms and mops and there were sheets and slips in cherry drawers built into the wall. She swept the room and made the bed for herself. He would get the room warm and sleep by the fire. She was thinking, stupidly, *Piano. Piano. Piano. Piano.* It would get dark in not-long. *Play it by firelight.* In another room she heard him breaking something. He came in with the splinters of drawers and the waxy paper from inside them. Usually he didn't destroy things, what was going on with him? But *piano. Fingers. Heat.*

When he had a flame rising up under the copper hood he went away and with the pine needles tapping the window beside her she tried an arpeggio, middle C up. It sounded honky-tonky from being cold and in the hard room without enough soft things. But not that bad—a couple of chords—it wasn't so bad. He brought in a huge armload fireplace logs that were crusted with ice from outside and she sat down Indian-fashion to chip the ice off them and tend the fire. Some of the pieces were too long to lie down without hanging off the tiles, over the floor. She stood them up against each other, like a teepee.

Keeping watch that the wetness of the big pieces didn't put out the kindling she went back to the piano and looked inside it again, this time for the tuning wrench. She was leaning over the piano, on tip-toe, her head in under the raised top, reaching with her left hand to the keys, with her right turning the wrench, just a little here and there, high notes. Her sweater rose up her back and she felt the hot light of the lowering sun coming in under the boughs of the pine tree outside, warming the small of her back. She drank it in.

How good was Bobby's ear? It didn't matter, she needed the piano to be in tune, pretty much, to be able to play it at all. She tried an octave, a short arpeggio, a chord, found the peg, loosened then tightened it, so. She pushed herself back off the piano, aware of her breasts lifted by the curved edge. She tried the middle and upper registers, and now that she had touched up a couple of strings it was *good*. She tried octaves down, way down. The low wound strings gave a rich, chugging vibration. The lowest C, E, F took her breath away, after so long. She looked toward the door. Did he hear that? A piano could be such an emotional powerhouse, even a baby grand. The sound could carry you away. She thought of that great picture where a woman pianist has just been accompanying a violinist, they're formally dressed, and they've both just been overwhelmed by the music, and she's risen and he's swept her in to a passionate kiss, the violin in the hand that has her around the waist.

She wanted to play Chopin, something not too hard. She wanted to play children's music too, the Mother Goose Overture, the easy stuff that she had been trying to get ready for her recital, last year, last fall, the recital which she'd never dared to schedule and was supposed to be getting ready again while she practice-taught, but hadn't been. She had that program all memorized, more or less. Maybe she could do it without music. And then something heavier, if she thought she could. Night on Bald Mountain? It would be messy though. She'd stumble, with or without the music.

Bobby'd been down in the kitchen and outside turning on the gas tanks and getting snow in a pan, the way he usually did, and heating it on the gas stove, because now he brought bouillon. Mr Dexter had his own heavy white china with a green pine tree on it, nice. There was no heat from the fire yet, so she sat on the piano bench. While she sipped he sat next to her and told her the story of Dexter. *Orrando P.* Dexter, such a name! He didn't ask her if she had anything else on her mind, he just told it.

"You know that old story, Leo. Why did he tell it to me? Some rich man from Connecticut who came up here and bought up a lot of the woods including this lake and built this place which was a copy of some royal hunting lodge in Europe. What do I care about that? He brought his bride up here and they hired servants and guides and gardeners and furniture-makers from the Falls and had horses and boats, bla bla bla.

"And this was all just woods then and nobody owned it and everybody hunted and fished it or took wood from it the same as they had for a hundred years. But Mr Dexter didn't want anybody else on his however many thousands of acres, so he posted it all against trespassing. And people ignored his posters and it was too big to fence so he hired a bunch of uniformed constables to keep everybody off it. And the poachers didn't like that and the people who had wood-lots completely surrounded by Dexter's didn't like it and he wasn't very nice about how they were to get back and forth to their pieces, or how they were to get their lumber off. Didn't let them build roads, didn't give them enough time.

"And so on and so on until somebody shot him, in the back, as he was riding his buggy out to town to get the mail. And the vet found the bullet that went through the seatback and through Mr Dexter and through the dashboard of the buggy, just under the skin in the rump of the mare, but they never did find the gun that it came from. And the whole thing was famous all over the country because Mr Dexter's father put up a huge reward and a lot of people claimed to know who the killer was but nobody peached and wasn't that peachy because it showed how these North Country people couldn't be bought. And I'm all the time thinking I wonder what's in the piano seat. I've got to have music to play!"

After he finished, she folded her arms across her chest and frowned at him.

"Just a story," he said.

"It is an ugly story and stupid and sad, with the moral that this isn't a safe town to try to introduce new ideas in. Like legal rights? Civil rights? Women's rights?"

Robert looked sharply at her. His face changed, without any feature moving. The thing that it changed to was just plain sadness.

"Ever heard of them?" she said, unrelenting.

"Yah," he said.

He didn't like that. Ooh how he didn't like that. Then she hung her head and not looking at him said, seriously, "You're the victim of it too, Bobby. That town's obsolete ideas—of independence, courage, man-woman things. What were you trying to do when you came back from California? Weren't you introducing something new? I don't mean the grass, that's nothing. I mean the touching, the freedom, looking into people's eyes and *seeing* them. Peace and love, don't make fun of it. All that stuff your ank stands for. And what you got was threats to beat you up and break your nose and kill you. I know."

He didn't like this either. She sort of telepathied, *Aren't you glad I haven't been talking all this time?* He took their bowls and spoons and disappeared downstairs.

She could walk out, he said. Except she couldn't. She didn't have much of anything left. She wasn't absolutely all right. And he would never let her, really. Not and leave it at that. She itched to play the piano but she had to think think think about what she really *could* do, and what he thought *he* was doing. When she played, she had to make it count.

She heard him come up and go into one of the other corner rooms. He went down again and she thought maybe she heard him going into the cellar, and then he came up and went into other rooms again. Was he starting fires in the other fire-places? Lighting all the lights? It wasn't dark yet. He was doing something, his thing. She dreaded it, whatever it was.

Because what was that business of making their snowshoe tracks backwards? Was that supposed to fool anybody? There were searchers. She knew that. She knew who they must be, mostly. Sic'd on by Peter's mother, of course. She knew what he'd been doing, leaving signs, letting them know where he and she had been, antagonizing them, but always staying one jump ahead of them. Now if they found these tracks going across this lake and came to this house they'd think they were behind him and in no danger but he would be here waiting for them. With his thirteen bullets. *This was crazy! Could this be?*

But this place did resemble a fort, a block-house, with its overhanging second story. Wasn't that the way the colonists built their places, to ward off the Indians? They had shutters over the windows and slits to shoot through. Here it would be the Indians on the inside. Peter and Francis and their friends behind every tree outside the house and inside Bobby going from room to room trying to make like he had one of his Indian buddies aiming at them from every window. Trying to get himself killed in some heroic foolish way over her and thus pay up for Ray and leave a story that they would tell forever. She knew him better than he knew himself. He didn't care about anything but the way his blood pounded when he kissed her. After all her teaching, he was still a ninny about that. And she really believed that he was getting ready for the end, he was luring them here, to this place, famous already for one murder. "I really think he was, Leo!"

Not tonight, though, right? She wished she could ask him, They wouldn't find our tracks today, would they? Maybe they would. What did she know? He wouldn't succeed. It wouldn't turn out the way he'd dreamed it, no matter what. You can't make other people crazy just because you're crazy. And then the other thing, which maybe made all of these assumptions true. Bobby was wise to her, her body. What changes from that? Or did he allow for that from the first? *"I didn't know!"*

Robert came up and went into the other rooms. He went down again and she thought maybe she heard him going into the cellar and then he came and went into other rooms again. She heard him at the door and raised her head to show him a smile. She couldn't see his face behind the armload of wood he was bringing but she thought, Maybe he has a little bit of the same idea that I do. That we should be warm, that we should be friends, that we should get down to it completely and utterly because this is it. It-it-it. She was a person trying to be an artist in her life and she had a feeling of the way this could end and be art, like truth and beauty, herself and Bobby going around the Grecian urn together forever in the truth and beauty of their struggle and they could also go on living their lives a million miles away from each other and this circle of flight and pursuit go on forever just the same.

The first thing she saw in the bench was a book of Schuman songs. She snatched the volume up to her chest. This was amazing. This meant—don't say it. Under the Schuman, Chopin! Preludes and Nocturnes! Not so amazing really, Schuman, Chopin, but— She took the Chopin up and lowered the seat and sat down and lay the volumes on her lap. She sniffled. Should she tell him what she thought? "Do you know what this means, that these are here? Chopin, sure, but *Schuman? Frauenliebe und Leben?* It means that we are okay, Bobby. It means that everything is going to be all right." No, he'd think she was silly. But it really did mean this to her. It meant that the great god pine tree here was watching over them, that things were supposed to be the way they were.

She put the music on the piano and brought the Chopin to the top and leafed through it. Hardly registering what she'd chosen, she spread the music open, pressed it flat. She took her hair on her thumbs and carried it behind her ears, which would not hold it long. She sat up straighter. Her eyes were clear now. She hooked her fingers together in front off her and pulled. She interlaced her fingers and turned her hands palm out and stretched them. For a second she held her hands above the keys, fluttering her fingers. A smile came to her mouth and she touched them down. Music! She'd almost forgotten she could do this! A high E-flat was still too flat, she learned to skip it. She could tune that string later, this was just testing. In the middle registers the piano was so nearly right she played with open-mouthed surprise. The room was hard and sparkly, but that made the sudden abundance of sound more exciting. She stumbled sometimes, but she played the nocturne through without stopping, not so badly, a re-discovery, all her senses alive. She held her fingers on the last keys and let the sound die down. Out of sight, he didn't move a muscle, make a sound. Was he still there? He was listening. She could feel him.

She found another nocturne not too hard and played it. She tried for the same feeling, where the impulse of every note seemed exactly timed and measured, but there were cross-handed parts and she had to look down, she couldn't look back and forth fast enough, she stumbled a little. She remembered what work it was, playing so that it seemed easy. She struggled and created it the hard way, but she felt exposed, caught out. This was what she told everybody she did and yet she wasn't really great at it. She should be great at it but she wasn't. She was searching with tiny hesitations these staves she had played a thousand times. Shit! Shit! And there was Schuman to come. But my God, music! She didn't stumble as much as she feared. It was like coming back the next day after a bad practice and it all being easy, clear, her hands doing what they were supposed to do. Robert stood up and came behind her. What was he thinking? She hoped he noticed her fingers stumbling, overcoming obstacles. She hoped he saw that she was trying with all her heart. She hoped that the music knocked him out and that he saw that she wasn't great and that this was her life just the same, and she hoped he loved her as a real live ordinary person trying to be good at something terribly hard. She was nervous. It was terrible, these nerves, this vanity, a sickness, she was terrible about this, she had played piano since she was eight and she ought to be over this, but she wasn't. But here they were, just two lonely people in this old castle and she was trying to show him that that's all that they were and then there was music and that was the whole idea, trying hard to be good enough to play it well enough to make you happy, Bobby, so you wouldn't try and try and try to get shot like that man who lived in this beautiful place and wasn't happy enough to be nice to his neighbors. He laid his hand on her shoulder, where she had to put her hair at every right-hand rest. Was he moved? Did he see what music meant? What she was, how different her world was? She could barely wonder because she was getting caught up in it herself. She was so starved—

He reached in front of her and stopped her hands. His head was down next to hers, held still. She turned her face toward him. He was tense. He was listening hard, open-eyed. To a spoiled chord fading? Her forehead touched his cheek, his ear, the ring, which called her to him. She let the pedal up. Then she heard the hum. A drone, some distant motor. She looked out past his head, through the boughs of the pine tree so intimately close, at the blue sky over the lake. The drone got louder and louder. It wasn't a helicopter, it didn't batter the air like that. An airplane. There! A little one, coming low. Slow. Near. Noisy. The pine boughs moved, their shadows on the keyboard stirred. The airplane went over the roof.

He was smiling. The drone got quieter and quieter. He let her hands go. She turned to make him look at her. She didn't say these things but she asked him with her eyes, back and forth to his. *That's them, isn't it? They will be here in the morning, won't they? What're we going to do?*

His eyes didn't switch back and forth. His were steady. He was calculating the answers without having heard the questions. She rose from the bench and put her arms around him, held him against her breast. Then she took his hands and led him to one end of the bed that she had made for herself. They weren't going to sleep that way, apart. She went to the other end and they dragged the mattress onto the floor in front of the hearth. She straightened up the bedding on it. The fire was high now and she thought that while the sun set and the light outside turned pink and then blue they would sit here, close together. She wouldn't try to say everything. Maybe not anything. Later, in the gas-light, candle-light, with the room still warmer, she'd play the Schuman. Maybe she could mow him down with the Schuman.

And after that, would they? Could they? In this nice room all warmed up, a tropical paradise? In the skin-colored firelight? With their starved new never-seen bodies? She didn't know if she even had it in her but in that case she knew she could pretend. She had pretended quite a lot for other people's sakes in her short life and she always did want them a little at least and enjoyed it at least a little. It was very easy to do stuff when it gave so much pleasure and it was very easy to fake ecstasy when you were almost having it. The idea was spreading through her. It wouldn't be ecstasy anyway it would just be sharing, comforting, loving. Just love. If love wouldn't save him nothing would. But would it be okay?

24

All Right, Mister

Souver Hubbard lives in an unfinished ranch up on a bare ungraded cement foundation in cheap swampy land west of town, with a hairdresser named Janet who is his third wife, his second since JoAnn Sochia. It seems as if the house is always being lengthened, for a beauty shop on one end, a three-vehicle garage on the other. Beyond a field of broken machinery, on gravel fill, is the cinderblock shell of his eventual car and truck washing facility, new roof-trusses stacked and weathering against its side. All around that are septic tanks, dry wells, piles of coiled plastic drainage tile. Unfinished as everything is around Spry Company, everything eventually moves forward. A load of dirt will be dumped in the yard, towards eventual grass. Some sunny day three or four roof trusses will be thrown across between the block walls of the truck-wash, tilted up and stayed against the wind. Souver's everyday work is heavy trucking, of logs and anything else. His shoe-leather worn through, he is up into one of his trucks and off on a sixteen hour day every morning before five. He goes through employees the same as wives. They'll get his spirit for a while, the camaraderie of crazy hard work and the relish of absurdity, but it doesn't last forever. No one goes away mad.

He's always putting one thing off to do another, so Peter's project is no problem. He'd been itching to fly that little Ercoupe. "Just didn't have no time!" said as a joke on himself. Time pronounced *toime,* and shouted with emphasis. It's a two-seater, very small, low winged, not ideal for studying the ground. You sit shoulder to shoulder in it and shout in each other's ear. Now and then, coming or going, they'd be near Dexter Lake and Souver would make a point of flying over Dexter's house, just to trespass and bother him, though he was dead and gone sixty years.

This time they'd been circling way down to Kildare and the fuel tank was nearing empty. They flew straight over the pond on a bee-line for the hangar. They went right over the tracks, low, without seeing them, but the steep-roofed house with the giant virgin pines around it was in bright sunlight to the right, windows flashing through the boughs, and Peter saw the smoke, or vapor, a thin spout from the tall brick chimney, bent off at an angle by the breeze. Souver put the plane over on his own side and wheeled around pointing a wing at the edge of the pond. They stood momentarily over Catamount Ridge and then were back over the white ice, still on edge, and there were the tracks below, in high contrast, right in the open, right in the middle, going south southwest and off into the balsam swamp near the outlet. "Was them there yestiddy?" Souver asked. "No," he answered himself. "Where's they come from?" He came on around toward the copper roof and passed beside it, low, looking overboard on his own side. The tracks came down onto the pond out of mixed-up trampings around the house. He hollered, "You see any tracks comin' *to* the place?"

"Hanh?"

"Any tracks comin' *to* Dexter's? Them's going away. Maybe he's been living there all the time. Hee hee."

Souver took this whole thing without displeasure. Peter yelled, "There wasn't any smoke before."

His father grinned. "How good we been checkin'? A nice fire don't always make smoke." They were leveled off northward. Souver said, "Mebbe we stirred him out of there, jest by flyin' over. We better go look at them tracks again, wouldn't we?" They circled again and dropped low beside the tracks, paralleling them. Thirty feet above the level snow they could see the pattern of the mesh sometimes, and long blue shadows of puffs that the snowshoes had thrown up, and imprints of the slender tails of the shoes. "Them are not old," Souver shouted. "Not by no means." He lifted the plane a hundred feet to clear the balsams. They cast back and forth over openings in the timber to the south and west of the pond and saw at a distance something coming in, from the south, but these tracks never came out in the clear. "Ain't he a bitch?" Souver yelled. "He's crawling on his belly in that stuff."

Headed home again he said, "We found 'em, by Jesus! Hah? Now you boys can get to work!" He slapped Peter's thigh, tight beside his own. "But holy shit I near forgot about the gas! We best throttle back and stretch the fumes, here." In an eery relative quiet, they glided over treetops, roads, then fields and buildings, listening for the first cough and splutter of the engine.

The plane died right about when they flew over the orange balls strung over the Risdonville road, and Souver had to nose up and risk a stall to drift over the snow as far as his bulldozed track. It hit too hard for one of the struts, apparently, because the plane tilted to the right and dragged a wing along the snowbank. It pivoted around the wing-tip and decelerated rapidly with the broken strut plowing a furrow and came to a sudden halt, sideways, Peter banging against his father, the plane leaning hard on its left wing, its nose in the snow, the black stick-forest just beyond.

"Well, we were done flyin' ennaway," Souver said.

They sat there a moment, Peter appalled at what might have happened to the plane, the incalculable cost of repair. His father read him deeper than that. "Aw, it'll be all right," he said. Peter didn't respond. "You always get behind a few points before you get to work. That's the way you are."

"I wasn't thinking about that," Peter said.

"What are you thinking about?"

Peter didn't answer.

"Patty. Her phone trouble, y'mean?"

Souver sat back. "Murdock parks his telephone van up or down the street. He goes in. But what do you think he does with her? He has a cup of tea. He's a tea-drinker."

Peter burst out, "He takes showers with her, Dad!"

"Son of a gun!" Souver didn't ask for an explanation of that unexpected statement. Peter must have walked in on them. The bathroom's right at the top of the stairs in that house, he could have heard them splashing around from the vestibule. So, if you combined Patty with that other young woman, Peter did have troubles. But still, he thought, *It ain't nothing but human life. We're in the middle of it all the time.*

"Women," Souver said, with a happy shake of the head. "You know what? They taught me everything I know. One pushes you this way. Good, you needed it. Next pushes you that way. Lo-behold you needed that too. Add it all up, it's an education. You'd think it was planned by a mastermind, no shit."

Peter remained sunk in his gloom.

Souver said, "That's how I jest be perfecter and perfecter."

Out of the plane, walking back toward the house, he exclaimed, "Jesus look what a trench we digged! I'll have to come back with the cam'ra for that."

"This is good," Clarence said. "We know he's left Dexter Lake before we start. So where do we go? Dexter Lake."

The posse was riding in on Dexter's long driveway from the Blue Mountain Road, Clarence toward the back in the blue smoke, clamping Clarkie Tharrett round the middle. "Good recipe for no stew."

Clarkie couldn't hear him of course, so he turned to internal monologue. *Maybe a experienced hunter wouldn't need to see the track now, which way it went from Dexter, to tell you some places the buck might be hiding in. Maybe if you looked at where the track pointed you would be wrong. Maybe somebody knows sum'ing Mister LaFleur don't know.*

He'd kept his counsel when LaFleur signed up a ragtag bunch, more of them than usual and this time some of them armed. Big argument there, about who's to have a rifle on a sling across his back. LaFleur took one gun right off the man and locked it in his truck. Pistols he excepted lest he have a rebellion. The pistol fellows said they had a license to carry them, so who's he to tell them not to? LaFleur didn't want any guns at all, said the best way to get hurt was stick a barrel in Robert Sochia's face. Said he would take the girl away from him with his two hands once he caught him. *Well, may be, may be not*, Clarence thought. Clarence regretted a certain Colt's revolver he'd been looking at for years, gathering dust under a glass counter in Arquit's store. A hundred twenty-nine dollars, not cheap. Worth it, but he didn't want his sisters calling him a fool, so he hadn't shelled out, and now he wished he had. He'd like to have one on his hip today, for the quick draw.

They passed the famous boulder behind which the casings of the bullets fired at Orrando Dexter had been found, no more than a quarter-mile from the house. They scattered out and went to a lot of trouble to surround the place just in case Mister Murder Man had come back. Clarence heard somebody up front call warnings to surrender and so forth but naturally there wasn't even a vibration in the sky over that chimney by then. Clarence sat on a stone in the sun until called. They assembled on the terrace on the lake side, which the wind had kept clear. Tried the doors, guess what, the place was locked. Finally Atkin banged out a pane of one of the windows, unlatched it, nudged the bottom sash up. Climbed in and unlatched the French doors, top and bottom, and pulled them open. After a pause there was a little sudden rush to get through it, and Clarence followed. He was genuinely interested to see the insides of this legendary place, a very nice house, so he had heard.

People he knew had worked in here, for Dexter and his wife. The Dexters were good employers, they kept their people working most the year, hired guides to row them in their boats on into November, cut logs and firewood after that, cut ice from the pond for the ice-house; in spring made syrup from their maples. A nice-mannered person, the wife was, so they said. Sad thing to have your husband killed, no matter if he did invite it. Clarence was a very small boy when the fellow was shot.

Not fancy but a nice lot of windows and nice scenes to see through them in all directions, woods and lake. Neat, bare, cold. Clean except dead insects and seeds brought in by squirrels, and that track of snow across the parquet floor to the wide staircase that turned twice going up. Clarence tramped up the stairs behind the other men, saying humorously, "Look, guess what, some'n's been up these stairs, not very long ago. Hnnn-nh."

He looked in each room after the others did, as if he was on a school tour, too far behind the teacher to hear what she said. He didn't register everything. Exclamations coming from the one room distracted him. When he came in there he thought the point was the open hearth with the copper hood over it, and he mumbled in agreement, "Well, goodness, nor did I ever. A fireplace like that." Started to say, "What's that he was using for firewood?" because the unburned ends of the legs of some piece of furniture lay around the ashes. They were from the wooden spool-bed, as nice a bed as you please, maple wood, broken to bits and the mattress drawn up to the fire and the bedding in a heap. And then he saw the piano.

Perfect it was, like new, untouched, but so close-by he feared for it in retrospect. The thought of it down off its legs and the legs in the fire just stopped him. Moved him a step backwards. Burning up the bed bespoke a callousness incomprehensible to him. So how close did that piano come to getting burnt? If his step-mother could have had a piano in their log home not far across the woods from here, when he was a boy, she would have been a happy young lady. If ever a person loved music. Not to mention himself, who might have learnt to play it too. Up to now, he'd had some sympathy with the fugitive, some admiration as you had for the buck that always slipped away. *But not no more.* Imagining him in here, burning that piano to light his mischief with that nice girl.

They all went down and out onto the lake-side terrace and round to the drive and checked the couple of pistols among them and looked at one another soldier-like. One fellow said he was going back to the truck to get his rifle, fuck LaFleur. Not starting a trend, he didn't go. They looked at their watches. They pulled on their helmets and got on their sleds. With Prentice in the lead they ran down onto the ice and strung out at good speed along the snowshoe trail across the pond. It was almost hot in the glaring sunlight, and Clarence with his arms around his young chauffeur closed his eyes.

No money in the house for such a thing when he was young, only a Jew's harp and your own voice. And your step-mother's, not much older than your older sister but as good to you as any mother, with a sweet voice she had no child of her own to inherit. *When I catch up with you, Mister . . .*

At the southwest side of the pond they bounced up among snow-covered rocks and into thick trees, a wall. Dense young balsams, the kind of place a wounded deer lies down when pressed and makes the hunter crawl. Good as a house against the wind, as Clarence knew. Somebody on a light, low-powered sled ran around the eastward side of the inlet swamp and the bog and the hardwood ridge that bordered it, to see where the track came out. Came back saying he had found the track but he thought it was going the wrong way, left to right. If it was this track it ought to be crossing right to left. Atkin said, "Shit, who cares which way it's going? If it's his track, let's go!" Harry said somebody better run around the other way too. So while they waited for that, Hubbard asked, "Where you thinking he would go from here, Harry?"

Clarence was only half listening but he caught that, best question he'd heard in a long time. Could answer any of three places and not tell all he thought. This country was rich. He didn't know that he was talking out loud himself until Hubbard came over. "What did you say, Clarence? I'm listening."

Clarence was already in the middle of something, another question of where someone might go from somewhere, started up by being in that house of Dexter's. He took a breath, now he had an audience. "Reason my father was to the court in the first place was this, them others come and fetched him, with a jug of liquor. All suspected of murdering Dexter, they were, or else paying some'n else to. What'd they do when in trouble, come to my father, get him to go and do their talking for them. B'cause it was well known how he could talk. That's why he was to the court. And when he got done talking, wasn't a case against any of them fellows."

"Yeah?"

"So that was when the judge stood up, looked at a map they had in court there, this territory right round here. Asked Father,

'All right, Mister Shampine, if 'twasn't any of these other boys, then where was you, that day when Mister Dexter got it in the back?' 'Where was I?' Father says. 'I was right to home.' 'Where's your home, Mister Shampine?' 'One big hill away from Cook's Lake on the road to the Falls, is where my home is. Not far from the broo-k.' 'Is that so?' says the judge. 'Looky here, then, Mister Shampine, here's the map, it ain't very fur crosslots betwixt Mr Dexter's house and yours. I see there isn't any road. Might be there's a trail. How long would it taken you to go over there and let daylight into Orrando P. Dexter yourself?' 'That, sir,' my father told the judge, 'would depend on how fast I walked.'"

"What's this bullshit?" Billy asked.

"From Dexter's to where?" Hubbard asked.

"The home place," Clarence said. "Where I was born."

"Where?"

Clarence stood up and simply pointed, as if with that pistol that he wished he had. West or a little south of west.

"How long would it take, Clarence?" Hubbard said.

"On foot, forty minutes to a hour, for a woodsman, but don't you try it. Surprised? That shows how much you know when all you know is the roads. Them two places are close'ter together than you think, since you reach them from different highways, different sides of town. That's the way the woods is, very interesting. All connected up, long b'fore the roads was ever built."

"Forget it, Clarence," Billy said. The scouts were back. Had found the track, going west down the valley, in the open. Billy said, "He's gone to Purryer's camp, on this end of Cook's Lake. That's what I think. That's the only fuckin' place left, lest he's just runnin' to the road. Come on, assholes." He jumped on his sled, revved it up until it started to move, then looking to Harry with his mouth in an *o*.

Hubbard was standing beside Clarence. "Ride with me now, Clarence, will you?"

"What?"

"Ride with me." Hubbard turned to Tharrett. "Clarkie, that all right with you?"

Clarence had gotten used to riding with Tharrett. He didn't know Hubbard. He didn't want to switch, but the boy was interested. He asked a good question. Tharrett turned him over, with a shrug.

Hubbard drove off quickly, right behind the leaders, and sat up stiffer with his hands out straight to the handlebars. Clarence rode uncomfortably with Hubbard's helmet in his face. He leaned out and looked ahead. They were going into country where Clarence's father had owned three small woodlots, now his sisters', which Clarence wished were his, squares and rectangles of second growth, worthless to his sisters or anybody else. If they'd been left to him, he could have logged them just the way he wanted to, the old way, with horses, and boarded himself and a team off the proceeds. That was all he would have asked in life. But oh no, Clarence was no good with figures, they said, those lots were too much for Clarence to be entrusted with. *Is that so, you don't know how much I've got in the bank.* Instead, had to ask permission even just to take stove-wood. Had to report to his sisters if he was only going in there to fish. Afraid he would stay too late, get lost in the dark!

For a way they followed the frozen outlet of Dexter Lake, bordered by another stump-filled bog. Then they veered to the south across a range of low hardwood hills and in the next valley hit the snowshoe trail. Sochia and the girl, for sure. They swept onto these tracks and ran right on top of them, Prentice in the lead. Then Atkin raced past Hubbard and Clarence, up beside the leaders, got them to stop, took his helmet off and shook his fists. "Wait a minute! Don't just chase after him!" he yelled.

"What's the problem, Billy?"

"That Purryer place is a fuckin' fort, that's all. We're being led right to it!"

"No we ain't," Prentice said, "we hardly found the trail. You don't know where it's going."

"Yas I do, he's going to Purryer Camp. You been to Purryer Camp?"

"I know where it is. Here, Clarence knows the place."

They were gesturing at him to take his helmet off. "Purryer Camp? The best log building ever built. Tamarack logs forty foot long and straight's a die, thick end of one laid on the thin end of the other, coped to fit without no chinking. My brother and I shoveled the snow off that camp for fifty years."

"I ain't listening to this," Prentice said. "Let's go!"

Hubbard turned around on the sled to warn Clarence, then accelerated after his friend, Clarence trying to snap his chin-strap one-handed.

He wasn't sure he was allowed to embrace this new driver around the waist. He worked one mitten under the seat-strap between them and clenched Hubbard's hips with his knees. He shut his ears to the tinny up-and-down whine. This was a rough trail, because it was no trail. He couldn't see ahead anyway, so he almost closed his eyes. But they opened wide when the timber pulled away to the sides and the pitching ceased and whiteness shot out flat beside them, brilliant, and at once he was afraid.

He knew what this was, they were crossing Mud Pond, they were running out on the open ice, two fellows on a half-ton machine, more of such behind, a thing he would not do himself alone, afoot or on snowshoes, though laughed at for a coward. No matter how cold it might have been, how thick you thought the ice was, because this was a spring-fed pond, just like Cook's lake, there were springs of water under here which might open up a hole, anywhere, or keep the ice thin even if covered by the snow. Dared not take loose a hand to pound the fellow's back. He held on tightly, stiff with prediction of sudden, balladless death. Thin ice beside them now, bare, black! Black water under there!

But here they were, still running on top, white snow underneath, racing toward the narrowing far end and safety. When the sled suddenly veered under him and stopped, still out in the open, way short of land, he didn't know what was happening; something just before drowning, he feared. Hubbard jumped up, knocking his head back. Hubbard was yelling at him. Get off? Off? Hubbard roughly dragged him off the sled, he caught his balance, afraid to go down. The fellow pounced behind him and dragged the back end of the machine around, like Charlie Chaplin for speed, straddled it again and roared away.

Clarence was alone where he didn't want to be, but the ice felt firm as the skating rink under him. He stood with his hands at his sides, turning around. This was his sister's pond, a beautiful place to him. You could come here in the summer and with a big fire on that rocky point where the other sleds were gathering, you'd catch a washpanful of bullheads. They were waving to him, to come on, come on. Pointing to something ahead, jumping up and down and yelling and pointing but he couldn't hear them. He took his helmet off. The walking wasn't good.

LaFleur's sled was still out there making a wide loop, and Hubbard's. Clarence could see somebody's helmet, just above ice-level, could see his bulky green-suited arms sometimes, reaching up slowly, one at a time, one and then the other.

"Where's his sled?" somebody said on shore.

"Gone to the fucking bottom!"

"Who is it?"

"Prentice! He went in!"

With one thick arm at a time Prentice seemed to be waving to them. It looked to Clarence as if the monkey-suit buoyed the fellow up. He could see that he was clinging to a deadhead that might have made that open place, a grey old pine snag that stuck up through the ice and drank up the heat of the sun and kept the ice thin around it. With the engines on shore idling or stalled, all but LaFleur's and Hubbard's continually moving out there, Clarence could just hear Prentice's puny yelling.

Now another roar and another sled racing out there, going too fast for Clarence to follow. Clarence could scarcely watch, for this machine went right back in the tracks and ran straight for the black hole with the other fellow in it. At the last second, it turned and passed close by it, very fast, the rider looking over sideways, shouting something. And now LaFleur was there too, on foot, too close to that hole for good health.

Then Hubbard came back past the hole the other way and what Clarence thought he saw was Hubbard fall off his own machine, sidewards and backwards. But he held on to it some way by his feet. Head and arms, upside down, he went right over the icy water and somehow he and other fellow took ahold of each other's hands, and they dragged the sled to a halt. But going that fast, it jerked the boy up halfway out of the water before it stopped.

Clarence understood the physics of that. Get anything going that fast, it takes some force to stop it, the more the bigger it is. That stunt was enough to give the boy a purchase on solid ice. Then here came LaFleur, another good man, Johnny-on-the-spot and fearless, grabbed the handlebars of Hubbard's machine, gave it the gas and hopped on, and skidded the two of them both away and clear. Cheers and whoops on shore. "A nice piece of work," Clarence said to nobody, "well-done, faster than you can say Jack Robinson. Good work for the one in the drink too. If that been me, sunk before you got near me."

Now Hubbard jumped up and dragged the other fellow to the sled. The other fellow couldn't move, it looked like. Hubbard got him bent enough to sit, pushed him on ahead of LaFleur, and the sled lit for the shore faster than Hubbard could skip. He fell, got up, stood on the ice, sucking his hands, which were bare. Wincing, shaking them, he started to run. LaFleur was hollering to them on shore, something Clarence didn't understand at first. "Fire! Fire!"

"Start a fire, start a fire!" LaFleur cried, coming up on the point.

"What with? Wet wood frozen through?"

Clarence had already turned to look about the point for anything to kindle. The day he couldn't find something to start a fire with, rain or snow, would be a very wet day, and colder than this. Those little hairs on the bottoms of the hemlocks would light, moss from under the snow too, but then what? You were going to need a fire to heat all outdoors, to save that young man. LaFleur yelled, "Gasoline!"

LaFleur, yes sir, good idea, Clarence thought. That fellow knows how to do in an emergency. Had that whole crew looking like the Army in a minute, and Clarence found himself standing in the middle of a storm of activity. Snapping twigs. Limbs being swung against tree trunks to break them short. He recognized a figure in green and yellow coveralls standing beside him, speechless. Embarrassed, he said, "Well, you're a good swimmer, good wor-k."

The flames stood as tall as a man for a moment and then there was just smoke. The man in green crawled into the ashes. But the fire died, didn't even make a slurry. Clarence would have done better if asked and given time. LaFleur told them to swing the fellow over what fire there was. "Smoke the bastard," someone said. "If he don't live at least he'll keep." But it was a losing battle keeping enough of the small dry twigs burning to get the larger ones going and melt the snow down to the ground and build up some coals in time, even with some of them stamping a kind of little fort in the snow and building up the sides to stop the wind. Hubbard was slapping Prentice's face and pinching his cheeks, yelling at him, "Stay awake, you dumb son of a bitch!"

Then Clarence didn't exactly hear right, LaFleur shouting: "Never mind. Forget the fire. Strip him. Every stitch! Off! Us too! Quick!" And they were doing it, Clarence saw pallor and hair and didn't look. The green snowmobile snowsuit spread on the ashes, dirty snow. "Us too! Every stitch, God-damn you! Every mother's son!" Clarence started to move his hands to his neckerchief knot though others were rebelling. "Hanh?" He stopped. But LaFleur irresistible, a force of nature. "Show me your cheeks, damn it! He's freezing!"

But of course that was right, no better way. Big LaFleur himself, white, booted, a tattoo on his chest, longjohns around his ankles, kicked the wood aside, threw his snowsuit in the trampled place, yanked others' out of their hands. Clarence's fingers stiffly worked the knot but at the same time he stumbled backwards. Naked men issuing steam and odor and giggling now, sniggering, massing together. *I don't think I—*

Against his will he saw between them LaFleur down on the suits with his arms and legs open like a woman's, a way Clarence would not have imagined but had seen in picture-magazines. The frozen man slung over him, LaFleur's hairy white legs clamped him in. "All right, pile on!" Other men crawled on top of them and beside them, bare, and more on them, laughing, rolling off and touching the snow and hopping back on, squealing, and then somebody yelling for Clarence, "Clarence! Where's Clarence? Cover us up! Keep us covered! Where the hell is he?" Swearing at him but he was already stepping around the edges of the mass, avoiding legs, avoiding sight. Picking things up and covering whiteness without touching, sympathetically muttering, "That's a cold wind, I wouldn't want—" Snowmobile jackets, opened like capes, the overhauls with the legs unzipped, he made what blankets he could of them, put them back on the pile of bodies as fast as they slid or were kicked off. Round and round, fast as he could go around the pile, a losing battle, amidst squeals and cries in mock-female voices, "Ooh, Jerry, I didn't know you cared." "Dis is pretty warm, by da Gee, you know dat?" "Not my ass ain't warm! Clarence, get over here!" "Hey Francis, you talking yet?"

Clarence closed his mind to it, talked to himself to cover it, "Suppose that was a live animal instead of a machine. Once upon a time a man that had no more sense than go right over black ice next to a stump, wouldn't been allowed to drive a horse. Run and fetch is all he'd been considered good for. Nowadays, every orangutang can do as he pleases. Now this pond of my sister's, it isn't the same no more, has a brand new pile of purple junk on the bottom of it that don't belong anywhere on earth, that's my opinion."

The pile got noisier and sillier, his name often called, but Clarence didn't listen. He stumbled round and round it, abstracted, picking things up. So many things to do at once, but you can only do one at a time. Made him think of the man that ran the evaporator in Wilfred Gonyea's sugarbush, had much to do and much depending on it. Keep the foam down and feed the arch and syrup off at just the right time, when the syrup aproned just so from the scoop. "Boiling sap, that is a job that I was never asked to do, and would not ask to do, much sap as I have gathered. Because for the simple reason, a maple syrup evaporator isn't a team of horses."

He saw, as if it were a dark cloud descending on them all, above and behind their shoulders, the story that this would be. The ridicule that would fall upon them all. Saw the very image of it that the whole community would soon have graven in its consciousness, even though it was only himself that was here to see it. All these bare bottoms in a heap, squirming and kicking, and himself going round and round. "Just like the maid in a whorehouse, attending to people without their clothes on. You think I never been to a whorehouse. Well, you're right. But I have been places where I couldn't miss hearing more than I wanted to know about them. My ears turned the color of the fire truck."

And somewhere in along there, he quit. He didn't notice when, himself. Only knew it when he said it. Already matter of fact and done without effort. Heard himself say it. "This isn't what I signed on for. Tomorrow, don't look for me to ride with this posse. I'll be somewheres else, on the same case, alone."

The pile surged. Clarence stepped back, a shirt in his hand. Someone crawled to him and grabbed it, and then they were all around him, dancing in their socks, looking for their clothes and the right snowsuit. LaFleur pushed Prentice upright, pinched his cheeks. He still couldn't talk. Somebody said, "Frank's suit's soaked, he can't wear that." LaFleur said, "Give him somebody's that's got bibbed bottoms. He's gonna ride in front of me. Give him clothes, come on, come on! Another wool shirt. Pants."

They were dressing the fellow. "Want to go home, Frank? Your mother and sister'll give you a nice hot bath in the tub."

"Spit out the marbles, Frank."

He was moving his lips. Dressed, he jumped slowly around in a circle.

LaFleur sat on his jacket, pulling on his pants. Atkin, all ready to go, stood beside him, wanting to have a conference. Slyly, Clarence listened. "We can't go on today, huh?" Atkin said. "He'll still be there tomorrow. Or maybe he's giving up, eh? That's what he's doing here, maybe. Getting ready to come out."

"Yeah, Billy," LaFleur said. "That's why he led Francis into a hole."

"We can't go on now though, ain't that right?"

LaFleur looked around at the group. He'd be the last dressed. Motors were already running. They weren't even going to wait for him.

"Got to go back to the trucks. Home. Get warm, get dry," Atkin said. "Then, it's too late to start again. So have a meeting tonight. Make a plan. Get some rest. Go up there by way of the lake in the morning. That's the way to hit Purryer Camp. Go in fast, on the lake. Early. A fuckin' fleet. Everybody together."

LaFleur couldn't zip his boots. Fingers numb. Motors were revving, sleds jerking and stopping. Clarence looked for his ride.

"Rilly," Atkin said. "What elst can we do?"

Clarence had already quit. It didn't matter to him.

Quitting, all privately, inside, was a thrill he'd never experienced. Wasn't sure how it had happened, but it had. The day was a waste to them but not to him. It wasn't noon. The bank would still be open when they got back, Arquit's would be open.

Hubbard, with a silly grin on his face, was waving for him to come get on behind.

25

Iceman Comes

They'd had a string of clear, cold, snowless days, ten in a row counting today when Prentice nearly froze. Now, the radio said, a front was coming through. First, by that evening, south winds and a wave of unseasonable warmth. Sometime during the night, warm rain, turning heavy, and in the early hours, a sharp drop in temperature, to well below freezing. Then deepening cold. By morning it would be clear, the coldest day since January, ten below zero, warming gradually under clear skies, bright sun. This would be the first ice-storm of the spring, and it would be a dandy. Tomorrow a snowmobile would be able to run anywhere in the woods or in the open, on the crust.

In the bars that afternoon (lightly attended at first—the Trailblazers went home to warm up) JoAnn was strangely sweet and amused. She wasn't saying much but she was wearing a soft green woolly top that somehow lifted each of her breasts, small but tantalizing, in its separate sling, supporting it from the opposite shoulder. This could be confusing, for a man with three or four dead-Indians lined up in front of him. She was mum but she had a private smile and everybody knew she would take charge again at the fire station that evening. Eleven o-clock. Everything was in suspense until then, they all felt that, and so they were surprised when the place filled up later in the afternoon and she went to work with her big shears.

Still with the sweetness, the smile that didn't for once seem so ironical. She was in high spirits but she went a little crazy with those scissors. She had to have a snip off everybody's shirt, a good

long snip too, twenty inches or so, long as a mink, tail and body.
She got under their jackets to the nice wool hunting shirts most of
them had on underneath, most everybody giving up the tail of his
shirt with pretended good humor even though this was wholly
unfair, and expensive. Billy Atkin wouldn't let her near him. He
was more than usually profane. "This sucks, JoAnn! I didn't miss
no buck. This is a forty-dollar shirt and you ain't cutting it." And
when she came at him again, "Fuck off!"

She'd been pretty sexy last night too, different, when they
thought they had RS pinned at Dexter. They'd all talked about it,
envying Harry. Her color high, how eager she looked. "Once this
is over old Harry gets his reward." "What wouldn't you give for
some of that?" Not that anybody would forget what she said when
somebody asked, "What we do with Sochia when they get him?" A
question on a lot of minds. JoAnn had answered, "Bring him to
me!"

They'd whistled at that. What in Jesus's name did she mean
by that? "Bring him to me!" Billy Atkin muttered, "That was fuckin'
final. Whew."

Now the shirt-tails from the cast of the whorehouse-scene at
Mud Pond were tacked like a great garland up the bar columns
and along the ceramics shelf between them, replacing last hunting-
season's snips, and she was all right again, more herself but still
exciting somehow, sexy. Always sexy but sexi*er*. It was like this
changing weather outside that you could feel, right through the
walls of the place, getting balmy, quite unfamiliar, giving you the
itch. The men commented on it to each other, indirectly. "That
was a little scary, JoAnn with them shears. Black handles and silver
blades, ten inch blades to them things."

Peter's shirt-tail among the rest of course though many of the
men had thumped him on the back very seriously, by way of
acknowledging what he had done out on the ice. JoAnn didn't give
him any credit, much less call it saving a life. But he felt good. He
felt surprisingly good. He only wished he could go home and get
his rocks off like some of the others. It occurred to him Francis
must be out of the bathtub by now and he left The Rapids to go

see how he was doing. Francis was probably full of brandy slings. If he wasn't still in the tub he would be on the couch in a bathrobe and slippers, propped up with pillows and covered with a comforter. He'd be watching hockey, or the car races in Florida, his mother and sister taking his temperature every ten minutes. His sister Carla might give Peter a kiss for pulling him out. He was hardly aware when he did it but it felt good after, he was proud of it. His father had told him that when he did something good in the middle of a ball-game, it wasn't just following coach's orders. No coach could have told him how to do it. *You* did it, his father'd said.

He was not that surprised when the Prentice women didn't thank him. They didn't even let him in. Carla wouldn't open the door more than to snap at him, "Oh, not you. Go away." She was an old flame of Peter's and still bitter, so. He pushed the door against her but hit the chain. He saw the shadow of Mrs Prentice's dressing-gown, swinging, on the hall floor behind her. They blamed him for this whole business. Their Francis could do no wrong.

"How's he doing?" At least they could tell him that.

"Just fine! And he's staying that way. He's all through with your hunt."

Peter hadn't even thought of this possibility. He called in past them, cried, "What? Hey, Frank. You quit? Huh? You can't quit."

But Carla said, "Yes he can quit! He has. Good-bye."

"But I need—I can't—Tomorrow—" Door closed in his face. Francis *quit.* Huh? You could quit? Could he? *Nah, nah. It's for Ma.* Ma and Julia. But he didn't know about Julia any more. It would be neat to swoop by on a snowmobile and save her like he did Francis. But he didn't know if she would want to be saved, anymore. He didn't know if she needed it. He didn't need to do it. He was over her. He could be a hero and forget it, didn't really care if he ever got in her pants or not. He wanted to get in somebody's pants pretty soon but no more Julia's than Patty's. He wanted to get it back like that with Patty and have it in bed with her the way they used to, belonging to each other and nobody else and having it as good as it was. Like the uncle who gave him his house had told him: "All right, you're married. Now, keep your pecker in your pants." Except at home. And the kids. It was all clear to him now, what he wanted. Try to be a family and make some money and get a better job and move along, upwards. Play some ball again, get in shape, get rid of the pot. Already he felt lighter, better, unburdened by that few seconds of action at Mud Pond. You don't have to brag, you just feel better, after you do something. That's what matters. And things get clearer.

Now what, though? Nothing happening until the meeting tonight. Time-out. Plan an in-bounds play. But it never worked. Things never turn out the way you plan. Something else happens you never thought of. You just go in and do what you do.

He was still on the Prentices' side-walk. What he wanted to do was go home, surprise Patty, see if she felt like it. But he couldn't. He had to finish this other thing first, so now he slipped back into the pickup and circled the block and came out opposite The Rapids again. Went back in and told them Francis quit.

"Frank's made *peace? Now?*" Billy Atkin had arrived by then. "I'd want to *kill* the cocksucker, if t'was me." JoAnn looked sharply at him, her lips pursed: even as applied to Robert Sochia, that language went beyond the standard at her bar. "That was a trap," Billy said, undeterred. "Another fucking cowardly murder, that's what that was. All but. Except for Peter here, hey?"

JoAnn brought Peter a beer, gaily, as if she agreed.

Later in the afternoon word came down from the bank and Arquit's and the gas company about another quitter, Clarence Shampine. He hit the three places one after the other. First, the bank. He came in there very much like a robber, had a kerchief round his neck that he only pulled down from his nose at the last minute. When asked if they could help him, he told them gruffly, Give him everything in his account, cash. No, he didn't have no checkbook, it was his money, however much there was of it, which they knew better than he did, and he wanted it, now.

One looked at the other, afraid to just hand him that much money. The teller said,"My goodness, Clarence, all of it?" She knew she wasn't supposed to bat an eye, but she felt responsible to Bess and Nellie Shampine.

He said, "Yes, all of it. Starting a new life, that's what I saved it for. How much is it, girlie?"

"Well just let me see. (Girly!)" But the one not talking to him had already looked up his account, and she put in, "It's ten thousand two hundred thirty-seven dollars and twenty-two cents, Clarence."

"All right, maybe you think that is a small amount, for a man who has worked hard all his life. But more than some clowns that ride motor-sleds under water could lay hands on that fast. Fork it over."

"You must be going on a spree. I could use a nice vacation myself." The younger woman, in the teller's window, raised a shoulder at him and touched her hair in back. But before Clarence could prepare a gallantry, the other one said, "Clarence, do your sisters know you're doing this? Taking out all your money?"

"No and I put myself to bed at night too. If 'twas up to my relations I would have kept that cabbage in a sock and forgot where it is by now."

The ladies exchanged looks, hunched shoulders. "Well! How do you want it?"

"Cash, I told you."

"Hundreds?"

"What?"

"Do you want it in hundred dollar bills?"

That seemed to rock him slightly, and he asked the teller to put in some fives and tens. And ones. They had to tell the manager and open the vault. The bank manager came out of her room and stood watching. He stuffed what he could in his pocket, and they gave him a bank envelope for the rest. The younger one came out from behind the counter and turned his neckerchief around for him. He went out holding the big envelope in both hands.

He must have thrown the envelope on the front seat of his pickup in passing, because he wasn't carrying it when he came into Arquit's. The clerk at the check-out noticed that he was dressed for the woods, with those laced high-topped boots nobody else wears anymore, and a red bandanna spread over his rounded back like a Boy Scout's. He headed straight for the sporting goods and paced around over there until they called Duke out of the meat room to wait on him. Arquit walked up the aisle in his white paper hat, wiping his hands and taking off his bloody apron, receiving orders all the way. "Give me that Colt's revolver in your case, Arquit. Quick, b'fore some'n else snatches it up."

Arquit leaned two-handed on the glass counter looking down through it. He bent down and slid the door open and brought out the weapon in its open box. "A hundred twenty-nine dollars," he said. "That's too cheap now," he said. "I ought to raise that price."

Clarence picked the pistol up. Didn't look closely at it, didn't even blow off the dust. "Now where's the hol-ster?"

Arquit found one in a drawer under the case, looked at its price, put it on the counter saying, "That ought to cost more too."

"Give me two boxes of ca'tridges."

Arquit could see he was dealing with a new man, but he went on teasing. "Gee, do they still make ammunition for that? Let's see." He found a box of shells, shoved it toward the customer on edge.

"Give me another."

"This is adding up," Arquit warned.

Clarence said, "Yes, I know it, you're a thief, and if 'twas twice as much it wouldn't make no difference."

So Arquit thought he'd better finally ask, he being *in loco sororis* too. "What're you buying that thing for, Clarence? It weighs ten pounds, you can't hold it up."

Clarence held the piece left-handed by the barrel and settled the checkered wooden grip in his right palm. He extended it at arm's length, drawing a bead on something meatwards. "Just possible," he said, "where I'm going, I might meet up with a she-bear. When that happens, say your prayers, Bruin." He mimed a gentle recoil.

Arquit moved around the counter and stood close to Clarence. He took off his paper hat. He said quietly, "You don't need to go with them tomorrow. They know where he's at now. That business is as good as over with. You've done your part. Come back on the town crew. Let me put the pistol back. You don't need that thing."

Clarence put the pistol in the holster on the counter. He pulled three hundreds out of his wad and let them fall on the glass. "Get my change. And another thing, you can look for a new snow-boy. I'll move out 'the cabin tomorrow." He gathered up his purchases and headed for the check-out counter.

"Well, all right, but hold your horses," Arquit told him. "If you're bound and determined to have that weapon, we got paperwork to do. This ain't the Wild West here."

When he finally got out of there he went around the pickup, threw that armload through the open driver's window, then got in and drove ahead about four parking places and stopped in front of the gas company.

Conlon Tidy said that he looked neither to the left nor to the right, marched straight through the empty store to the office in back, and told Tidy, "Give me that cooker in the window, how much, hundred dollars, I can read, all right here's your money," all before Tidy could remember that he had anything you could call a cooker in front there, or anything else. Once in a while he has a stove or a water heater in the window, usually in its crate. Then he did remember what he had there. He said, "You mean the barbecue?"

"Don't care what you call it, I call it a cooker because it cooks, and that's what I want it for."

"Sure, glad to get shut of it." But then again, remembering more about it. "You had a good look at that thing, Clarence? It's a sort of a fancy model."

Clarence said, "So what, sum'ing wrong with my money? Put 't in the truck."

No please, no thank you. Before that rudeness, Tidy'd been going to point out that it was the kind of a cooker you mount on a concrete pad on your patio and pipe the gas to it underground. It had no provision for a portable tank of fuel. But now he just said, "All right, sir!" and led Clarence out to the front of the store.

Clarence opened the street door and let in the cold, impatient while Tidy climbed into the window and lugged the thing onto the floor, saying, "You think it's summer, Clarence?" He put on a jacket and hoisted it again, out the door and onto the tailgate of the pickup, tipped it over on its side among some icy hunks of firewood Clarence carried there for traction. Clarence slammed the tailgate back up and pounded his hands together with finality. Tidy said to wait but he was already roaring away, slipping his poor clutch, before Tidy, back inside, could write out the sales slip and add the tax. He turned around at Lenny's garage and went past without turning his wooden head, Tidy outside again waving the slip at him unnoticed.

Some head-shaking along the bar, grins exchanged that seemed to mean that something unkind could be said, we all know what, but kindly wasn't said. Old Shampine was a wonder for dumbness, but only his own problem and he'd never know it. Peter saw more in him than that. Funny, sure, but also— He didn't know; he liked him. He enjoyed him.

"Ma. You all right?"

Weller was still over at the far end of the bar with his Coke, but everybody else had gone home. Peter wondered, is she really cool with this? With waiting overnight? Himself, he'd just as soon be doing something. In the dark? Yeah, in the dark. He'd had a couple of beers, he was restless. He liked this warm dark night, somehow. Darkness might be good. He surely wasn't going to go and do his shift, not tonight. Maybe she'd like to talk.

"What kind of a question is that?"

"It'll be all over tomorrow," he said.

"Will it."

"Yah. I mean don't you think so?"

She pointed with her nail-file at the bar behind her, meaning Ray. "He'll still be dead."

"Yah." He wanted to stay with his own focus. "I'm gonna get right with Patty after this."

"That's nice." She turned around and looked up at the garland of shirt-tails. "I think I'll make a braided rug." She flashed him a really bright smile.

"You know how to do that?"

"Of course I do!" Then she said furiously, "Nobody knows me!"

He thought maybe she would go on if he waited.

"Nobody! I'm back here behind the bar, running things. Running everything."

"What do you mean, Ma?"

"Billy was so shocked, at my reaction to his ugly speech. If he knew how I'd like to choke him! Running things: it would all just stop if I stopped. Nobody else could do this. I could never sell this stinking business. The cooler, the washer, the help, if you could call it that. I'm the mother of a pubescent daughter—did you know you have a sister?"

"Yes, Ma."

"You have no conception! I even have to run your hunt for you. Nothing would happen if I didn't provide the leadership, the gumption! Harry? Don't make me laugh."

Peter was strangely warmed. Maybe it was coming from outside, through the thin walls.

"Do you know whom I am thinking of calling into my bed?"

Wow. "No, Ma."

She'd made herself excited but now she looked away and slumped.

"Without me people could talk like animals and get raped, get shot, shat upon and nobody'd do anything about it."

"Who, Ma?"

"Royal Sochia seduced me at sixteen and walked on my face at seventeen. I made a toy out of his son for that. I had his balls in my teeth and I let him go. And he shoots my brother in cold blood. What do you expect me to do about this?"

She let that flurry go by and said, cooly, "Whom, Peter, with an m. Object of the verb. Whom would I take into my bed. Terry O'Neil."

"Yah?" Peter was open-mouthed with surprise.

"A clean, hard, boney man. I'd like his body, I think. I'd like his *brain*. It's the only *mystery* around. Nobody knows me. Nobody has the least little idea what it is to be me, what I want, what I'd like. I *do want*. Wouldn't you know, I want a man who is utterly speechless with contempt for me. I'd have to give him myself to show him there's nothing there! Nothing but an injured, whimpering girl. Did you hear all this, Mister Big Ears? Are you listening, Leo?"

Weller over there was draining his Coke, rattling the cubes. He banged the glass down on the counter. "What? I missed it," he said, smiling.

JoAnn put her hand to her brow and, removing it, gave her head a shake.

It was over, Peter knew. She was tense because everything was coming to a head, that's all. Harry came in. It must be time for Peter's ride. He got up from his stool suddenly, slapped the bar, and went out under the streetlights. Something was different. He walked out on the bridge, in the middle of it, brightly lit. He felt sharp. Something was different.

The evening had warmed *way* up. He hadn't quite noticed before but the evening had warmed way, way up. Weird, how there was like this warm breath from somewhere, like a soft touch on his face. That was what the difference was. How much had he had to drink? He wasn't sure. He didn't usually notice any effect. He looked into the dark, upstream. The black water slid from under the ice and molded over the top of the dam, shining in one long line of reflection. Nearly under the bridge it started rocking and pointing up into little points. Patty's little pointed tits which he preferred to Julia's big soft ones, now that he thought about it. How come? He had wanted Julia so bad. Just to fuck her. What was the big deal? He just wanted to fuck her! Once is all. Because he loved her and so that he could know that he was all right with her. Now he understood that he couldn't, so, okay. He was over it. He had a house and a wife and kids.

He turned around and crossed to the other side of the bridge. There the water was all in commotion, upwards and sidewards and backwards at the same time as it was all bashing down past the back of his mother's place and a store and a couple of empty houses to where it leveled out in a widening bend. Then it went under the other bridge where the Wellers' house was on the opposite side and dropped out of sight down beside the campground. There was a street-lamp there and a big pile of snow but in the dark beyond the snow-pile he saw, at the entrance to the campground, a window that shone with light the orange color of wood. That was the cabin where Clarence lived.

Clarence must be sitting in there by himself. He was up pretty late.

A car came down the hill from the south and paused beside him. The back door opened for him. It was his ride, his and Frank's. He waved them on. One of them opened a door and said, "Grab him, he's shitface." Somebody with a cigarette in his mouth got out and scuffled with him. Suddenly the person quit, wincing, holding the fingers of one hand with the other hand and hunching over both hands with his head down to his knees. They pulled the other man back in the car and it spun away.

Peter turned and walked off the bridge. Past The Rapids he turned the corner towards the campground. Clarence was from the old days. He knew everything about lumbering. He knew how to drive a team of horses. The only thing that Peter had ever known how to do well was play basketball. That was not equivalent. He walked on down past the lower bridge and passed into the shadow behind the snow-pile where he couldn't see his own feet. The roof of Clarence's truck glistened over the snow with light from the cabin window. Was it raining? So unfamiliar, warm wind, now something like rain on his face.

In the dark beside the truck he found the porch step. What was he doing here? He'd walked down here without thinking. It was as if South was yelling at him in the noise of the river, with his yellow tablet in his hand, telling him to do something, he didn't know what. He stepped up on the porch and knocked.

Clarence hardly looked at him. Peter wondered if he even recognized him. He offered him a chair and a cup of tea and sat down with his own mug up to his face in both hands. But he started right in talking, around the mug, as if he had been talking to nobody before Peter knocked and now just went back to it. "So you heard

I've quit. Ha-ha word gets around. Perhaps heard worse, I'm leaving town, right again, what of it? 'Never been anywheres else, Clarence, what will you do? How will you find your way? Where will you go?' Hnnn, well, you sound just like somebody I know. So if you come to try changing my mind, good luck, don't bother."

"I just come to visit," Peter said.

"I will show you sum'ing, young man, 'f perhaps you don't think—" He got up and set his mug on the table and went to a curtained closet at the back of the cabin. "Used to be, you would leave anything you wanted to in your truck. Leave a camp unlocked anywhere in these woods. You did that, by common agreement, just so anybody that happened to need shelter in the winter could go in and get warm and get sum'ing to eat. Anybody that come in and used your camp, he'd leave a fire built for you when you come back, and if they used any of your supplies why they would leave some change on your tablecloth."

"Not no more, huh, Clarence?" Peter said.

"That's right, not no more." Clarence swept the curtain to one side. "So I brought these things in, even for a short while. There now, Mister," he said. "This year, I am going on the first vacation of my life. I will carry that along with me, and wherever I stop, set that up and there's my cooking arrangements. It runs by gas."

Peter got up and went to see. It was an outdoor grill on a pedestal, with a cover. "That's a nice one," Peter said.

"'f I ever come back around here, I'll set that up at the home place, and we will have some good eating. Invite you and your wife over and we will have a barbecue. You name it, spare ribs or steak or chicken."

"Yes, sir," Peter said.

"But now, look here." Clarence reached something down off a hook and turned with it in both hands. It was a brand new leather holster with a pistol in it, heavy looking dark blue metal with checkered wooden handgrips.

"I have spent all my life in the woods and never owned one 'til this day. Luck'ly, I was never cornered by a pan-ther."

Peter was impressed. It had a long barrel and a cylinder for six shells and a hammer you cocked with your thumb. Clarence said, "I had my eye on that a long time. That's a Colt's revolver, what that is. Many a Injun laid low with one of these."

Clarence fit his right hand around the checkered walnut. He stooped as if he was hiding behind a tree. Reached it out at arm's length, pointed up. Then standing up straight he let the long barrel make a downward quarter-circle until it steadied level. Clarence's lips pursed, his eyes narrowed, the hammer fell with a clear loud *clink!* He brought the barrel back up vertical, as if the recoil lifted it, but in slow motion.

Peter reached out for it, and Clarence set it in his hands like a baby. He rolled the fluted cylinder, to feel the quiet clicks. Clarence, good-humored now, imitated somebody, some woman, asking him, "'Clarence, what do you want that pis-tol for?' 'Well, ha-ha, I can't run so fast's I used to.'" He held up the fat round-nosed bullet from his belt. "If that hits you, mister, say good-bye, just from the shock wave."

Peter offered back the pistol. "You been on quite a spree, Clarence."

Clarence pulled up one foot, bent his back and rested the foot on his other knee. "See them new solds to my boots. I have just had them put on, to Moira, this very afternoon, special delivery, nine dollars just the solds. Some people would say that's too much. But those are still good boots, no need of a new pair. Only one thing left to do, and I'm ready to travel."

He undid his belt and worked the new holster over it and took the pistol back and shoved it down into the holster across his body so it hung butt forward. The thongs on the bottom of the holster he tied around his leg above the knee. He crossed the cabin to where his outside clothes hung on pegs by the door. There he fanned over his narrow, rounded shoulders a red neckerchief. He knotted it under his Adam's apple, and put on that ranger hat of his, wide green felt, with the crown pinched to a hollow-cheeked point in front. He faced Peter, spread his feet and stood a moment. He seemed to be posing for a photograph: ready for anything, laced leather boots nearly knee high, the dark grey wool pants, the wool shirts flaring out like skirts below the wide, tightly cinched belt with the big grass buckle, and the huge revolver hanging on him backwards. Peter wondered why he wanted it butt forwards, wasn't that wrong? But maybe some cowboys did that. Clarence reached across his middle with his opposite hand and drew the pistol up straight until it cleared the holster, then completed the spiral draw. He pointed it at some imaginary enemy off to the side of Peter. "All right, mister," he said, "I'll take the girl. If you want to die, say so. Other wise, keep your mouth shut and don't make a move." He held the pose for several seconds, then gave a sort of cluck, put the revolver back in its holster and took his hat off. The hat had already pressed his grey hair in a dark cylinder around his head.

He sat down. Cast his eyes this way and that around the floor and drummed his chair arms. He opened his mouth and took a breath, but then he pursed it shut.

Peter said, "You mean you're going after Sochia by yourself, Clarence? Tonight?"

Clarence turned his head away from Peter with a jerk.

"Are ya?"

"Just so happens I know exactly where that scalawag was heading. Too late now, to get there first, no thanks to them that don't know how to listen. He will of been and gone before I get to it. Therefore, I have to make a giant circle round the spot, a walk not many men could make, and in the dark of night, without no rest, to make sure he hasn't done the light fantastic, before I close in."

"Where's this place? That big log camp at the end of the lake?"

"Purryer Camp? No, that isn't where I mean."

Clarence took a deep breath, and tucked his chin down on his breast. "I seem bound to see his ugly face everywhere I go. This time I'm talking about, I see him when he thought he wasn't watched. A place he shouldn't been. I went in behind the home place, to a spot I thought was secret to me and my sisters, of all folks living. I went there to get a jar of spaghetti sauce. You wonder what I'm talking about? A mud spring, good as a refrigerator for keeping anything cold. Not everywhere will you find one, but this is what we had to keep things cold in when I was a boy."

"No kidding?"

"My step mother sent me to that spring a thousand times if she sent me once. Well, I've got some cans in there, put up by my sisters, good cooks as there is. Once in a while, lonesome for home cooking, walk back in there and pull some up."

Clarence took a breath, moved his hands back and forth on the chair arms. "Back of the house a third of a mile, and longer by the brook. At the end of a softwood ridge, sharp as a hog's back, that runs parallel to the brook. This time, I got just to the end of the ridge, that overlooks the spring, and the brook running right beside it. It's a place I always go slow, for deer cross the brook there, and I salt a stump for them in season. Sometimes, don't tell nobody, put out apples. And guess who's there ahead of me? Hnnn. Mister Murderer, putting down sum'ing in cans of his own. Venison, it looked like from afar. Dark colored meat which would be lighter colored in a year and tenderer too."

"Sochia? No shit? When was this?"

"Yes, under a hat like mine there, only black, with a taller crown, and beads around it. How he knew about our mud spring, you tell me. Young man but a old-time woodsman, a rare bird nowadays. Had his sleeve rolled up, arm as white's that teacup, and three glass Mason jars of meat. All right: What was he putting that meat down for, if not to dig it up some day and have a stew? Some day when he was on the run and didn't want to go to the store. He never knew I saw him. I turned right round and come away without my supper. Now you ask, when was that? When that was was several weeks ago, 'fore he ever run off with the music teacher. I have kept that secret ever since, waiting for him to come into this territory."

"You think he's going there tonight?"

"Very certainly he's in the vicinity, and there's his food supply. What's any animal going to do, you tell by food, especially after a spell of deep snow and slim pickings."

Peter could almost picture the place. It would be a great way to end this, to surprise Robert with his arm stuck in the mud. Two men would have him surrounded. He was smiling. "You going after him, Clarence? Tonight?" Clarence didn't answer. "You want somebody to go with you? I'll go with you."

Clarence seemed to be continuing his thought. "For carrying you, you've got two things the Lord provided you, that's all, your feet."

"I've got my snowshoes," Peter said. "I've got my hunting clothes in my truck."

"We won't come back for supper if it takes two days or three. The animal we are going to hunt, you have to have respect for, it's at home where you're a stranger. Me, I have been there some. I thought I was a woodsman when I ought to been in school."

"I'll come with you if you'll take me. Take me along, Clarence. Huh?"

"I only mean to rest a few more minutes," Clarence said. "Then all right, Hubbard, come if you are a mind to. If you do, I'll have a watcher on the main runway, very good. If I was to tell you where you're going, you wouldn't know."

"I'll go get my stuff." Peter jumped up and strode to the door. "Do we want both trucks?" No answer. Outside again in the warm night wind, Peter shook fists overhead, hearing the roar of the river. South would approve. This was what he was supposed to do. After one more day in the woods he and Patty would take a deep long bath together, wash each other good, then get into bed all clean and red and wet.

Leo in turn noted, as he walked in a rather comfortable rain over to the office of the Feed & Coal at nine o'clock, that the warm front had come through on schedule. It was positively balmy! Bug-eyed behind his spectacles, the corners of his mouth irrepressible, he felt that this story was like a cube of ice on a hot stove, riding on its own melting. My sakes, that was a nice metaphor, where'd that come from? The wonder of unexpected supply. Another good phrase! Could he have invented them himself? He would crow them to his worried Père, who wouldn't know where he got them any more than he did.

But his father had a surprise for him. Mr Weller said, "As it happens, Terence O'Neil is taking steps to get this over with tonight. He's gotten John Pelo out on parole, or something of the sort, to help him bring Robert and your teacher out."

At which Leo exploded, through his nose, so that he had to take out his large, red, polka-dotted handkerchief and busy himself with it for a minute. He emerged red to the hairline. Truly, this thing was on its own. Cube of ice on a hot stove indeed. The author, if Leo any longer felt like such, had fallen behind. But not far. He must rush to provide. Pelo! Yes! He suspected his father's meddling. "Did you do this?" he cried. "Did you tip off the law at last?"

"I can't say I did," his father said, guiltily. "I've told him everything I know tonight, however."

"Such as where the hero and heroine are," Leo said. "And Helen?" Leo said. "She in on this? She agree to this?"

"Helen was doing her damnedest to keep Pelo in prison, apparently."

"Good girl that she is, too!" said Leo, tolerant.

"Terence had to—"

But Leo overrode. "Are O'Neil and Pelo out there already? Do they know what's happened, today and yesterday? Oh, sure they do. Are they off in dark of night?"

"Terence seemed confident of Pelo's finding the way."

"I should say so!"

Should he tell his father this? Plain as day to himself, Pelo would give O'Neil the slip, nothing easier; needless to invent that. He would rush to the aid of his friend, everybody knows where, and there he'd do something stupid, probably, and dangerous to everything and everybody. Leo had no idea what.

His father said, "I wonder if you oughtn't to stay up, tonight."

Leo intended to. He had thinking to do. Still he stared at his father. What did he mean?

"Go to that meeting."

"Up to the fire station? And?" That would be a waste of time; he knew what they were going to decide, attack on the ice in the morning. He'd be ashamed to think he had to be there to learn that.

"Tell them it's all over," his father suggested, a trifle querulously. "Shouldn't you? Tell them O'Neil has everything in hand."

"But he hasn't! He can't keep Johnny on a leash. If Robert Sochia is sitting there at Purryer's waiting for a shoot-out like they think he is, he'll be getting reinforcements."

"Don't tell me so!" Loyal Weller said.

"I do tell you so."

"Well then perhaps if they knew that, they wouldn't go up. Leo, we don't want any bloodshed. I'm sure nobody does."

"Oh, I wouldn't go so far as to say *that*," Leo murmured. He wondered if he should mention Clarence, another wild card. Mr Weller knew of his raids on the bank and stores and assumed Clarence had simply and reasonably, in disgust and embarrassment, quit. Leo knew the old ballad-lover better than that.

Mr Weller said, "What *do* you think your Mr Sochia is up to? He must have known about that airplane for days. Coming to Dexter Lake and sending smoke out the chimney in daylight. Leaving tracks straight across the pond. I don't believe he was surprised there. And then moving so obviously toward the lake. After all his skilled evasion."

Now his father was getting to the point, the crux, the whatyoucallit. "I think he changed his plans at Dexter," Leo said. "I think something happened there. Something he hadn't foreseen."

"Eh?"

"I think she's come around him," Leo said, improvising rapidly. "Got him. Beat him. Triumphed." He liked it.

"How? What?"

"You ever see that teeshirt she used to wear? She got it from one of her motorcycle professors. *Triumph*, blue on white, underlined, all across the front."

"I don't recall it."

"She's triumphed. She's got him to quit what he thought he was doing." He liked it. And yet, maybe not. "Or else the other way around." Leo was thinking aloud. "She beat him, he beat her. I don't know which."

"I hope not."

"She played her ace, maybe," Leo said. Thinking immediately, *Or he played his.*

Father staring at him, aquiline. "What's that? Do you mean—"

Père, Victorian, didn't like to say the word. But Leo did. "Oh, sex, you mean? I hope so. Good for sales. But I was thinking of her other ace." *If she had one. If she was. Is.*

"What's that?"

At that moment, the lights dimmed, there was a sort of an ozone hum, and Leo looked up, alert to any new input. He glanced over his shoulder at the black front window and listened for the forecast sleet. No sound of ticking yet. The lights came back up.

"Her *other* ace?"

Leo hesitated. Maybe not hers, maybe his. Hadn't they covered this? Not in so many words. There might be a baby in the picture, RS's or somebody worse's. His father didn't want to face this thought, and Leo didn't bring it forth aloud. But how would that play? At Dexter Lake, where, if anywhere, a fellow would have set up for a good losing battle. And she would have pulled out the stops to save him. But if there was a baby in the picture, *whose ace was that?"*

The globed light, suspended by a dusty chain from an escutcheon in the pressed-tin ceiling, dimmed, went orange, went out. Simultaneously the street-lamp down by the bridge went dark, and the lights of the houses up the back street. The office of the Feed & Coal was pitch-black.

They waited a moment, wordless. Then Mr Weller pulled out a bottom drawer of his desk.

Leo heard the squeak of the cork and a slop of liquid inside the bottle. He stood and turned around twice in place, looking for the windows. By the time he went to sit down again he'd lost the bearing of his chair, so remained on his feet.

"Is it sleeting?" Mr Weller said. "It don't feel any colder yet." Leo noted the return of farmer-dialect. In the wash of Florida air he'd turned the kerosene stove way down.

They listened. There was only light splashy rain on the windows, still not the ticking of ice. Through the pane in the office door Leo could now make out the river, a dull glowing grey in the blackness without.

"There's no wind," his father commented. Leo heard him take another sip. "You wouldn't think, with no sleet and no wind, we'd have a power outage just yet."

Yes, interesting. A power outage a little later was to be expected, if the wind and sleet did come as promised. A power outage in those conditions was a near certainty. A series of them, in fact, night-long. But this one's previous.

His father, stirring around, had lit a candle. Starting as a mere yellow point, its illumination slowly expanded to suggest the walls of a cave around them. They sat in silence, waiting for the lights to come back on. Usually they came on rather quickly, only to falter and go off again, several times before a durable blackout. Then, in a bad storm it might be out for an hour or two. Over in Eugene's, Leo knew, they'd be watching for the Niagara-Mohawk truck, with the cherry-picker on top. Eugene's and Mavis's son, David, would be on it. Somebody would be saying, "David'll be earning his pay tonight."

Leo sat twiddling the thumbs of his hands clasped across his belly, roaming in his imagination, doubly in the dark. She won, he won. Clarence. Pelo. Ice storm. His fingers knit together, his thumbs rolling one over the other. After a while he practiced the more difficult art of twiddling them in opposite directions. Once he had got it, a skill which he always lost between infrequent practices, he resumed speech.

"By the way, I've been working on a title."

His father didn't rise to the bait.

"Lotsa candidates: *Desperate Characters, Water and High Places, Pounding on the Gates.* The one I like best is just simply *Florida.* Wake up, Père."

"Florida makes no sense."

"Misleading, I'll admit. But it's perfect. The question is, do I dare? Anyway, imagine the dust-jacket, *Pounding on the Gates*, if you prefer. Then, 'A Novel.' I love that. 'Aye Novel.' Then, another line: 'By.' Another line: 'Almo P. Smith.'"

He waited for a response. "I say, 'a novel by Almo Smyth.' You there?"

A very faint, "huh." Not very interested in his pseudonym apparently.

"You don't think I'm going to put this out, in this town, under my own name, do you? I have no vanity, I need no kudos. I'm gonna put the phrase 'almost-myth' in the text somewhere, casually, and see if anybody gets it. What do you think?"

That man over there with his back to him in the dark was more interested in his port. Almost under his breath Leo muttered, "Subtitled, 'How Stories Like This Help Small Town People Hold Their Heads Up in This Here Busy World.'"

But Mr Weller did respond, first clearing his phlegm: "What's happening out there is probably pretty mundane. Pretty Squalid, I expect."

Leo opened his eyes and mouth in astonishment, partially put-on and self-satirical. "I beg your pardon!"

"Two trashy young people without any principles—"

"I really do protest!" His father was a little bit in drink tonight, poor man. "You don't respect my subjects?" What he had out there, for subject, was a classic confrontation! A certified 60s-70s Now-person, female, versus a certified Old-Time, uh, uh, male person, a regular flying shaman, from the late Primitive-Archaic. Read your Eliade!

"Let's say I don't see them as outstanding candidates for literature. I wouldn't want to read a word about either of them. I wish them both at the devil!"

This was rather vehement for Père. More disturbing, it was Leo's first hint that there might not be an immediate, general embrace of his prospective opus! "Father, you're talking about people I love!"

"You may love them. I do not. And I think it would be better if you didn't try to make this story into something it isn't. I wouldn't get so excited about it if I were you, Leo."

Oh that's your problem is it? Me getting high. Leo sat there momentarily deflated, non-plussed, listening to the sleet just beginning to tap against the windows. But not truly shaken. He was sure that those two out there were not what his father said they were. They were terrifically significant figures, in terrific opposition. No! He was right. It was going to be great! Maybe he shouldn't get too excited about actually *writing* it. There was that problem, hereto unfaced. His father was just trying to protect him from disappointment.

And then, too, Père was scared of his own shadow; of his responsibility, and of Aunt Sarah. *Who*, Leo realized, *would be involved in the ending, the outcome, the come-down, some way!* Yes! He would be seeing Aunt Sarah, very soon. And likely his father was thinking of that very sight, her dear, trembling, downy jowls, her dangling earrings shaking with the fervor of her scolding, her cane, which she wouldn't lift for all her anger, thumping on the floor. He smiled. An image for the ending came in view: The Cadillac, turning the corner at The Rapids, bringing the old girl herself to dictate the denouement.

"He's at large," Leo said, suddenly, quite sure whereof he spoke.

"You say?"

"He's here."

In the dark, Leo shook his head with admiration, just short of giggling. If Robert hadn't wanted them to know this power outage was his doing, all around the town, in Eugene's and The Rapids and the fire station, and in the bedrooms and kitchens as they felt for their flashlights and candles and kerosene lamps, if he hadn't wanted them all to know he was at large, he could have waited for the sleet.

26

South Wind

An ordeal getting through the snow with her toward Purryer Camp.
After their crawl through the balsams where they had to leave her
snowshoes behind, she couldn't keep up, he was really half-carrying
her most of the way. The cries of her breath, at his back, cut into
him, went through him in a new way. New, this whole set of
feelings. They had to get to Purryer's quickly and he forced the
march, both of them breathing deep, together.

It would have been easier the old way, the way he'd planned
it. He'd come to the end of his life. He'd been ready for that. How
it would have surprised them, a gunshot from an upstairs window
while they milled around in their own smoke. A hole in a gas-
tank, maybe starting a fire. They'd have scattered behind anything
solid— He'd have forced them to do it, to save their own skins.
Nothing else he wanted: to fall at her feet, feeling what he felt.
That would have been forever.

Now he had to live. He had to get to Purryer Camp. He needed
time to go fast, night to come quickly; and then he needed time to
slow down and almost stop for all the things he had to do in the
dark, for his new life to start in the morning.

From the high ground between the outlet drainage and the
next valley south, which led to Mud Pond, they heard the whine
of snow-machines coming in on Dexter's road. Those others could
follow at ten times his and Julia's speed, overrun them, swarm
around her, take her from him before he could even get to Purryer
Camp. Everything he hoped for now would vanish. He had
everything to lose for the first time in his life. Down into the next

drainage, over a beaver-meadow, onto the pond, her small cries at every breath.

They would probably think he planned this but he didn't. He didn't see the hole himself, carrying her as fast as he could, head bent, eyes down. It was invisible from a distance, skinned over with ice, frosted white just like the surrounding snow. From above, it was black, the flowers of rime like white roses scattered over it just in front of his snowshoes, and ahead, a circle of black water, open around the dead-head. He backed up, put her down carefully in the track and stepped around her. He told her not to move. She nodded, biting her lip, eyes as dark as the water. Back to the beaver-meadow for two limbless dead young trees rotten at the root, which he pushed over and carried back, one under each arm, balanced so the tips wouldn't drag.

He slid them ahead across the black hole onto the gray ice beyond, and farther; and she ran across bravely not looking down and pitched herself ahead on hands and knees. He walked over teetering, more scared than she. Then carried the poles on to the narrow end of the pond and pitched them as far off the track as he could. Not far. She clung to his back again and they went on.

That was the only hope. He just had to leave it at that. It made his scalp crawl.

His other plan probably wouldn't have worked, either. He'd have had to shoot from window after window, ping bullets off rocks and trees and snow-machines to get them to shoot back. If they even had guns. He figured they would, some of them. Or go get more. But probably they'd just run home to their wives and it would all peter out into nothing. This was better even though the hope was so thin.

There was hardly a chance and still he felt this newness, this *lift*. How did this happen to him? The music? He didn't understand how anybody could do such things, make anything like that. It was beyond him. He was right to feel what he had always felt for this person. It would carry him past the stars. But it wasn't the music that changed everything. The long long night-long talking hadn't done it either. Her talking, not his, fast and intricate, rising

and falling like the music, making feelings come and go, syllable
after syllable telling him all that about himself, true and not true,
and all that about JoAnn true and not true, so that it went by like
a stream or a song, and you couldn't remember it all. He just
floated along in it, washed and lifted, and the room was always
warmer and warmer and they wanted to touch each other and
then they were out of their clothes as if they had been trees and
the syllables were the bright-colored leaves blown away from them,
swirling around them, drifting in piles. But it was already different
by then, they were naked differently and touching differently. He
didn't want to trespass on the child. Neither of them wanted to do
anything ungentle anywhere near.

No problem breaking in at Purryer Camp; the screen door on
the verandah toward the cove was hooked from the inside but he
had only to jerk it hard enough to pull the hook-eye out of the
jamb. The main door was unlatched, couldn't be closed for the
heave of the sill. Swung inwards, it caught against the floor, where
it had worn an arc. She slipped in under his arm, stopped just
inside to let her eyes adjust, the great room was so dark.

As it always was; he knew it well, from winter break-in parties
back when he was in school, dark on the brightest of days and colder
than outdoors. The log purlins of the high roof and the roundwood
railings of the balcony shone faintly silver, all you could see at first.
She was scanning, he followed her eyes. Deer heads, up high in the
dark. A stuffed owl, a bobcat on high shelves. Lower down, tasseled
lampshades, wicker rocker, the tremendous hearth and chimney
almost lost in blackness between windows over the lake. Now she
was staring at something in that darkness around the chimney, rolling
her lips together. On a shelf, in the dark space between a window
and the fireplace, the radio? He remembered a gray metal box with
many knobs and a round cloth-covered speaker, a 9-volt battery on
the shelf beside it, a pair of wires leading out through the chinking.
The wires went down from tree to tree to the roof over the boathouse
where there was a little wind-mill on the peak, to charge the battery.
It was always charged: he and his friends used to turn on that old
Hallicrafters radio and listen to Montreal.

But it was the clock she'd noticed, a dark old wind-up clock, its wooden case hexagonal, a dim face with Roman numerals behind its glass door, and under the face an ornamented silver pendulum, hanging still. He followed her there, into the shadows. She turned to him, her eyes going back forth between his. She didn't speak but she was asking, *Is it okay? We're coming back into the world, aren't we? We need to know the time now, don't we?* Suddenly finding energy, she pushed the ottoman from in front of the sofa and stepped up on it. She fingered a key from the bottom of the case and wound the mainspring. She pushed the pendulum to one side with a precise finger, and turned to him. "Bobby, watch!" Nodded three times and let it go.

She swung her head with the ticking. "Now to set it! Does the radio work?" She moved the ottoman over to the radio and stood on it again. The radio only hummed. It was an old radio; it needed to warm up. Just as suddenly tired, she stepped down and sank on the ottoman.

He wasn't ready for these things, clock, radio. But they didn't change anything; the change had already happened. Time was unwinding steadily and those others could be here any minute, and the long life ahead with the child by his side could vanish. But maybe not. The wood-box was full of good dry chunks, there was dry kindling and the *New York Times*. More firewood, he knew, under snow outside by the outer hearth of the same chimney. You couldn't heat this huge room but you could warm people and things with the radiance of a big fire. He pulled the wing-back sofa close in front, a reflector, and lifted her onto it.

She was so light, so little. She shut her eyes and he covered her up with a loosely-woven wool spread from the back of the sofa. He tuned the radio. At first there were just blips of sound when he turned the knob but then he remembered the second knob, that moved the needle slower, and he stopped at the first weak station, French. He didn't care about the time. Light and dark was all. "I need to eat," she cried.

Outside the kitchen door, intense bright day. Back toward the carriage barn, among the tall columns of the pines, the deep snow unmarked; the air just like it, unmarked by any sound or motion but the chickadees. No, no whining machines. They weren't coming. If not yet, not at all? He couldn't assume it. Maybe it wasn't that at all. A missile, a bomb. An attack on the United Nations or something. A blackout, an earthquake, the President shot. When you were away in the woods and came back you never knew what might have happened. He lifted the steel cover over the tanks and turned on the gas. The people who owned this camp now stripped the cupboards but he had tea in his pockets somewhere. That would have to do until he came back from his travels in the night.

Meanwhile this day in which nothing must happen, no one must move, and yet time must fly, though it wouldn't, it would trickle out second by second, interminably. But they weren't coming. It was as if he knew what he couldn't know. During that new and differrent, amazing day Robert felt a kind of rest he had never known. Like marriage, almost; a kind of marriage? No striving in that day, no hurry even, nowhere to get to. He couldn't leave her, and he couldn't have borne to. An unhurried day of closeness, warmth, talk, intimacy, sleep, accord, concern for one another, in the company of the unborn but already adored child. He had no terms for it. Her body as much his as his own, and his as much hers, without need and urgency. He hadn't imagined that either: that there could be any intimacy greater, any feeling stronger, any acceptance more complete than in sex. He'd always thought that was the way sex was designed: to be an end beyond which there was nothing left to want. But how blind. You could shame yourself with sex, you could waste yourself. It was nothing.

It wasn't from Julia's teaching. It was from the child inside her and contrary to her wish. She'd argued as hard as she could against it, in tears at the end. But it had seemed to him that all her best arguments were for it in spite of her. He'd found it in them. And finally she'd accepted it. She'd said okay. In tears but not whining. She'd do it. And there was no more hardship between them. He thought she was glad herself, deep down.

The clock's ticking was the waves falling, one after the other, on the sea beach where she'd lie waiting, under a cabaña, her belly weighing her down to the sand more and more each day. Himself in the background, earning, cooking, feeding her, ignoring his father's preening in front of her, his mother's lust to take the baby out of their hands the moment it would be born. Years later, himself a working man, back in the Falls, with a growing daughter glued to his side. Or a son, but he pictured a daughter, like her. A life, making up for Ray. The town wouldn't have to remember his story then. They'd be looking at it every day.

She would go back on their deal if she could, he knew that; if they came after all, if anything happened. But if he could keep control, if he could balance and juggle and get through this night, and then if he could keep her with him all the way to Florida, it would happen. As she said through her tears last night, looking at him and touching his face, "Then there will be no more loneliness forever." He was never lonely that he knew of but it made him cry too.

He hated it to end, this day he had needed to pass in a flash. She clung to him, held him down, her arms around his neck, squeezing as hard as she could. As if she were thinking too, how lucky he would have to be. How lucky they had already been, to have this day, so how much more luck could they hope for? Outside he felt the wind warm and in the south. They'd heard the forecast; this was the south wind coming in. He was in his element. Time would stand still now and he would fly. All else would be suspended while he made his giant circle over the dark country. Then the sleet would come and coat it all in ice.

He lifted a chainsaw out of one of the loggers' pickup trucks parked outside the Blue Mountain Tavern, on the Stark's Mill road. From there he crossed northeastward through the old farms grown to brush, toward the river. When he picked up the power line he followed it toward town. Down along the river road, it turns behind a low hill, cutting off a sharp bend. There he notched three poles, the one that was guyed against the tension of the bend and one each way from that one. One by one he sawed them almost through, from the side opposite the notch. Then he simply sawed the many-stranded steel cable of the guy, anchored to a dead-man in the frozen ground. The chainsaw cut or burned the cable strand by strand, and when the cable parted, the tension of the lines pulled the three poles inward. They cracked at the hinges he had left uncut and the central pole went down. The lines draped into the tops of wet trees and sizzled. After a while, white sparks began to shower out in various places, illuminating graceful young poplars. Smoke and steam spewed out of the treetops and there was a humming sound. Then a sibilant buzz. Then the busses blew, somewhere, and he was in the dark again. He dropped the ruined saw and went on, keeping to the right of way, which climbed another hill and then descended toward the town.

27

Kiss the Cowboy

Clarence was scarcely conscious of Hubbard behind him, or of his own snowshoes, his benumbed stride in them, even the dark leafless branches that jogged toward him and tugged at his shoulders, hat, face, turning him sometimes halfway around before they let him go. He wasn't even thinking about where he was going, wasn't navigating at all, just getting across the ground, turning freely, thoughtlessly, to take the open way. His mind was away beyond the event he had armed himself for, himself already a desperate character, a fugitive just like his prey. In his rests, seated on a fallen tree, rubbing his sore knee, telling aloud how, to make good his escape, he would break in anywhere he needed to, take anything he found, shoot any animal not man or woman, for food or to defend himself. And when caught up with, told to come peaceful, pushed too hard, do something worse he wouldn't name.

Not Hubbard he was talking to, even while Hubbard was there, hearing. Not even himself. It was that same audience as always, the one he'd never had, the past that was gone for good, the future that ought to be right at his shoulder with a tape machine, otherwise they miss their chance. *I done the worse thing a man can do. Don't look to find this old boy living among decent people no more.*

Or if he wasn't ahead, he was behind, straightening up old injustices, his future flight forgotten and some incident with the wife of a past landlord angering him, something about the kerosene that was stolen from the drum on the porch of an old house he rented, and he knew who had taken it, her own son, but who got accused of it, right in the public thoroughfare where he felt obliged to hold his tongue? *That's right, me myself and I. I will meet you, Missus, later in some place where I can speak my mind. That's a nail I will be very happy to drive. Because, h'nnn, that woman walked on my neck in a pair of spike boots. Said I'd set the stove too warm, the oil went up the chimbley, hnnn. How many winters do you think I've heated my own quarters?*

But never derailed long, always making good his course, always coming back to his line. Hubbard had to jog or skip now and then to keep up with him. They had driven way around the string of camps on the northwest end of the lake, far as the campers's road was plowed, farther than it ever used to be, for the sake of the snowmobilers. Left the truck there and made their way by skidder roads and hunter's trails, back in to the Stony Brook Club line. Southeast to Center Camp, then north around Miner's Hill, country he knew like his own name. In the pitch dark he seldom switched on his light, never looked at his compass. After two hours' tramping they arriving at the service road to Purryer's Camp from Stark's Mill. Of course there were the expected tracks on that road, he turned left and walked directly in them to the low plank bridge over the outlet brook, just audibly trickling among snow-capped rocks beneath the dark spruces. There, not an eighth of a mile from Mr Purryer's carriage-barn, he stopped and placed his watcher, strict and clear in his instructions, even if too short and swift, you don't waste words when the buck might hear you: "Set right there, watch that way, your game'll be coming pell-mell when I jump him, don't let him over that brid-ge. Very likely, we'll put sum'ing in the ket-tle."

Scarcely hearing Hubbard's urgent whisper, which rose to a cry as he left him in the dark, "What? What? What am I supposed to do? *Shoot* him? I can't even see! Wait, Clarence! Where are you going? You coming back for me?" And a last despairing "How long will you be?"

Now he followed the brook, taking the camp itself and even the whole two and a quarter-mile-long lake inside his circle, going on around east of it, east even of the shoreside hills, back towards the home place. *How long will I be? Good question. I am making such a large circle nobody would know what I was after. That's the way*

I hunt, I've been laughed at for it before today, so what? Sometimes the buck goes out the side of the drive, not past the watchers, to live another day. That's luck. But he knew where this animal was going, sure as shooting. He had to loop that mud spring into the drive, to be sure he hadn't got out before it started.

It was a big circle, the biggest he had ever made, hungry himself now and good food where he was going but not for him tonight. Would have liked nothing better than to fetch up some of Bessie's spaghetti sauce and take it on to the home place where he might find noodles to go with it. Eat it plain if not and go to bed. That's what called to him, food and bed. *But, signed on to this deal. Nowadays, 'f you try to help somebody, you are asking for trouble, yes I know. Dare not even help a person get up that's been hit with a car, sue you for more than you're worth for interfering, hnnn. If I wouldn't come to the aid of a woman in distress, I might's well shoot myself, I'd be ashamed to draw another breath.*

He was unconsciously looking for sign now though he couldn't take time to go slowly and quietly. Found the old trail back from the house, marched along it, in due time cut over to the brook. *Just as I thought, not yet. Good.* No sign at the spring or on the trail, so now he could turn back, first through a long stretch of low swamp where he could sometimes make out the old blazes when the tree was right beside him, a trail he and his brother used to keep so clean you could stalk through here silent as an Indian. On the far side of the swamp the trail gave out and he had to bushwhack up the back side of the hill. Then, hit the old tote-road, otherwise called the hay-road, easier going and still no sign. Looked like he had him dead to rights, the only way he could escape was the lake, where Clarence dared not go. *You might's well come peaceful, you're surrounded. Otherwise see what I've got on my side, a side-arm, ha-ha. You won't get two chances. After which*

> *I'm going to the Indian Territories, and live outside the law*
> *I'll bid farewell to the canebrakes in the state of Arkansaw-w.*
> *If you ever see me back again, I'll extend to you my paw-w,*
> *But it'll be through a telescope, from hell to Arkansaw.*

Once he would have made this hike over the tote road blindfolded, known to touch each tree along it as sure as you reach for the light-string in your woodshed. Now he banged his shins on crisscrossing deadfall in the lightless night. When he stopped and leaned on his knees again he was high on the hill. Could see downward to his right, a lighter, more even grey, the open expanse of the lake, frightening to him even at this distance. No man unpressed would go that way any more than a deer would, such hard going where your feet cut through to slush and water on top of the ice, how thick you never knew. Luck. Maybe luck was on his side tonight.

Luck like that time he'd shot a buck when he was sitting down resting, carving a stick. *Mid morning, set down on a south slope to eat my lunch. Then, ten minutes, heard a step, right behind me, tramp-tramp, so loud I thought it was a man. I twisted my neck around so I could see him, and what do you suppose it was, a six point buck, mister, no further'n from me to you. Had his nose right down in my footprints, coming right up my trail. Left his doe's track and followed mine. That was b'cause I had mare's urine on my boots, just cleant out her stall. Well, I says to him, Johnny-boy, I didn't know a mare's bedding made such a very good buck lure. I had to shoot left-handed. I put that ball, sir, right between the antlers and into the top of his back. He rolled right over backwards, dead before he knew what hit him. That was good luck.*

Now he was tramping steadily downward, knees sore, nearly to the level of the lake. There he bent again to rest, with his hands on his knees, rubbing, the big camp not three-fourths of a mile from where he stood. It began to look as if he was going to accomplish something never done by him in his life, though done by others worthy of admiration, shoot a buck right in its bed. You didn't do that without stealth. Most of his hunting life he had been a guide, another good name for dog, expected to make a racket, no chance of sneaking up on anything.

Smelled smoke, good. He stumbled on, the old road skirting the last cove of the shore, suddenly the trees were larger, all pines and spruces and hemlocks, the woods picked up clean and the trail suddenly a level, kept-up road for car or truck. He passed the skiff-house, as the Purryers called it, on the shore well away from the main camp, where the canoes and guide-boats were kept, all painted green, black trim, nice old boats too tippy for him. The road turned to go in back of the camp toward the barn, so he left it for a path through the pines. He was amid black pillars towering around him up into the rain and snow not so deep. The first he'd noticed it raining. How long had that been going on? He caught a smoky glimmer of light, a window-shape of amber, appearing and reappearing among the dark columns of the trees.

He headed for the darkest darkness, the mass of the building. Came up on the terrace around the outside hearth of the great chimney. Beside him now, a widening blanket of dim, reflected firelight lay on the wetted snow. He leaned both hands on the knee that pained, held his head down for a minute, blank, then stuck out his chin and peered around him. A lit tree-trunk stood out like a partner. He heard nothing from inside, only the pops of heavier raindrops hitting a railing. *'What, you here, Shampine?' That's my name, surprised to see me? You aren't no more surprised than I am. I would of thought I would make up a reason to visit New York City first.*

He thought, *'f you're in there waiting, I might just's well put my eye up to the muzzle of your gun and tell you to fire. Good-bye Clarence, you've caught your last bullhead my boy. That's all for your family name in the history books, unless somebody write up a song, 'The Last Pioneer.' I wish't I was married, for the first time in my life, do you want to know what for? Just like Alexander Macomb in the battle of Lake Champlain, whilst he was across the water licking the British, she was making the song of it. 'My elbow I leaned on a rock near the shore, the sound of the guns nearly parted my heartstrings asunder, I thought I should see my dear Sandy no more.'*

Now he was feeling clever, light-hearted. He turned his neckerchief around and pulled the fold up on his nose. He held his arms away from his body and looked down, saying, "All right, boys, what have you done with my pis-tol?" It was there, heavy and true, loaded but never been fired. He crossed his right hand in front of his body and drew it up nearly to the height of his face before the muzzle cleared the holster. Very slowly, and now listening intently, he brought it in front of his face and turned it muzzle up.

He turned the corner where the verandah began, two steps higher than the terrace, under the overhanging roof. Started to climb the half-log steps forgetful of the snowshoes worn so long. Had to kneel now and undo the straps one-handed, not to put the pistol down.

Boots were slippery on a slope of painted boards, and any step made a crack. He slid his feet inch by inch up the slope and pressed his body against the log wall, his weight where the boards were firmest. One way, to his left, a window throwing out light that would shine on him if he tried to look in. He angled back from the wall staying in the shadow and scanned inside, bringing the end wall in view, a little more and more of it until he saw the high-backed, flowered sofa close before the fire, the source of the light. He knelt and crept beneath the window, rose beyond it silently, and scanned the room from the opposite angle. He knew the room better than he could see it; the balcony railings picked up the firelight, but little else, and beneath them everything was deep in shade cast by the back of the sofa. *Watch out for a ambush there.*

Then under that window and up again, the pistol now carried high, next to his ear, like a tomahawk ready to throw. In two steps he had opened the screen door and, committed by its spring's noisy stretching, tripped the latch and thrown the heavy wooden door inward. It stuck against the floor, halting him rudely, but no matter, he stepped sideways around it into firelight, gun descending, searching for its object, expecting sudden death from the dark. He heard a cry, a rush, his pistol hand was swept aside and he was lassoed, his head pulled down, a cheek was against his cheek, he felt skin through the kerchief. Warmth and fragrance filled his nose, bare arms were around his neck, knocked his hat to the floor.

He did not know what song this was, maybe one he hadn't heard. This was the girl, he did know that, grateful for her rescue, naturally. Barely he remembered his foe, probably in under the balcony in the dark. He waved his pistol behind her back, but could not separate himself, couldn't try. If luck held, the fellow wasn't there. "Shoot me now," he joked, "I'll die happy."

"Before we go," she said, "I've got something to show you, Clarence. It's a big surprise. You'll never guess."

Before we go, hnn. Who says we're going. Clarence had rejoiced in survival, the discovery that the rooster had flown. Had a moment to rest and drink a cup of tea. Sure, set down with you on the sofa in the heat, though hot enough, too hot the minute he stepped indoors, in his layered woolens and boots, with her in her underthings, sock feet. Embarrassing if anybody looked in the window, him sitting with the other fellow's girl. Away on errands, good, but he'd be back, and Clarence hadn't forgot what he'd come for. Something to show him? All right. What?

"Paintings," she said. She was close beside him, turned to him, looking into his face, her eyes going back and forth too fast to follow. "Two water-color paintings, Clarence. I know who painted them. And you do too."

Paintings. Water-color paintings. The idea was oddly familiar, awakened an old sentiment long dormant in him. He used to know something of the furnishings of this camp.

"Come see!"

Just got set down comfortable, hot mug to his lips, but all right. He got up and let her lead him by the hand. Back along the dark inside wall, made of peeled logs like the outside walls but these smaller, straight as a die. Above a sideboard there, two framed pictures, not well lit but yes, familiar to him as if he lived here, not just the scenes but the hand of the painter too. Both were of the lake at the Narrows, ducks flying low over the water, in the spring, probably, twilight, the water dark blue and the upper sky dark blue and in between, the mallards silhouetted against the pale part of the sky at twilight. Different but the same. They made a pair. The work of Jack Arden, sure as shooting. He hadn't thought of that . . . person . . . in a long while and didn't want to. For why? Because the deepest pain of his life had been inflicted by that man, a man he took for a friend.

"Do you recognize them, Clarence?"

Yes I know who painted them pictures, Miss. Could do a painting like that, or one of your camp or house, in fifteen minutes, more like the thing than the thing itself, sell it for ten dollars, the easiest money Clarence ever saw made. Or, just as likely, give it to you. Clarence had guided the fellow all around these woods, showed him his favorite places to fish, rowed him in a round-bottomed tin rowboat all over the lake though afeared to overturn every minute; that was how well he thought of him. The thanks he got— Never mind. That was a friendship betrayed, his sister—

He didn't finish, didn't want to think of his sister, youngest and everybody's darling, misbehaved with by that artist, taken away not to return.

"I know what happened, Clarence."

You what? You don't.

"But it wasn't how you think it was. They were fine, those two, my Gramps and your youngest sister. Don't you worry, they were fine. My grandfather knew how to let a woman be herself, not mistreat her, not take power over her. I know she died too soon, way too soon. Women died a lot from having children, Clarence. But they were happy, your sister and my Gramps."

Well, how many times did she have to say it? Heard her the first time and didn't believe it then. She would have to excuse him if she wanted him to react. But she'd caught his attention, put him into a sort of numbness, enough that he let her lead him back to the sofa, when he knew better: ought to take up his ambush. He sat down beside her numbly, forgetful of the danger from without though trying to remain in the present. *Come here to face a killer. Now she wants me to believe something impossible, then walk two mile over the ice. Almost sugaring season, the ice thin under a long winter's blanket of snow.* Women always sending him on some work he didn't care to do.

Yet he was gradually taken with something akin to bliss, side by side with this young person on the high-backed sofa in front of

the fire, the coals a glowing heap and one new log at a time aflame
on top of them, put there by her, no need for him to stir. She was
drying her things, stripped down to her underwear, bare-legged
but for thick socks, close to him, hugging him, touching him,
calling him what he'd never been called. *Uncle.* A deep pleasure-
pain that he didn't know by any name burned through his weariness
and misanthropy.

It seemed to him that those days when Jack Arden was here at
the lake and he was young had been the sunniest, sweetest days of
his life, all three sisters working together at the Lodge and himself
the handyman, the best of it the friendship of that artist, the trips
afoot and by boat everywhere Jack wanted to go, with gun and
pole and paint-box. A kind of companionship and respect he'd
never known 'til then nor ever since. Everything shared as equals,
always a smile showing that the man took pleasure in him too. *So
that was your grandfather. Well hit me with a— Do I remember your
grandfather, Miss. I guess I would. Nobody would forget him.*

He didn't want to tell her everything. The fellow was a
laughingstock in some ways. Tall, skinny, freckled red-head, didn't
know how comical he appeared to natives. Telling stories at the
dinner table in the Lodge, he would wave his long bony arms,
blue cotton sleeves rolled up past his knobby elbows, so wildly
that Milly, waiting on him, had to stand back, blushing for him,
looking for a safe chance to set down his pie in front of him. His
accent when he talked—he had no idea.

He did tell her of the cabin on the shore they built together.
"Jack Arden, oh he loved the lake. Nothing would do but he had a
piece of the shore. Bought it from the Wellers, how he persuaded
them I'll never know. Hard man to resist. Well, had to have a cottage
on it. But the shore is steep and rocky there, no room for anything.
No matter, we built that little camp on top of the boulders at the
water's edge. Very small, no bigger'n a shoe-box, a crazy criss-cross
of posts and braces among the rocks to hold it up. He could dive out
the window from his bed, right into the lake." Clarence chuckled in
spite of himself. "I never saw it myself, but he claimed he did that
before he put his clothes on every morning."

"That's my Gramps all right."

Well, if you say so. "That fall, decided he needed firewood. Well guess what, that steep rocky hillside's not so easy a place to cut and haul wood. But, never say die. 'Clarence,' he says, 'we'll build a slippery-slide. Planks and crossbucks, from up the hill there, right down to the back door. Cut wood up top, on the level, pile it next the slide. When we get some freezing rain, why, send the firewood down the slide. Won't have to lug it at all.' Your grandfather (did I say that?), he'd try anything, not like me."

She gave him another hug. "I'm so glad you liked my Gramps and did things with him. I'm so glad you're my uncle."

Not a very good one. Had no practice. No children in my family that I ever knew about, so where do you come from?

"Now can we go? Let's go now, Clarence. I'll put my clothes on and we'll go? Right?"

But he couldn't bring himself to do it. Set in his ways, and scared to lose the cover of the fort. Scared to walk on the ice. He couldn't do it no matter how she pleaded. "Clarence, you came to save me, didn't you? You're saving my life! We have to go!" No thanks, sister. I'll sit here in the shadows and wait. I've got the 'vantage here. Comes in that door, meets this pistol, pointed at his heart. If I go out, either up the trail or by the lake, bad lu-ck. "Oh no no, we have to go." *Oh yes yes yes, we stay.* He found a chair back under the balcony, one of the good wicker armchairs that go on the verandah in summer.

Very comfortable. Can prop my elbow steady on the arm, like so. You sit there with most your clothes off, in the light of the fire, plain sight of the window. Who'd you say you was, don't tell me. Not the man to have the world turned upside down in a shake. Whoever you are, pretty good bait.

28

Pelo Perforate

JoAnn's daughter Karen, beautiful girl, huge eyes, doe-like, shy. Could be a model, everybody agrees. She dresses well, under her mother's eye. She has been brought up technically innocent in this profane setting by means of dire threats. She's usually kept out of the bar, and that is why we haven't seen her before. This night during the blackout Karen and some of her friends are sitting at a table in the dining part of The Rapids with a kerosene lamp. For her and her friends' sakes JoAnn suppresses with stern looks even the milder profanities of the men in the bar. The rest of the place is all dark as are the streets, the whole town outside. The telephone, however, has just rung. Not the phone behind the bar; it's the public one in the telephone booth in the little-used front entrance hall, at the foot of the stairs to the second floor. Karen gets up, still speaking to her friends, walks backwards through the archway to the bar, then catches her mother's eye and turns toward the hall, which has only what light falls on its carpet-runner from the two mantel-lanterns in the bar. In the darkness to one side of this wedge of dim illumination she reaches out her hand to push in the folding door of the booth. The phone has not rung again, and she supposes the caller has hung up, but when she raises her hand toward the receiver, she touches wool and instantly feels a finger on her lips. There is in fact enough light to see him. Robert Sochia has already removed the finger from her lips to his own.

She checks the passageway to the bar and steps in close to him. He asks her who is at the bar. Her mother, she says. "Who else?" "I don't know them all." "Your brother Peter?" "No."

"Prentice?" "No." He doesn't ask more but she offers, "Not Harry either, he's at the hospital. Somebody in his family is sick. What do you want?" She is excited to be so close to him. She has always assumed her mother's hatred of this person who killed her uncle who was always sweet to her. But she doesn't feel hatred now, close to him. He seems smaller, shorter than she thought he was. She would fit him perfectly. But he's a coward, he shot Ray, out of fear, so of course she does hate him. There's nothing all that attractive about him.

"Go tell her her whoever it was hung up."

"Huh?"

"Tell her he hung up."

"I don't want to go into the bar and say that. It's a lie."

"Then go whisper in her ear. Tell her he wants the key."

"What? Who?"

"Just say, 'the key.' Go."

He's so intense, she thinks she'll do it. Her mother would want her to. Her mother will guess who it is. This is exciting. She'll have to keep it secret from her friends, go back and tell them the same lie, the phone went dead.

O'Neil, driving the woods roads, like a poacher. Luckily for him, the cruiser has been fitted with studded snow tires—by two A.M. the rain has turned to sleet, the roads are glazed. He keeps the heat on high and mostly on the windshield and never turns the engine off even when he stops somewhere to wait, give Pelo time.

Pelo's word was worthless, there'd been no holding him back. O'Neil expected that. He even understood John's need to go his own speed. He'd thought he might keep up with him on his skis. He had dressed in his whole Nordic costume, North Face parka, layers, gaiters, plus his head-lamp. He's still dressed this way—off duty. Pelo laughed at him. And he was certainly right: the old skidder-trail that Pelo took off on was much too rough and overgrown for the skis. So he's fallen back on Pelo's last over-the-shoulder yell, "Drive the roads! Watch for a light!" Droive the roads, watch for a loight.

Actually it is one of his normal winter duties to patrol these roads, check these camps at the Lake and along the Blue Mountain Road, empty for the winter. His headlights pick up, on the doors of dark garages, under gables drooping with snow, yellowed notices to this effect, tacked on doors and shutters by himself, warning the larcenously tempted. He drives the Lake road, the Stark's Mill road, the Blue Mountain road; back and forth through town to each of these in turn, feeling an edge of excitement new to him, the result of his meddling creativity.

Like a poacher looking for the amber reflectors of a deer's eyes in the pitch black night. Still more like the poacher's wife, looking for the red six-pack carton, hanging in a low green bough, that tells her where her husband's waiting with the doe shot in the eye. A quick slide over the snowbank as she slows to a stop, a swing up into the opened trunk, her husband jouncing onto the seat beside her, the car already moving. That's the way he will pick up the fugitives, Pelo and Robert and the girl, quicky, wordlessly, when on one of these roads he finds them signaling.

He's ridiculous, wandering the roads, of course, not in the action at all. He doesn't know why Robert Sochia should come out just because, through Pelo, he has offered his protection. If not then the danger is that once he finds his friend, Pelo will forget his wife, his kids, his parole, and join Robert in his purpose. Whatever that is. In the darkness, with his vague information, he can see only that Robert's project is terminal, irrational, makes sense only to him, within the past, the forest. He suspects it couldn't stand the light of day. Pelo wouldn't know the difference.

Nevertheless, at least he's acted. He's injected dumb innocence into the dark machinery turning. He feels connected to events despite lost contact with his agent.

Now coming up on the high point of the Falls road, nearly out to the highway, he sees, far to the north and unexpectedly, a clear horizon under the heavy low overcast from which the freezing rain still falls: the lights of the plants along the big river and the city of Cornwall beyond. He stops the cruiser and steps out, feet flown from under him so suddenly he couldn't even grab the door for support. Down on his right shoulder, hard, hard enough to question his bones. Pains in neck and rib as well as the shoulder, which however still works. Once up, shaken, he stands by his cruiser watching gusts of northern lights flutter under the edge of the cloud-mass. The sky is opening, rapidly, from the north; he watches shimmers and tatters of light that seem blown by a polar wind. The rain clicks and patters on the car and all around him and then, with a waft of much colder air, draws away, with a rustle like an opening curtain. Or like static dying out, the signal suddenly coming clear. How sudden, the forecast change.

There's been time enough. More than time enough. He's just come from the lake but on a hunch or a memory—*did he see a light? Halfway back?*—hurriedly he turns the cruiser around and heads back. He pushes the car now, faster, as he had done when Pelo was with him, and pays attention only to driving until halfway in, when he is coming downhill toward the narrow culvert over some small stream. What does he remember that was odd, here, the last time he passed? He slows going up the other side and begins looking closely at the snowbanks and the crowded sticks of hardwoods briefly lit by his passing headlamps. He might be going too slowly to make the hill. On the other hand, too fast to see everything, anything. They will step out and flag, yell as he goes by, as soon as they identify the car. He tries to watch out of the corners of his eyes, both sides, checks the rear-view mirrors. The car is hot, all the heat blowing on the windshield to keep it clear.

Was there a light here, back behind this long pile of polewood just over the snowbank on the right? He knows the place, the name is Fisk, it's a trailer, up there under some shade trees. In the summer, small brown rabbits would be feeding by the road here. Mr Fisk had decided to walk home from The Rapids one night, too drunk to drive his pickup, and O'Neil gave him a lift and helped him to his door. Mr Fisk explained the rabbits, pets that had gone feral but still lived around the place, slowly being picked off by coyotes. Would have been foxes, but the coyotes had driven off the foxes. Yes, there is a light, faint, reddish, from a curtained window in the trailer. Why, at this hour?

The patrol car doesn't make it much beyond the entrance of the drive, even steeper than the road. The headlights at least shine up toward the trailer. He leaves the engine running and walks tenderfoot in his slippery square-toed boots up the light-beams, arms shooting out for balance. He uses the railing to pulled himself up the three glazed steps to the small platform outside the trailer door.

The grizzled, erect little man opens quickly, blank smudged eyeglasses opaque in shadow. O'Neil sees false teeth possibly in a grin. Mr Fisk doesn't try to shield his guests. There they are, big wet bodies like out-of-place horses, John Pelo sprawled on the short sofa with his arm in a red bandanna sling, eyes closed, the knot of the sling in his teeth, and, getting up from a stuffed chair, nervous, not Robert Sochia but a giddy, mouth-breathing longhair O'Neil recognizes after a moment's confusion as Mrs Hubbard's son. He looks for the girl, the young woman. Peter Hubbard shakes his head, spreads his hands in helplessness, as if he knows even less than O'Neil, cannot explain. Solicitous, he puts a hand on Pelo's shoulder.

So it was Pelo who told it, Johny Pelo the beautiful dummy, winged, watched over by his wife. He insisted on going first to get Helen, who had been sweeping out the chickenhouse again, getting it ready for his homecoming. At the intersection by The Rapids, Peter Hubbard leaped out, saying something about his truck. Helen, eyes blazing, nostrils wide, took his place with John in back. Then to the Rescue Squad garage, where the competent Terwilliger, working in the ambulance for its battery-powered lights, stabilized the arm and narcotized the victim sufficiently to get him by until Dougherty, the hand surgeon from Saranac, could meet them at the Emergency Room at six o'clock. In that interval O'Neil, still in his cross-country ski outfit, took what evidence he had over to the Wellers. Mr Weller, on the school board, somewhat responsible for the music teacher, would want to know this.

Leo was at the door before O'Neil even knocked. They all filed into that small den, Loyal Weller in his bathrobe and slippers offering chairs but standing, himself, before the fireplace with the civil war musket hanging over it. O'Neil stayed on his feet too, and Helen stood behind her husband, hands on his shoulders, bending down sometimes, her hair hiding his face from them, Pelo writhing in discomfort on a chair too fragile for him. Mr Weller said, "John, is this all right now, can you talk?"

"It wasn't him," John said.

"You mean who shot you?"

"It wasn't Bobby."

"I shouldn't think it would have been. Start at the beginning, why don't you? Take your time."

So Pelo bawled it, heatedly, his wife seeming to want to deny, revise, correct it but mostly holding her tongue. How he went right to the place, deep snow no problem, you just had to go fast, use your arms, pull yourself along by the trees. Came at it from the side toward the cove at the end of the lake, crossed the ice to it there, went up the path from their little dock on the narrows. There was a big snowdrift along that side of the porch, where somebody shoveled off the roof. He took off his snowshoes in the shadow of it. Then climbing up the drift he saw right in, some of the big room lit by firelight, nothing else.

He couldn't see anybody in there at first. Then saw her hands waving above the back of the sofa that was in front of the fire. Gesturing, he said, like leading a band. He got back away from the building and crept back around the corner of the veranda and came up to the window next to the chimney. Found a block of wood to stand on. To see her from in front.

Helen stiffened up. This person he didn't know, never saw before, long hair and a lot of it, she was sitting Indian-fashion on the sofa, in her underthings. Nobody else there but she was talking, and waving her hands, her hair all spread out and her head nodding up and down or turning back and forth. She was talking to herself, for all Pelo could see, or else to the chimney, eyes right on it, as if it was somebody there. Talking loud enough so he could hear, not the words, but like music, he said. Up and down, slow sometimes, sometimes fast, always going, like a steady stream . . .

"Talking to the chimney?" Mr Weller interjected in the pause.

Pelo said it again. "Yes, to the chimney. Up to it. As if it was a picture there. I couldn't see what it was. There was an old pair of snowshoes up there. On the chimney. I see that from the other window. Like, for decoration."

"To a picture, you say?"

"I didn't see no picture. Did I say picture?"

"The old Indian," Leo said.

"What?"

It took a while to get this straight, what was up on that chimney that she might have been talking to. Pelo's description brought back to Leo remembered nights at Purryer Camp in his childhood when he would stay over with a cousin whose mother rented the place. They all sat in front of that fireplace, with the Ouija board on an ottoman between them, Aunt Nancy, his cousin Phillip, Phillip's sister Dianne, and Leo. Aunt Nancy believed that her daughter had spiritual gifts, and Leo and Dianne would put their fingers on the little table. He would fix his eyes on the wood-burned portrait of an Indian on a wooden disc up on the chimney, like a huge wooden nickel, between those desiccated, fine-mesh Michigan snowshoes crossed at the tails. Aquiline nose, hair gathered into a bound cylinder by the ear, four or five feathers tied to it quills-up. He would stare at that old Indian and try to channel something from it onto the Ouija board, but Dianne would be pushing the little table all over the board, spelling out predictions of tall dark strangers coming down the lake tomorrow by mahogany inboard, her dreams come true.

But that was by the bye. "The head of an old Indian, on a wooden plaque," Leo said, efficiently. "Carved, or wood-burned rather, I think it was. I remember it well. That's what she was talking to."

"All right," Mr Weller said. "Talking to this wood-burned head of an Indian, up on the chimney, John, is that it? But you couldn't hear what she was saying."

Pelo tossed his nonexistent mane and dug his good hand over his scalp. "I didn't see no Indian. But she was talking to somebody. I figured Bobby was in there, I just couldn't see him." Something, maybe a twitch of Helen's fingers on his collar-bone, made him add, "But he wasn't there. It wasn't him."

"You mean to say Robert Sochia wasn't there with her?"

"Yeah. I mean no. It wasn't him that shot me."

They waited. Pelo lifted his arm and let it down. Helen kept her hands on his shoulders and looked angrily at Leo. At O'Neil.

"Take your time, John," Mr Weller said. "If it doesn't hurt too much. Just tell what you can."

Pelo lifted and dropped his arm again. The person on the sofa had been putting on her things, that had been draped around her on the sofa, drying and warming, he guessed. Long-johns, socks, wool shirts, wool pants that didn't fit, she was putting them all on, while she talked. "Getting ready to go outdoors, looked like. All the time she's still talking to the chimney, singing at it, like. But she's really getting dressed, like, out of his sight, see. And in between she's listening, like. Thinking. She looks scared, or worried. But when she's talking she's all happy and smiling. She's talking loud, and then she's listening, hard. So I finally get what she's doing. Wait a minute, I says. She's talking to somebody back there in the dark, behind her. She's fooling him, she ain't telling him what she's doing. She's getting ready to run for it."

Consternation! "But—" Mr Weller began.

"Robert wasn't there, you said," from Leo.

"I don't know!"

Mr Weller said, "You think maybe he was, John? Robert was back there, behind her somewhere? Couldn't see her?"

"I—"

"She was getting ready to run away from him? Is that what you think?"

"I don't know! I just figured, Go in. I wasn't going to stand around out there."

He'd vaulted up onto the porch, no drift on that end of it, and not worrying about the sharp cracks it gave, or the thumps of his weight, he made for the door. He heard her yelling inside, right away, as he ran: "No-no-no!"

"What's that?"

"Like that, I swear! I no sooner made a noise than she was hollering."

She got to the door before Pelo did. "Slippery, that porch! I near slipped on my ass." She pulled the door open, and he'd have had her, but the door caught and he banged against it. She was pushing at him, out, pushing him away down the slope of the porch. He had no traction. He turned around, slipping, "And *bam!*" He held up his elbow again, as he might have thrown an arm out for balance. Too quickly. He winced and hauled it in to his chest and hugged it, rocking, and Helen bent her head to his and patted his other cheek.

"I didn't hardly feel it. It was like something jerked my arm. Picked me right off my feet. I pitched down that drift head-first. Then I heard the shot, like roll of thunder, roaring back off the hills, two-three times. Double-echoes because the hills are so close. You couldn't believe it, how loud it was. My ears hurt with it."

He'd just lain there, evidently in shock. Deaf, numb, amazed. Then somebody rolled him over, or tried to: turned him enough to look at his face. "And this voice said 'What? *What?*' Higher, like that. Like my face was messed up. I had ice in my mouth, I know."

Then his shoulder was let go, there was someone talking, a man's voice he didn't know, but it wasn't Bobby's, but he didn't get any of it, he was out of it, he wasn't sure if he was conscious or not. "'til Hubbard come and found me." He hung his head.

"There were other voices, John, do you say? I'm sorry."

"It wasn't Bobby. It wasn't him, that's all I know. You don't have to say nothing about it, do ya?"

Mr Weller glanced at O'Neil. Of course a gunshot wound had to be reported. The medical people would take care of that. He said, "Nobody will ask us, I'm sure."

"I didn't do anything wrong, did I?" Pelo looked around at O'Neil.

Mr Weller said, "Not at all, John. Now you go along and get your arm fixed. That's the important thing. We're very much obliged to you."

After the deputy helped the Pelos down the icy front steps and into his cruiser, Leo and his father stayed out there on the round-cornered porch of the house, taking in the change. Everything below the streetlamp down by the bridge now gleamed in a pebbly coating of ice. Above, the stars crowded a sky profoundly clear. Mr Weller tilted his watch toward the streetlamp. "Nearly four o'clock. What do you think?"

Leo didn't think. He might have been there, he was so sure. "The Colt's revolver spoke."

O'Neil had explained how Hubbard happened to be close by. Hunting with Clarence. Clarence had set him to watch a runway, just as if he was hunting deer, and went off to make his drive. That was Clarence in there. Had to be.

"The old woodenheaded Indian. That was our boy."

"So I thought too, until the fellow shoots Pelo."

"Not Pelo, Father. Robert."

"They said Robert wasn't there. It's Pelo that has the extra elbow."

"It's who he thinks he shot that counts. Clarence the Clear, Ragnar the Rough. Refused to run away. Had to bring him in." He could already hear her telling him this part. *He wouldn't go, Leo! That stupid old man! He wouldn't go! We could have run right down the lake, oh up the lake don't interrupt! He could have helped me, we'd have made it. But he couldn't make a new decision. He had to do what he came to do. Sit there and wait for him, and capture him! Can you believe?*

Mr Weller was cold, in his bathrobe, out there on the porch. "I'd rather think that was the kind of ambush Robert would have set, for whoever dared come after him. Your Pelo protests too much."

"Oh, he thought it was Robert too."

"Clarence is no homicide," Mr Weller said, through teeth clenched against rattling. "Let's go in."

In the den again, while his father lit a fire, Leo rubbed his hands together. "All right, that's settled. What happens next? Nobody else around. Hubbard helps Pelo up. Naturally they go into the camp, where there's firelight and warmth at least, and first-aid supplies somewhere, and between the two of them they have enough sense to rig up a bandage and a sling and get Pelo out of the woods. He wasn't bleeding badly, I gather. Pelo's tough as a deer, and you know how a deer can run with a broken limb. How they come out at old Fisk's, I don't pretend to guess. A short cut of Pelo's maybe. Doesn't matter. They're out. They're done.

"What counts is Clarence and the girl. Where are they? Once he's killed the outlaw, he takes charge, heroic, tells her 'Pack up, cutie, we're out of here. You want to split, let's split.' Back to his truck, wherever he left it? When? They would have made it out of the woods as quick as Pelo and Hubbard, or not long after. But Father, here's the thing. I've watched this bridge all night. I've sat by my window watching, never took off my clothes and never slept. And Clarence never came across the bridge."

His father had his slabs alight. He fanned the flame a little with a folded newspaper, cranked his knees straight and moved to his chair. "I am unconvinced he was there at all, but if he was, and got to his truck, he could have gone out the other road, to Risdonville. Anywhere."

"Wait!" Leo said, who was not listening. "I'm getting something. The ice! The ice! He'd bring her to this end of the lake—"

"You say he won't go on the ice!"

"Different ice. Right, he made her walk the hay road, because he won't walk on the lake, and he's in charge, he's the hero now, remember. There's some time there. They get to the truck. Out the road to the Shampines' home place, where what'll you bet he takes her in, builds a fire, makes them a cup of tea. They rest. Might both fall asleep sipping it. More time. Still raining then? Don't know, doesn't matter, somewhere the rain turns to sleet."

He jumped up suddenly. "Come with me while I get my things on." He brushed past his father's knees, led through the parlor. He dug in the hall closet, threw outdoor clothing out onto the floor.

"What, you're going out? Where?"

"Breakthrough, breakthrough," Leo muttered.

"What?"

As he chose his things he chattered. "I told you. Ice. When they're rested up, have drunk their tea, he's falling asleep. She's saying 'Clarence, Clarence, wake up, we can't stay here! Get me out of here!' Well, he tries. They go out and get in the truck, still in the road. They cross the brook. They start up the hill."

"Nobody would get up that hill tonight," his father said.

"Good for you! Nor the other one, back toward the lake. He's stuck, Father. He can't get out of there. If he didn't know better than to even try, what'll you bet his truck's in the ditch, or the creek. He'd spin out, lock his brakes, lose control trying to back down." Leo was dressing as he would for shoveling snow. "They're at his lair, keeping warm. Best they can do."

"Are you sure?" his father said.

"Does a bear shit in the woods?" Leo had his helmet on, ear-flaps up for now, his overshoes, his coat and gloves. Took the car keys from the cardholder by the mirror. Looked into the closet one last time to stir up a scarf. Made a crank of his elbow and wound it round his neck. His father stepped out of his way, then followed him out the door.

Leo's teeth and glasses flashed in the blue-white light from the street-lamp down by the bridge. He backed down the ice-coated steps holding onto the rail and let that go to tiptoe unsupported to the garage. One foot flew up, he turned, slid halfway down the walk in a pirouette. He had to throw himself on one of his glans-shaped cedar bushes to stop. Far from chagrined, he turned and beamed at his father, who watched from the top of the steps.

Mr Weller said, "If you go down in there between those hills, you won't get out either."

"Tire chains! In the trunk."

"Do you think you can put them on by yourself?"

"Father."

Leo used to put on chains for everybody, when he worked at Lenny's Shell after his breakdown. "Well, I know," Mr Weller admitted. "But tonight? You'll freeze your fingers. And in the dark. I don't like this."

"I know it," Leo said. "But don't you think I'd better find those two before Robert Sochia does?"

"Oh! Oh!" Mr Weller hadn't thought of Robert.

"Robert will be in this somewhere, Father. It isn't over yet."

Leo sidestepped carefully over to the driveway and up it to the garage. Held onto one of the doors and slid back downhill with it while it opened. Pulled himself along it, back up to the bathtub-fendered Chevrolet.

"Maybe you'd better put the chains on before you start?" But Leo was out of sight in the garage. "Didn't hear me," Mr Weller said to himself. He watched him back out, turn around and, the braked front wheels sliding much of the way, ease the car down to the highway. At least the main road was well-sanded, salted too: the trucks had been out all night. He didn't like this at all. Should he have gone along? Was there any need of his staying here, holding the fort? His son's adventure seemed perilous and lonely to him and Leo wasn't necessarily capable of everything a normal person might be, alone. He was brave and buoyant but he didn't necessarily have good sense, or appreciate the seriousness of everything. From a bag just beside the door Mr Weller sprinkled some rock-salt on the steps. Then he thought he'd better dress himself more warmly, put on his rubber boots and try to salt the driveway, too; if he could stay upright well enough.

29

As Big a Mouth as Anybody

He wanted the town to know it, so that it could weave it, even this
last part of it, his pride, into "that garment, that threadbare tapestry
of rumor and jabber and gossip" (as Leo calls it) by which he would
be held forever in these hills, after he was lost in common ordinary
love and time. He told Marcia that he felt like a knower himself
that night. He was everywhere, saw everything. Seemed to think
he could fly, in the dark, like a demigod, the distances that he had
in fact to trudge, step by step, in snow, in rain that turned to ice.
She says he seemed to think that his tasks required no time, or that
the night was infinite. All that had happened, all that had yet to
happen, was wound on a ball that would unwind to the end that
night, no matter how much there was to unwind. Time would
hold still for it so that he could even go out of his way, not directly
back to Purryer Camp, to tell it.

He went there to tell it to Old Herman, Herman Plumadore,
the Repository, the Authority, the Curator of that tapestry. But it
wasn't Old Herman anymore, living in Herman's house, on another
back road off the main road west of town. Old Herman was doubly
legless now, still in the hospital from his second amputation. He'd
sold his house and barn, or they'd been sold for him by Social
Services to pay for his care. So Robert Sochia found there in the
early morning, long before daylight, not Old Herman but this
pregnant black woman who tends the fires and reads books all
hours of the night, while her husband sleeps a few feet away in a
downstairs bedroom.

Maybe her baby kept her up unusually late this night, or the power-outage did, and she had lost a sense of time herself, lulled by comfort and the whisper of the Aladdin lamp on a table by the arm of Herman's old sofa, near the new air-tight Norwegian stove full of maple chunks that were turned into charcoal by now and would last all night, the draft shut as tight as it would shut against the pull of the warm chimney. Legs up under her, all under a crocheted throw, she heard over that low hiss of the lamp his steps on the frozen ground even before his boots crunched on the single step of unpainted wood outside the kitchen door, which doesn't seal too well.

(Firewood's cheap, her husband says, the fresh-air fiend. He'd rather feed the stoves than tighten up the house. He rises early, washes shirtless outside on the porch, shaves in a shard of mirror. He does his reading by the cookstove, before breakfast. Between the two of them and the tow-headed kid there are books on every level surface in that lair.)

Two icy-sounding footfalls and a clatter of the loose door being tested without first a knock. She closed her book over her marker, pushed herself up out of the sofa, carried the lamp to the archway where you step down into the kitchen, a low shed on the back of the house very like the kitchen of her family home in South Carolina. No more sound from without; but sure of what she'd heard she stepped down, set the lamp on the drain-board, and crossed the linoleum feeling bark and chips of wood-hauling under her slippers. Lifted the latch, looked out, spoke, but no one was there. So she turned around to find him standing out of her light, but in the penumbra of its shade, back by the cookstove, its oven door propped closed with a stick.

She's a person with reserves of calm. She knew who he was even before she saw the dark glint of gold. But he stared at her unknowing. "Herman? Where's Old Herman?"

She raised the lamp, but the cone of light still missed his face. She thought she saw something like war-paint on it. She told him to come nearer where she could see him better.

Her voice has a flicker in it, a click, part of its richness. He did move a step. She might have seen a flinch. He said, "I came to see Old Herman."

Shorter than she expected, slighter. Swarthy from being outdoors, but beneath the sun- and wind-burn, she thought him pallid, face framed in shaggy, glinting black hair, black beard. He did have a straight nose, long enough, and breathed through it, mouth closed until he spoke.

"I have to tell him the story."

She explained that this was her home, bought quite some time ago from Herman by her husband. Mr Plumadore was in the hospital. He didn't bat an eye at that, or at her particulars if he noticed them. He said simply, "You then. I'll tell you. You got as big a mouth as anybody."

Just then the kitchen wall gave a heavy thud, the house adjusting to encroaching cold—extreme cold by such evidence. That as much as anything caused her to ask him come into the living room. She paused in the archway to advise him that her husband was asleep, in the downstairs bedroom behind the sofa, then stepped up onto its floor insulated with overlapping braided rugs and bits of carpet. She put the lamp down on the end table and sat down again and brought her feet up and pulled the afghan over her. Let Robert Sochia sit opposite, deep in Herman's, now her husband's, sagging armchair. From there he looked around the walls at Herman's moth-eaten deer heads, deer-foot gun-racks, hat-racks, mirrors, maps. His eyes closed, and what seemed a tremor of accidental sleep went over him. His eyes opened again but he didn't move. She was sure of the scratches on his cheeks now. But Marcia is not one to jump ahead or pry. She assumed they'd be explained.

It would be a while before he got to this night. "You remember that jurywoman that used to come and stay the nights with me? You heard about her? I told her all of it up to Canada. I have to tell you all of it after that."

"I have to go to bed some time."

"Not 'til I'm done. Old Herman would have heard it all."

He talked. He told it simple and fast, with ellipses he didn't seem aware of. He didn't hurry but he didn't explain things either and not everything made sense to her, a requirement she didn't make. He wasn't exactly in the regular world, she thought, but in some ancillary pouch where Time would hold still while he told it to her and slow way down for the rest of it, so that there would still be night and time for everything yet to be done. And then he seemed to think the pouch would empty him out into the new day with all clocks ticking. She thinks he was hardly present in his own body, to notice anything like exhaustion or hunger or pain, or the pull of barbed wire on his wool pants, perhaps when he crossed into their pasture, back behind the barn. At least he'd torn them somewhere, a cornered flap was open on his inner thigh, a flash of pallor there, a spark of blood.

Talked plain and fast, in the barest statements, telling her the things the town had to know, about that trip to Canada, about the way he couldn't breathe and then how he could, with the other person, "like two pipes to one tank," and then when he got back, maybe he assumed she knew all about the fire, the Pelodome a pile of embers, didn't even tell her where he had slept, only that when he woke up that morning "after Canada," he knew something, he felt as if he had been operated on in the night, something taken right out of his body, he had an awful knowledge of removal and loss and sure enough when he went to Days' he found her packing up to leave, and without knowing anything, knew everything, knew what he was doing even though he hadn't thought of it in advance, and shut her up and shut Neva Day up and did it.

"You got it up to there?"

"Yes," Marcia said.

"Okay. I don't have to tell you everything about the woods, what that was like, they can figure that out from what they found, and if they don't know everything that's okay, I don't care. They don't know where I was all the time, how I traveled. That's okay. They can guess. They can imagine. It was good. She slept like the woods. She didn't eat. I could do anything. I could fly. I knew everything. I wanted it just the way it was, her not talking, not eating. That was leading to an ending. That was good. It was cold. It was beautiful. She walked. I had her with me. That thing that was taken out of me, it wasn't gone. I had it. I could look at her and it would shake me. I was promised that with my mother's milk, only my mother is a liar. You aren't promised it at all. But I had it. That was all that mattered. I was up to it. I did everything just so. I don't have to tell you all of that, they can guess. They will anyway. They can imagine, they'll know when they make it wrong and try to take something away from me. It won't do them any good."

"Go on," she'd say, when he went on like that, wasting his own time and hers. And he went on, fast, erratically, with geographic references she didn't understand yet. The centerfolds, the cold cow, Dexter Lake. But she knew he was coming closer, he was coming to tonight, tonight was the main thing, after which it wouldn't be a story any more, wouldn't have to be told because it would be witnessed, it would just be present history.

He came to it quickly, Purryer Camp, the power-line. Then he was in the town and it was almost the present, it was only moments ago and the main thing yet to tell.

JoAnn would see the lie, Karen saying the caller hung up. She'd know who'd asked for the key, and what key he meant.

She would make nothing of it for a while and then leave one of the men in charge and go back into the kitchen and pick out a knife. She'd always brought one up to the room, and put it in the drawer of the bedside table, and left the drawer open while they fought. He was afraid to touch a knife when they were struggling. She could threaten him with it and he wouldn't even move. He couldn't run because Ray would be out there at the top of the stairs keeping watch. But he wouldn't run anyway. He started out not wanting to do the things that JoAnn also pretended not to want, or maybe she started out not wanting them either, but it changed and soon he was pretending not to want them too, and making her want them worse, until they were both fighting each other for it not against. He never told anyone. That was what the knife was about, picked up and held in his face when they were done fighting for it. "If you ever tell, you little shit—" And he was a coward and he was afraid of it all right but it was more complicated than that, because although he was afraid certainly, right inside the fear there was the want, and the knowing that he could make her want it too, make her turn against herself, both of them shaming themselves to reduce the other to scum afterwards. More complicated than that too because each was the only one that was worth doing it with, or to, both being Sochias, both from the same unforgiving blood; only Robert a coward, afraid of pain, afraid to fight except to fight her. Not afraid to do it. Afraid to not. And afterwards afraid to tell and ashamed to tell, and yet proud, inside. She knew that, too.

A corner room, not large, high-ceilinged, its gold and silver wallpaper only a little stained, a pattern of shaded columns and vines. Fancy wallpaper because the man who built The Rapids was a state senator and friend of Teddy Roosevelt and this hotel was where the rich people rested on the way to their big camps or fancy hotels in the South Woods after having come up Lake Champlain by steamboat and from there to Moira by train and from Moira by horse-drawn coach. In those days when the town was young and booming, with a milliner and a haberdashery and even a newspaper, they rested here overnight before the last leg of their journey into the woods where they would stay, or at least the women and children would stay, two months or more, the whole season away from the pestilent cities, the heat and the coal-dust and the polio. And the lumber-buyers and the land-dealers too, and Orrando Dexter and his wife stayed here while their house was being built at Dexter Lake.

Robert had heard of the room, growing up. How as the place had changed hands, as the old shops and offices of its long clapboarded back part, along the side street, had been boarded up, the other rooms emptied in auctions, the grounds graveled and the widened main street crowded up against the porch, through all that change and entropy one room had been closed off and kept the same. As the outside of the place had been sided with asbestos shingles, its porches torn off, its inside, even the pressed-tin ceilings, painted maroon and green and white and its bar paneled in knotty pine, all through the decline of the town itself, one room in The Rapids kept closed, unchanged, almost-secret, described authoritatively by people who never saw it just the way it was well known who shot Orrando Dexter but nobody ever heard anybody actually say.

But it was actually there, true, The Rapids having come into JoAnn's hands, not down through family, though one antecedent Sochia had owned it too, and others further back had doubtless worked for the senator's family, the original owners. Bought cheap, with the help of that first husband who worked on the St. Lawrence Seaway, always shadowy, long gone; bought cheap and only the bar really run, no business for a hotel in the town anymore. On certain occasions, dinners served. A band on Saturday night. The room was there and it was to the room that JoAnn made her younger brother bring their cousin, his coeval; there she served him out for wrong done to her, tempting, seducing, flattering, rejecting, humiliating the younger cousin, the fine-nosed son of her own betrayer.

Hating him all the more for this duty, threatening to break that nose if he told, Ray would bring him secretly up the service stairway, to the dark hall of closed doors, the floor like a warped bowling alley, the shade rolled down in the one window at the sunward end overlooking the down-plunging river. And sit at the top of the stairs and wait, make sure nobody came up while she took Robert at fifteen and sixteen into the room.

Inside, she locked the door, the shades already drawn, and lit the lamp while he stood there watching, the register already turned up, the room already overheated, to make their bodies sweat. She made him look at the pictures on the wall, told him of those women in the old-time pictures, with jewels at their throats and curls at their ears, with their clothes buttoned right up to their chins and you couldn't even see their shoes under their skirts. This room was where all that stuff came off of them, and did he know what was underneath? Had he ever seen? Did he wonder? Under this mantle lamp in a wall sconce with its tall clear chimney reaching up through a china globe their fancy men took all that stuff off. Was he man enough to do that? With her sitting on this cane-seated rocking-chair without arms, or lying on this little fringed white Persian rug. Or kneeling? In front of this vanity skirted the same as the bed, its oval mirror, held in two arms like the curve of a woman's hips, large enough to reflect a whole human body.

What did he think the women did? Did they fight? Did they like what was happening? Did they help? Did they undress the men? Did Lucille Dexter open the fly of her fancy Orrando, like this? What do you think your father did to me in this room, Robert; would you like to see? Would you like to do it to me too? Or have me do the same things to you? Do you think you're as much of a man as he was? That shit! Are you any better? Here, what are you looking at? Want to see them? Tear this apart! Never mind the snaps, here's a knife! Cut it!

It smelled like hot fur, in that room, the dust on the radiator heating, unless it was her, heating. Skinny then, high-breasted, cobra-like. There was always jewelry, painted toenails, shoes that the painted toenails peeked through. She would always have something on that made you think of her body under it, even a boy who'd never seen a woman's body. In the room she would tease him with her body, show it and hide it, get him to touch her and then fight him off. After the first time he knew what was coming but it wasn't a game, it was real every time, a fight to stay out of it that he would lose and then a fight to get it that he would win with a feeling of loss and then her threats and belittlement, the knife always there in the drawer of the bed-table under the sconce.

At first, he was just a kid, fifteen, she would start to do it herself, saying what was the matter with him, here's what his father would do. Tear open her dress herself. Pull a strap away from her shoulder. Don't you want to see what's under there? Flick your finger over it until it's stiff? Stick it in your mouth? But if he did what she taunted him to do, it would start a fight. If he protected himself from her fingers it would start a fight too. She would start tickling him and hurting him to embarrass him and make him mad, and she would be hissing insults and comparisons and belittlements, the radiator hissing and clanging too, and he would just try to hold her off. But she would have his shirt out of his pants and her hands down his tummy and it would change, she would be tearing at her clothes and his at the same time and it would be like a fire, he would catch fire too, he wouldn't care how much it hurt. It hurt just to have it that hard at that age. But it would make him proud, that she would seem like it was going to kill her, she was the one that was hurt and afraid. He would be all bitten and scratched when they were done, and proud of that too.

For just a minute, her dying and him strong. Then she would have his balls in one hand, squeezing them, calling him a little shit and telling him what she would do if he ever opened his mouth to anybody. And she would open the drawer of the bed table just in case he had forgotten what was in it, lying there, whetted on an oil-stone. She took his hand one time and held it still and shaved the hairs on the back of his wrist with it, dry. He'd get dressed and go out and pick up her brother with a whack on the back of the neck and the two of them get down the stairs and out of there.

He never told. Ray would brag that he had made the marks on him. He would say the same thing, Ray had been beating him up. His mother would say, "Did you fight back, for once?" and his father would leave the house in disgust. Then for weeks and weeks, through Ray and in person, JoAnn would give him nothing but scorn and bitterness and insult again until some day the hate and bitterness would grow into a summons again and Ray would threaten him and tell him that she called him a piss-yellow coward and his father something worse, and he'd tell Ray his sister was a slut, why doesn't she tell it to his face? and they'd go, and Ray would keep watch, and in that room they'd fight again and the fight would turn out to be for it, not against. Followed by his balls in her hand, squeezed hard, and the threat. And he'd say, Do you think I'd brag about fucking *you*? And she, you didn't fuck me! You never could! What with? Do you imagine you are half the man your father is?

For a while she had probably been thrilled with his father's flattery, his indulgence, his professed infatuation. He had taken her far away, to Montreal, even to Quebec City, in his luxurious Imperial. He had spent money on her, dressed her, fed her at the Café de la Paix, himself finely dressed with tailored suits and wing-tipped shoes. His father did have style, he had class however phony and saved for women. When they came to their room in the Chateau Laurier or the Reine Elizabeth, he probably worshiped her with new negligees, perfumes, candles and champagne, with lavish seductions that took hours. Robert could see him doing that, the hypocrite, the faker, the lady's man. Making her so desperate for him—to hear him tell about it, around the poker table in hunting camp, with little Bobby and Ray all ears, listening from the bunkroom—that when he would finally let her have it and it dripped out the corners of her mouth, she'd catch it on her fingers and rub it on her tits, to get it all. Robert now confused in imagining, his father or himself, the same lips, the same fingers, tongue.

He would leave town completely for half a year or a year at a time, to get away from that. He'd be glad to be sent away to reform school, a relief. He would come back for it too. Because it was something. It wasn't nothing. JoAnn was wild. It didn't have to make any sense. That was what a woman was, to him. Somebody who had to have it and couldn't even tell you how furious it made her. That was what it was between men and women. All he had ever wanted was for it to be as much him as it was her, with one of them. To feel that wildness in himself. Until then every woman was measured against JoAnn and the strongest thing he'd known was the fear, the wildness, the hatred, the smell of fur in that room in The Rapids.

He heard her, behind him, coming up, not up the main stairs but the service stairway. No light. Her steps on the hard wood, slowing. Stopping. He just waited in the hall at the door of the room. Fingers touched his side and quickly withdrew. He felt her brush past him. She smelled the same. Heard the clicking of her nails on wall, on the door casing, the key finding the lock.

He followed her into the room, different now from any other time, no silhouette of her, no streetlight beyond the window. He stopped, unable to tell where she was. He felt the air move around him, heard the door closing. Now the movements of the past, exactly the same but in blackness. She passed him to draw the window-shade down to the sill, black eclipsing black. Turned the knob of the radiator. He didn't see or hear her move but next, beside him, the sound of something put into the drawer and then the cover of the china box on the bed-table gave a little scrape. The snap of her thumbnail, flare of match-light. Her face and hair, hand and arm bringing the match up to the lamp in the wall sconce, the other arm lifted too, the loose sleeve falling back, to lift the chimney, let it down over the flame. A puff from her lips put out the match and she turned to him straight. He felt as at a distance how scared he used to be, of fingernails, pain, how fear fought with the other thing for control of his blood

He had never faced her alone since she tore her brother's coughing, spattered torso from his knees. The same, tall, long-legged, high-waisted, high-breasted JoAnn, same long crinkly hair, curly on her forehead over the dark level brows. A girl's face, pretty to others but family to him, all clear quick feelings for which he felt a family pride. A turquoise top of some fuzzy soft material, in two parts that started on one side at the waist and crossed to the opposite shoulder, with soft short puffy sleeves. In the vee between them, her sharp collar-bones and a place between them where he could see her pulse. If he ripped those soft turquoise crossings apart, would it start? For a second he thought he would do it, was going to do it, was supposed to. Felt his warm blood squeezed through the valves already. He held his breath momentarily. It had always been JoAnn who started it, ripped things apart.

Then he breathed. He didn't know what released him at first, then felt it, as if within him: the new life. He felt a sort of comfort with JoAnn, flesh and blood, his partner in past history. He remembered he was tired, hungry. Like Julia, just like her. Had to spare himself, for her. Warm indoors even though the room was only starting to heat up, he shrugged off his parka, sat down on the armless rocking chair, rocked back.

"You can call off yourdogs," he said. "I came to make peace with you."

She was not surprised. She pressed her lips in a hard smile, shook her head. "Make peace, that's an interesting thought. Now."

"Yeah."

"Why would I do that? You're caught!"

"I'm sorry about Ray. I couldn't help it. I was scared."

"Are you afraid now?"

"No. I'm not afraid now."

"What does that mean?"

"You can do whatever you want to me. Just call off your dogs."

It took her a moment to answer. She breathed like it was coming, a long way off but the old stuff coming. "For what? You can go. Nobody cares about you."

"You don't care about her."

"There you are right. For letting *her* go?"

"The two of us. Just stop your crew. That's all."

"I want your balls in my teeth, Sochia!"

"Just stop your crew."

"Why? You are scared."

It was true but it was a different fear from what she thought it was, from what he'd always felt. Everything hung by a thread. If they came, in the morning, he'd lose everything. He knew it. Whatever happened, the end of it would be her disappearing on the back of one of their snowmobiles, everything lost.

"Then we're right where we always were," JoAnn said. She took a deep breath, slowly. Her face was rich, fierce. Her nose and mouth and eyes belonged to him. He was proud of her. She turned and bent down and opened the door of the night-stand and set on top a decanter and glass. There never used to be a decanter and glass. He didn't see another glass. The decanter was half-full of something, brandy or whiskey.

"No," he told her, "it's different now." She gave him a look askance that was perfect, rich, drew him to her even more. He watched her drink the liquor with fine control and put the empty glass down on the bed-stand. Then she came to him and framed his face in her hands and drew her sharp nails down his cheeks. He felt his blood well out and run behind them.

"I wouldn't have minded to die, out there in the woods," he said, closing his eyes. "I would have been just as glad. If your clowns would have had the balls."

She laughed, a sort of snort, still with his face in her hands. They were veterans of an old time no one else had had. She was still faithful to it even if he was new.

"I wasn't afraid. All the time I was out there, with her, I could feel it coming into me, a bullet, mushrooming, plowing through me. And my blood, red and warm, going out of me, just like Ray's. I would have been just as glad. If they would have found me."

"You shit. You were running for all you were worth."

"That was what they would have had to do, to get her away from me. I was waiting for it. I wasn't afraid. It would have been the way I wanted it."

JoAnn said, "Cheap, cowardly tricks. You were running." She stood up over him with her hands on her breasts, nails against her skin, slowly starting to pull the green vee open.

"I was showing them what good they are."

She didn't wait, she pulled one side of her top away, showing him a see-through brassiere, black lace. She lifted the breast by its strap and leaned it toward his face, yanked his face against it. She always had a perfume that made him dizzy. His blood would be on the black flowers and the white skin between them.

"And now you're caught and you'll do anything to get out of it in your skin."

"Yeah. That's right. I need to be alive." The green stuff was off either shoulder, her breasts fatter now above the black lace, she was older but the remembered dark nipples pushing the bruise-colored aureolas back from it like always. She was great, always.

"What changed?" One hand was on his belt, behind it. Blood moving inside him, flowing through an opening, filling up a space, the same. He couldn't change that. He didn't want the blood contained, he wanted to let it flow on out, but it was contained, and his parts tightened, swelled in her hand.

She felt, squeezed, let go and withdrew her hand, smiling with the old despair. She used to do that, check on him, make fun of it. Pretend she hated it.

"That isn't me." He didn't mind that she could make that happen. She deserved it. But he had to tell her how he'd changed. He was full of this. She was the older and stronger of the two of them and he had to show it to her. "I'm needed to be alive."

"Jesus," she said. She knew, now, that this was something more. She poured from the decanter again. She sipped, swallowed, then took a bigger swallow. "What are you telling me?"she suddenly commanded, in a different voice. "You better say it."

A woman would figure it out, wouldn't she? "We'll go away. We'll go to Florida."

"And—?"

"She won't stay with me. I don't expect anything like that. She'll have it."

"Have. It. And then."

"I'll take care of it," he said. "I'm going to raise it."

She slammed the glass down on the little table. "I want your balls, you filth! Stand up!"

She was breathing harder and on every breath spitting into his ear, while her hands went inside his belt, pulling out his shirttails, plunging back there and grabbing. "Your father wouldn't give me his juice. Did you know that? He made me take it in my mouth, that scum! There is no peace for you and me. And there is no baby, stupid! A girl like that is on the Pill. She's been on the Pill since she was fourteen! If she did happen to get caught, she'd know how to get rid of it without your help. She's making a fool of you."

He was hardening again in spite of himself, in spite of what she was saying. He felt her nails, the thin edges against his skin. She loved to claw and draw blood there too, and the fear and the perfume and the pain used to make him so stiff it hurt. He'd break and evade her, all over the room, until it came over him that there was never anything else as strong as this, and he was feeling it just as strong as she was, proud at how strong it was, and she couldn't take it from him because he was taking it from her. But he was different now, hard but passive. It wasn't him.

"You think you're going to be a father? Let me tell you, even if she was pregnant, it wouldn't be you. You would be the last person it would be. It would be even worse than you."

"I know it isn't mine," he said. "It doesn't matter whose it is."

"Just because it's hers? That sloppy little brat's? Just because it's *hers?*"

"Because of the way I feel."

"I don't believe this! What's this in my hand?"

"I can't help that. I love the baby," he said. "I'm going to raise it. That's the deal." He added, "I'll get some help."

The mantle had begun to smoke, the wick was up too high. She was still breathing fast but she pushed him away and shrugged her things back over her shoulders. She turned to the wall and lowered the flame and while she was there she opened the little drawer of the bed-table, pulled it out half-way. The kitchen knife lay there half in the light.

"You don't think I ever meant it, do you?"

"Yes. I thought you meant it."

"You were right. Well. You've said it several times. I can do what I want to you. So it's up to me, now, isn't it." She refilled the glass and handed it to him. "You better numb yourself."

He sipped it first; brandy, he thought, no expert; then drank it in several swallows without pause, eyes on JoAnn, she watching him. He was ashamed, handing the glass back to her. This was from fear of the pain, he shouldn't have drunk it. He needed to be clear, all night. For Old Herman, for navigating. He had such distances to travel. He shouldn't have drunk it but it was only because of fear of the pain, not anything else.

He didn't want to make her uncomfortable. He didn't need to tell her everything. There was no pain. Little pain. Not much. They'd done this to a boy horse once out at the Pelos', following a book. There was no blood to speak of and the colt got right up as soon as they untied him and ran around, and also he healed in no time. Anyway he didn't need to tell her all how it was, just some. Just so it would be known that there was some of JoAnn's crew there. She called downstairs to them to come up. They were falling all over themselves that they had him, LaFleur sent somebody for a rope to tie him up. Oh they were shitface, they thought it was all over. They didn't know JoAnn.

They couldn't believe her. They didn't want her to do anything, they wanted to tie him up and go get the girl. But JoAnn was in charge. They had to see it. One or two of them left. LaFleur left, he wouldn't stay. It wasn't with the knife. It was with a safety razor blade, sterilized in a candle-flame. Then after the first one Atkin said that was enough, he'd get the point. That's what they all thought. But JoAnn said, "They don't know us, do they Bobby? There's a lot they don't know, isn't there?" They were all out of there then. They couldn't believe it.

Afterwards JoAnn sat down in the little rocking chair looking at him. He stayed still too, looking at her. He thought nobody had ever done anything like this before. What he'd done, for the reason he'd done it, the baby's life. He felt great. He didn't feel any different.

He was strong. He could fly. All right. But she said, "Lie still, Bobby. Just a minute or two. I'll call my sister to come give you a shot of penicillin. Seriously. I'd be scared to death of you getting an infection."

He told Marcia, "We're going to my father's. He's got a business there and I can work for him. Just for a start. I do sheet-rock. I do wallpaper."

He was spelling it out, the rest of the story, correct version. "I'm going to live there and work until it is born. I'm going to bring it back up here and raise it. I will come and see you. I will bring the kid. My kid and your kid can play together. You and I can drink coffee and talk."

"Sure," she said.

"While I'm gone, you can tell the story."

"Sure."

"Can you remember it all?"

"Enough of it."

"You can tell it to Old Herman when you see him. He'll remember it."

"I will do that."

"Well, I better be going."

She followed him out into the kitchen and to the door. Outside, he turned. "Good luck with that one of yours."

She nodded.

"We'll see ya."

30

Diamonds on Every Leaf and Twig

The car lights had come slowly down the farther hill with the sound of the tires on the loud ice, along the valley bottom and across the bridge. The lights stopped moving, the sound stopped. The door opened with a groan, then was slammed. The person who got out of it knew where he was going, right through the gap in the snowbank for the house, the bright star-light all he needed and then some. Clarence kept him covered, within a finger-squeeze of sudden death, through the glass of the kitchen window. He was seated at the little square table, with the red-and-white checkered oilcloth, squinting, one eye closed, his pistol-hand supported by his other forearm held shoulder-high in front of him.

The fellow came gingerly up the icy cellar-mound and made a study of the frozen footprints on and off the step, the big front blade of the pistol's sights bisecting the top of his leather helmet. Clarence saw the dark ends of glasses frames behind the man's protruding ears when he looked straight down.

Leo finally looked up, grinned brightly at sight of the hero within, and directly let himself in. "Oh good," he said, "we've got a gun."

Clarence turned his head away, tight-lipped. "At first I thought 'twas some'n else, Weller."

Leo stepped past him, looking around. "That right?" he said. "Who's that?" He noted moisture on the linoleum, wet bootprints on the bottom step of the steep narrow stairs, above which a curtain served as a door. A register in the ceiling let the heat of the cookstove go up to the bedroom under the roof.

"Never mind. You'd been a ghost if you was him."

"You mean Pelo?" Leo said. "He's all right. Dougherty'll put his elbow back together." Leo pulled off gloves, his helmet, untucked his scarf ends from under his arms and unwound the scarf from his neck. He unzipped his jacket and flapped it by its pockets.

"Pelo? No, I—"

"You put the safety back on that thing?"

"What? The safety? No, I forgot to. I tremble to think—" Clarence lifted the revolver out of the shadow of the kerosene lamp suspended over the table, looking for the lever. Had never checked where the safe was on this side-arm. Leo's hand was out for it. He handed it over and watched, embarrassed but humble. The hammer was still down, on the spent shell in the chamber. Leo pulled the hammer back, the cylinder clicked to a new chamber, loaded. He released the hammer to half-cock and handed it back.

"Good man," Clarence said. "Thanks. I never—"

"It's ready to cock and fire," Leo said. "You keep watch."

"Yes, that's what I was doing 'fore you come."

Leo went into French-Canadian. "You god dat dere girl, eh? I see her track out dere. You sauve her, by da Gee. You portay her to your cabine, eh? By da Gee you done good, ennaway!" Leo swept aside the thin curtain of the stairway to the loft and spoke English. "Hullo up there, anybody home?"

Clarence wanted to get clear who he'd killed, but suddenly he knew his duty. He stood up and put an arm across the stairway. "See here, Weller, you talk softer. She might be sleeping."

"Sleeping? Then we'll get her up. We've got to skedaddle, boy."

"No, we haven't," Clarence said. "You might's well slow down. You don't know." He took a breath. Swallowed. Cleared his throat. "What's happening to her."

Leo turned his ear, held still. Clarence said, "I'm glad you come, Weller, a good man to have beside me in a pick-le. You can ask her what it is, not good. I know what it is in a horse but I am not so familiar with a female person. I have seen a mare thrash around so, she got a knot in her intestine, died of starvation in a week. That was two good animals gone, in a flash, the colt and the mother. I will feed the stove. If you need wat-her I will fetch snow and melt it."

Leo closed his eyes and took a breath.

"I killt the outlaw, so we haven't got to worry about him."

"That was Johnny Pelo. You hit him in the elbow."

"What? Where's the—?"

"The other fellow's still on the loose. He will find us here, if we can't leave right away. You stop him, Clarence. Don't put any more balls through that thing, but don't let him inside, either."

Clarence sat down at the table. Laid the pistol on the oilcloth and folded his stiff hands over it, sweating in his layers of wool. He put his bafflement out of mind, mumbling to himself, "You can't keep track of everything."

After a minute he turned his neckerchief back around and pulled it up over his nose. He wished for his hat, left up there in the loft. She had asked him to bless the baby and he had taken it off to oblige and forgot it. It would have shaded his features when the killer came to the door.

He imagined what he would say to him. He was having his tea, all by himself, that's right, and no you could not come in, to try it would invite a big hole in your chest, how big, thirty-caliber. This was his home, though in his sister's name, and he had a right to protect it from intruders.

Or, "Already shot you once tonight, so what are you doing in the land of the living?" But he felt false, hokum, sitting there with the revolver under his hands. "Weller says I only winged somebody and it wa'n't you. If I ever meet the other person, this side of the pearly gate, I'll apologize, very certainly. I never meant to shoot a honest man."

Time passed. The other man seemed to be sitting outside the door, forlorn, denied entry. He pitied the murderer now. "Your baby is sliding off without saying hello, and you lost the girl you wanted. That's a sad song twice over. Deserves to be set to music and sung forever, much more than my troubles. Many a good song tells the hard life of a outlaw."

Leo called down and had him heat some water, and forgetting the danger Clarence went out and broke the crust with a hatchet. Filled a kettle with snow and set it on the stove. He went out again to dig up more blockwood from the pile. He leaned it up against the door-stone and split it by starlight, rolling his axe as it hit so the flat of it rang against the top of the block and it sent the sticks flying apart, telling the imaginary student of old-time skills, "that way, see, your blade doesn't get stuck in the blo-ck. You never have to prize it loose."

Inside he banged the stovelids, cranked the grates around, opened up the draft and damper. The stovepipe crackled inside, he heard creosote from the half-chimney drip in the closet overhead, and smelled it too.

Sometimes when it was quiet for fifteen minutes or so he would numbly climb the stairs. He was past all shame or nicety. He wouldn't just stop with his head above the level of the floor, he'd come up all the way, bending his head under the roof, and ask after her. He did not blush or talk about the weather. Her face was shining. She would make him come and sit on the bed with her, and he would bend and brush her forehead with his mustache, first sweeping the damp hair back from it with his hand. She told Leo, "We're married. Isn't that right, Clarence?" Clarence chuckled and said, "Well, h'nn, all right, 'f you think so, Miss Muppit. If thoughts was deeds, no less." Once she told him, sing-song through tears, "Don't forget your ha-at!"

Then he would clump back downstairs, yank the door open and step outside. Below zero. Every footfall creaked. Looked off into the dark, around the house and up the valley to the east, watching for the loom of dawn.

Leo Weller had been involved in other operations of this general sort. He'd been on hand to cheer and knead a mother out of begging for Demerol or pitocin for an extra hour or two, where the father wasn't handy. He'd watched happily from behind a doctor's shoulder the sewing up of a tear. He'd seen a womb brought forth to light, a very basketball in size and shape and almost the leathery color of one, and sung the first lullaby to the child unfolded out of it. Moreover he had put two and two together long ago and had been reading up, in case of some such emergency.

This is his subject, after all. Women. He does get carried away by his enthusiasms, but within a certain small range of reference he is likely to know what he's talking about. Interested in sex like any boy, he has made a lifelong study, really, of the physiology and taxonomy of the reproductive parts, starting when most boys had only hearsay and knot-hole imagery. By now, for instance, he would have made a dizzyingly prolix informant on abortion, "folk methods" included. If that had been the question here, he'd have been resourceful, matter-of-fact, exhaustive. Chattily amusing at first, philosophical, but ultimately maddening and exhausting, so that any normally helpless girl would either give the idea up or shriek him away from her sight.

Here where the miscarriage was already in train all that was needed was sympathy, an air of competence, no shame, some knowledge of efficient positions, useful accessories, hygiene. A loving voice, the art of complicity. It was a thing he had not only imagined but rehearsed, being the irreverent doctor of the goddess embarrassed by accident, or sin.

No surprise to Julia what Leo knew, how concisely he questioned her, she hurting and scared, of course, and completely taken up with herself. He relaxed her with massage, helped her keep her head with talk. She knew she was on the verge of relief. After this horrible night was past, she told him, she'd wouldn't have any "valence" again forever and ever.

"Do you know where that's from, Leo?" She was making talk.

"What, dear?"

"Not having any valence. I might have it wrong but that's the way I remember it. It's from a book, a great great book, the first hippy novel. The hero says it. 'I possess not valence.' Do you know what valence is?"

"Faintly. Chemistry?"

"It's being charged, plus or minus, so that you are attracted to other molecules, or whatever."

"So to not have valence means you're never going to be attracted—"

"Or attrac*tive*. It works both ways."

"Ever again."

"Yeah. No more of that for me. No more men, anyway."

"That would be a sad loss to us."

"I mean it."

"You are the most charged particle I ever knew, sweetie. Sleep a bit?"

"This is work, man."

"That's what they say."

She was ready, seated on the edge of the bed, when they heard Clarence begin to climb the stairs again, sluggishly, his boot-toes banging against the risers. He brought his head only just above the level of the floor. Not looking at them, nor the arrangements (only things to kneel or squat upon and a receptacle), he said, "Excuse me, I just come to say Good morning. Clear sky. Diamonds on every twig and needle. You can't look, well, it will wait, a long day ahead and very beautiful, no more than one like this a year."

Without an answer he was gone down backwards. Leo helped Julia lift her hollow-flanked body up, helped her squat over the ash scuttle from beside the kitchen stove. It was over quickly then. Suddenly she was strong in Leo's hands. She wanted to step back and look. But he stepped over the scuttle and pushed her back into the bed. He pulled the covers over her, then called down for another basin of warm water and a dishtowel.

Julia was still deep-breathing, holding each breath a second, blowing out. Not crying now, thinking, her eyes open; rolling her lips together in worry. Clarence came up, two footsteps per riser, with the dishpan carefully held high. He stooped to set it by the bed and saw the scuttle, the substance in it. He stood a moment, head turned away, eyes closed, mouth pursed.

He didn't look at anybody as he spoke. "A thousand thanks for coming, Weller. Me, you might as well have asked me to drive a locomotive. Now, soon's the lady's ready, you take her to your people's place. She's got the best people to look after her there is in the world, you and your family. My part, I know, take care of this. Then, what do you think? Bid adieu to home and family, not fit for civil company no more." He bent and lifted the bail of the scuttle now, the arm holding it stretched numbly at his side as he straightened up again. "Farewell, Miss, and don't get up on my account." He clumped sidewards back down the stairs, the scuttle ringing dully as it swung against the steps.

Leo helped her dress and bundled her further in a blanket. He had to let her negotiate the narrow stairs alone, waiting below to catch her if she fell. There was no sign of Clarence. Outside, the bottom of the valley was in gleaming shade, the tops of the trees eastward sparkled like a breaking wave of light. The cold came through their wraps at once. They crouched to slide and skip down off the mound, in their hardened tracks to the road, the Chevrolet glaring green just beyond the shadow of the hill.

Leo opened the back door for her. He wanted her down flat, out of sight, but he didn't need to say so. She curled up with a *whoosh* of relief and he fixed the blanket and the car robe over her and closed the door, conscious of the loudness of its click.

Now with the chains from the trunk, he lay down on his side on the road. Dazzled by glare, he could hardly see up in the cave of wheel-well. With his mittens in his teeth and his fingers sticking to the steel he draped the chains over the tire and wedged one cross-chain in under it. He squirmed out, rolled over and did the other side.

He scrambled up, flung open the driver's door, bounced himself in on the high seat. He started the motor and drove ahead about a foot and a half, measuring by the edge of the open door passing over the gravel. He set the brake, climbed out, fell down flat, taught himself to see again, sucked his chopper's mitts, counted the links, inserted the latches, levered them over and slipped on the keepers. Squirmed, rolled, did it again on the other side, efficiently, humming all the while under the quiet stitching of the motor. He'd never felt so close to earth. In love with the hard and soft materials, warm and cold, light and dark.

Then, there being no place to turn around, he backed down, around the curve at the bottom of the hill, across the bridge over the brook, across the beaver flat, up the other hill to the first curve. With the chains clumping under the cold tires, the Chevy felt like a bulldozer on cleats. He shifted ahead and made his run, humming, imitating the engine, spitting off rpms between gears. Two frost-heaves on the flat before the brook gave his back-seat cargo a toss, forced a cry from her lungs. At the curve right after the narrow bridge the rear end slewed out despite the chains. He counter-steered with both hands, humming higher, pushing on the pedal. When the chains chewed into something he wrapped his forearms across each other the opposite way, pressing on. Then he straightened the big wheel to the climb and leaned up to it, chinning on the circle with his elbows out. Past the home place the road roughened, steepened, and in second gear now, pushing the accelerator hard against the firewall, he rocked back and forth as if he were jacking the vibrating Chevrolet up the hill. The motor was silent, smooth, the small-bore, long-stroke six, yes! The chains stuttered and slipped. He double-clutched down into first and pushed himself back in the shaking seat. He let off the gas just a little. The chains lifted the car one bar at a time. Then they began to sing again and the extra links to tick the fenders. The vibration rose into a hum and the hum gradually quieted, the chains just ticking now and then. Going the wrong way, toward the lake, the long way home. But they were out of the hole.

When they came out on the main road, she felt the change and sat up, partly. He felt his seat-back pulled. "Where are you taking me?"

"Risdonville's back there. Seven miles to the Falls."

"I don't want to go to the Falls. I don't want to go to Neva's."

"Where do you want to go?"

"I just want to be *away* from this place, these people."

"I figure our house."

"I've got to get my things, my car, and get *out* of here, Leo."

"You can't drive."

"Yes I can."

"You shouldn't. Our house, hm? No one needs to know you're there. You need rest, a bath. I'll take care of you. Just a day. We'll get your things, don't worry."

"Where's Bobby?" She didn't seem to notice what he'd said. *"Where's Bobby?"*

"Don't know," Leo said. Looked for her in the rear view mirror but she was out of sight again though still attached by a hand to his seat-back. "Johnny Pelo got hurt, but you know all about that." He felt her sudden tensing behind him, caught out at having left an injured person, saved herself. He forgave her freely: starved, weak, miscarrying, her guide the horseman already high-tailing it, what could she do? "He'll mend," he said. He heard her exhale.

"Stay down. Here's civilization."

Back at home he put the car into the garage before getting her out, then made sure no one was on the street across the river before he led her in. His father had a napkin tucked into his collar which he nervously pulled out to hold her by the shoulders against his chest. Leo helped her up the back stairs to his bathroom full of manly lotions and shaving gear. He set her on the toilet, started drawing her bath, fetched towels and washcloth from the linen closet in the hall. He undressed her and handed her into the tub. She crouched and hugged her knees. He soaped the washcloth, rinsed her back. She got her feet out from under her, and he laid her back and washed her arms and breasts and belly and crotch. Drained the water and filled the tub again for a luxurious soak. Then left her, to make ready his room.

His trombone, always polished, horn-down over its stand beside the record player—that needn't be hidden. He put out of sight the books he'd been studying. Remade his bed with clean flannel sheets. Closed the Venetian blinds. What music? He chose to his own taste, Tommy Dorsey, very low, Woody Herman and Stan Kenton and Roy Eldridge with Anita O'Day in a stack on the changer. On second thought, he took all those off and put on his Bobby Hackett records, two of them. Brought out from his closet a folded wood-and-canvas army cot and a sleeping bag, for himself, the nurse. Father was already calling Aunt Sarah, he was sure. He'd have her to himself, until Aunt Sarah came. Story! Story! In through his ears, out through the tip of his pen, or the top of his head.

31

Can You Amagine?

In the middle of the day the light was blinding in the streets of the town. Lenny LaBounty had stationed his bleached and faded Toronado across the gas pumps, to discourage business. The parking space in front of Eugene's was full, mostly pickup trucks, Amos's with two snowmobiles in back. Murdock, the lineman, had angled the telephone van into the snowbank in front of Eugene's house next door.

Inside, the talk was low in spite of a bar nearly full. No one played shuffleboard. The hunt was over, that was understood. Hunting party evanesced overnight, suddenly no interest in Robert Sochia, or the girl. How did that come to be so? No rumors, no knowledge, short answers.

Innocence everywhere you looked, a bar full of open faces. Hear about The Rapids? Closed, owner on vacation, said to have gone where everybody goes. Peter Hubbard's truck in the driveway of his own house up the street, for a change, so that Murdock incurred mild kidding when he came in. "What, no phone trouble to fix, George, after such an ice storm as this?"

Amos Cheney and Millard Frary hunched side by side, over their hands, at the far end of the bar, their backs and arms thickly clothed in outdoor wear, down vests under their wool jackets. Their elbows touched, they drank warm coffees, not their usual mid-day beers. At noon the alarm siren went off, down by the river on the roof of the fire-station. Their faces rotated up to meet each other. They looked into each other's eyes.

They turned to Eugene, upright behind the bar across from them, in a creased Pendleton shirt, not leaning on the bar but keeping both hands on it, watching them. The three of them had talked of going to look for Clarence, if they hadn't seen or heard of him by twelve o'clock

Amos asked, "Think that crust would hold us up?"

"I think so. I say, I think so."

"Would mine, prob'ly," Millard said. He rides an early, lighter-weight Ski-doo.

"It'll hold you up," commented a neighbor along the bar. "It's half an inch thick, or better." And it had stayed very cold.

Amos, then, to Eugene: "Go for a ride?"

Mavis would take over the bar. Millard stepped back off his stool and went toward the door, slapping his hat against his pants in rhythm. Amos stopped next to Lenny and stood there in his unzipped galoshes, jingling his change. "You ain't got anything you can't leave to tomorrow, have ye?"

"I got to take the engine out of Phillips's dump-truck, I'm behind two weeks on grease jobs and inspections, I ain't got any help and I can't hold down my food. Shit no."

"We might take a run up t' the lake."

"Cook's Lake? We goring after Robert ourselfs?"

The minutest shake of head. "Clarence."

"All right, sure, I'll come wiv yez. I ain't ben anywhere all winter."

Eugene was cleaning up their places. Amos asked him, "You got an extra suit for Lenny?"

The lake road had been salted and sanded by then, heavily on the hills. The sun was as high as it gets in March, the woods a fairy spectacle, the ice encasing everything. Too heavy for the younger birches and poplars along the road, borne down into bows and hoops they mightn't ever straighten from. Lenny, riding with Eugene, marveled at the sight.

No truck at the Shampine home place and no vibration above the chimney. At the intersection with the camper's road they took the left turn, sharply back and around the foot of the bay lined with cottages, and along the other side of the bay to where the plows turn around. They unloaded their machines, yellow and black, purple and black, blue and white, in the sharp air. Started their engines, put on helmets, got aboard, checked with each other by hand signals. Millard nosed over the snowbank, leading. Up and down, one after the other, over the moguls to the end of the snow-filled road and down the driveway of the last camp at the narrows, then down a steeper path and over the dock, deep under snow, onto the flat white expanse of the lake.

Out a hundred yards Millard paused and they gathered in a line abreast. They were on a hot-white sheet between the wooded slopes on either side. Beyond the farther end, Blue Mountain was an azure mound in a vee of lesser hills. A light wind hummed over the shiny plain. Amos waved a chopper's mitt forward. Ice spraying up behind, the phalanx raced down the lake.

They left the machines out on the ice, like boats, in front of Purryer Camp. They climbed on foot under the tall pines, and found, opposite the door to the verandah, down the snowdrift toward them as they approached, the blurred and reddened patch where Pelo bled, thankfully small. Lenny went round the drift, sprang onto the porch at the terrace end, looked in a window, couldn't see. Got to the door and stepped around it into the great room and paused to let his eyes accustom to the dark. He turned all the way around, awed, saying, "This where you was holding up, Robert? Hah? This where you was goring to stand and fight?"

He heard others on the porch and went back out, saying, "Can you amagine?" But they were coming for him to saddle up. Amos had found Clarence's snowshoes at the corner of the building, his chain-sole boot-trail faint under the crust, or on it, here and there sunk or broken through. If there was anybody with him it was somebody light, who didn't break the crust; or else he was carrying her.

Simply a matter of tracing it then, on their machines; over the hay-road, off that and down the back side, through the swamp, where it wasn't so simple finding a way for the sleds, to the Shampines' old trail, which Millard knew about. They went some distance toward the house and the Falls road on that trail before Millard, leading, questioned a print and halted, to dismount and

look closer. Amos, off his machine and looking too, saw that Clarence
had come back over his own tracks. They left the machines then,
turned back on foot. They found where he had slanted off the
track, the ice crust cracking and sagging under his weight if not
accepting the imprint of his boots, and occasionally, the part-circular
mark of something he set down on the crust whenever he stopped
and planted both feet.

Finally, except for Eugene who stayed up on the ridge, they
came down through the almost waist-high deadfall to the place
where dark green boughs had been laid at the edge of a small circle
of bare black mud, recently thawed but hardened again and
sparkling with frost. Among the boughs, two glass jars with metal
caps shone in the sunlight. Near-by, on the ice beside the mud, a
little pile of something orange-red, already tracked around by tiny
feet of chipmunks, squirrels, mice. Blood? No. Millard says it.
"That'd be Bessie's tomato sauce. Now why would anybody pour
that on the ground?"

They worked it out the best they could. They did it well enough,
knowing their man. Leo would go them something better in due
time, knowing more. Possibly better than fact itself. Here he was,
having come back along the trail with the thing that thawed its
circular imprint into the crust of ice, so warm the contents, *the
scuttle in his hand steaming in the cold morning air, so long the bearer's
pauses for his hurting knee. The sky deep blue and still half dark.
Accompanying him that green interior smell he knows from cleaning
deer and is in no way revolted by. Where else is he to bury something on
short notice, without a pick and shovel?*

*Here and there ahead of him the brilliance of the rising sun strikes
the high trees, and every twig and bud is a prism, a diamond, shooting
rainbows. He keeps up a patter as he might to ward off bears.* "Where
I am taking you is up the brook, where we used to go fishing, my brother
and my sisters and I. We would catch a washtub of brook trout on an
overcast day, just after the black flies come out. That's when the trout
will start biting, six or eight weeks yet 'til then."

Each time he puts the scuttle down, puts hands on knees, and rests, he speaks.

"*Back here next to the brook, in a certain place known to but few, is a mud spring, so called, where we put canning jars down in mud so cold it numbs your arm. No use to try to dig a grave for you anywheres else. No shovel sharp enough. Too much ice, and stony ground, and some'n might locate where you lie.*

"*To show no disrespect, either to the spring or you, I will pull up a canning jar. I have not put anything in that spring in several years, but what'll you bet I will find something? Quart or pint will do. Pint-size, that's what you are. Put you in place of what's in it, a sad deal for you but a necessary swit-ch. Then, push you very far down, with a branch from a tree, lest you ever be fetched back up to the light.*

"*I don't know if I could do justice to a prayer but I will try. 'Here lies so and so, don't know the name or who the father is but I will take the blame.' Where you're going, 'f they ask you whose you are, just say Clarence Shampine's and never mind the laugh-ter. I've got as good a right as anybody, if scorched ears could tell tales. Your mother asked me to kiss you, and I come as close't as I could. I feel as if I was you, myself. I nearly come in there with you, where you were. Good place to be, however short a while.*"

He stumbles forward in the frozen track, bent sideways as well as forward, to keep the scuttle from his knee. "You missed very little, my boy. The big trees are all gone, it is just pulp-cutting now, done by men that wouldn't know a peavey from a pike-pole nor ever saw a river-drive. All the work done by big machines. You had to know sum'ing in the old times, or elst, may be, you lost your life to the logs and icy wat-er. Or supposing you were a teamster, injured your horses or broke equipment. Then down the road you'd go.

"*Anything like me, you wouldn't be any good for these times. Some men could handle horses and also machines, Eddy LaVigne was one such. Soon's the Linn tractors came into the woods, Eddie went to driving one. That was a good man, could play the fiddle too. He kept right up with the times. If you can't change, you are lost, that's the law of the world. Yours truly, born too late. Just like the old songs, only way they will be remembered is by 'lectric machines. When the 'lectricity goes, where are you then?"*

He climbs over deadfall in the trail, or skirts it, now speaking aloud as he goes, following no logic but his feelings. He makes his departure from the trail unconsciously, zigzags through all kinds of wind-throw and new growth, down to a balsam swamp. Follows the edge of the swamp and comes to the ridge along the brook.

"I would trade places with you if I could. I don't need to live no more. What is the life of men and women, when they show it all right in the picture magazines? I was brought up to respect a woman. That is, not take advantage of her weakness, go to her aid if she was in distress. Now, treat a woman no better than you would a man you didn't like, and get into bed with a stranger. If a baby comes of it, go and see the doc-tor.

"Your case, special circumstances, no offense. Your mother is the most heartbroken person I ever see."

He is on the ridge now, in the thick of it where he has to push through small softwoods. Sometimes they web him, claw at him, and he has to turn and bring the scuttle through behind him.

"I have known harder times but I preferred them. I have worked for a skinflint farmer all winter just for a place to board my team, the only way I could afford to own a pair of horses. Now, if you don't get forty dollars a day sitting in a chair, cry just like a baby. Minute you get laid off, straight to Moira, sign up for the unemployment. My sisters told me to go get the unemployment one time. I didn't want to, but I went. I got confused, right in the line in front of other people. I didn't answer right, and they made fun of me, there behind the window. Come home and my sisters said I didn't stand up for myself, hnnn. Didn't get as much as the other fellow. No, of course not, other fellow signs up to get his check and then he goes and cuts wood for money under the table. Next week, sign his name to a lie and gets another check. I would work, I said, for Philip Arquit, on the Recreation Progr'm, federal government money, before I would go back and be made fun of again."

Habit of stealth now makes him close his mouth and move the branches quietly aside. He is on the brow of the ridge, approaching the *pulpit, as he calls it, above the spring. The spring is close beside the brook and the swale around it makes a natural crossing-place for animals. "Every hunting season for forty years I have put out salt and apples on an old pine stump, and from what I call The Pulpit I would watch for deer. Is that legal, did you ask, salt a stump for deer? Well . . . I don't want you to think I'm a angel, ha-ha-ha. You'll see, here just a minute, how they've tore apart that stump, to get that salt. They'll winter in here too, a balsam swamp all round. Might see one now, if we haven't made too much racket—"*

He stops at the brink. The sun breaks over the pointed tops of spruces up the valley and partly blinds him. But he sees an animal down there, too thick-limbed to be a deer. A bear, come out of her den to see the ice-show? No, no bear. "Look who's here," he says.

Robert Sochia kneels forward on a pallet of hemlock boughs. He has broken them from trees near-by to spread his weight on the unfrozen mud. He has hung his jacket on a dazzling alder bush behind him, so Clarence for a second thinks there are two of them, or a man and a bear together, in silhouette against this glitter of new day. The man has one wool sleeve pulled up and that arm down in the mud. He raises himself slowly and brings up a jar that glistens in the sun. He sets the jar down with another two beside him and leans across the boughs to scoop handfuls of snow from underneath the crust to wash his arm.

Clarence is not frightened, nor surprised. He has seen the fellow here before, by chance, expected him again, forgotten him. He has a mission there and is being delayed. There is, also, something left in him of the conviction that he has already disposed of this man. New to himself, he clambers downward, the scuttle dings against a rock, twigs break, he steps on downed timber and crushes it out of his way.

Robert Sochia is unscrewing the sealing ring of the last jar. He puts the ring aside, brings a jack-knife from his pocket and pries the blade under the seal. He takes a piece of the meat, puts the jar down, and with two hands brings the meat to his mouth. Then flings himself on his back, half on the bed of boughs, half on the icy crust, his arms out wide, what's left of the morsel in one hand, his legs still folded under him.

The sudden motion causes Clarence to flinch but he doesn't stop. He studies his way. He holds the pail over the next obstacle, then follows, stepping on downed branches to clear his way.

Close now, he stands. The man lies still, facing up, not taking another bite, not even chewing, not moving even when Clarence sets the scuttle down. He says, "You've done half my work, made just such a bed as I would make to hold me up. I'll do the rest if you'll get out the way."

The other doesn't move. Clarence looks directly at his face. It is scratched as if by claws. The blood has dried. War paint, but Clarence is immune. "This is my sister's property, posted legally, so you are off limits, my boy. You got what you come for, you don't need to stay and watch what I am doing. One reason, it would make a man cry, that had a heart of anything but flint."

Clarence gets down on his knees beside him. He picks up the jars, one by one, and sees that one of them contains his sisters' tomato sauce. Perhaps the outlaw was going to put that back, it wasn't his. Good, it will do for Clarence's purpose. He unscrews the sealing ring, pries up the cap, shakes the contents out. Robert Sochia turns his head to watch a moment, then looks up at the sky.

Clarence reaches behind him for the scuttle. Its circular base scrapes against the ice. He puts the jar down among the branches so they'll hold it. Then he rises on his knees and lifts the bail to pour.

Robert has rolled up on his side, he's scrambling to his knees. "What're you doing there?" Clarence's arm is whacked, the scuttle almost spilled. Clarence sets it down and looks away up the valley east, where the dark timber slopes intersect, and above them the sun has risen clear.

The sound that Robert Sochia makes embarrasses him. He talks over it. "Well, Mister, you figured it out. If you are looking for some'n to blame, here I am. If I had stood by her like a gentleman, come by the lake, easier going, it would been a different story. But I was always afeared of the ice. Harder going over the hill, she fell too many times."

Stands up straight, and looks away. "This is a day for such a thing to happen on, sad but beautiful. Look how them birches are bent over, thick as your thigh, turned right round toward the ground. Many of those will break. That will make a sound like a rifle shot. 'f you walk in the woods today, keep sharp look-out, wear a hat. I see you got a good one, just like mine."

The other's hat is on the snow. He lifts his own hat off and looks inside it. "You and I are in agreement here. Thick felt, high crown, wide brim. Only difference, color, and you got a fancier band, made of beads. Very good-looking." With one hand he sweeps the top of his head. He puts the hat back on firmly, by the crown.

"All right," he says, done killing time.

The other's still bent over the scuttle, doesn't move.

"I done the services along the way. I can do what's left to do, alone. Then, my mouth is sealed, you needn't worry. Besides which, I won't be around no more."

The dried blood on Robert Sochia's face isn't so dry any more. He ignores Clarence, sets the jar that Clarence emptied upright between his knees. The sleeve has fallen down his wet arm.

Clarence says, "Now see here, I asked you to step aside. Last thing I want is you to do my wor-k."

Robert Sochia lifts the scuttle from beside him, leaning his torso as if it took all his strength. Clarence has reached across his body to his left hip and drawn the revolver. He holds it pointing down, a little to the side. He is reluctant to tap the other man's shoulder with it, but he means to. But Robert ignores him, brings the scuttle in front of him and pours the contents into the jar. The liquid wells over. He puts the seal and ring back on the jar and twists the ring.

"What have you got there, Clarence?"

"Never mind. It has got one not-ch already, that I ha'n't had time to carve, and it would have another quick's you went for it. I told you to stand aside."

Robert Sochia holds the jar in the hand of the arm that was bare, and with the other hand he rolls the cuff of his sleeve back up. He pushes up the sleeve of his underwear and then both sleeves together, up to his shoulder.

Clarence moves the gun toward him. He points it near the arm, the pale edge of it. "Mister Sochia," he says, "I come to bury this baby. I'll put him down for keeps, and then, may be, you'll hear the sound this Colt's revolver makes. That's how I feel, so now you know I'm a *desperate man. How long d'you think I'd hesitate to send you out of this world?"*

Clarence feels himself lose balance. He feels as if he hasn't lived. He hardly sees the other man lean forward on that arm and sink the jar in the mud until his cheek and his dark shaggy hair lie on the surface. The bloody face turns into the mud.

The pistol hangs from Clarence's hand. Robert Sochia lingers there as if he can't bring out his arm, or wouldn't if he could. Then slowly draws his body up. He pulls the muddy cuff of his underwear down. The wool sleeve falls after it, heavy with mud. He says something Clarence doesn't understand.

"What?"

"Put it on the stump and go away."

"Not so quick." Clarence brings the piece up in front of him. "Hard-earned money paid for this, after a long wai-t."

"You can come back and take it from my hand."

"Sure I can. After what?" Clarence starts to understand, and to object, move away, jealous already of the other man's intended use of this treasured possession.

"Lay it on the stump."

Clarence is behind a little. "That'll look good. I already got a Wanted poster up for me." But suddenly this is no play, no song, the bloody, muddied face is terrible, the motions too fast, the words crude. The revolver yanks his hand, his arm. "Huh!" Had to let go or his finger in the guard would have—

Clarence is stumbling, too stiff to protect himself. He has left the ground and now the ground runs into him from behind. He is looking at the sky, landed soft on boughs, hat-brim on edge under his neck. He hears splashing over the murmur of the creek. Three steps and Robert Sochia must have been across, he can hear only three or four steps beyond, up the slope under the thick small balsams where bucks sneak down to drink. He thinks he hears twigs break. Then nothing but the stream. Slowly, he covers up his ears.

The older men have been standing around the spring talking softly, keeping their feet out of the tracks. They haven't surmised the last part of the scene, for there's no clue to it. They see that

Robert walked away after the encounter, leaving Clarence on his back; unhurt, with luck, for he's gone too. Lenny moves beyond, following frozen bootprints that lead him toward the brook. He sees them also on the other side, eight-ten feet across. Squats down to look up through the crowded stems of balsams, where the bootprints disappear, underneath the furl of weighted boughs.

He doesn't say anything right away. He waits until he is sure. Even then he doesn't quite know why he is sure. He's only seen the boots. And then he doesn't say it very loud; just loud enough. "Shit, boys, there he is."

In a moment Clarence removes the gloved hands from the sides of his head. If there was a shot, it was less loud than expected. No echo of it booming away up the valley. Still on his back, he moves his hands to shade his eyes against the sun.

He gets up, slowly. Supposing there had been a shot. The other fellow doesn't deserve to come off with everything, but he doesn't know if he could touch the pistol in the cold muddy hand. Besides which, the judge would say, "Here's the bullet kilt him, Mr Shampine, from your Colt's revolver, what're your last words?" He picks up the scuttle, not to forget to take it back where it belongs. Ought to rinse it in the brook. Numbly he goes to the edge of it.

No, he's surer now. The fellow's just up there in the dark timber. How does he know he won't decide to kill him first, the man that caused his grief? Suddenly he fears even to hear the sound, to smell the powder burnt. There's no way for flight except the open brook. He is splashing, wading, pushing his legs against a medium going the same way he is, as if he knows it's coming. As it is, the concussion first, whitening the daylight, then the stunning amplitude of sound carried by dense air, and then the long reverberations off the hills on every side, chasing him down the brook. He's slipped, he's down in it, over his head, lost. But here, it beaches him. There's footing, small gravel, quiet voices. No, only the rippling water. The scuttle's lost, but he's out of it, and hardly wet, under his woolens, the woolens hardly heavier.

The three of them, Eugene too, back up on the ridge, are stooping, straightening, shifting sideways, trying to see what Lenny is looking at.

"I see his boots. His pantlegs. See them, boys?"

"I don't," Millard says.

"That's him, boys. Shit. He done it. You believe this? I think he fuckin' did it."

"Clarence," Millard calls. "Yo, Clarence."

Lenny looks round at him. "It ain't Clarence. I don't *think*." Serious, heroic now, he says, "Set still, boys. I'm goring over there."

"Look out," Amos says. But Lenny unhesitating wades the brook and climbs the slope on hands and feet. In a moment he is only an inference to the others, up behind the low bows, something dark moving across the few interstices of light.

But they can hear him clearly, speaking in a normal tone. The brook's gentle murmur is one of those background sounds that make the human voice more audible. "Aw, shit, Robert." It comes as if he were next to them. "Aw shit." His voice goes thin in complaint. "What did you do that for?"

Amos says, "Don't touch him, Lenny."

"I ain't," Lenny says. "Come over here wiv me, men. I can't stand this. Jesus, Robert. Christ. Why'd you do this? Hey? He shot his self. Wiv Clarence's new gun, it looks as if."

Millard and Amos look upstream for a way to cross dry-shod.

"Right in the fuckin' heart. His shirt's unbuttoned. You know what, boys? He opened his cloves and put that muzzle right to his skin."

There isn't any way to cross on stones. For minutes they stand this way, Lenny concealed by the boughs, Millard and Amos halted on the near side of the brook, Eugene on the ridge. Amos squats down, then Millard, the better to see up there. They can see him then, well enough. Eugene starts to work his way down the face of the ridge.

Finally, when Eugene has joined them, Amos leads through the water. On the other side, they edge their boots into grainy snow under the hemlocks where the sleet never reached the ground. Small twigs break on their shoulders.

Lenny turns away, ashamed of himself. "Hey," he says. "Hey. I didn't know nuffin' about the poor fucker, really. What is he to me?"

They crouch shoulder to shoulder, their hands on their knees, breathing deep, looking up. Robert is sitting like a man asleep in the sun, his head a little bowed, and no rest for his arms but his lap, where the pistol's loosely held. His domed hat is set on straight, his nose lined up with the trees, the red scratches on the dark face symmetrical, the ring untarnished, the curly beard and mustache dry.

Lenny cries, "Why did he have to do that?" Millard reaches a hand out to him. "I ain't sick," he says, "Shit, a dead man don't make me sick. I was sick before I come. There, Christ, I'm all right. I just felt sorry for him a minute." But he is overtaken again for several seconds, and then clears his nose by closing each nostril in turn, with his thumb, and leaning over and blowing. The mucous comes out in a string, which he wipes from his face with the edge of his hand, and from his hand on the bib of Mavis's suit.

Amos squints at Robert, tips back his cap and rubs his forehead. He cocks his eye at Millard.

Millard doesn't speak, only looks at the body, blinking slowly.

Eugene, behind them, clears his throat, says something. Then repeats, "I say, he never did get his nose broken. Did he?"

Now Millard and Amos turn to go back down, and Eugene turns down ahead of them. Lenny speaks again. "You know what, boys?" They turn.

He has found a place to sit, in company with Robert Sochia, in a patch of warmth where the sun falls clear to the ground. "I never realized all this month, two months, whatever it's been. I never realized it but I ben ridin' all over the fuckin' woods wiv him. No shit, I have. My own life hasn't amounted to nuffin'. I ain't even been wiv a woman. Now that's an awful thing to admit, but it's the God's honest truth. I ain't. My wife, you know about me and her. I did have a nice little woman over Risdonville treated me very good, but she lives in a trailer wiv her kids. I can't see putting one of them kids out of bed and making him sleep on the floor. It ain't that warm of a trailer. I ain't done nuffin' but work day and night, and get drunk once or twice. Today's the first day I done anything, really. But I ben trying to amagine his life out

here. I mean he's had some idea. I don't know what it was. I wish't
I could ask him. Robert! What was the idea? I guess whatever it
was come to a end. Or else what he done here, kilt his self, was
part of it too. I bet it was, you know it? But all winter I been really
enjoying that fucker and all he thought up to do. No shit. I have!
He weren't no coward. Coward's the last thing he was. Do you
think if you were blowin' yourself away you'd set there and
unbutton your shirt and put the steel right to your tit, 'stead of
quick and painless up the top of your mouth? I mean if you was
just plain discouraged, what the hell would you care?"

Amos starts back across the brook. Millard and Eugene follow
quickly. On the other side they turn back to see that Lenny is
coming now. He sloshes across to them and they stand together,
solemn, for a minute.

"She'll be awful upset," Millard says, "She always saw
something in the boy." They all know that he means Grace. But
they'd been on another errand before this discovery. Amos has
been studying the ground and now sees something more.

He says, "You expecting Clarence to help you sugar?"

"Oh, if I do it at all this year."

"Look here." Downstream a few paces, a scallop out of the
edge of the ice. "I think your help walked right down the brook."

That had been a morning of bliss for Leo: clinical ministrations,
physical intimacy as if without gender, their heads-together
reconstruction of events, her bouts (as now) of pure and child-like
sleep, between fits of volubility which were heaven to the
story-gatherer. Once, Neva Day marched up the stairs and shooed
him out of his room and shut the door on him. But she came out
in less than fifteen minutes, dabbing her eyes, having been sent
away. Julia told him, "I only want you, Leo. Nobody else. Don't
let her back in here."

Finished with this town, no tolerance left for anything or
anybody in it. "Except you, Leo." Her eyes already on her future.
Everything she had to do now, before she escaped the last clinging

strands of connection to this, this, this *place*, was onerous to her. Everything except telling her story to Leo. Even that was onerous, but she too believed in it. It was urgent, necessary, part of culture, education, hope. This that had happened to her *mattered*. "It mustn't be lost in ignorant frivolous gossip, guessing and opinion."

"I beg your pardon!" Leo said. "Gossip is not ignorant and frivolous, it's the very—! But never mind, go on."

"Leo, I mean this! It mustn't be made into some romantic myth!"

"Heaven forfend."

"Don't joke! And people mustn't say bad things about me." What people thought and said, here, was still contingent to her life, even to her future life, far away from here. "This matters, Leo!

"And people have to know that it is *my* story. It's Bobby's of course but it is mostly mine. Do you understand that? Because I'm the something trying to be new, to change things, against terrible odds. I'm the one against whom the worst crimes were done, that people don't even know are crimes! Do you understand that, Leo?"

"Sure, no problem, goes without saying. Sleep, sweetie."

It was mid-day before she awoke suddenly and asked again, "Where's Bobby?"

"Don't know," Leo said again.

"What time is it? What day is it?"

Leo told her. She rolled her lips.

"Didn't he ever come to find me? At Purryer Camp?"

"Don't know."

"Didn't he ever come to Clarence's house?"

"Not while we were there."

"Since then!" she cried.

"Don't know! Clarence hasn't checked in either, by the way."

"Have you looked for him?"

"Clarence?"

"*Bobby! I don't know why Bobby didn't find us there!*"

She pushed his hand away from her forehead. "I don't believe this!" She fell back on the pillow, rolling her lips.

Leo got a chap-stick, put some on them. "You may not care, but my Aunt Sarah'll be fit to be tied if Clarence is still missing when she gets here." She was coming, Cousin Whitney was driving her up from Westchester in the Cadillac.

"Who *cares*? Clarence is all right, for heaven's sake. Where is Bobby, Leo?"

"Sweetie, go on now, go back to sleep."

"He was my best pupil."

"Yes, sure he was."

"I don't know if you even know what that means! I don't have any confidence in anybody! Will you find out stuff while I am sleeping?"

"Neva's downstairs on the telephone. Sleep. She'll find out everything."

"Don't let her in here. I don't want to hear it from her."

In the afternoon he put on his favorite records of the big bands, Tommy Dorsey especially, but also other trombonists, Jack Teagarden, Kai Winding and J.J. Johnson. Wetting his large lips and hooking his slippered toes behind the legs of his folding metal chair, he put the mute in his bell and brought his horn to his mouth and played, softly, along with his heroes, note for note, his favorite solos, those slowly swinging old dance tunes that he had played with his high school combo in the darkened gym. Very soothing, he was sure.

She'd fallen into a sleep less and less troubled, more and more childlike and sweet, when from his window, over the bell of his horn, he saw Amos's and Millard's two pickups, returning from somewhere, the lake road probably, cross the bridge. He put away the trombone, brushed his sore, swollen lips over her wispy temple, rumbled downstairs humming. He gave Neva orders as from Julia, not to go in the room unless the girl called out for him, then just to say he'd be right back.

His father watched him dress for outdoors, wondering aloud whether he might find out anything of Clarence over-town. Clarence-shmarence, that all he could think about? Clarence was all right, Julia was right about that. He jogged and skated down the drive, across the bridge, over to the intersection, whammed his shoulder against the door of the hotel just for form. *Fermée* indeed. Up Main Street to the restaurant. He pushed in somewhat out of breath, found the place crammed, doubly, with the usuals plus the people who would have been at The Rapids if open. He sensed at once a post-revelation lull and contemplation, the instinctive reticence of the knowers. Lenny LaBounty wouldn't even look at him.

Amos and Millard took him aside, into the restaurant part. Neither one could seem to get it out. Stood there looking at each other instead of him. He had to do his part and say, "I'll trade you. I know something too." Amos squinted at him. "I've got the girl," Leo said. Hadn't planned to spend that capital, but it would do some good to add, "She's fine," and it loosened Amos's tongue.

He stumbled out of the restaurant stunned, brimming, pounded his mittens together. A thriller! Terrible! He didn't know if he could handle this. He would have composed this very differently. He liked his own plot better, much! Felt horror, fright, shame, as if he'd been playing with guns and caused a tragedy. Nonetheless, revise, revise! But not everything. Omniscient now (almost!), he made a snap decision, Julia not to know. Home to tell his father, but Neva'd gotten it, already, on the kitchen phone. She and Père told him before he could tell them, *Julia must not know.* They had half a dozen condescending sexist reasons, she couldn't take it, she was weak et cetera. His was better: authorial instinct, inexpressible.

The stack of records wasn't even done playing. He picked up his horn and licked his lips and nestled them into the mouthpiece. She suddenly asked, "What about JoAnn? Has anybody asked her where he is?"

He swept his tubing in the negative.

"Why not? Didn't *she* see him at least?"

He took his lips away to say, "Gone."

"Gone? JoAnn?"

He nodded with the horn.

"*She's* gone?"

"Car's gone, anyway. Rapids locked up."

"Aiee! Where does she go when she goes?"

"Where does anybody go this time of year?"

Dully she said, "Don't tell me. I don't believe all this."

Her eyes were large, she rolled her lips compulsively. She reached out from the bed and held the slide of his trombone. "I made a deal. I lied. I made a deal, Leo, and then I ran. I tried to save him when he came up on the porch but then I simply ran." Added impatiently, since he'd already told her it was Pelo, "I know it wasn't him but I thought it was. I thought I heard him, I thought I saw him out there and I was trying to tell him that there was somebody there that I was talking to and to not come in." Sniffled, stopped. Let go his horn and crashed back, to sleep, for all he could tell.

Later she said, "We even had the radio, did you know? We knew the weather. It said, 'Ice storm.' 'Yeah, right,' I said, 'no school.'"

She said, "And I thought he ought to not go anywhere and we ought to stay right where we were while everything got coated with crystal. We'd stay in bed late in the morning, *this* morning, looking out the window at the jewelry and listening to the necklaces clacking on the panes, so we would be fixed together forever eternally like that. And just let them come if they were coming, so what if they were coming? I'd talk to them. I'd tell them the deal. He didn't believe I would but I would have. Then (today!) we would have gotten here somehow and of course I would deny everything I promised him and run away and we would be forever back there at the end of our travels in the wilderness, in the log camp, in front of the fire. Or back at Dexter Lake. So that one Now could never change. But *now* where is he? Leo, where? *Where is he?*"

Leo had to offer something. He said, "He just left, is what I think. He was one step ahead of you. He just let it go. Wouldn't that be neat?"

"Do you think he really did?"

"Yeah, sure. You thought you had Robert fooled, sweetie, but you didn't. I know that hombre. Say one thing and do another. He brought you to Dexter Lake and Purryer Camp to get the boys to come after him but he wasn't ever going to be there. They'd find you alone."

"Do you think so, really?"

"Sure! Robert Sochia raise a baby? Who fooled whom? He was finished. It was perfect already. You just said so. See?"

She bit her lower lip.

"He couldn't change you. He didn't even want to. He knew you'd betray him." She didn't like that much, turned away from frowning. "Semantics. Point of view. It isn't even you. Time is treachery enough. It runs down. So he just said, 'She will do it all over again to somebody else. Over and over again all of her life. Because she can. I would just prove I ain't ever had her if I tried too hard to keep her.'"

"Bobby isn't that ungrammatical," she said, pouting. "You have to listen carefully if you intend to write about people."

"He was thinking of getting himself killed over you, but your perfidy restored him. And he's just sitting back and smiling to think of it, wherever he's gone. Maybe he's gone to Florida, too, at last.

"How do you know this?" she asked.

"I made it up," he said. "Something wrong with that?"

"I didn't perfidy anybody."

"You can't help it."

"Do you really believe he's gone to Florida?" She was beginning to smile. "He really was my best pupil, you know," she said.

After a while, after more rolling of her (irresistible) lips together, she said, "You said he said he had it. You said he said you just prove you didn't really have it if you keep on trying to hold on to it."

"Yeah so what?"

"I don't like that, Leo. Change it. That's his old way of thinking about love and I taught it out of him. Change it, change it, change it!"

"Stroke of a pen. Consider it done. But it's your way of talking about time, isn't it? Never mind, go to sleep. Aunt Sarah be here soon, take you home. Everything all right."

That was one more handy trick she possessed—being able to believe what she needed to believe.

32

Artists Like Us

Leo reclined on a wicker chaise-longe on the porch, bundled in blankets to the chin, sniffing the ozone like a cure patient in Saranac Lake, watching for the Cadillac from Westchester, due anytime this hour or next. Leo had re-salted the driveway and path in preparation. The late sunlight of the gorgeous day burning on the ironwork of the bridge, shadows long and blue over the river. His father looked out on him from time to time, wondering, "Any sign of them yet?"

It came with all expected dignity, crossing the bridge in silence, turning, turning again up the drive. Of course not the great old gray '38, that he used to pretend-drive in Aunt Sarah's dirt-floored garage at the lake, with the bare-breasted woman-figure on the hood, her arms sweeping back into wings, the deep vee of the old V/8 symbol, the fine-mesh nickel of the radiator grille, the tall white-sidewall tires, the curious gaps in the rim of the ivory steering wheel, showing the steel hoop inside. (What happened there, does ivory evaporate?) Too late to immortalize that. Sarah'd eventually had to get a new one, no-account, hard to tell from any other Body by Fisher, with the woman-figure streamlined to a blur that could be a boat or bird.

Metallic green, ho-hum, with ho-hum tires all solid black. Sandy slush frozen heavily all along its sides. Cousin Whitney backed and filled to reverse ends in front of the garage, and the car bobbed to a stop (the '38 swept to a stop), Sarah's door right at the end of the salted walk. Good boy, Whit! Young Whitney in a suit helped the dear old lady up out of it, where Leo used to help her down.

Dark blue veiled hat over the yellowish silver bun of her hair, dark blue coat, black gloves and bag, black cane, black shoes too small for the stocked-up ankles, over which the usual brown stockings sagged. Leo bent to kiss her downy cheek near her long ear-lobe whereby hung a pearl, vibrant with her tiny palsy. She pushed him back by the shoulders. "Let me look at you. Ah, smart! You've been grinning like that through this whole mess, I know you have!"

She went straight to the kitchen where Neva had a turkey in, had made two pies. "Good!" Sarah said emphatically. She herself put potatoes on to boil. "We'll go out to the girls' tomorrow. Clarence better show his face by then, or I don't know what I wun't do to him." Julia she'd force to eat a proper meal. Then they'd have a heart-to-heart talk. Plenary session right after that in the den. While the potatoes cooked, show her to her room and Whitney to his. After eight hours in the car, she needed twenty minutes with her feet as high as her head. Loyal, come tell her everything he knew.

Goodness! Leo thought. He was right to have told himself the end was coming in the Cadillac. The little old woman breathed conclusion. The very house felt different. He was dying to get back up in his lair with his sweetie, but he was sent instead across the river to check Clarence's cabin, Sarah having chidden his father, "Haven't you done that?" No good to tell her Clarence had cleared out of that two days ago.

Door not even closed. The light lit, it looked as if looted. Emptied even of that picture Clarence always had on his wall, and called, incorrectly, *The Last of the Mohicans*. Indian on his pony, both drooping, looking out over the Pacific. He'd taken it with him! Did he identify? "Where have you gone, you coot! When did you slip by me and where did you head? The Land of the Setting Sun?"

Back into this new regime, rigorous organization, his cutie denied to him by fiat, transported to another room. He and his father were embarrassed in each other's company, useless and powerless, their bachelorhood demolished. Three women in the house most of the time and nothing the men could do but brought criticism, belittlement. They began to blame Clarence just as much as Aunt Sarah blamed him, for not showing up.

The days continued clear and cold and everything remained encased in ice, the branches of the elms and maples arching over the streets, bowed but glittering, vehicles pouring out white steam, their tires loud on the unsalted side streets. Otherwise the town was quiet, people blinking at the brilliance as if they'd just come from a long night in caves.

The second morning, the jurywoman in her Buick passed through the town again, out to the Gokey Road and back. She had heard the barest information on the radio and came just to see the places again, to think, privately pay her respects. She passed the smooth mound of snow on the site of the Pelosphere, saw signs of life in the chicken-coop, did not stop but turned around at the end of plowing. Returning through town, she would have gone into The Rapids to inquire about the service, but finding the hotel closed she went on up the street to Eugene's, where she was kindly recognized and greeted, and informed as to time and location. Then, surprised it was so soon, that day, in fact only minutes away, had a cup of coffee at the bar while she waited. Then when everybody moved to go, she went out too, and waited, to follow in her own car.

She inferred from the sign at the iron gate that this cemetery, at the northern edge of the town, was not the Catholic one. Really, she wondered, do they still ban such ones as Robert Sochia from their holy ground? But it was well enough. Who could want a nicer resting-place? Naturally uneven terrain with splendid trees, and views both north to Canada and south to the mountains, giving a feeling high and remote.

Leo found her there, and stood with her, her hand looped inside his elbow, at the back of a surprisingly large crowd. He'd slipped away from the Weller house unknown to Julia and Aunt Sarah, who were closeted together in Julia's room. A surprising crowd, especially considering how much of the tale was still under wraps, scarcely even to be gossiped about until the journalists' interest in it, not to mention the law's, blew over. O'Neil seemed to have suppressed any compulsion to locate the recent purchaser of the fatal instrument. Care of the body had been an inside job (Merrill Sochia in the business). Interment the very day after death was a relief to all. The priest had apprenticed under the deceased at poaching trout, and so seemed fit for the office though he didn't mention the past. The service had little to do with the particular dead and nothing to do with the manner of death.

One other surprising attendant caught Leo's eye. She glanced at him at the same time, around the fringe of the crowd from him, and held him with her look, long enough to convey a dark significance. My goodness, he thought. What has she to say to me? He wasn't long in answering himself. She lives in Old Herman's house. Could Robert have—? But yes, of course! She's wondering, she's asking me, Are you the one I ought to tell? Oh my, oh my! I am to know it all. He caught her eye this time, and held it, and nodded at the coffin as a question. She closed her eyes and nodded yes and opened them.

At the end, Marjorie turned in front of Leo and leaned against him for a moment. He put his arms around her, way around, palms on either shoulder. They swayed a little together for comfort's sake. Then she separated herself, smiled off to one side, and drifted away to her car without talking to anyone else. She had wanted to know the story, earlier. Not any more. Nor did he stay to reminisce. He had to get back lest Julia gain even the barest idea that he'd been out of the house. His meetings with Marcia Beardsley would come in time. *Oh God how Fate (or Luck or Life, whatever it is) does lavish upon me arrows to the heart!*

He found Whitney assembling survival gear for an expedition to the lake. Whitney was going to heat the camp for one night with the woodstove, cut a hole in the ice for water, contribute to the ancient stalagmite in the out-house, sleep on the hide of a bear, its plaster-filed head for a pillow. Be Alone! Oh, my, thought Leo, what's Whit become now, some *poet*? But Whitney was well out of the way. He was irrelevant and he sensed it, good boy.

Neva getting lunch, his father staying out of the range of high and stertorous voices so unfamiliar in the house. Was his nose a trifle red? Perhaps during Nanna's interview with the patient, Père had escaped to the office for a nip of port. Leo could not blame him. Aunt Sarah had been *shocked* at all that had been *deliberately* kept from her. And nothing *done* about it! So that now, when the worst had happened, nothing *could* be done about it, except take the child home and make her rest; a full recovery under proper supervision; in due course make some arrangements for her finishing her schooling.

And Clarence! *Of course* Clarence was confused by such goings-on! How did her brother ever let him get involved! Why hadn't they taken him in hand! Oh, if she had been here! If she had not been betrayed! Oh!

She wanted Julia's story from Julia's lips, and once she'd rested and they'd had their conference, Leo had helped her up the stairs to his room. He'd tried to stay, of course, but of course been sent away. He'd hovered on the service stairway but only got painful gusts of Aunt Sarah's crackling voice, "Serves you right! What did you expect?" Otherwise, only Julia's murmurs. He could not imagine the conversation. What truth could Julia tell? How could she paint herself, so as not to hear, over and over, "Serves you right! You've only yourself to blame!"?

Yet soon enough those audible, predictable outbursts ceased, the murmuring was two-sided, conspiratorial, inaudible, and he gave up and stole downstairs lest Neva find him snooping. Was it possible that those two, old Sarah, new Julia, were more united by their femaleness and their experience of males than divided by their different centuries and civilizations of origin?

He guessed that Julia would paint herself the victim, the survivor, tell Aunt Sarah how she coped, walked, tell her how proud she was of her stellar navigation, her care of herself, her fasting in protest. Maybe she'd boldly turn the tables on Nanna herself. *Why did you make me go to that school? Why did you make me come up here to the frozen north at all? And who set it up for me to practice teach in this town? What were you thinking, Nanna?*

Maybe they talked truth, but he doubted it. He was sure that they did discuss the immediate future. Nanna intended, no matter what, to go on with her original plan for Julia to inherit the Shampine girls' property, openly discussed at lunch. That was the only possible decent economic basis for the child's future, so Julia, even in her weakened condition, was going to meet the sisters. The sisters, more to the point, were going to meet her. One more day for Clarence to reveal himself, then tomorrow they'd all drive out to the sheep-farm for a mid-day dinner, before the return to Westchester. Julia would be on her very best behavior with the girls, did she hear? They were her betters, though uneducated, no better people in this world. "You'll be polite, and modest; leave the rest to me."

Sarah went off to put her feet up. Julia heard him, quietly as he had entered, and croaked, "Lock the door."

He'd already done that, silently. She was rolling her lips, her eyes were large and dark. "You have to come close," she said, with a sniff. "Lie down here," patting the bed beside her. As she rolled away on her side, "Behind me. Put your arms around me."

Oh my. What is this? What has the old girl said to her? It doesn't matter, Leo rates!

"Hold my boobs. They're just there, you can't avoid them."

She talked into her pillow. He heard it through their bones, skull to skull, his face in her sweet-smelling hair. "I'm so unhappy, Leo!" He nodded in her hair. "Nobody knows how much I love children, Leo, nobody knows how much I am giving up to be a musician. Do you think that I don't care about ever being able to have babies? It is a terrible cost, Leo! But if I had had this baby I would have gotten attached to it. I would breast-feed it, naturally, and I wouldn't have been able to leave it, to give it up to him to raise! Him, by himself? I'd get attached to it and even to him, either that or hate him. Sit there on the beach and get fat and have a kid, be a mom, wash his work-clothes live on a sheet-rocker's wages *no no no no no!* I want to be a pince-nez scholar, city-dweller, feminist, *no more men* unless maybe gay ones. Or very old. And only artists! Like us, right, Leo?"

"Right."

"I want to practice with a baton, in front of a mirror, hours and hours every day. Learn three hundred scores by heart. Be the first woman ever to conduct the Berlin Philharmonic! *I want these things! No one can know how badly!* If I compromise one little bit with my adoration of kids it will never happen, I'll just be a vegetable."

Why was she even thinking of this?

"I lied to him, Leo," she said.

"No you didn't."

"Yes I did! I let him think I'd go through with it. I said, 'How would we do this?' He had it all figured out. I pretended to give in to him. But maybe I should have gone through with it. Do you think I should have, Leo?"

"I can't imagine it."

Suddenly she was brighter, animated, she moved in his arms. "It was so great of him to do that, just go to Florida without me, Leo! Without even saying good-bye. It was so brilliant. Wasn't it?"

"Yes."

"But do you really see why? How brilliant it was? To realize that he could do what he was going to do without me. He could have a baby. He could sit on the beach with some other woman in Florida and she could have a baby and he could be a father. A father, Leo! Do you see what that means?"

"I think so. Sure." Her breasts were warm and soft and abundant in his hands, the only ones he had ever cupped, and cupped wasn't the word since if his hands were cups her breasts were a quart apiece. He wondered if he could feel her nipples.

"I am perfectly sure what happened now. Leo. I can *see* it. He believed in the deal that I made with him. But he also really knew that I would get out of it if I could. I didn't ever really fool him, but he believed in it, with his *will*, Leo. That's what makes belief belief, that's what belief *is*, it has to have *will* in it, you have to *want* to believe. And he did. This proves it. He really did believe in a future, for the first time in his life. Right?"

"Right."

Roll of lips, he could feel her jaw moving and hear a little liquid squish, passed bone to bone.

"I mean because he just left me there! He'd made sure everybody knew where I was. He told me he was going in to see JoAnn and tell her the deal but what he did was go in and knock out the power. How cool was that? And how symbolic, don't fail to point that out."

"Mm-mm. I won't."

"And he never came back! He just left. (They won't respond, Leo. Listen to what I am trying to say.) He knew I would figure it out and understand. I would have done what I agreed to if I had absolutely had to but it wasn't going to happen, it just wasn't. And so he left."

She sniffed. A perfect time to sniff, and Leo smiled.

She detected it. "Don't smile. I'm really sad. You don't know."

"I know."

"No you don't, nobody does, but I want to get this across to you, Leo, because it's important, it's everything. Let me think, please. He realized everything and he still had the idea of the future, of Robert Sochia a living breathing human being who could go anyplace he wanted to and be a father if he wanted to and make peace with his father and work and earn money and have a child with some other woman, he could do all that just as well as raise that child of mine all alone. Better."

"Well . . ." Leo said.

"No, not 'well,' Leo. Better. I know what you're thinking but you're wrong, Leo. Are you still a romantic after all this? Yes he wanted the child because it was mine and he thought he had this once-in-a-lifetime thing about me. You know what a GPC is, Leo?"

"Nope."

"Grand Passionate Connection. That's what one of my professors said he had for me, and I called it his GPC for short. I gave him no mercy. An educated person like that, at his age. That's a solo thing, that isn't love. Look how Robert had it, he didn't need me to do it, he had his GPC whether I loved him or not. Glad to raise my baby *without me!* Without having to really love *me* every boring day and hold my hand when I'm crazy. The kook. If anybody ever does love me with real plain love they're in for hard work, not thrills; except I'm not having any more men, I think I'm a lesbian. I could be. I'll see."

"What about me," Leo said. "Don't I love you?"

"You love me. You're pretty good to me, Leo."

He gave her boobs a grateful squeeze. Still, he kept his pelvis back away from her bottom. His stiff prick was something on another plane, it threatened to interfere with his notation.

She was rolling her lips, her body tense, trying to get out the last point she had to make. "Because you see Leo he really did love the baby. That is the best kind of love. (That's why I'm so sad.) And he will be able to transfer this love that he had for it. He's already over me because I betrayed him which he knew I would do. But he will never be able to get over the feeling that he had for the baby. For life in the form of the child, and for the future that he imagined for himself and it. He'll find another way to have that future. He was my best student, Leo. He was my best student ever. He will be happy. Robert Sochia, a dad!"

Sniff. Another good place for a sniff, but he didn't smile this time.

"Right Leo?"

"Right sweetie."

"I did pretty good, didn't I?"

"Yup."

"You make sure it comes out that way in the book?"

A nod.

"Because I believe in your book, Leo. I'm an artist too and I know about these things and our generation will have its artists who will be great and they could be us if we try very hard and believe in ourselves. And each other."

"It's going to be great."

"Thank you! It is. But you have to *do* it. You can't just not and say you did. It'll be hard. It'll take a long time. But we deserved it. It's important, Leo."

"Right."

"I love you."

"I love you too. Feel up to going to meet your great-aunties tomorrow?"

"No. But don't worry, I can fake it. I know how I am supposed to feel about them, they are my never-known grandmother's sisters and so I love them but I feel light-years away from them and Clarence. I am so many light years away from here Leo you wouldn't believe. Now go away please. I'm going to cry for myself for a little while. Come up and get me in the morning when it's time. You can give me a bath. Has Neva brought me some clothes?"

Give her a bath, good luck.

33

Spring's Work

Aunt Sarah didn't like the look of him. He was slobbering a little (noticed it himself!), told his stories too fast, grinned at what wasn't funny. He couldn't be serious about lost Clarence ("Gone west!"). It wouldn't do. The girls mustn't be distracted from falling in love with Julia, and Nellie had to be made to understand certain things about property, blood, and taxes. They took Julia out there to meet the girls without him.

After that, they would put the potatoes and carrots into the pot with the lamb and come get him for a drive in the country to visit certain Weller family shrines, winding up back at the sheep-farm for the banquet.

And then she would be gone.

She would be gone. It would be all upon his shoulders and nothing to look forward to but his interviews with Marcia. But that's not nothing, he thought, that will be thrilling in fact, the last notes of Robert Sochia from those lips!

Whitney would drive her Valiant, loaded with her college-kid possessions (posters and books mostly, scores, records, record player), following the Cadillac, which Julia herself would drive, in her first dress of spring, the old gal beside her across the armrest. Julia would look like a lady, too fine, civilized, sophisticated for words.

No doubt they'd talk about what comes after. After she regains her strength, catches up her credits, gets her degree. Where she will apply to graduate school, how she will prepare herself, with whom she will study conducting.

Though he wasn't sure she'd confided this dream to Sarah. Sarah might well not approve, or give it any credence. She might well think it vain of Julia to dream any such dream. To be an Artist, what presumption! And it was an impossible dream, Julia'd told him so herself, symphony orchestras were the most retrograde, sexist organizations in the world. Almost all the mere players in them were men, never mind conductors. But who's to say she couldn't do it? With her charm, her power over men, her ability to draw them after her, her intuition, feeling, her passion for music. Who better? Could she convince Sarah? A tiny start, some children's orchestra while she's in graduate school, then a contest win, a fellowship, then some small city orchestra. Step by step, a visiting turn at the Pittsburgh, the youth orchestra at Carnegie Hall, someday the BSO, the Philadelphia—it wasn't impossible. He believed; but could she sell it to Sarah?

She needed plenty of money just for graduate school. But for the conducting lessons besides it was on another scale. She'd told him how complicated this would be. She needed to start her lessons in secret from her other teachers, soon, next year, "right after Europe." How much would they cost? Oh God! The lessons would have to be with a great conductor, in the City. "Do you know what an hour of Maurice Abravanel's time is worth?" She'd have to commute, from wherever she got into a musicology program, Yale, Brown, Harvard, Brandeis? From Boston, say (the pits), to Manhattan, every week. She'd be in *desperate* need of money, lots and lots of money. Lots more than she could earn as a T.A. That's what she'd be telling the old gal, on the way down-state. What would Nanna say to that?

God bless the child that's got her own.

She would be gone on her way, and he would write write write! He was simmering. The story was bubbling up in him, beautiful, complete, irresistible! Write, play his horn, masturbate, sleep, get up to write again, what a life! With his own little postage stamp of territory all to himself. Olmstead County! Fictitious, wedged in between Franklin and St. Lawrence, partaking of a little bit of each. He knew it like the palm of his hand. Not another novelist for a town or two on either side.

On the sentimental tour, with Julia between the sisters in the back seat of the Cadillac, they were too many for one car. Behind, Leo drove his father in the Chevrolet, to pick up Neva when they passed through town.

They drove in thawing sunshine, out north of Risdonville to the Weller family farm—a small green-trimmed white Greek Revival house of the dearest proportions, woodshed attached, huge barns, the tenant house across the road. Good land, well-chosen by the Vermont native great-grandfather, but Opel scarcely thriving on it, by the look of things. They didn't get out. Then to the cemetery along the river, here beyond its boisterous parts, flowing serenely by the leafless maples under which Wellers well known to the living were at rest. And then back roads to town. They turned at the school, paused in front of Days', and Neva, in a dress that hardly let her move her legs enough to walk, came out and got in the back of the Chevrolet, behind Leo's father.

Leo imitated gearbox noises and muffler patter as he turned at Lenny's garage, following the Cadillac, and headed for the sheep-farm again. This was Leo's favorite road, following the north side of the river, a piece of the military turnpike from Lake Champlain to Lake Ontario in the War of 1812, when the North Country almost became part of Canada. It used to be so pretty, along here, in Leo's childhood, the small houses and barns kept up, the land well-tended. Too sandy for nowaday farmers, going back to frontier. Pride, character no match for economic forces! Bucolic scenes exist to make milk, and who drinks milk? Ah, but it was still pretty. Leo'd rather have depopulation and decay than nowaday prosperity, which belonged to no culture at all! Which destroyed anything lovely in its own unholy name. He whistled. Nobody, least of all his two passengers, would have understood why Leo was so perilously gay.

Ahead the good Whitney drove carefully the icy crown between shrunken snow-banks. The river was deep out of sight in its valley over the edges of the fields. There was a schoolhouse converted to a home, next to an overgrown dugway down to an absent bridge, just piers in the quick water now. On one of the old farms, or rather several of them strung together by one late-come consolidating owner, scattered beef-cattle of mixed breed and color. What's wrong with this picture? Just a little further on, Nellie's husband Rob had raised sheep, shot neighbors' dogs, grown alfalfa, sugared, hunted deer and caught trout, all on his own land. He once trapped a wolf and kept it in a dark stall in the barn. His border collies, raised in the same dark barn, were so neurotic they pissed when spoken to, then dragged their rear ends over the linoleum like a wet mop. Just as well Rob and Nellie had no children. Ever since he died Nellie wore a black bow in her hair and left the parlor as it was. Let the sugarhouse fall in, the barn roof collapse, the house rust and weather and rot. No comforts for her, no sir! No more than she had when young in the home place, or cooking at Center Camp or at the Lodge, or newly married and farming in the Depression. The beautiful shady pastures down by the river grew up to pin-cherries and poison ivy. She let someone tap the sugarbush. The beef-baron neighbor cut off her hay. Bessie had lived with her for a decade; Clarence too, at times, under duress. The two old women bundled themselves up and hauled their own firewood on a rubber-tired wagon behind Rob's old Allis Chalmers, from long piles in the meadow across the road, passed it hand to hand into the woodshed. Everything just got older along here and ran down lovelier and lovelier. What would follow?

He said to his father, "This is what it's about, today, eh, Father? Not Clarence. We all know Clarence is all right. He's just still trying to get back from trying to find the Injun Territories. This is what's serious." Rob's lovely pastures, under snow that sparkled red and green, coming into view.

Mr Weller said, "I don't know what you're talking about."

"You know the broker in Moira, Lyle what'shisname, brings Nellie an offer, every now and again. Some big paper company wants the farm; diversifying into real estate, planning river-front condos, hey! 'Would you sell it for *this*?' Lyle asks her, and she says, 'I'd hate tuh.' The broker tells the paper company, 'That's a tough old lady. She drives a hard deal.' And in few months he's back, offering a little bit more, and she says, 'I'd hate tuh,' again. Until it's got to where they're offering her pretty near what it's worth, even to them. Not as a farm, never again as a farm, or even a place for the owners to actually live on it and take care of it or even care if it was good land or not, or hardly if it laid outdoors, since it would be all little cubicles for people to not even live in anyway but trade living in for a chance to live in some other cell just like it in some other earthly paradise, like Spain or Baja California, two weeks out of a year. Now you see it, now you don't." Was he slobbering again? Leo steered with one hand and wiped his lips with a handkerchief, familiar gesture to a trombonist.

"Ain't that what Aunt Sarah told Nellie yesterday?"

"Don't say 'ain't' when we get there, Leo. They'll think you're making fun of them."

"Isn't it, though? She'd have said, 'You wouldn't want that to happen, Nellie, would you now.' Not even a question. 'Would you now. No you wouldn't. When you could sell it to somebody now that you'd want to inherit it anyway. And have it to live on in peace the rest of your life, and no taxes to pay.' There wouldn't be any question at all, would there?"

Neva chimed in primly, "I think it would be very nice if it stayed in the family."

"Well gosh, so do I," Leo said. "Here we are." At a distance the barn was a torpedoed ship, ends up, middle down. The fields behind it rolled half a mile toward the riverbank. The tin roof of the old house rose above the snow, rusted the color of dried blood. On the other side of the road, the long, train-like pile of firewood, cut from the north sugarbush two years ago and stacked in the meadow to dry. Nothing now but to drive in after the Cadillac and eat roast lamb and watch the charmer at work. Kiss her good-bye after dessert. Oh the tristesse after. He'd take his pills perhaps.

Until it comes around again. Retold and reiterated. Regenerated in the yakking of your neighbors. Only Leo was going to improve on mere gossip-immortality and put it between the covers of a book, published by, say, Alfred A. Knopf, and get rich and famous in the bargain. Infectious ambition! *"If we don't do it, Leo, who will?"* Momentarily empty there for a sec, now he almost brayed with a sudden access of self-love. The interest, the keyed fitness, the consistency of his visions! The gifts that he had, known only to him! Grateful Leo! No one could know what raptures he felt in his mind every day. It only required a certain ration of deaths and dismemberments, shot-up plumbing and other heartbreaks, the usual truck of humanity. Over the falls with you, Jean Saint-Jean Baptiste! Around the stone foundation of the house some of the sand and burlap with which it had been insulated for winter was now exposed. The rain had settled the snow which Clarence or some other boy had banked around it for the girls. The rotting sills were slipping outward, bowing. Lilac bushes, leafless but still glittering in skins of ice, engulfed the porch piers. The clapboards were grooved and curled, and decades of frost had pushed out their rusted nails a half-inch. If you didn't look close for a tremble in the sky over the chimney, you'd think nobody had lived in the place for forty years. But Bessie's gray Ford station wagon, all of its chrome corroded, flowers of rust even on its top and hood, stood on hard packed snow melted into ice, facing the road, licensed.

Someone had preceded the two arriving cars. Around back, in the sun, between the woodshed and the barn, where the wind sweeping round the house kept the ground almost bare, an unfamiliar truck. Not a pickup, an old stake truck such as you used to see more when milk was hauled in cans. More brokenbacked farmers then too, and here was one, leaning in apparent pain against the tractor which the girls left out there in the open, with feedsacks tied over its radiator. A short, bent man in high rubber boots and a thick, dirty denim coat that hung to his knees. He had his arms flung up against the fuel tank and his face in his arms. Only turned his head under the engineer's cap enough to raise one eye clear of an arm while the two cars crunched to a stop.

Whitney ran around opening doors for his carload of women. Leo went forward to offer his arm to Aunt Sarah. Heard Bessie croak, "Goodness, who's that? I don't think I know him."

"Why, I believe it's Wilfred Gonyea," Nellie said mildly.

"Whut's he doin' here?"

Sarah Bryant said, "Is that who that is!" Leo took her cane, got her feet outboard, hauled her up on them and gave it back. Her memory sharp as tacks for land and families around. "I haven't seen him since he was a wicked boy. Bessie, you let the men see what he wants. We'll go right in and put the dinner on. Julia, hold my other hand." Julia's bright smile to him, over the top of Aunt Sarah's blue straw hat, like a spear in his breast. *Careful with that!*

Now Mr Gonyea faced around with a grin much like a scowl, still leaning on one padded arm against the tractor. Nellie paused and told him, "If you're looking for help in sugaring, Mr Gonyea, Clarence isn't free." Aunt Sarah saying to Leo, "I know the family, they had no learning, but they had a very good farm, worked hard and wasted not. This one was just a mischief! I can step up by myself, thank you! You find out what he wants, and send him off."

But Leo, followed by his father holding Neva's elbow, helped her through the woodshed up into the kitchen, where she inhaled with satisfaction. Everybody entered, went on into the parlor to throw down their coats. Bessie leaned on a kitchen chair-back to pull her rubbers off, saying, "My, doesn't that roast smell good?" Sarah put a saucepan on with water for the peas before she unpinned her hat.

But then the lamb's aroma fled before a reek of lime and manure. They could already feel it adhering to their clothes and faces. They turned and saw the farmer close, his gold eye-tooth, his three days' growth of iron whiskers, the filthy hat he wore to milk his cows, shiny with the polish of their flanks. Unkempt grey hair stuck out from under it, long enough to tie a bow on. Bessie started to say "Whut?—" and Sarah Bryant ordered, "See here, you step right back outdoors!" But Mr Gonyea only closed his eyes and sniffed. "I come 't the roight toime, en't I? Invite a man to dinner, Bessie, won't ye?"

Bessie's low voice cracked uncertainly. "I didn't know you was comin' in."

"Either that," he said, "or else come over to my place and cook for me. I en't et home food in seventy hours."

Nellie stopped in the parlor door, her hand up to her face. Gonyea went on, "I can't run the highways no more. Not and milk m' gon-demn caows. You want to milk m'caows, I'll keep after 'em and bring her back. Otherwise I'll have to call the troopers."

Sarah Bryant demanded, "What're you talking about? Go on out and tell your business to the men!"

"M' *cook*," the farmer bawled, "m' *cook*, gon-demn it! I reckon he'll have enough of her 'fore long. He wun't never get to Alasky with her. Not the way he's headin'. But it's too fur. I can't do it n' more."

Bessie croaked, "Well pardon me, but I don't think I heard yuh good. I didn't understand yuh."

"—Clarence?" Nellie asked.

Mr Gonyea bawled at them in wicked glee, "Yas, Jayses Chroist, y'r con-demn brother, 's run off with m' *cook!*"

Nellie said, "Do you mean Hester? Isn't that your daughter's name? We haven't seen her in so long—"

"Yas, Hester, damn him, the only one I got!"

"Why, I can't imagine—"

"Way there beyent Sudbury now, they be!" He put a finger in the corner of his eye and twisted up his face. "Hester! My girl!"

So after a moment while comprehension soaked in, and relief, they got him out of his barn coat and hat, which Leo was ordered to hang in the woodshed, and set him down at the table. Bessie lifted out the roaster and transferred the lamb to a waiting platter. Took up the potatoes into a serving dish, went to making gravy in the pan. Loveliness slipped in and sat down at her place, silent, flattering Leo again with a bone-tingling smile.

Gonyea started over now. "You remember how he come a-courtin' my girl, a few years back, running her to all them picture shows. And then he up and dropped her soon's he got another place to keep his team? I never thought that was right, ye know. No, sir, I didn't jest like that."

"Yes," Nellie said. "That was awful bad of him."

(Not the way it was, Leo remembered. Hester fell once, getting out of his pickup at the home place, and rolled half the way down

to the brook. Clarence said, "If I'd had holt of you, sister, I'd been
flattened like a cookie." That's when Clarence thought better of
his engagement, not his idea and never agreed to in the first place.)

"And yet I loiked him well enough," Gonyea said. "I would of
welcomed him, if he'd of been up straight and honorable."

"He would have been cheaper than a hired man, you mean,"
Aunt Sarah said.

"Now now, Sairey Weller, I know you!"

"I know *you*, and don't I! Don't you filigree this story. Tell it!"

Clarence's pickup had rattled into his yard, slid almost to a
halt with its wheels all locked, and Clarence flung himself out of it
already marching while the truck turned itself around on the ice.
"Like one of them Hell-drivers at the County Fair." He never said
so much as how d'ye do to Wilfred Gonyea. Just came in and
stood with his boots wide apart, in the middle of the linoleum.
Red bandanna under his chin, an empty pistol holster mounted
backwards on the wrong side of his belt, that silly ranger's hat of
his. He didn't even look where he was talking, he just made his
speech over everybody's head. "All right, miss, some time ago you
wanted a man and thought you had him sewed up-p. Come to his
senses, took flight and didn't come back. Now, second chance,
jump quick without no argument or else stay, I haven't got time to
ask twice."

He didn't wait for her to answer, either. Went right on, "Where
we going? That's my business, if I told you you wouldn't know.
Dress warm but travel light, for we are going further'n you ever
been from home. And you," he said to Gonyea, "keep your mouth
shut, nobody asked for your two cents."

Then he just covered his ears while Hester cackled at him,
from her rocking chair pulled up to the table, out of that round
Boston-bull-dog face behind her round and thick-lensed glasses.
"You know how she cackles," Gonyea said. "'You can't do this, you
got to do that.'" But the man didn't pay any attention. Looked off
out the window. When he could tell see she had finished, he took
his hands off his ears and said, "Very good, so long, there's plenty
of fish in the ocean." And Hester said, "Wait! I never said I wasn't

comin'!" She rocked herself up out of her chair and paddled out of the kitchen faster than her father would have believed she could travel.

"In case you're wondering," Clarence told her father, "I'm carrying off your little girl, only she isn't so little. I have lived a long time without a cook, now it's your turn. Any other questions?" And he yelled into the parlor, "Get a move on, sister."

Julia shot another arrow, rosy lips, gleaming teeth, into Leo's overflowing heart.

Hester'd had her trousseau ready years before, packed in a trunk, and hadn't disturbed it since. Now, puffing through her nose, her mouth clamped shut, she came dragging it and half the scatter rugs across the parlor. Before Gonyea could stuff what he already suspected would be his last hot cornbread into his mouth and follow them outside, Clarence had thrown the trunk in on top of his blockwood and shovel and junk, and Hester had opened the passenger door, got one knee on the sill. As he watched, Clarence put his shoulder to her buttocks and drove her up into the cab, his head bent sideways in distaste. The engine roared, and the pickup slewed out onto the road.

Gonyea pauses to grin now, right at Sarah Weller Bryant who glares at him, her cheeks shaking with doubt and affront. The food has started going round, but only Mr Gonyea has touched a thing, clearly famished. Masticated carrots and potatoes fall from his long, dark-rooted upper teeth. His forehead above the soiled deep wrinkles is pale, smooth and shiny. The sisters say, "Well, my land," and, "Goodness gracious." Leo looks down the table at his darling, lovelier and calmer than he has ever seen her look, deep color in her face, dark riches in the skin around her eyes, abundant, fragrant hair, a hand hooking it over a seashell ear. She's watching Gonyea with large eyes that sometimes slowly blink. Mr Gonyea pushes out his chin and claws that black-and-white stubble on his neck, showing his gold tooth.

Of course he jumped in his own old truck and followed. Tail-gated them clear the other side of Canton, fifty-four miles west, before Clarence pulled off to a diner. They all three got out of the vehicles and went in, Gonyea at least noticing the black-and-white patrol car of the State Police. They passed the taut gray back of the trooper at the counter. The farmer drew up a chair to the end of their booth.

"I was going to welcome him, ye know," Gonyea says. "I was going to say no need of going ennawheres. Always thought the world of Clarence Shampine." But Clarence didn't even hear him. "Hunched down out of sight, his mouth pursed shut like a turtle's. Scairt of the law, some reason. Mebbe I should have had the trooper grab him, eh?"

The girls inhale in alarm. "But no, Sairey Weller, I didn't. Clarence ordered four eggs, ham, and potatoes, et like he never learnt no manners at all." He paid up, got past the trooper and out, told the father and daughter following him, "'Next stop, the liquor store.'"

"Oh my *land*," says Nell.

Gonyea saw liquor stores in Dekalb and Richville, but Clarence didn't stop until they were on the west side of Gouverneur. There, when Gonyea pulled up beside him, he said, "What, you again? Haven't you got gutters to clean somewheres?" Both of them went in and bought bottles, Clarence's blackberry brandy, Gonyea's Canadian whisky. Then both got back into their trucks.

By Watertown, well over a hundred miles from home, Clarence was driving slower and wandering some. Not from drinking that fruit-juice of his. "I believe the man was tired. Tired in advance, mebbe." He parked in the No Parking zone in front of the Hotel Woodruff, right downtown, and went in, same as ever, empty holster tied to his leg by a thong, three shirts open halfway down his union suit, red mask fanned out on his back. He took a double room and paid in cash from a bulging wallet. He couldn't see close up to count out fifty, let the clerk do that and hand the excess back. He said, "If that's not enough, here's more," and fetched a separate roll of bills out of his back pocket, the size of his fist.

The clerk told him to go around the block and put his truck down in back, by the bus depot. As they went outside where Hester waited, Gonyea tried to draw the line. "Clarence Shampine, hold on a minute. Let's be reasonable. I'm her father. We got a good farm there. What is your intentions?"

Clarence said, "Intentions? Not honorable, that's all you need to know, mister. Don't you think it will be milking time 'fore you get back, unless you hot-foot it pretty soon?"

So Gonyea drove around the block and parked too, and went up behind them to the room and followed them in. "It's three o'clock," he said. "Ain't no time to go to bed." Clarence answered, "Three o'clock cow time, so what, I'm headed for the midnight sun." He lay down on one twin bed in his clothes and was asleep and snoring within half a minute.

"Well, that's good, anyway," Bessie says.

"Yes," says Nell. "You had a good chance to take your daughter right back home."

"Well naow jest hold on a minute, girls," Gonyea says. "I had to think of m'cook. I was always fond of your brother, you know. By golly, if she wanted him, I didn't want to spoil it for her. I figured, well, I'll wait for Clarence to wake up. Moight be a little late home for milkin,' but most m' caows are droey this time of year."

He didn't talk to Hester. Didn't usually have to start a conversation with her. He didn't know what to make of her, exactly, but it was kind of nice, the quiet. The television low and Hester silent. It was interesting. He thought to speak to her, many a time, but every time, he caught that look of hers again, as if it might be better if he didn't.

Came to be evening, six, seven o'clock, and it looked as though Clarence would sleep the night long. It was already three hours past milking time. So finally he said, "Hester, we got to go. We got to milk the caows and get our supper. Come on, girl. We got to git."

It was only his ordinary way of talking, hers too, but blew up in his face. She said, "Don't you never say 'Got to' to me, never more!" She said, "The only thing we *got* to do is die."

And Leo almost bursts with sudden grief for Robert Sochia, as easy a mark for Hester's point, and the way it is pronounced, *doy, doie, doe-eye,* as he is for Julia's smiles.

Gonyea says he couldn't believe what was happening. He was driving a hundred and ten miles to milk thirteen cows five hours late. When he finished, supperless he drove a hundred and ten miles back to Watertown. Clarence was still sleeping. Hester had lain down in her clothes on the other bed. So Gonyea sat in a chair and went to sleep too.

In the early morning he drove home and milked and drove back again, with a loaf of bread and a can of milk. Clarence was just waking up. After he'd had another gluttonous breakfast it was almost noon. Full of jokes. "Which way is north?" Jumped into the truck, and headed for the Thousand Islands Bridge.

"You en't got to go to Alasky, Clarence," Gonyea told him when he stopped for refreshments, somewhere north-west of Kingston. "Go ahead and marry her, it's all right with me. We'll all go home and live together on the farm. Spend your money on a team of horses, hell's to Betsy."

"Ha ha," Clarence said. "Funny but I didn't hear nobody ask. How is a fellow supposed to be that sure, about any particular female? First night might tell, might not. I am taking a good gander at every person with the right kind of clothes on that comes to my attention on this expedition, Indian or white. Besides," he said, patting his pockets, "look at the money I'm packing. A wife might get a notion I was worth more dead than alive."

Sarah Bryant cries, "I don't believe a word of this! Take him to the woodshed, Loyal. Get!"

But nobody moves. Mr Gonyea goes right on. He traveled along behind them that afternoon too, up along past Sudbury, further from his cows than he had ever been, and no arrangements made to get them milked. Clarence never looked at a map and Gonyea suspected that he couldn't read one if he had one. When asked where he was going, he said, "'f you don't know where Alaska is, you wasn't educated very good." And then as the sun got low, he bought some groceries and rented a cabin off on some plowed road in the woods, near a lake. Gonyea was two hundred and fifty miles from the cows, but he was hungry too.

There was a steak in that bag of groceries, and he'd seen some sort of cooker or grill in the back of Clarence's truck. But Clarence didn't move to set it up, didn't issue any orders to the cook to see what the cabin had, to do with. He left the groceries sitting on the bureau. He found his blackberry brandy, took a nip. Gonyea thought of his rye, but resisted the temptation, thinking of his cows, the longest drive yet.

Then Clarence clapped his hands together and rubbed them. He looked all around the floor, and then he spoke. This was suddenly another man. "Humble, like. More like himself. The gentleman he al'ys used to be. 'All right,' he says. 'Appears I've shook any posse that was following me, except for you, the father of the girl. Whilst I had any pride, I lived without a woman. But now, same's a cave man, not changed myself but deserted by all my kind that ever roamed the ear-th. What's a cave man do, hits a female over the head and drags her after him. Enough of that, and there's your human race. Which, that's one responsibility that I have never thought was mine. But now, some reason, maybe that I can't be brought no lower, I decide to shoulder it. I am hungry. I would rather eat that steak with you than fish a springhole on a cloudy summer's day. But when your time comes, you're a fool if you don't know it. I have taken her off, sir, to do with her what people do in private, man and woman. 'f you haven't got the sense to see that that is what she come along for, well, a cow is just the animal for you to associate with, brainless. So good-bye, go milk your herd before they tear apart the barn."

"Fiddlesticks!" cries Aunt Sarah now. "Wilfred Gonyea, I know you from way back, and that will do! The idea, coming into decent people's kitchen and telling any such a tale as that!"

But Gonyea looks at her seriously, takes a moment, shakes his head. "No, Sairey, it's the truth. My girl was thrilled to hear it, what he said. I see her in there behind him, rolling down her stockings. Unbuttoning her sweater. Door's open but it en't that cold. And Clarence he goes on, still humble-sounding, kind of sorry, even though his words was kinder harsh, to me. 'I know your next argument,' he says, 'as if 'twas my own name: what a ugly-tempered bossy bird she is. And I'm not blind so I can see how fat. At least it will be a home-town girl, second best to not going nowhere at all. What, you still here? I thought if I'd say enough and look again I wouldn't have to see your ugly face. I would just as soon see a octopus. What's it take to get you to leave?"

"Clarence Shampine never said such words! Now quit your pranks and tell us the truth! He's at your place this minute. Don't you dare say he isn't. You go right home and send him here. Let him know it isn't only Nell and Bessie he's worried sick with his shenanigans. Tell him Sarah Bryant's waiting too, to take a cat o' nine tails to his hide!"

But the old lady is mistaken. She senses it. The cramped and mischievous old farmer, whose stable smell was always familiar and now is inoffensive to these people, does not invent. He is arrested, even himself, by what he sees. By his lifetime habit, never before bearing the aspect of devotion. His very body craves the milking now. But just as much a habit are the greasy spiceless cooking of his daughter, her obese and odorous presence, the racket of her implacable faultfinding, as reliable as the very walls of his old house. So he must go, but he must also try his last card on Clarence.

He says, "I told him, 'Well, Clarence, if you're truly sure you want her. I only come this far just to be sure that I was shed of her. Now you know where Alasky is, but I doubt you could find your way back, so I reckon I am. Shed of her, that is. So I'll go home now. Maybe Bessie will come cook for me. I know you wouldn't want to eat your sister's cooking anymore, but I en't proud, it's good enough for me—'"

"Wilfred Gonyea I am warning you!"

Gonyea grins at Bessie. "'But, ennaways, Clarence,' I says. 'If you could let it go, I know you would. If you've got to do it, well, you've got to. That's all there is about it.'" Clarence picked up his head but didn't go for that bait either. "'She does talk, normally. I expect it'll come back to her how to do that, so's to keep you company when this other thing you got to do is over. So I best be running along. I was just waitin' to be sure. It's getting to be a long ways to run to do the chores. Tomorrow, it'll be just too con-demn fur to come fetch her. If you decided you didn't want her, up there in Alasky. Talkin',' you know. She'd be your'n to keep.'"

He had touched Clarence a little. He'd touched him, maybe, with his own loneliness. The man sitting on the bed cast his eyes about the floor, his hands turned inward on his knees, his head thrust forward in uncertainty.

But Gonyea had almost forgotten his daughter, sitting there behind him on the bed. Hester had toed her shoes and stockings off. She'd shrugged off her sweater and started to unbutton her blouse. Now, behind Clarence, she was suddenly under the covers, sitting up against the pillows, not a thing on her plump white shoulders or arms, both hands clamped over her mouth.

"I don't believe I've seen her shoulders in thirty years," Gonyea says. No, nor thought of her as anything but a source of noise, a warrant for his meanness, a personification of his fate, to serve back with wickedness for the hardness it has dealt him. Now, in his empathy for Clarence, it comes to him that, as he puts it, "Clarence en't so much to be pitied after all. He's gettin' my daughter. Once a baby, then a girl, now, soft flesh, lots of it, unblemished, warm, whatever else it is." He looks to Sarah for a scolding but it doesn't come.

"At the last, there, he stood in the door of the cabin, with his back to the lighted room, in his high laced boots and hunting pants, his many shirts, but without his hat. Says, 'I am sorry you have to drive home hungry, Wilfred. But, 'f you have to go, well, a good march 'fore daybreak, regards to hometown folks. It's a nice evenin' for your drive. Clear and cold, high pressure. 'f you've got a good heater you'll be comfortable. I'm much obliged to you, certainly. If you are ever in the place I'm in, you're welcome. That will be another country, very interesting. Learn something every day. Here I haven't been traveling but two, been through three counties and a foreign land, not bad for a beginner. You see that woman, well as I. She's after me for something good. What you call a volunteer, that's me this evening. If I ain't quick, look out for my ne-ck. So here I'll say good night. Good night. Good night. Sweet dreams to them that sleep."

Mr Gonyea pauses. Fills his mouth with lamb, potatoes, the peas that have just been served. He shakes his head, chewing. He's still the only one who's eating. "Alasky," he says with his mouth full. "Mountain like we never seen. They wun't be back. No. Never will. Bessie, come cook for me."

"Well, I'd hate tuh leave my sister, Wilfred. No."

"Knew ye wouldn't." Bursts out, "Damn it all!"

He seems to be done, with this last profanity, forgiven perhaps for being so heartfelt. Leo catches Julia looking warmly at her old protectress, Aunt Sarah's jewelled ear-lobes trembling. Julia raises her eyebrows, brightens her smile, nods yes? in a way of asking for permission to begin. No one else will start until Sarah lifts her fork. Only Leo has snitched a buttered roll, dipped it in the gravy-well of his mashed potato, lifted it to his mouth behind his napkin, leaning back. No grace has yet been said. Sarah Weller Bryant takes a sharp look down the table to see all plates in readiness. "Thank you, Wilfred," she says sternly now. "We're relieved to hear he's alive, at least. Let's hope Hester can teach him sense. Now let's everybody concentrate on what's in front of us. Dear Lord make us ever grateful for thy bounty. Amen."

Everybody, excepting Mr Gonyea, repeats, "Amen."

Leo says, "Amen. Amen. Amen." He cannot stop. "Amen. Amen."

She's beside him, holding his hand, wiping his eyes with his napkin, until he steadies up.

THE END

AUTHOR'S NOTE

The National Endowment for the Arts, The MacDowell Colony, and the New York State Council on the Arts awarded fellowships and stipends for the composition of this work. I am especially grateful to Betsy Folwell, who funneled the NYSCA fellowship through the Adirondack Lakes Center for the Arts and brought me back to the area that was always, give or take a hundred miles, my home. I was generously supported and encouraged at the beginning of a long task by my then publisher Alfred A. Knopf and my editor Bob Gottlieb. Pat Ryan at *Sports Illustrated* and Ted Williams at *Gray's Sporting Journal* helped keep the wolf from my door with many enjoyable assignments. Candida Donadio tried her best to sell this book in an earlier form, and Gordon Lish, as an editor at Knopf, tried to buy it. Joel Ray gave me helpful alerts from two careful readings along the way. Eventually I was thrown back on my own resources and the immeasurable help of my first wife Ann and my second wife Hallie and the refreshing company of our children, Haze, Sean, Reuben, Alex and Maggie.

There's a borrowing in the book from a piece by Andrew O'Hagan in the *London Review*, about delinquent boys and "the depth of their wish to be remembered."

Inasmuch as the work has been dedicated really to the dream of itself completed, I could not do better, as you see up front, than offer it in memory of my sister, the singer Jane Gartner (Sooky Smith) and my boyhood friend Lou Curtis. The point is that, playing in that little dance-band (of which I was the manager), they set the example of aspiring artists, living intensely in anticipation of their futures as such. I love my memories of them both.

The characters in this book are with one exception wholly fictitious. I have used a real name or two that I liked, and there are a few slant remembrances of my mother's family, but I made no attempts at portraiture except in the case of Ambrose Stark, who always did want a ballad sung about him. I have certainly not known enough about any real town to have disguised it as Sabattis Falls. As for the geography of the story, this imaginary Olmstead County wedges Franklin and St. Lawrence apart without much disturbing the ground; it overlies familiar space.

—Long Lake, 2005